Also by Alexandra Potter

alexandra potter

THE love detective

HODDER

First published in 2014 by Hodder & Stoughton
An Hachette Livre UK company

1

A CIP catalogue record for this title is available from the British Library.

B format Paperback ISBN 978 1 444 71214 8
A format Paperback ISBN 978 1 444 78747 4
Ebook ISBN 978 1 444 71215 5

Typeset in Plantin Light by Hewer Text UK Ltd, Edinburgh
Printed and bound by Clays Ltd, St Ives plc

Hodder & Stoughton policy is to use papers that are natural, renewable
and recyclable products and made from wood grown in sustainable
forests. The logging and manufacturing processes are expected to
conform to the environmental regulations of the country of origin.

Hodder & Stoughton Ltd
338 Euston Road
London NW1 3BH

www.hodder.co.uk

For AC

Who holds my hand to walk down the street,
and makes every side feel like the sunny side

ACKNOWLEDGEMENTS

I want to say a big thank you to my editor Francesca Best, and the fantastic team at Hodder for all their hard work and enthusiasm on this new book. As always, huge thanks to my wonderful agent Stephanie Cabot for her wise words, unfailing support and belief in me as writer. Also, to everyone at The Gernert Company for working so hard behind the scenes.

To all my friends who live through each book with me (and there are now ten books!) thanks for always being so kind and encouraging. To Dana, a big hug for all the brainstorming and the pep-talks. Cheers also to Sara, a great friend and travel buddy, with whom I went on a truly memorable road trip across India, and from which this book was inspired. We must do it again!

As always, I couldn't do this without my beloved mum, Anita and big sister Kelly. Thank you from the bottom of my heart for all your endless love and support. The same goes to my dad, Ray, who left this party called life way too early, but is forever in our thoughts and hearts.

And to Aaron, who only went for a pint and ended up changing my life in so many wonderful ways, I want to give the biggest thanks of all. I'm so lucky to have you by my side; *Te amo*.

Finally, I want to give special mention to India, and all the wonderful people I met and friends I made there. I will never forget all the laughter, the joy, the kindness and the smiles. Thank you.

I

His dark hair glinted in the sunshine as he turned and reached for her hand.

'I love you, Suzie, I've loved you since the first moment I met you. Will you marry me?'

Suzie gazed at Rich's handsome face. Her breath caught inside her.

'Suzie?' he whispered, slipping a stunning diamond ring onto her finger. 'What do you say?'

For a moment she couldn't find the words to reply.

Then suddenly she found them.

'I say you're a lying, cheating bastard who's been sleeping with Miriam from Marketing!' and, tugging off the ring, she threw it so hard it bounced off his forehead. 'Go to hell!'

Argh, no!

That's not what she's supposed to say at all!

Staring in horror at my computer screen, I hit DELETE. Holding down my finger I watch my cursor race backwards, eating up the words like Pac-Man, until they've all gone.

And I'm looking at a blank page again.

Shit.

Still dressed in my flannel pyjamas, I'm sitting at my desk in my office. My office being a corner of my living room, which consists of a rickety IKEA bookcase, a printer which never has any ink (it's forever running out and have you *seen* the price of ink cartridges? Seriously, you'd think they were gold-plated) and an orchid, which was my attempt at designer chic but has now lost all its blooms and is just a bare twig in a pot.

Funny, but I never see them looking like that in *Elle Decor*.

Hugging my hot-water bottle to my chest (the central heating has gone on the blink again), I look at the flashing cursor for a few moments, hoping for inspiration to strike. Then give up and log into online banking to check my overdraft.

And to think most people believe being a writer is glamorous.

But then, so did I.

For years I worked in an office and dreamed of writing a novel. Of being a novelist. How exciting would that be? From the dreary confines of my local council's town-planning department, I imagined a glamorous jet-set lifestyle that would consist of penning bestsellers whilst wafting around in designer clothes. Of attending glitzy literary parties filled with scintillating conversation and free-flowing champagne.

Until one day I wrote that book I was always talking about, got a publishing deal, moved to London and my dream came true!

And I realised that in actual fact being a writer means rarely getting changed out of your pyjamas, buying a lot of things you don't need on eBay, and talking to yourself a lot.

'Woof . . .'

Or to Heathcliff, my sausage dog.

Another high-pitched bark interrupts my thoughts and I look across to see Heathcliff, his nose pressed up against the window, furiously yapping at my neighbour's cat, his arch nemesis. Heathcliff has a type of body dysmorphia in which he seems to think he looks like a scary German shepherd. In real life he looks more like a comedy draught excluder and is forever taking on animals twice his size. Even next-door's tabby is bigger than he is.

'Hey buddy, just ignore her, she's only teasing you.'

Scooping up his little sausage body, I tickle him under his belly and he licks my face appreciatively. I rescued him from Battersea Dog's Home, though, to be honest, after the events of the past year, I'm beginning to wonder who rescued whom . . .

Leaving Heathcliff to declare war on Mrs Flannegan's tabby, who's now parading up and down the garden in a feline equivalent of sticking her thumb on her nose and twiddling her fingers, I turn back to my computer. Absently I reach for my morning coffee and take a swig.

And spit it out again. Ugh, it's stone cold!

Grimacing, I pad into the kitchen, flick on the kettle and tug open the fridge, which is papered with a mishmash of take-away menus, 'to-do' lists and photos. As I reach for the milk, one of the pictures catches my eye – it's me and the gang, arms round each other, grinning drunkenly at the camera.

That photograph always makes me smile. It's not often we get together these days, what with everyone having busy lives and living in far-flung corners of the globe, but this was taken on my birthday last year when we all managed to convene on a pub in London. I pause to look at it for the millionth time.

On the far left, inadvertently showing off a little too much of her famous cleavage, is Harriet, who recently relocated to Paris for work and has embraced all things French, including a diet of red wine, cheese and anything that's full-fat.

However, it seems she might have embraced things a little *too* heartily, judging by the email I received from her yesterday complaining: *So it's true, French women don't get fat. Alas, I am not French. Merde!* As evidence she attached a photograph of her wearing baggy jogging bottoms along with the caption: *I'm now having to wear elasticated waists.*

As someone who wears baggy yoga trousers to do

everything but yoga, I'd replied telling her not to worry. To which she'd fired back: *You don't understand! This is Paris! Style Capital of the World! I'm like a pariah!*

Mental note to self: never move to Paris.

Next to her, with the kind of arms that make me want to lunge for a long-sleeved cardi, is Milly. Milly's a Pilates teacher and now lives in Los Angeles, but she used to teach a course in London that promised to 'Invigorate, Transform and Empower'. Personally for me it was more along the lines of 'Exhaust, Ache and Give Up', but that's got nothing to do with Milly. She's a brilliant teacher, and now a brilliant friend. Even if every time she sees me the first thing she does is nag me about my core strength. Or rather, lack of, I muse, feeling that little roll hanging over my waistband and automatically sucking it in.

Then there's Rachel. Squinting myopically into the camera, as she hates being photographed wearing her glasses, she's still in her work suit as she's come straight from the office. She's a lawyer for a big firm in the City and always working on some case or other. Personally, I think she works *too* hard. She's constantly stressed and travelling for work and never takes a holiday. Apparently she has so much annual leave due from work, Human Resources recently banned her from the office for a week. So she worked from home and put in *even longer* hours.

On the right is my little sister Amy, though you'd never know we were sisters. Whereas I'm a brown-eyed brunette, she's blonde and blue-eyed. She's also a whole ten years younger. She was what my parents call, 'a happy accident'. Which describes Amy pretty well, as she can be a bit ditzy and is forever having accidents. As her big sister, I've always been responsible for her. From the day she was born I was told 'look after your little sister', and I've spent my whole life taking care of her and getting her out of trouble.

However, what she might lack in common sense, she makes up for in brains. Academically, Amy's super-bright. She wants to be an archaeologist but, despite graduating with a first-class honours degree, she can't get a job and has spent the past year sending out CVs whilst lurching from one temp job to another. She's been a bicycle courier (she was terrible, she has no sense of direction), a waitress (terrible again, she can barely balance her mug of tea on her plate of toast, let alone carry four main courses and a side-salad) and dog-walker (worse than terrible, she ending up losing two dogs; thankfully they later found their own way home).

Then, six months ago, she decided she'd had enough of job-hunting and sleeping on friends' sofas and opted to go off travelling, much to my parents' consternation. If they didn't have enough sleepless nights about her before she went, ever since she put on her rucksack and cheerfully waved goodbye at Heathrow, they've done nothing but worry themselves sick about her. I keep trying to reassure them – after all, she's twenty-two now; she's big enough to look after herself.

Plus, judging by her Facebook page, she seems to be having a great time. I mean, how much trouble can you get up to lying around on a beach all day in Goa?

Actually, on second thoughts, I don't think I want to know the answer to that question.

Anyway, the good news is that one of the museums she sent her CV to has been in touch offering her a place on one of their research programmes. Not only that, but it's the most prestigious archaeological research and archive centre in London and it starts in two weeks! So she's coming home. I don't know who's more thrilled. Amy. Or my parents.

Which leaves me, Ruby Miller, squished up in the middle of the photo, arms draped around everyone. To be honest it's not the most flattering picture of me. I'd bought some of that face illuminator after being convinced by the sales assistant in Boots that it was the only thing standing between me and the kind of dewy, shiny model skin you see on the front cover of *Vogue*.

Except when I got home and read the instructions, it said to just dab it on your cheekbones. Easy for them to say. I don't *have* any cheekbones. So instead I rubbed it all over and ended up with a big shiny moon face. I'm not kidding. The flash is actually reflecting.

Single and thirty-something, I live with Heathcliff in a basement flat in a converted Victorian townhouse in West London. It's not the biggest flat, or the brightest, but it has the cutest garden, with a real-life apple tree and a camellia bush that blooms all summer. Though in England, 'all summer' seems to amount to a week at the end of May. Still, Heathcliff likes to sniff around it even in the rain, and I like to look out onto it when I'm working.

Saying that, writing never really feels like work. Not just because I get to do it in my pyjamas, but because it's more than just a job, it's like stepping outside my world and into another. I get to meet all these new people, I get to laugh with them when they're happy and cry with them when they're sad. I get to make best friends with my heroine.

And – *this is the best bit* – I get to fall in love with my hero.

People always ask me what kind of books I write and I guess you'd call them love stories (unless you're the evil journalist from the *Weekly Telegraph* who called them something unrepeatable), but I also think of them as mysteries.

After all, what makes two people fall in love? It's a question people ask all over the world, in a million different languages. Last year, *What is love?* was the most searched query on Google. And yet no one seems to know. Even experts can't agree. Scientists offer complicated chemical theories about pheromones and neurotransmitters, philosophers eulogise and psychotherapists analyse. But it's impossible to define.

Like George Harrison said, it's '*something*'. An elusive feeling that knows no rhyme or reason. No rules. No boundaries. It can be different for every person and yet for every person it feels the same. You can't explain it. It's like faith, or hope . . .

Or magic.

I've written three novels on the topic and I'm still looking for the answers. I guess, in a way, I'm a bit of a love detective. Not in a Sherlock-Holmes-in-a-deerstalker type of way. I'm not out searching for clues to solve crimes, though I did once spend hours with my friend Rachel, trying to discover why her online date never called her again. Which is a sort of a crime.

As, trust me, she was a *million* times nicer than him.

My friends are always telling me about their love lives and I've lost count of the times I've spent with them dissecting an opaque text message from a guy or Googling someone to see if he really was divorced (and no, he wasn't, there were photos of him with his wife all over his firm's website; poor Harriet was devastated).

But it's not just about being good at Google. When it comes to love I'm a bit of a detective because I'm fascinated by people's stories of love and romance. I love discovering how they met and what brought them together, listening to how they talk about chemistry, whilst trying to figure out exactly what chemistry is, marvelling at how – by some incredible stroke of luck, timing, fate, or all three – two people fall in love.

And because detectives are always exploring mysteries, and what is love, if not the greatest mystery of all?

Seriously, just look at Charles and Camilla!

Or me and Sam.

At the memory of him, I feel a familiar knot in my stomach. Because that's the irony. Whilst my heroines always fall in love and get a happy-ever-after, the same couldn't be said for me. They say you should always write about what you know, but if that's the case, I should be writing a horror story.

Well, how else do you describe walking in on your fiancé having sex with another woman, a week before your wedding?

I know. It sounds like such a cliché, and it was. But just because something is a cliché, it doesn't make it hurt any less. It just means you're humiliated *and* heartbroken.

But anyway, that's all in the past now.

Grabbing the carton of milk, I close the fridge and turn back to the kettle. It's doing its usual thing of boiling away merrily and refusing to switch off, filling the kitchen with clouds of steam that are rapidly turning to condensation on the cold window panes. Which reminds me, that's another thing I need to add to my to-do list.

Snatching up a pen I scrawl Buy new kettle on one of the bits of paper on the fridge door.

I'm a big fan of lists. I love that feeling when you get to cross something off. It makes me feel all super-organised. In fact, I have a secret to confess: I sometimes even put things on there I've done *already*, just so I can draw a line through them.

Like, for example, 'Lunch with Diana Friday @ 1230'

See, I can just take my pen and cross it straight off.

Wait a minute . . . I pause. Working from home makes every day roll into the next and I quickly scroll through the calendar in my head. Oh crap, Friday's *today*! I glance across at the clock on the microwave. And is that the time already?

Double crap.

Abandoning the half-made coffee, I dash back into my bedroom, throw on some clothes and attempt to drag a brush through my hair, before giving up, sticking on a woolly hat and grabbing my coat.

Heathcliff starts yapping; he hates it when I go out and leave him. 'Heathcliff look! There's the pussycat!' I fib, to create a distraction. As he races over to the French windows, I race out of the front door.

Honestly. Lying to my own dog. What next?

And, taking the steps two at a time, I reach the street and begin hurrying towards the Tube.

2

Outside it's a typical January day in London. Cold, grey and damp, the city feels grumpy and lethargic. Even the weather can't be bothered to make the effort to pour with rain, and instead is just lazily drizzling. But I don't have time to go back and hunt for an umbrella and, even if I did, it would probably only blow inside out. I grimace, pulling up my collar and dipping my head into the wind.

I take the Tube to Baker Street, then walk to Marylebone High Street. Diana's my agent and we've arranged to meet at a little Italian café on the corner. Before I was a writer, I thought lunch with an agent would be terribly glamorous, all fancy restaurants and big business deals, but in reality we meet in cafés and spend the whole time gossiping about men over the house white.

Only, in all the rush I'm actually a few minutes early, and Diana hasn't arrived yet, I realise, glancing in the window. In which case I'll just pop next door and buy my parents a card – it's their wedding anniversary in a few weeks.

Next door is my favourite bookshop in all of London. In all the world, probably. Feeling a rush of pleasure I push open the door and walk inside. An original Edwardian bookshop, with beautiful floor-to-ceiling oak shelves, a creaky wooden staircase, and books organised into their different countries, it's more than just a bookshop, it's like taking a trip around the world.

Heading past Malaysia and Africa, I reach the rack of

cards and, twirling it around, find the perfect one for Mum and Dad. Pleased, I make my way towards the till.

Then pause.

Hang on . . .

In the shadowy depths of the bookshop, a statuesque grey-haired woman, wearing a Columbo-style mackintosh raincoat with the collar turned up and oversized sunglasses, is acting very suspiciously over by Great Britain. Grabbing several books from a shelf, she's nervously chewing gum and looking from side to side to make sure no one is looking.

That's Diana, although she hasn't noticed me. What *on earth* is she doing?

I'm about to call out her name when suddenly, in a swift and seamless move, she swipes the books quickly up inside her coat.

Oh my god. *She's shoplifting!*

I watch in horror as she starts heading towards the exit, head down, avoiding the eye of all the sales assistants. I can't believe what I'm seeing. For a moment I'm frozen to the spot in disbelief, then abruptly I come to. I can't just stand here; I need to take action. I have to stop her before she gets caught. Diana isn't just my agent, she's also a dear friend.

I suddenly see the news headline flashing before my eyes:

SUCCESSFUL LITERARY AGENT ARRESTED FOR SHOPLIFTING IN A LONDON BOOKSHOP.
'I don't know what came over me,' wept disgraced agent Diana Diamond as she was led away in hand-cuffs. 'My reputation and career are now ruined!'

Prompted to act, I charge towards her like a rugby player. She might be six foot tall, but I'm prepared to tackle her to the ground if need be.

'Diana!' I say her name out loud, blocking her path.

She looks up in surprise and, seeing me, creases her face into a huge smile. 'Hey sweetie!' she cries in her strong New York accent. 'You're looking great as always!'

'So are you,' I smile, trying to avert my eyes from the large bulge under her mac. I don't know what to say. It's like the time a girl at school had terrible halitosis and no one knew how to tell her. In the end I bought her a packet of Polos and hoped she'd take the hint.

But this is going to take a lot more than a breath mint.

'I just thought I'd pop in, check out the competition,' she laughs. 'It's a habit.'

Maybe she's a kleptomaniac. Maybe she can't help it. Maybe it's a bona-fide medical condition she's never told me about.

'But hey, listen, let's go next door and get some lunch and catch up.'

Shit. I have to stop her. But how?

She goes to step forward and there's nothing else for it: I block her.

'Oops,' she laughs as we almost bump into each other, and steps to one side. I do the same. She laughs again and steps back. I mirror her move. Back and forth we go like we're doing some kind of dance, until finally she gasps with impatience. 'Ruby, is everything OK?' she asks, pushing her sunglasses onto her head and peering at me intently. 'You're acting really weirdly.'

'*I'm* acting weirdly?' I reply indignantly, before remembering myself and hastily lowering my voice. 'You have books underneath your coat,' I hiss.

'I know,' she replies evenly.

I feel a beat of shock. Gosh, she's so *brazen* about it.

'They're your books,' she adds, and gives me a quick flash. I see a whole pile of my latest novel hidden in the lining of her coat.

I gape at her in total confusion. 'But why would you steal my books?' I whisper.

Throwing back her head she erupts with throaty laughter. 'I'm not stealing them silly!' and sweeping past me she moves over to the 'Weekly Promotions' table and starts moving books around.

'So what *are* you doing?' I hiss, rushing over.

'Well, no one's going to notice you if you're sitting on a shelf, now are they?' she intones, roughly shoving several best-selling celebrity tell-alls to one side and plonking my books on top. Spreading them around so there's a whole display, she picks one up and starts waving it around.

'Come and buy this book by Ruby Miller,' she says loudly to an elderly woman in tweed who's browsing the Russian classics section. The old lady looks up from her copy of Dostoevsky and peers at us through her spectacles.

'It's fabulous, lots of sex,' adds Diana with a wink.

Oh my god.

'I'm so sorry, please ignore my friend,' I fluster apologetically, my cheeks blushing bright red. 'She's American,' and, grabbing Diana by the elbow, I start steering her towards the exit.

'What's wrong with lots of sex?' she protests.

Is it just me or is her voice getting even louder? Several other customers are turning around to stare now and it's all I can do to get her through the doorway.

'I write romance, not porn!' I gasp, once we're outside.

'So what?' she shrugs. 'Sex sells.'

I shoot her a look. After the furore surrounding *Fifty Shades of Grey*, she's been nagging me to try my hand at erotic fiction, but I can't. Not in a million years. I once tried talking dirty with a boyfriend – it was his idea not mine – and it was so embarrassing. Plus I was useless at it. I'm not a prude, I'm not still calling it 'my front bottom' like my friend Harriet, but I can't even say the *you-know-what* word, let alone write it down. Imagine my mum and dad reading it?

I feel a flush of embarrassment. Oh god, no. On second thoughts, best not.

Dashing out of the rain, which has now obviously decided it should put a bit more effort in and is coming down in stair-rods, we step next door and are seated by the waitress who swiftly takes our order.

'So, how's the new book going?' asks Diana, getting down to business.

I feel a beat of anxiety as my mind flashes back to earlier, sitting at my computer, staring at the blank screen. 'Slowly,' I say vaguely.

'How much have you written so far?'

'Um, you mean specifically?' I try stalling.

'Because I'm dying to read it!' she continues swiftly. 'I thought if you emailed me the first few hundred pages, or whatever, I could read it tonight on the flight back to New York.'

Diana works for a literary agency based here in London, which also has offices in New York, and she's always back and forth. Which *sounds* exciting, but in actual fact it just means eating a lot of bad airline food and being constantly jetlagged.

'Well, that's the thing . . .' I swallow hard. Fuck. I'm going to have to confess. 'There aren't any pages,' I blurt.

For a moment, there's a pause, then . . .

'*None?*' Even unflappable Diana, who will fight a publisher to the death for me and is never fazed by anything, looks slightly alarmed.

'Not yet, no,' I add hastily. 'But it's just a bit of writer's block. I'll be fine,' I say reassuringly, though I'm not sure if it's her or me I'm trying to reassure.

'Of course you will,' she agrees confidently, swiftly remembering her role is to support and encourage. 'What you need is some inspiration and I have just the thing. There's this guy—'

'No,' I shake my head, cutting her off.

'What do you mean, no? You don't even know what I was going to say.'

I throw her a look. 'Is the Pope a Catholic?'

'What?' She stares at me all wide-eyed and innocent. 'I'm your agent, I can't believe you don't trust me.'

I feel a stab of guilt. 'I'm sorry,' I apologise quickly, feeling bad for misjudging her. 'I thought for a moment you were trying to set me up on another date, that's all.'

Her face colours. 'Well, I wouldn't call it a date *exactly*.'

Wait a minute . . .

'Why, what would you call it?' I ask suspiciously.

'A favour. He's a friend of a friend and he's going to be coming through London at the end of next month and doesn't know anyone,' she says briskly, before I can get a word in. 'And I said you'd meet him for coffee. That's all,' she adds, smiling brightly.

'Well, now you're going to have to tell him I can't,' I reply firmly.

She frowns. 'C'mon Ruby, it's only a coffee.'

'That's how I met Sam. In the queue at Starbucks, remember? One minute he was buying me a cappuccino and asking me out on a date; eighteen months later he was cheating on me and I was calling off our wedding.'

'I know, and it sucks, but that was over a year ago—'

'And it still feels like yesterday,' I reply quietly.

Reaching across the table, she gives my hand a sympathetic squeeze. 'I know, sweetie,' she says, softening, 'but you can't give up on love.'

'Why not?' I say impulsively.

'Because you'll end up on the shelf like one of your books,' she quips, trying to make me laugh, but it just makes me more resolute.

'Fine. I don't care,' I shrug, leaning back into my chair. 'Maybe it's better that way.'

Diana looks at me, shocked.

'Well, why not?' I demand again and, as the thought strikes me, it suddenly catches like an ember from a flame, and takes hold. 'I've always been such a hopeless romantic, I've always dreamed of love and marriage and happy-ever-afters . . . and yes, I know it's not always easy,' I add quickly, before she can. 'But I've always had hope – it's like the Beatles said, "All You Need Is Love" . . .' I break off and stare down at the table, twisting up my paper napkin as my mind races. I can feel the emotions rising inside me, all the hurt and disappointment and heartbreak. 'But you know what? Not anymore, the Beatles got it wrong, it's all bollocks—'

'But you can't say that!' protests Diana.

'Yes I can,' I fire back.

It's like a revelation. It's as if everything I've held onto my whole life is crumbling away around me and I've suddenly seen the reality. 'And it's not just about what happened to me, look at all my friends!' I cry, my emotions spilling out of me. 'They've all been disappointed in love. Look at Harriet – she just found out the guy she was dating was still married! And then there's Milly: her boyfriend's a commitment-phobe and after seven years he still won't propose. And what about Rachel? She's been single forever, because every date she goes on ends in disaster—'

'And that's exactly why you can't write,' interrupts Diana simply.

I break off and look at her.

'It's not because you have writer's block, it's because you don't think any of it is true any more. You've lost your faith in love, Ruby,' she says, and gives me a long look. 'You just don't believe in love any more.'

I fall silent, her words sinking in, only this time I don't try to argue.

Finally I've admitted it to myself. For so many months I've been trying to ignore a fear deep inside of me, to hold onto that person who, despite everything, believes in love. Real, true love. Move-heaven-and-earth, can't-live-without-you love. The kind of love that makes people do incredible, ridiculous, wonderful things. And, despite everything that's happened, despite her being bashed and bruised and badly shaken, I don't want to let that person go.

But she's already gone, I suddenly realise.

'You're right,' I say quietly. 'I don't think I do believe in love any more.'

We're interrupted by the arrival of my gnocchi and Diana's spaghetti marinara; Diana's distracted as the waitress fusses around her, laying down a plate for the shells and a finger bowl with a slice of lemon. The waitress leaves the table, and we both fall silent as we make a start on our food.

After a few moments, Diana breaks off between mouthfuls. 'What you need is a vacation,' she says decisively. 'Why don't you take some time out? Shut the laptop, turn off your phone, go relax on a beach somewhere.'

'A beach? I can't go and sit on a beach.' I make a moan of protest, but she railroads my objections.

'It'll do you the world of good. Seriously, when was the last time you had a break?' She looks at me pointedly.

'The year before last. Sam and I went on a cycling holiday around Norway. You know how he loved activity holidays.'

'That's not a vacation. A vacation is lying on a beach in a bikini, not wearing a fleece and a backpack.'

I smile, despite myself. 'I know, but I can't, I have so much to do here—'

'Trust me, I'm your agent, I know what's best for you. *See . . .*' With her fork she gestures towards the window.

I glance over and see the little old lady from the book-shop. Sitting at a table, she's sipping a cappuccino, deeply engrossed in a novel. Only it's not Dostoevsky's, it's mine.

I turn back to Diana, who raises her eyebrows. 'Now will you do what you're told?' She waggles her fork scarily at me. 'A vacation will do you the world of good. *Go!*'

3

It's already dusk by the time I arrive back at the flat. It's still raining heavily and I'm just putting my key in my front door when I hear a loud thudding coming down the steps behind me. My heart jumps into my throat and I twirl around, terrified.

'Who's there?' I demand, in my deepest, gruffest voice.

I see a dark shape. Hear a rustle in the bushes. Oh my god! Just when I think things can't get any worse, I'm going to be mugged! And on my own doorstep!

Gripped with panic and fear I try to scramble my brain into action, I need to act fast, surprise my assailant, attack before I'm attacked—

'Ruby, is that you dear?'

Suddenly I hear a quavering voice.

'Mrs Flannegan!' I gasp, my voice coming out in a rush of relief. 'What are you doing?'

'I'm sorry, did I scare you there for a moment?' The security light flashes on, and across the hedge her face abruptly comes into view underneath her plastic rain hood.

'No, not at all, don't be silly,' I fib, feeling silly myself that I could have been scared by my tiny, silver-haired neighbour. Mrs Flannegan's nearly eighty, a widow and a heavy smoker, and has lived in the flat next door for fifty-eight years. I often chat to her over the garden wall, as she likes to go outside for a cigarette. She has to use a walking stick now, as she's unsteady on her feet, but three times a day she stands by her back door, blowing out clouds of smoke, like she must have done for over half a century.

'I was just coming back from the shop, I had to get a few things.'

'Here, let me help,' I offer, rushing across to her and grabbing the shopping trolley, which she's attempting to drag down the steps behind her.

'Oh, you are so very kind dear,' she smiles. 'I was rather wondering if a big strong man might come to my rescue, but you'll do . . .' She lets out a chuckle, which turns into a rattling cough.

'You should stop smoking,' I chide, hitching the trolley over the crook of my arm so I can help her down the rest of the steps, which are all slippery in the rain.

'Then I'd have no vices left,' she grumbles.

I scoop her key from underneath the geranium pot on her windowsill – despite my constant nagging that's it's less a 'hiding' place and more a 'come and burgle me' place, she refuses to move it – then unlock her front door and help her inside. We're greeted by her tabby cat, which immediately begins rubbing herself on Mrs Flannegan's stockinged ankles.

'What's yours?'

'My what?' Turning on the hallway light, I walk through into the kitchen and start putting away her groceries: teabags in the cupboard on the left, fruit scones in the bread bin, milk in the fridge . . . I've done this so many times, I know where everything goes, including her tins of treacle pudding which, for some bizarre reason that she's never explained, she keeps next to the shoe polish. I'm always worried she'll get mixed up one day and end up eating black gloss polish and custard.

'Your vice,' she says, as if it's obvious. Having changed into her tartan slippers, she shuffles behind me into the kitchen and flicks on the kettle.

'Oh, I don't have one,' I laugh, reaching for the teapot. Mrs Flannegan likes her tea brewed properly: 'None of that horrid bags-in-cups business.'

Resting a bony hand on her walking stick, she peers at me through her large, thick-rimmed glasses. 'Every girl should have a vice, you know,' she says with a click of her tongue, 'whether it's drinking, cigarettes, men . . .'

'Mrs Flannegan!' I laugh, feeling myself blush a little.

'Don't be so shocked dear! I was young once you know . . .' She trails off and gives a little chuckle as she reminisces. 'There's plenty of time for being sensible when you get to my age. You've got to walk on the wild side a little, be a rebel.' Her eyes flash wickedly behind the thick lenses of her spectacles. 'Do something daft, impulsive, *bad for you.*'

'I take sugar in my tea,' I counter, heaping a teaspoon into my cup, 'and if you promise you won't tell anyone, I'll let you into a secret . . .'

Mrs Flannegan leans her silver head closer.

'I haven't paid my TV licence.'

She looks appalled.

'But I'm going to,' I protest quickly, 'it's on my list!'

'And to think when I was your age I was kicking my heels up,' she mutters, shaking her head with disapproval. 'In my day, you'd never catch me indoors watching telly – not that we had it in my day, but still . . .' She looks at me with something that looks suspiciously like pity.

Our walls are paper-thin and, since I broke up with Sam, I seem to spend most of my evenings watching crap TV. I've lost count of the number of times I've fallen asleep on the sofa and woken up in the early hours with it still blaring.

Avoiding her disapproving gaze, I busy myself with the tea as she makes her way into the living room and eases herself into her armchair by the fire. Immediately Snoopy, her cat, jumps into her lap and curls up like butter wouldn't melt in her mouth.

'You know she's still teasing Heathcliff,' I say, passing her a cup.

'She's a terrible flirt, like her mother,' she smiles, patting her affectionately.

I laugh and take a few sips of tea. Next to her, on the sideboard, are dozens of photographs, mostly of her grand-children (at the last count she had nine), but tucked in the middle, in a heart-shaped frame, is one of her and her husband Alf. Taken not long before he died, they're sitting in deckchairs on the seafront holding hands. I feel suddenly sad. They don't make love like that any more.

'Well, I'd best be getting back next door . . .' Glancing away, I look at my watch. It's getting late and I need to feed Heathcliff.

'Of course, I mustn't keep you, I know how busy you young ones are,' she smiles. 'It's Friday night, going out somewhere nice?'

I hesitate. I was supposed to be meeting Rachel for a drink, but she cancelled as she had to work late again on some big case. Poor Rach works such long hours, I haven't seen her for weeks; but, to be honest, when she called to cancel I didn't mind. In fact, to be honest, I felt relieved; I'm just not in the mood to go out these days. Actually, I can't remember being in the mood to do anything much since . . .

My mind flicks back to my engagement party, me in a red dress, drunk on champagne and happiness, my arms wrapped around Sam as we slow-danced to an old Sam Cooke song around our living room. It was a summer night. Everything was warm and fuzzy. Our future was glistening ahead of us, filled with hopes and dreams that shone and sparkled like the stars in the night sky.

And in that moment everything seemed possible.

Everything was wonderful. And although it was late and all our friends and family had left, I remember feeling that everything I had ever wanted was there in that room.

Well, anyway. Like I said, it's been a while since I've felt in the mood.

'Yes, out on the town,' I fib, crossing my fingers behind my back. I hate lying to Mrs Flannegan, but I can't admit the truth that I have no plans except for another evening on the sofa with a takeaway pizza and Heathcliff, watching repeats on TV.

'Well, have a lovely time dear,' she smiles.

I feel a stab of guilt. 'Thanks, I'll try,' I smile and, giving her a little wave, I let myself out of the front door.

Arriving back at my flat, I kick off my shoes, scoop the post off the doormat and pad into the living room. Heathcliff is waiting like a sentry by his dog bowl. Having fed him quickly, I flop down at my desk. The blank screen of my computer is waiting to greet me like a sulky teenager and, ignoring it, I set about opening my mail.

Bills, bank statements, junk mail . . . Just the usual, then. I'm about to shove it all onto the growing pile to deal with later, when I spot something else. A postcard. I perk up. On the front is a photograph of a beautiful, palm-fringed beach in Goa, Southern India. I turn it over.

Hi Rubes! Having an amazing time! Wish you were here! Amy x

The rain lashing against the window distracts me and I turn to gaze outside. Dusk has given way to darkness and so I flick on the desk lamp. My little terraced garden recedes and I see my figure reflected back at me. Pale-faced, shoulders hunched, hair scraped up into a scrunchie, I look about a hundred years old, and for a moment I barely recognise myself.

I'd always assumed that by the time I hit thirty my life

would be sorted out, I'd have a career, a partner, *a future*. And for a while everything seemed to be going to plan. Getting my first novel published, meeting Sam, falling in love, planning our wedding – all the foundations of my life were falling magically into place and now all that was left was to build a future upon them.

And for a few dizzying months, everything was perfect. I had what every magazine article says you can't have: *I had it all*.

Until one day, in the split second it takes to turn the handle on a bedroom door, I discovered that those magazines were right after all. I didn't have it all. I had a fiancé who was sleeping with someone else.

And *boom*, just like that, all those foundations I'd carefully laid, all that future I was happily building, brick by naive brick, came crashing down on top of me, burying me underneath the rubble of broken dreams, betrayal and more tears than I ever thought it was possible for a human to shed. Forget breaking my heart, Sam pretty much destroyed it.

Luckily for me, the emergency services were on hand to pull me out of the wreckage. Though in my case it wasn't the police, ambulance or fire brigade that saved my life, it was my girlfriends, Gordon's gin, and a trip to Battersea Dog's Home. And in time I got over it. Well people always do, don't they? It happens all the time. Now I'm fine. More than fine. I've got my career, my health, my friends and family, plus Heathcliff if I need a cuddle. I'm really lucky.

And yet . . . I stare harder at my reflection. And yet sometimes I can't help feeling like I lost myself somehow. That I'm just going through the motions. That the old me is still lying buried underneath that rubble and, try as I might, I don't know how to find her again . . .

A gust of wind makes the French windows rattle and they suddenly blow open. I mustn't have shut them properly earlier and I jump up to close them, shivering in the blast of cold winter air as I fiddle with the old catch. Gosh, it's horrible out there. Maybe Diana was right. Maybe all I need is a holiday. Some sun, sea and sand. Maybe a change of scene will inspire me. Fix my writer's block.

I glance down at the postcard that's blown fluttering onto the floor. I pick it up. I've never been to India. It seems so magical, so exotic. And I have to say, that beach does look inviting . . .

Impulsively I sit back down at my desk, snatch up my mouse, click onto Expedia, and search for flights to Goa. My sister's coming back in a week's time, so it's probably a crazy idea, I mean, I probably won't be able to get a flight last minute anyway . . . Oh look, there's one leaving first thing tomorrow!

I hesitate, a list of all the things I need to do running through my head, all the reasons why I can't possibly just drop everything and jump on a plane. Every sane, sensible, careful bone in my body is telling me it's a ridiculous idea. A holiday isn't going to fix anything. I need to stay here. I have deadlines, bills to pay, a pile of laundry, my annual check-up at the dentist's . . .

'*There's plenty of time to be sensible when you get to my age.*' Mrs Flannegan's voice rings in my ears.

And it *is* only a week.

Before I can change my mind, I click purchase.

After all, what can happen in a week?

4

Two long-haul flights squashed on the back row, next to the toilets, in a seat that won't recline, a delayed stopover in Doha Airport where a cappuccino costs a small fortune, and some severe turbulence later, I finally arrive in Goa.

Phew.

If I looked a hundred years old when I left Heathrow, I look double that now, I wince, giving myself a fright as I catch my bleary-eyed reflection in a mirror as I wait at baggage reclaim.

Still, I'm here, I quickly remind myself. In India! On holiday!

Despite my exhaustion, I feel a surge of excitement. It was all a bit of a rush, but I got everything sorted:

To Do

1 Water plants

(aka half-dead spider plant in bathroom.)

2 Put lights on timer

(though let's be honest, does this really fool a potential burglar?)

3 Leave Heathcliff with Mrs Flannegan

(She offered to look after him and I gave her strict instructions on how he likes being tickled under his belly and not to give him too many treats. Last time she had him for the weekend he came back twice the size and couldn't even fit through his dog door. Admittedly he didn't look best pleased to be left with his arch nemesis, Snoopy the cat, who promptly got into Heathcliff's basket, but I'll make it up to him. Somehow.)

4. Buy Immodium

(also insect repellent, antiseptic ointment, plasters, hand sanitiser, headache tablets, tampons . . . I didn't have time to go shopping so I had to do it all at Heathrow . . . in fact, sod it, just throw in all of Boots to be on safe side.)

5. Buy guidebook

(I like to be prepared. See above.)
And last but not least.

6. Shut laptop!

Spotting my suitcase, I grab it off the conveyor belt and, stifling a yawn, set off, wheeling it determinedly towards the exit. A few days of sun, sea and relaxation and I'll be a whole new me.

It's like walking into a sauna.

As the automatic doors slide open, I step from the cool, air-conditioned building into the tropical humidity outside. It's still early in the morning and darkness is clinging on around the edges of the new day, but the heat is already stifling. I'm greeted by an excited crowd of people waiting for their friends and relatives, arms waving, faces smiling, voices shouting.

I smell the air: it's a pungent mix of diesel oil mingled with incense, and I take a deep lungful. It *smells* like India. My excitement ratchets up a notch and for a moment I pause, trying to slowly take it all in. To observe. To let myself acclimatise. But it's impossible. It's like being on a diving board, I just need to jump straight in.

Gripping on to my suitcase, I charge forwards through the commotion. Busily I scan the crowds. I texted my little sister yesterday to tell her I was coming out and she texted back excitedly, asking for my flight details and saying she would pick me up at the airport.

Only I can't see her.

My gaze passes from face to face, but there's just a sea of shiny black hair and not a blonde head in sight. I feel a familiar tug of annoyance. Why am I not surprised? This is so typical of Amy. She's always late. Or in the wrong place.

Or she's totally forgotten.

I get a sudden flashback to last year, waiting for her in the pouring rain in Leicester Square. It was just after I'd broken up with Sam and we'd arranged to see a movie, only she never showed up. Or answered her phone. (That's another thing about my sister, she has this infuriating habit of never answering her phone because she didn't hear it, or she's run out of credit, or she's forgotten to charge it. Or the classic excuse: *she forgot to turn it on.*) I ended up spending Saturday night on my own, sitting amid a row of snuggly couples, watching *What To Expect When You're Expecting*.

Trust me, I still bear the scars.

'You need taxi?' A small, wiry man appears next to me.

'No thanks, I'm fine,' I smile politely, and try to keep moving.

But I've barely gone two more paces before I'm swooped upon by another man. 'Taxi ma'am?'

'Um, no thank you,' I shake my head, dislodging the beads of sweat that have sprung up around my hairline. They start trickling down my face in big fat rivulets. 'I'm fine, thank you.'

He stares at me dubiously, and who would blame him? I'd left my flat dressed for the weather – as in, the weather in London in January, not the weather in Southern India – and I'm wearing black leggings, a black jumper and a pair of black boots. Believe me, I couldn't look less fine.

Fine is sitting on the sofa with your feet up, drinking a cup of tea and flicking through *Grazia*. Fine is not melting in thirty-five-degree heat, encased in Lycra and sporting a pair of swollen cankles.

And now I'm being dived upon by a whole crowd of taxi drivers. 'Miss! Taxi! You need taxi? I give you ride! Where you go? *Taxi! Miss!*'

It reminds me of a wildlife programme I once saw where all these lions were circling a herd of elephants and one became separated and was all lost and vulnerable and *boom*, they pounced.

In my head I can hear David Attenborough's voiceover:

'*The taxi drivers circle the crowds of arriving passengers, hungry for a fare, until suddenly they spot one . . . jetlagged and disorientated, it's been left stranded . . . and as it moves away from the pack and starts looking for its relative, it leaves itself defenceless . . .*'

Just as I'm identifying with the elephant (trust me, you haven't *seen* my cankles) and thinking, that's it, there's no point trying to resist, I might as well give up on my sister and be bundled into a cab, I hear a voice:

'Rubes!'

At the sound of my name I twirl around and see a tousled blonde head bobbing up and down in the crowd and a pair of tanned, skinny arms stacked with lots of sparkly bracelets waving in the air. I watch them both getting closer, until suddenly the crowds part, and my little sister bursts forth.

'You're here already!' she gasps breathlessly, flinging her jangly arms around me.

My sister always acts surprised to see you when she's late. As if it's a complete mystery to her how this could have happened.

'Well yes, my flight arrived an hour ago,' I reply, hugging her back.

'Oh, was it early?'

'No, it was on time,' I bristle as we break apart. 'Didn't you get my text?'

She looks at me blankly.

I'm about to remind her that I texted her my flight details, but I don't want to get into an argument already, I've only just arrived. Plus, knowing me and my little sister, there'll be plenty of time for that later.

'So how are you?' I ask, quickly changing the subject and standing back to take a good look at her. Her hair has gone even blonder in the sun, her skin is tanned and, instead of her usual Topshop wardrobe, she's wearing an embroidered pink kaftan and a pair of brightly patterned silk harem trousers. Next to me in my head-to-toe black combo she's like an explosion of colour.

'Wicked!' she grins back, her teeth looking super-white against her suntan. 'How are you Rubes?' She jumps around exuberantly.

'A bit jetlagged,' I reply, feeling like her ancient, ashen-faced big sister. It's times like these I think there are more than just ten years between me and Amy; it's like we don't even speak the same language.

'Well no worries, we can get a tuk-tuk and head straight back.' Grabbing my suitcase she starts negotiating her way through the crowd.

'A *tuk-tuk?*' I repeat uncertainly.

But she's already sped ahead in her flip-flops. I hurry after her, sweating profusely in my boots and leggings as she charges towards the busy road.

'Be careful!' I shriek, as she steps into the melee of traffic and starts waving her arms around. 'You'll get knocked down . . .'

Oh god. I've been here five minutes and I've already turned into Mum.

As a brightly coloured rickshaw comes hurtling towards her, I have to cover my eyes.

'Here we are!' she says cheerfully, and I open them with relief to see that yes, I still have a sister and no, she's not squashed in the middle of the road, but is instead shoving my bag into the back seat. 'Hey, are you all right?' She glances at me, curiously. 'You look worried.'

'Of course I'm not worried,' I protest.

Which of course is a total lie. I'm always worried when I'm with my little sister. The two go together. Like PMT and chocolate.

'I'm just a little nervous . . .' I stare at the tuk-tuk, which is belching out exhaust fumes with a deafening noise. It's basically a scooter with a sidecar perched on top and has no doors or seatbelts. 'Is it safe?' I ask warily.

'Of course it's not safe,' she laughs. 'This is India! Come on, get in!'

I falter, then, putting aside my fears, I start trying to shoehorn my hand luggage into the back. Only, whilst my Samsonite carry-on might have been made to fit into the plane's overhead lockers, the designers obviously haven't given thought to the space in a tuk-tuk.

'Damn, it won't fit, we'll have to get a cab instead,' I say regretfully, whilst feeling secretly thrilled by the prospect. I take back my earlier David Attenborough fears. An air-conditioned cab seems like a much better option.

But I hadn't bargained on the driver's determination not to lose a fare. Before I know it, he's jumped out of the front seat and is shoving my luggage on the roof.

'Is it going to be OK on there?' I ask, somewhat anxiously, as he ties it on with a bit of string.

'No problem,' he beams, shooting me a blindingly white smile and swinging back behind the wheel. He motions for me to get in.

'Because there are a few breakables,' I continue, clambering onto the back seat behind my sister, who's already hopped inside with the ease of someone for whom climbing into a tuk-tuk is now like jumping on a bus, 'and I'm just a bit concerned—'

The driver slams his foot on the gas and I'm catapulted forwards as the tuk-tuk accelerates off.

'Ouch . . . oomf . . . sorry,' I jabber, bashing my leg as I lose my balance and crash headfirst onto my sister's lap.

'Will you stop worrying!' laughs Amy, as I resurface. 'You're on holiday!'

'I know I'm on holiday,' I nod, lurching onto the back seat and clinging on for dear life as we career around a corner. 'It's just . . . you know me . . . I don't want my camera to break . . .'

'Are you seriously trying to tell me you don't have insurance?' Amy gives a little snort of disbelief.

I colour. I'm renowned for being prudent. I have insurance for insurance.

'I'm just being careful, that's all,' I say, a little stiffly. 'If you were a bit more careful, I wouldn't always be having to . . . *ow!*' We bounce over a pothole and hit our heads. I hear my luggage bang up and down on the roof.

Amy stifles a giggle. 'Well anyway, you're going to be too busy doing yoga to be worrying about anything for a week,' she replies.

'Oh I don't think so.' Now it's my turn to laugh. 'I'm terrible at yoga. You know me, I can't even touch my toes.'

'You will be able to after a week at Rising Bliss, it's one of the best yoga retreats in Goa.'

'A yoga retreat?" My laughter trails off and I peer at her uncertainly. 'But I thought we were staying in a resort.'

'Resort, retreat, what's the difference?' She gives a tinkly little laugh and for the first time I notice something glinting underneath her fringe.

'What's that?' I ask, pointing to a little sparkly thing between her eyebrows.

'My bindi,' she shrugs nonchalantly.

'Your bindi?' This, from a girl who left Heathrow six months ago wearing skinny jeans and a Scouse brow and with her beloved hair straighteners carefully packed in her hand luggage.

'I can get you one if you like,' she offers.

'Thanks, but I don't think it would suit me.'

'You need to chill out a bit, Rubes, let go of your negativity, open your chakras.'

Oh god help us, my little sister's gone all hippy on me.

'My chakras are already open, thanks very much,' I say, a little huffily.

'Wait till you meet Shine, he'll sort you out.'

'Who's Shine?' I ask. 'And, by the way, I don't need *sorting out*.'

'He's the yoga instructor. He's amazing,' she gushes, going all limp-eyed.

'Oh-oh, someone's got a crush,' I tease, in big sisterly fashion.

But now it's her turn to get all tetchy. 'Don't be a teenager,' she says huffily, and changes the subject. 'So how are Mum and Dad?'

'Good, they're driving down to France next week with the caravan,' I nod, remembering the conversation I'd had with them at Heathrow this morning. Well, I call it a conversation, but it was mostly Mum running through a list of all the terrible things that can happen in India, from rabid dog attacks to tourists having their kidneys stolen. It ended with her saying if I needed a holiday, why didn't I go with them to Brittany instead? Thankfully my flight started boarding and I was saved from answering. 'It's their anniversary at the end of the month,' I add. 'Thirty-five years. They're going out for dinner with a few friends, I said we'd join them.'

I'm expecting Amy to be all enthusiastic – being the baby of the family, she's close to our parents. But instead she seems to hesitate.

'Um . . . well, I'm not sure when I'm flying back . . . I can't remember the date . . .'

This is nothing new; despite Amy being able to carbon date a three-thousand-year-old Egyptian mummy with ease, when it comes to the modern day, she's useless with dates. I'm always having to remind her of birthdays and anniversaries and even then she forgets and I end up signing her name on all my cards.

'It's next Saturday, I checked with Mum, she's got your flight details.'

'Oh . . . right, of course.'

'I've booked myself on the same return flight as you, so we can travel together,' I say cheerfully. 'I got the last seat so I was really lucky.'

'You did?' replies Amy, but she doesn't look as pleased as I'd expected. In fact, if I didn't know her better, I'd think something was troubling her.

But this is Amy we're talking about. Nothing ever troubles her and, as if to prove me right, her face quickly relaxes back into her characteristic grin.

'Brill,' she enthuses, 'Can't wait!'

5

Oh god. Are we nearly there yet?

We've been on our way now for about forty-five minutes, bumping along narrow dusty roads through towns and villages, narrowly avoiding wild pigs, goats, stray dogs, even people. And I'm not liking this. I'm really not liking it at all.

Oh, who am I kidding? I'm absolutely terrified.

Gripping my sister's hand so tightly I'm probably going to cut off her circulation, I try to steady my thudding heart. I'm all for new experiences, but driving in India is something else. Forget pedestrian crossings, pavements, even traffic sticking to their side of the road, it's like a game of fairground dodgems. Cars, tuk-tuks, motorbikes, trucks, all swerving around each other, in one constantly flowing insanity. It's a miracle everything doesn't collapse into one big pile-up, I wince, as we narrowly miss another crash.

And then there are the horns. Everyone has their hand on one, our driver included; there's constant honking and blasting at everyone and everything to get out of the way. It's like being in the loudest club I've ever been in, and then multiplying it by a thousand. My eardrums are pounding. My nerves are shredded. My eyes are . . .

Argh . . .

As the tuk-tuk swerves violently to avoid a couple of cows, I squeeze my eyes tightly shut. There are cows everywhere. I read a bit of my guidebook on the plane and it explained how, because they are sacred to Hindus, cows are allowed to roam freely. Not having to stay stuck in a field, they can stand anywhere they want, go anywhere they want, do anything they want. It's as if they've been given a VIP all-access pass. Unlike in the West, where they're just walking beefburgers, here they're worshipped, revered, untouchable.

Opening my eyes I see a couple of tourists taking their photograph . . .

. . . and a great big truck heading towards us – Fuck!

Finally, after the hair-raising, white-knuckle ride, we pull up outside where I'm staying for a week. At least, I presume it's where we're staying. My eyes are still screwed tightly shut in fear as the driver turns off the engine on the tuk-tuk and suddenly, there's silence.

'Rubes, we're here,' prods Amy, elbowing me sharply in the ribs. I open my eyes and clamber out after her. The brightness hits me. The sun has risen during our journey from the airport and I blink rapidly. After the British winter and months of it getting dark at 3 p.m., I'm unused to bright light and hastily rummage for the cheap pair of sunnies I bought at the airport.

'So, what do you think?' she asks impatiently, hopping up and down on one leg, just like she used to do when she was a kid.

Sticking them on, I take a deep breath and look out through a gap in the palm trees. I can see the glint of the ocean beyond, shimmering in the distance. My heart's still racing after the journey, but all at once it's as if the adrenaline just disappears and is replaced by a warm, calm feeling of joy.

So what if it's a yoga retreat, it's also paradise.

'I think it's beautiful,' I murmur, taking in the view.

'I told you!' she beams. 'I knew you were going to love it here.'

'See, we do agree on something,' I smile, turning back to her. 'Though I'm still not sure about that bindi,' I tease.

'Well, I'm not sure about those sunglasses.' She pulls a face. 'They're like something Mum would wear.'

'I was in a rush!' I protest, clutching at them. 'Are they that bad?' Being ten years younger, my sister is my fashion stylist. She's saved me from more than a few horrors, including a pair of furry boots that I thought were really nice but . . . well, anyway, the least said about those the better.

'Worse.' She pulls a face. 'In fact, I'm not sure even Mum would wear them.'

I glance at my reflection in the window of the tuk-tuk. Oh god, she's right. They're terrible. What was I thinking? I look like Elton John during his Rocket Man era.

'But it's the only pair I have,' I wail.

'I promise I won't take any photographs and put them on Facebook,' she grins.

My sister is a Facebook fanatic; she's forever tagging me in embarrassing photos. She can be very annoying like that.

'*Promise*, promise?' I demand.

'Cross my heart . . . Elton,' she teases, reading my mind.

A giggle escapes. It's impossible to stay annoyed at my sister. We both start laughing and, having grabbed my bags and paid the driver, we throw our arms around each other and walk inside.

After the noise and madness of the journey from the airport, Rising Bliss is an oasis of calm and relaxation. In fact, if you looked up 'bliss' in the dictionary, I wouldn't be surprised to see a photograph of this place instead of a definition, I decide, as we walk through the garden, which is filled with hammocks strung from palm trees and the scent of frangipani flowers, towards reception.

Inside I discover the scent of incense, and the sounds of soft chanting, and Biju, the small, plump owner who, after checking me in, shows me to my room. The retreat has a main guesthouse perched on the cliff overlooking the ocean, but I'm staying in one of the individual huts, which are reached by a steep path leading down from the cliff top.

'I trust everything is pleasing for you,' puffs Biju, who's insisted on carrying my suitcase and is sounding like a steam train as we finally reach the beach. Mopping his brow with a huge red handkerchief, he opens the door to a small hut tucked underneath a palm tree and ushers me and Amy inside.

Being a yoga retreat, I've been expecting a single bunk and no-frills accommodation, but instead there's a large double bed with pristine white sheets, across which are scattered a gorgeous arrangement of flower petals.

Even better, it's all mine, as Amy's checked into the main guesthouse. As much as I love my sister, I still haven't quite got over the shock of having to share my bedroom with her when she was born. Plus, she's so untidy, you need a map just to locate her bed underneath all her clothes.

'Wow, this is so lovely,' I smile.

There's just one thing.

'There's no mosquito net,' I say, looking up at the ceiling where one should be hanging.

'Oh, you don't need one here, you will be fine,' smiles Biju, whose cherubic face boasts a big grin and an even bigger black moustache.

'Are you sure?' I say uncertainly, 'it did say in my guidebook—'

'Rubes, stop worrying,' chastises Amy, 'I don't have any bites, look!' As evidence she waggles her long bronzed limbs at me.

'Hmm, it's just, you know how mozzies love me . . .'

'No mozzies!' beams Biju, rolling up his sleeves to reveal two hairy forearms as he makes a noise like a mosquito. '*Zzzzzzzzz*. No!' He looks delighted.

'OK, well if you say so,' I smile, reassured. 'You should know.'

Biju smiles even more broadly, his chest inflating at the compliment. 'I will be at your service at reception,' he says, giving a little wobble of his head, before leaving the beach hut.

The beep of a text sounds and I automatically reach for my phone. But it's not mine, it's Amy's.

'Who's that?' I ask out of interest.

'Just a friend,' she says casually, but I notice her quickly texting back in a way that tells me it's more than just any friend. 'OK, well I'll leave you to unpack.'

'Where are you going?'

'Oh . . . um . . . I've just got a few errands to do,' she says quickly. 'Let's meet down at the beach in half an hour.'

'OK, great,' I smile, giving her a hug goodbye. 'See you soon.'

She gives me a little wave and I watch as she hurries across the sand and disappears behind a palm tree. Yeah right, errands indeed. I wonder what she's up to? And more importantly, knowing my little sister, should I be worried?

Yes. I should.

I should be very worried.

But not about Amy.

Fifteen minutes later I've finished unpacking and am facing the unfaceable.

OK, Ruby, deep breaths.

Standing in my room, I screw up all my courage. There are lots of ways people are brave. Rescuing children from dangerous riptides. Parachuting out of aeroplanes. Facing illness. Even getting a big hairy spider out of your bath commands a great deal of courage (well, for me anyway).

But this has to be the scariest of all.

Wearing a bikini.

And worst, in the middle of January, when I've spent five months not seeing the sun, my legs haven't been out of 60-denier opaque tights and my body has not been exposed to sunlight. I'm like a vampire, only without sexy Robert Pattinson to keep me company. Even worse, I have to walk outside, into the bright sunshine, around a lot of tanned, fit yoga bodies.

Personally, I'd rather jump out of an aeroplane. *Without a parachute.*

Pulling on my bikini bottoms which, as always, are never big enough, I then hoick the triangles over my boobs and tie them securely in place. OK, now for the mirror. Bracing myself, I gingerly open the door of the small wooden wardrobe. Hanging on the back is a full-length mirror and, screwing up one eye, I sort of tentatively squint through the other at my reflection.

I've learned this trick from watching scary movies, or reading my book reviews, and trust me, this is *much* scarier.

I catch a blurry glimpse of pale limbs, a jiggly bit above my bikini bottoms that I could have sworn wasn't there last time, and inner thighs that prove Zumba twice a week is simply not enough.

I wince, but remain stoic. But not brave enough to open both eyes, I decide, as I do a reluctant twirl so I can check out the back view. Oh dear. It's all I can do not to jump cowering under my duvet.

Only there's not that option, as it's thirty-five degrees and there *isn't* a duvet.

Is it just me, or does every female look at their bottom in a bikini and just despair?

I mean, it should be up *here* . . .

Grabbing my bum cheeks with both hands, I hoist it up a good few inches and instantly I'm transformed. The ripple effect at the back of my thighs is smoothed out. My bum looks pert. I can even open both eyes and give a little nod of satisfaction. OK, so it's not Gisele, but it ain't bad – until I let go and it all just, well, 'drops' would be one way of putting it; 'sags like rice pudding in a string bag' would be another.

But I have a secret weapon. *The sarong*. I bought one at the airport, along with my sunnies, and whereas those might have been a mistake, this purchase most definitely wasn't.

God love a sarong, I cheer, wrapping it around me like I'm auditioning to be an Egyptian mummy and covering up all the white jiggly bits. *Correction*: dry, scaly, white jiggly bits. Honestly, what central heating does to your skin should be illegal.

Finishing tying the sarong tightly, I give myself a final check in the mirror. There, *much* better. And feeling a lot more cheered, I slip on a pair of flip-flops, grab my sun lotion and towel and head out onto the beach.

It's still early, but the small sandy cove is already a hive of activity. Several dedicated sunbathers with nutbrown limbs are stretched out on sun loungers, their oiled bodies glistening in the early morning sun like mahogany sideboards while, in the ocean, several guests from the resort are taking their morning swim.

For a moment I watch them, their heads bobbing up and down on the waves, until a very fit-looking blonde woman jogs into my eye-line, and I follow her progress along the shore to where another holiday-maker is doing his morning stretches.

Oh dear. My morning stretches involve bending down to put my slippers on and reaching for my coffee pot, but his are somewhat more advanced, I muse, feeling ever so slightly intimidated as I watch him do a handstand. I'm going to have to limber up a bit before I go to a yoga class.

Dropping my towel, I try to touch my toes. And come to

an abrupt halt by my knees. But of course that's only because I've just been sitting on a plane for god knows how many hours and my hamstrings are tight. I'll be fine once I've had time to relax, unwind, loosen up. I know, I'll do a bit of swimming first: that will do the trick.

Kicking off my flip-flops, I trot down to the water's edge. No one's looking, so I drop the sarong and step into the ocean. It's like walking into a warm bath, and I stretch out my hands and let my fingertips glide over the sparkling water.

Wow, this is bliss. What an amazing way to start the day. I think about my usual morning routine in London, but already that feels a million miles away and, closing my eyes, I tip my face to the sun, feeling its warmth on my face. My agent was so right. As always. I should have known to listen to Diana. I feel so much better already.

Stretching out my arms I dive into the waves and start swimming further out, relishing the feeling of water and sunshine on my skin, until after a few minutes I stop and turn back to look at the shore. Bobbing up and down in the warm waves, it seems a long way away, but I can see a couple of figures walking along the seashore. I squint, trying to bring them into focus. From the outline it looks like my sister. And is that a man she's with?

I peer harder, but they're too far away. Plus, I have salt in my eyes, making everything all bleary. For a few moments I tread water, watching their blurry shapes bending close, then I begin to swim back.

As I near the shore they come into focus. Yup, I was right, it's Amy and she's deep in conversation with an Indian man. An extremely handsome Indian man, I can't help noticing.

'Amy!' I call, as I walk out of the waves.

At the sound of her name she looks up, startled. 'Oh, Rubes, hi,' she says, and they break apart quickly. 'I didn't see you there.'

'I was just having a swim, did you finish your errands?'

For a moment Amy looks at me blankly. 'Oh . . . yes . . . my errands,' she nods, seeming to suddenly remember, 'yes, they're all finished.'

'Good,' I nod, wringing out my wet hair and brushing away the water that's trickling into my eyes.

There's a pause, and I wait expectantly to be introduced to the handsome man standing next to her.

'And then, would you believe it, but by total coincidence, look who I bumped into!' she exclaims.

Yeah right. I've seen better acting in a pantomime.

'Who?' I prompt.

'Oh! Right, yes . . . silly me, I haven't introduced you,' she says, all flustered. 'This is Shine, the yoga teacher I was telling you about.'

'Nice to meet you, I've heard so much about you,' he says in a perfect English accent, extending his hand.

'Likewise,' I smile, shaking his hand. He's wearing a white shirt, hanging open, and I catch a glimpse of his muscular torso. He doesn't just have a six-pack, he has an eight-pack. I'm both impressed and embarrassed. There's him with his amazing body and here's me with my wobbly bits, I cringe, thinking about my sarong lying only yards away and wishing I could teleport it.

'So I'm excited to hear you're coming to my sunset yoga class later,' he smiles, interrupting my thoughts.

'Um, I am?' I look at my sister.

Who's gazing dreamily at Shine. 'Absolutely,' she nods. 'His class is amazing.'

'Thanks,' he smiles, and they exchange a look.

Oh-oh. There's something going on here, and it's a lot more than a few sun salutations.

'Super,' I say, feeling rather green and hairy.

They both turn back to me, as if suddenly remembering I'm there.

'Wonderful, well see you later then,' he flashes me a handsome smile, before turning to Amy and giving a little bow of his head. '*Namaste.*'

'*Namaste,*' she chimes back, all doe-eyed.

He strides off up the beach, his white shirt billowing in the breeze.

'So come on, spill the beans,' I demand, as soon as he's out of earshot.

Still gazing dreamily after him, she gives a little startled jump. 'What?' She looks cornered.

'I might have saltwater in my eyes, but I'm not that blind.'

She blushes, despite her suntan. 'We're just good friends,' she protests.

'That's what everyone says,' I counter, giving her a long look.

She avoids my gaze and tosses her hair over her shoulder. 'We bond on a spiritual level,' she replies haughtily.

'Oh come on,' I tease, 'I saw his six-pack!'

'Really? I hadn't noticed,' she replies innocently.

'You fibber!' I laugh.

'Look, I don't know what you're talking about,' she says, all agitated. 'And I'm not going to stand here all day, I'm going to breakfast. Coming?' And without waiting for my answer, she turns on her heel and stalks up the beach.

6

Breakfast is a feast of fresh fruit, banana pancakes and masala omelettes, which are made of a mixture of delicate spices and the most delicious things I think I've ever tasted. Most of the other guests seem to be couples, though there are a group of guys from Manchester; I hear one of them talking loudly about a silent rave he'd been to on the beach, where everyone wore headphones.

Which, considering the volume of his voice, is probably what the people at the neighbouring table wish they were wearing.

But that's most likely because it's just so quiet here. Anything would seem loud against the backdrop of bird-calls and gentle ocean waves, I reflect, as I go for a walk with Amy along the beach afterwards. After the noise and fast pace of London, Goa is like a shifting down of gears to a much more relaxed pace of life. With the warm sand between our toes, we pass fishermen bringing in their nets, wide-smiled stallholders inviting us to 'just look' and beach-front cafés with names like 'chill-out zone' right on the water's edge, where it would be impossible to do anything else *but* chill out.

As usual, Amy snaps back like an elastic band to her normal chatty self, and the next couple of hours are spent catching up on the gossip from home and hearing about her trip.

'It's been incredible, Rubes,' she enthuses. 'I've seen so many things and met so many people! Like this great group of South Africans I met in my hostel in Bangkok . . . we had so much fun . . . you'd love Thailand . . . all the temples, and monks in orange robes, and this huge, giant Buddha that's made entirely out of gold . . .'

I look across at my sister as she gesticulates wildly, her face shining with enthusiasm, and feel a sudden beat of pride. My little sister's all grown up. It feels like only yesterday that she was so homesick on a school trip, she clung to my hand and refused to get on the minibus. And now look at her! Travelling to far-flung places like Thailand and seeing all these amazing cultural sights.

'And we went to this wicked full-moon party in Koh Phangan . . .'

'A full-moon party?' Of course, it's my sister, there had to be a party in there somewhere.

'Yeh, it was totally crazy,' she laughs, then pauses. 'Actually, on second thoughts, I'm not sure you'd love that bit.'

'Hey, I like parties!' I protest indignantly. Honestly, Amy thinks anyone over thirty should be in an old people's home.

'Not twenty-four-hour ones with rave music,' she points out.

I pull a face. 'OK, perhaps not,' I agree, 'but I seem to remember you're the one who can't handle a party.'

'Huh?' She frowns.

'Jamie Richardson's sixteenth birthday party?' I prompt.

She lets out a loud groan. 'Oh god, I'd forgotten all about that!'

'I haven't,' I tease, laughing at her cringing. 'And I'm not sure Detective Sergeant Harrison has either.'

At the mention of his name she lets out a loud shriek.

'I couldn't believe it when he rang the house to tell us you'd been arrested,' I continue.

She clutches at her face. 'Oh Rubes, it was awful!'

'I know! I had to come get you,' I remind her.

'It wasn't my fault!' she protests, 'I was only fifteen, I'd never drunk alcohol before, but someone gave me a glass of cider . . .'

I raise my eyebrows.

'Well OK, a few glasses of cider,' she concedes, 'but how was I to know the neighbours would call the police about the music—'

'And you'd get arrested for underage drinking and causing affray,' I finish.

She blushes bright red. 'Oh god, I was so scared about Mum and Dad finding out, I knew they'd kill me!'

'So did I,' I smile, 'which is why I never told them it was the police on the phone, but said it was you, calling for a lift home and not to worry, I'd pick you up.'

'You saved my life,' she says with a grateful smile.

'Well, it wouldn't be the first time,' I grin, 'though remember when we nearly got caught out when I bumped into Detective Sergeant Harrison with Mum in the supermarket and he asked after you—'

'And you told Mum it was because he'd come into school to give a talk on women's self-defence and how to keep safe and defend oneself against an attacker,' continues Amy, picking up the story, 'and I was a star pupil—'

'And that evening Dad asked you to give him a demonstration,' I giggle, remembering, 'and you hit him with an umbrella—'

'Right where I shouldn't,' she gasps, and breaks into a fit of laughter.

'And Mum had to give him a pack of frozen peas,' I guffaw loudly, wiping away the tears of mirth from my eyes.

'Poor Dad . . . I felt terrible,' she wails, between fits of laughing.

'Not as bad as he did,' I burst out, and we both dissolve

into heaps of laughter, as people walk past us, shooting us funny looks.

Finally, after a few moments, we manage to get control of ourselves again.

'Honestly, what would I do without you?' grins Amy, wiping her face with her sarong. Her kohl eyeliner has bled and smudged down her cheeks, making her look like a panda.

'I dread to think,' I grin, leaning over to help her. 'Here, you've missed a bit.'

Digging out a tissue from my purse, I rub it away as she stands there patiently, like I used to do when she was a little kid and got chocolate on her face.

'There you go.'

'Thanks Rubes.'

I smile. She might have travelled halfway across the world and be all grown up now, but she'll forever be my little sister. And, linking arms, we set off to walk back.

After we return to Rising Bliss, Amy goes off to meet some backpacker friends and I take a snooze in a hammock. Then I relax on the beach a bit. Goa's laid-back vibe is infectious, and whereas normally in London I'd be rushing around doing a million different things, the rest of the day slips by in a delightful haze of doing nothing.

Until I notice the sun starting to sink lower in the sky and realise it's time for the sunset yoga class.

OK, so I wouldn't say I'm scared, just more – how can I put it? – *trepidatious*.

'You'll be fine, don't worry,' reassures Amy, as she cajoles me into my baggy sweatpants and T-shirt. 'Shine is an amazing teacher, he works with all levels.'

I shoot her a look. She's wearing shorts and a white vest that show off perfectly toned limbs. Seriously, sometimes I wonder if Amy and I really are sisters, or if Mum brought the wrong baby home from the hospital.

'There's levels, and then there's me,' I reply.

'Oh c'mon Rubes, you can't be that bad!' she admonishes.

'I'm worse,' I reply, glancing at my reflection in the mirror. Not only do I look like a shapeless baggy thing, but I hadn't realised how strong the sun was and, despite my SPF 50, my face is bright red. I couldn't look less like the people you get on the cover of those yoga magazines.

'Ready?' I zone back in to see Amy waiting by the door, a bundle of energy and eagerness.

'As I'll ever be,' I say, forcing a bright smile in an attempt to hide my nerves. Which I know is a bit ridiculous. I mean, come on, it's only *yoga*.

'Trust me, you'll feel tons better after you've done a few *vinyasas*.'

I feel a beat of alarm.

'A few *what*?'

But she's already set off briskly flip-flopping across the sand and, quickly grabbing my towel, I follow her.

Outside the sun has sunk lower towards the ocean, transforming the sky into vibrant streaks of pomegranate pink, blood-red and orange. It really is beautiful, like flames dancing on the horizon and, distracted, I stop to stare at it for a few moments. Until I realise Amy has charged far ahead and I have to race after her.

Which means I'm already sweating by the time I arrive at the class, which is on a large wooden deck with a spectacular bamboo and palm leaf roof, built right in front of the ocean. It's a bit different to the one yoga class I went to at my local sports centre. Oil lamps are burning and incense drifts through the large open space, which is already filled with brightly coloured mats laid out across the floor, on which people are doing lots of stretching.

I grab a mat and look for Amy who, to my horror, has gone straight to the front of the class and is already limbering up. Oh god, this is going to be embarrassing. I was at least hoping I could hide away at the back, preferably in a darkened corner, where no one could see me, but this way I'm going to be on full show.

But it's no good, Amy turns and, spotting me, beckons me over.

'Hey Rubes, over here,' she calls loudly. Amy's voice has always been on the foghorn side. Something to do with a perforated eardrum she got from standing too close to the fireworks. Apparently she thought the rockets were real rockets, and would take her to the moon if she caught one in her mittened hands. Well, that's the kind of thing you think if you're seven years old. *And Amy.*

I can't pretend not to have heard her, the whole class has, so I start picking my way through the lithe, yoga-honed bodies. On closer inspection everyone looks terrifyingly good, as if they came out of the womb in the lotus position. There's a few model types, with their hair tied back and skyscraper limbs; lots of men with beards (not the geography teacher sort, but the fashionable media sort) and those rich, hippy trustafarian types with ankle tattoos and expensive yoga clothes who look as if they live in Notting Hill or Manhattan.

And then there's me.

I can almost feel my chakras tie themselves up into a knot. There's intimidating, and then there's a yoga class in Goa. Finally reaching the front, I squeeze in between Amy and a man who's so bendy he could be a contortionist in the circus. My anxiety ratchets up another few notches. I glance at Amy. Honestly, this is tantamount to sibling cruelty.

But she doesn't notice, she's too focused on staring over at the entrance, like a meerkat. Along with everyone else, I realise, following their gazes until mine lands on Shine, who appears from the beach and walks onto the deck.

It's like watching a rock star walking on stage.

Bare-chested, with his shoulder-length hair hanging loose, he strides barefoot across the room. He's wearing only a pair of white drawstring trousers and his muscles literally ripple like a racehorse's. The breeze from the ocean, which acts like a wind machine on his flowing tresses, blows them off his face like something from a slow-motion music video.

Every female in the room is transfixed, and secretly wanting to be with him. Every male is envious, and secretly wanting to be him. He's like the Adam Levine of yoga.

'*Namaste*,' he intones, pressing his hands together and doing a perfect bow.

'*Namaste*,' the class chimes back.

Taking a length of material from his wrist, he expertly ties his hair up into a neat, black bun and, taking a deep breath, fixes the class with his penetrating gaze. 'This class will be about honouring yourself and your practice . . . connecting to our divine essence . . . awakening our true inner energies . . . and transforming and enlightening our beings . . .'

That's another reason I'm rubbish at yoga. I'm never quite sure what they're *actually* saying. Still, it sounds really good, and he's got a lovely calming voice.

'. . . in this ever-unfolding mystery of life and love . . .'

Oh, well I get *that* bit, I muse, nodding along with everyone else. I couldn't agree more. Love's a *total* mystery.

'So we'll start by doing a short *vinyasa* in praise for the sun.'

Oh-oh. It's that *vinyasa* business again.

I shoot Amy an urgent look but she's totally absorbed by Shine, who's dropped down onto his mat and is beginning a sequence of effortless moves, while all the time instructing in his soothing tones:

'*Surya Namaskar,* the Sun Salutation, is a flowing sequence of twelve poses. Each movement is synchronised with the breath. It is the motion of the breath which drives these postures. Inhale deeply as you extend and exhale as you contract . . .'

He makes it look so easy with his flexible limbs and upper body strength, and I try to follow. I really do. With crunching knees I attempt to wrestle my limbs into one pose, then sort of half-collapse into another. But it's hopeless, it's like my body doesn't want to get into these poses.

I have a sudden image of trying to put the ironing board down, grappling with its stiff board and rigid legs as it refuses to bend. Oh my god, that's me! I *am* my ironing board! I'm not wearing a flowery cover, but I might as well be for all the flexibility in my back and hamstrings . . .

'. . . all the time focusing on *pranayama* . . .'

What? On all fours I look frantically at Amy.

'It's ancient Sanskrit,' she whispers in explanation.

Which makes things a lot clearer because, of course, I'm fluent in Sanskrit.

'. . . and now moving into *Parivrtta Trikonasana* . . .'

I watch Amy twisting her body into a triangle with apparent ease and try to copy her. Big mistake. She was the one who did gymnastics at school, not me.

I feel a sharp pain in my lower back. 'Ouch!'

'Are you OK?' she hisses, looking startled.

'Yes . . . fine,' I grimace. God, how embarrassing. I catch several people glancing over with concerned expressions.

'Great,' she beams, 'I knew you'd love this class once you'd warmed up.'

Warmed up? It must be a hundred degrees in here. Sweat is literally running down my back like water over Niagara Falls. And my body is *still* doing its impression of an ironing board. I look at Amy, she's barely broken into a sheen.

'He's amazing, isn't he?' she continues, gesturing towards

Shine, who's contorting himself into yet another unfeasible position.

'He's very supple,' I nod.

'He's just so inspiring.'

'Mmm . . .' I make a sort of vague sound.

Actually, this probably explains the real reason why I'm so useless at yoga. It's not just that I'm physically hopeless at it, but I've tried to get into the whole spiritual side of it and, call me a Neanderthal, but the only thing yoga has ever inspired me to do is go home and lie down with pint of Häagen-Dazs.

Or in this case one of those delicious fried banana pancakes. My stomach rumbles. Only it's not hunger pangs, I think it's the masala omelette I ate for breakfast, which isn't agreeing with me. I knew I shouldn't have eaten it as I'm not brilliant with spicy food, but I just couldn't resist. Saying that, I'm going to have to be a lot more careful in future, I realise, as my digestive system gurgles loudly in complaint. I don't want to spend the whole week eating Imodium tablets like sweets.

'. . . with your palms outstretched and keeping your shoulders strong, move into *Chaturanga Dandasana* . . .'

Flopping onto my mat, I try to push myself up with shaky elbows. Sweat drips onto my outstretched fingers and my chest feels as if it's about to burst. Oh bloody hell, this is so hard *and* I've got jetlag. I'm exhausted already. I really need to lie down.

But I can't give up without a fight, so for the next hour I concentrate hard on fighting off jetlag and desperately trying to mirror Shine as he flows from one position into another. It's a struggle. Out of the corner of my eyes I can see the rest of the class are all managing to keep up, whilst I constantly lag behind, abandoning one impossible-to-get-into pose for another hamstrings-are-killing-me pose.

Until finally . . .

'Now it's time to relax, lie or sit on your mats and close your eyes . . .'

At last! A position I can get into! With utter relief, I flop onto my mat as Shine begins circulating the room, giving people shoulder massages and rubbing their temples.

'. . . feeling your breaths, take a moment to thank yourself for committing yourself to this class . . .'

A pair of feet appear by my head and I feel the expert pressure of Shine's fingertips as he gives me a little massage. It's like heaven for my sore, aching shoulders and I feel myself drifting off. Actually, maybe I've been wrong all these years. Maybe I could totally get into yoga.

'. . . and tomorrow's class at sunrise . . .'

Sunrise? I'm jolted from my reverie.

'I hope you all will join me here on deck at five a.m.'

There's a loud murmuring of agreement and I feel all thoughts of a lie-in flying out of the window as I try imagining doing this all over again. At the crack of dawn tomorrow morning.

On second thoughts . . .

'Now, if you'd like to finish our practice by joining me in chanting Om . . .'

Probably best not to rush things. It's important to honour my divine energy and all that.

'*Ommmmmmmm,*' I breathe out and, closing my eyes, I fall fast asleep.

7

'Ouch.'

The next morning I can barely move and have to hobble into breakfast.

'Are you OK?' Amy looks at me with concern.

'Yes, I'm fine,' I wince, easing myself down into the chair with trembling thighs. My entire body feels as if it's been run over by a truck and as I try and reach for the orange juice it takes all my resolve not to let out an agonised yelp. 'I'm just a little stiff after yoga, aren't you?'

'No, I feel wonderful,' she smiles brightly, springing onto the seat next to me. 'I did the sunrise class before breakfast.'

'You did?' I stare at her, aghast. Once again I wonder how we can share the same DNA. After yesterday's class, I can barely reach to pour the orange juice, let alone do five a.m. Sun Salutations.

'Why don't you go for a massage?' she suggests, picking up the jug and starting to pour two glasses. 'My treat.'

I smile gratefully. 'Thanks Amy, that's really sweet of you, but I'll be OK.'

'No seriously, you should have one,' she enthuses. 'There's this really amazing Ayurvedic centre five minutes away where they drip oil onto your forehead. It's a traditional form of Indian medicine and is supposed to be great for rejuvenating frayed nerves and eliminating bad thoughts . . .' She trails off awkwardly.

'Are you trying to tell me something?' I raise my eyebrows.

'Well, I know things have been rough for you . . . ever since Sam . . .'

At the mention of his name, I fall silent. 'I thought I'd hidden it,' I say, after a pause.

'Maybe from everyone else, but I'm your sister. You can't hide it from me,' she says quietly, her bright blue eyes meeting mine.

I smile appreciatively. 'I love you, sis.'

'Ditto,' she grins, and passes me my juice.

'Though I should have known,' I add, 'I've never been able to hide anything from you. Remember how I tried to hide all my make-up from you and you still found it?'

'I was only six,' she protests.

'Mum and Dad couldn't stop laughing, you looked like a clown . . .' and now I start giggling at the memory, 'I've still got the photo somewhere.'

'Oh god,' she groans loudly, 'promise me you'll never show anyone that.'

'What's it worth?' I demand, laughing, then clutch my side as a pain shoots through my aching muscles. 'Ouch.'

'A massage,' she fires back, without missing a beat.

I take her up on her offer – well, it's too good not to – and after breakfast Amy calls up to make a booking for me, and gives me the directions. Which I attempt to follow and promptly get lost. Damn. I try retracing my steps, but that only makes things worse, and after a few minutes I end up down some little side street, completely lost. I look for someone to ask, but there's no one around. Bollocks, I'm going to be late, oh hang on.

Ahead, I notice a car parked up with the engine running. It's an expensive-looking car, a dark grey Mercedes with tinted windows; as it's mostly tuk-tuks and mopeds here, it sticks out like a sore thumb. I stare at it for a moment, wondering if I should go up and ask for directions, when the rear passenger door swings opens and someone gets out. A figure dressed in white. A man.

Hang on, I recognise him, isn't that Shine? Feeling a beat of relief, I start to hurry towards him – what a stroke of good luck, he'll totally be able to give me directions – then suddenly pull back.

He's not alone. As he slams the door behind him, a window buzzes down and I hear someone call after him. It's a woman's voice, and although I can't understand what she's saying, I can tell she's angry. But he's not listening. Ignoring her, he begins walking away, when suddenly the car door is flung open and a figure jumps out. It's an Indian woman. Stunningly beautiful, with long black hair to her waist and wearing Western clothes, she rushes after him, yelling, and grabs hold of his arm. Flinging herself at him to try and stop him leaving, she tries to embrace him, but he pushes her roughly away.

I feel suddenly embarrassed, like I've been caught watching something I shouldn't. Their body language is so passionate, so urgent, so *familiar*. They're obviously in some kind of a relationship. She must be his girlfriend, or wife, or maybe she's just his lover.

I shrink back. It feels so clandestine. I don't want them to see me looking, and yet, it's impossible *not* to look. They're making such a scene. And now they're arguing! Hearing their voices loud and urgent, I turn to see her gesticulating wildly and grabbing at his clothes. But Shine is having none of it. Shaking his head, as if refusing to listen, he's trying to fend off her hands and calm her down.

Crikey! What's all that about?

Finally they break apart and as she gets back in the car looking tearful, Shine strides away angrily. I watch him, his face set hard as he heads towards me . . . Oh shit! I look around desperately for something to dive behind, but it's too late, there's nowhere to hide.

'Oh, hi, Ruby.' Shine looks startled to see me.

'Hi,' I smile brightly, trying to cover up my awkwardness. 'Fancy seeing you here!'

I feel my cheeks flush bright red. Oh god, I am such a terrible actor. I really am.

'I was just taking a walk by myself,' he says, recovering quickly. 'I like the solitude.'

Why is he lying? What's the big secret? Who exactly was that woman and what were they arguing about?

'I was just looking for the massage place,' I reply, my mind racing. 'I . . . um . . . got a little lost . . .'

'What's the name of it? Maybe I can help you,' he suggests, seeming pleased to be taking the focus off himself.

I tell him and he quickly gives me directions. 'Enjoy your Ayurvedic treatment,' he nods then, seeming eager to be on his way, he bids me goodbye and strides away down the street.

I watch him for a moment, my mind turning, trying to make sense of it all . . . before snapping back. I'm already late, I can't stand here all day. Plus, I've got better things to think about than Shine's love life, like spending the next two hours being massaged with delicious perfumed oils. And, brushing the thoughts out of my mind, I hurry on my way.

★

Dear Diana,
Took your advice and am on holiday in India!
Having a fab time, doing lots of yoga and
getting super-fit. Just what the agent ordered!
Be back in London next week. Hope all is well
and speak soon.
Ruby xx

Well, that's the official line on my postcard.

In reality I only make it to just that one yoga class, and instead spend my time lazing around on the beach, having massages, shopping for souvenirs and drinking rather too many of these delicious cocktails served in coconuts.

Still, everyone fibs on postcards, don't they?

The rest of my holiday passes in a relaxing blur. Goa is stunning, the people are wonderful, and waking up every day to the constant blue skies and sunshine is better than any medicine. The knot in my shoulders disappears, the pale grey pallor goes from a bright pinkish tinge to a reasonable light tan and I sleep better than I have done in months.

Despite my best intentions, however, my sightseeing list remains untouched. The furthest I make it is to the string of stalls lining the beach where I buy a few souvenirs. Well OK, perhaps slightly more than a few, but it's all so colourful and glittery it's hard to resist.

I mean, who wouldn't want a silk umbrella embroidered with all these gorgeous twinkly mirrors? I muse, picking it up from the chair in the corner of my room, opening it and giving it a little twirl. Admittedly it's probably not *that* practical for London. In fact, now I'm thinking about it, is silk waterproof?

'That's bad luck!'

I look up to see Amy's head popped around the side of my door.

'Hi,' I smile, pleased to see her. Despite staying in the same resort, I've barely seen her all week as she's always doing yoga. Honestly, I had no idea she was such a yoga bunny! Whenever I'd suggested doing anything, she said she couldn't as she was busy working on her lotus position, which, I admit, has been a bit disappointing, but still, at least it shows dedication.

And thighs that are a damn sight firmer than mine, I muse, feeling a beat of regret that I didn't stick at the yoga a bit longer. Oh well, there's always next time.

'You're not supposed to put umbrellas up inside,' she cautions, coming in and sitting down cross-legged on the bed.

'Superstitious rubbish,' I pooh-pooh, giving it a last admiring glance, before wrapping it back up. 'I don't believe in all that.'

'Well, don't say I didn't warn you,' she shrugs. Pushing her sunglasses onto her head, she casts an eye around the clothes-strewn landscape. 'So, ready to go back to London?'

'Almost . . .' I smile, looking up from my packing. 'It's been a lovely break, just what my agent ordered, but I suppose it's time to get back to reality . . .' It's true, it's been a relaxing few days and physically I look and feel so much better than I did when I arrived, though mentally not much has changed. From the outside I might look different, but on the inside I feel pretty much the same as I did before I left London.

Still, what did I expect? A life-changing experience? It was just a week's holiday, after all. I couldn't expect miracles. Just a suntan and some souvenirs.

Speaking of which . . .

'I've just got to finish this last bit of packing.'

Putting down the umbrella, I try to shoehorn a set of wooden coasters and a hammock into my bag. Maybe I have gone a *little* overboard on the souvenir shopping. Do Mum and Dad really need more coasters? Even if they are really beautifully carved. And am I really going to use a hammock in London? OK, I've got a garden, but don't you need sunshine as well?

Then there are the three pashminas I bought for Rachel, Harriet and Milly, that turned into six as I couldn't make up my mind which they'd like best . . . actually, no, make it seven, I realise, spotting another one hidden under a large pile of incense sticks.

I stare at them for a moment. Crikey, did I buy all that? That's a lot of Nag Champa. Mrs Flannegan is going to think I've turned into a hippy.

'What about you?' Deciding to deal with my souvenirs later, I look up and shoot Amy a smile. 'Excited to be going home?'

There's a pause. 'Well, I wouldn't say excited . . .'

'No, you're probably more nervous,' I smile encouragingly, 'what with the new job and everything.'

'Yes,' she nods, fidgeting with her hair. She seems worried, but that's understandable, it's a huge deal for her.

'You'll be brilliant, don't worry,' I quickly try to reassure her. 'You're so talented, Amy, that's why they hired you! And we're all so proud of you, me, and Mum and Dad – we know how hard you've worked for this.'

'I just don't want to let anyone down—' she begins, but I don't let her finish.

'You're not going to let anyone down!' I admonish. 'Amy, you could *never* let anyone down!'

She throws me a thankful look. 'Thanks Rubes.'

'Hey, what are big sisters for?' I say, giving her arm a quick squeeze, before turning back to my packing. 'So, what time shall we get the cab for?' My buttocks have only just recovered from the tuk-tuk ride a week ago, so this time I've insisted on taking a taxi to the airport.

'Well actually, here's the thing . . .'

I pause from squeezing the fifth pashmina into my suitcase. Whenever my sister says 'here's the thing', it usually translates from Amy-speak into 'here's the problem.'

'What thing?' I say suspiciously.

'Oh, it's nothing,' she reassures me quickly. 'It's just that I want to say goodbye to a few people, just some of my backpacker friends, so I thought it's probably easier if I meet you at the airport.'

'But it seems silly to pay for two cabs when we can share one,' I frown.

'Biju offered to give me a lift,' she replies. 'So it's no problem, and I just thought I could leave now while you finish your packing. I've done mine already, I didn't have that much.' She glances at my overstuffed suitcase with a worried expression, 'And it looks like you might be a while.'

'Well, OK I suppose so . . .' I shrug. She has got a point. After all, there's no reason in her hanging around whilst I try and beat my Samsonite wheelie into submission.

'And there's another thing . . .'

I raise my eyebrows.

'Could you lend me some cash?' She shoots me an apologetic look. 'I'll give you it back, I promise. It's just my debit card won't work any more.'

I roll my eyes, I've lost count of the number of times I've bailed my sister out because her debit card won't work, or it's been eaten, or she's lost it. Of course, it's always the card's fault, and never because she's useless with money and has spent all of it.

'Look in my wallet,' I say, gesturing to my bag next to her. 'Just leave me enough for the taxi.'

'Thanks sis, I knew I could count on you!' She takes a bundle of rupees then, jumping up from the bed, gives me a big hug.

'This is just a loan,' I warn, hugging her back. 'To add to the other loans.'

'I know,' she nods, then, breaking away, turns to the door. 'Bye Rubes.'

'Bye Amy – oh, hang on.' But she's already gone rushing off up the beach. Standing at the doorway, I yell after her, 'Just don't be late!'

For a moment, she stops running and turns. 'I won't!' she yells back. Then she's gone, disappearing up the steep path that leads to the guesthouse and I go back inside and return to my packing.

Now how on earth am I going to pack that umbrella?

8

It's not until much later that I realise we never arranged what time to meet.

But that's OK, I'm sure it's fine.

I manage to brush this troublesome thought to one side until I reach Goa International Airport. After all, it's not rocket science, is it? Everyone knows you should get to the airport two hours before your flight.

Even Amy.

Still, just to be on the safe side, I send her a text telling her. Followed up by another, reminding her which airline we're flying with, the flight time and number. Another saying I'll meet her at their check-in desk. And another asking her to confirm she's received all my texts.

She doesn't reply to any of them.

An hour later and I'm still waiting in departures. Checking my mobile phone for the umpteenth time, I let out a gasp of frustration. *Where the hell is she?* Glancing up from the blank screen, I scan my eyes across the crowds of people at the airport. Any minute now she's going to come dashing towards me, an apologetic smile on her face, one of her excuses spilling out of her mouth.

OK, I'm going to count to ten.

No, twenty. Make it twenty.

I start counting. One, two, three . . . maybe I'm going too fast, I'll slow down . . . ten *elephant*, eleven *elephant* . . . No need to panic. Amy's always late. She'll turn up. Just stay calm.

Be patient. Keep counting. *Niiiinnnneeettteeenn* . . . I'm like a record on the wrong speed . . . *Eleeeeppppphhhaaannnttt* . . . I take a deep breath . . . *Tweeeennnnntttttyyyyy* . . .

I stare at the concourse. No Amy.

Shit.

Hot with annoyance, I scroll down my list of contacts to call her. Honestly, she is so irresponsible! She is always late! In fact, I feel like I've spent my whole life waiting for her. She was even late being born, too – three weeks overdue, apparently. Poor Mum was the size of a barrel.

The number connects and starts ringing. Irritation stabs. This call is probably going to cost me a fortune. God knows how much I'll be charged, but I don't have any choice, do I? If she doesn't turn up soon we're going to miss the plane.

Argh! *No answer!* I listen impatiently to the ringing tone. Why doesn't she ever answer her bloody phone, for Chrissakes? Just for once. Pick up your bloody phone . . .

'*Hi, this is Amy, I'm away travelling so can't get to the phone right now . . .*'

As her voicemail message clicks on, I hang up and stuff my phone in my pocket. Impatience gives way to unease. I'm actually getting worried now. I hope nothing's happened to her. The journey to the airport was pretty nerve-wracking, even in a cab. What if there was some kind of accident? What if—

Damn, I knew I shouldn't have let her go off on her own. I should have insisted she came with me.

'*This is a last call for the flight to London Heathrow. Any remaining passengers need to make their way to check-in immediately.*'

As an announcement sounds over the loudspeaker, I zone back in and turn around to look over at the check-in desk.

I do a double take. Hang on, where is everyone?

Before there was a long queue of people waiting to check in, a whole crowd milling around with suitcases and passports, but now they've all disappeared. There's just an empty space where they once were.

Surely everyone can't have gone through security, can they?

Can they?

I check my watch and my panic level moves from amber to code red.

It's that time already?

'Excuse me.' Grabbing hold of my suitcase, I quickly wheel it over to the check-in attendant sitting behind the desk.

She looks up from her paperwork, as if surprised to still see a passenger. This is not good. Inside I can feel code red starting to flash. 'Yes? Can I help you?' she enquires politely.

'I hope so,' I reply, giving her a big smile. I once read an article about how the power of a smile can break down religious boundaries, open doors of opportunity, and change people's lives. Personally, I'm just hoping it can hold up a plane for a few minutes. 'I'm flying to London but I'm waiting for my sister—'

I mean, compared to religious boundaries, what's a little delay?

'The check-in is closing,' she exclaims sharply.

OK, maybe a smile isn't *that* powerful.

'I need your passport,' she continues, her hand shooting out towards me.

'But I'm just waiting for someone,' I hear myself bleating.

'There is no time to wait!' she almost yells at me. 'You need to check in your bags and go to the gate immediately!'

I stare at her, frozen. For probably the first time in my sensible, practical, organised life, I have no idea what to do. I can't miss the plane, but I can't leave without Amy. And now my flashing code red has started sounding that loud foghorn alarm noise inside my head, like in a scene from one of those blockbusting Matt Damon action movies when the nuclear bomb is about to be detonated and all these men in suits are running around in front of computer monitors yelling and screaming . . .

Actually, that's not a bad idea . . .

I'm stopped by my phone, which suddenly springs to life and starts ringing.

Amy.

I snatch it desperately to my ear.

'Rubes, it's me.'

As I hear her voice, relief washes over me. 'Oh thank God you're OK! I've been worried sick,' I gasp, before turning back to the check-in attendant. 'Sorry, excuse me, just a sec.' I step quickly to one side out of earshot, then, '*Where the fuck are you?*' I screech into my handset, any thoughts of big sisterly love flying out of the window. 'You're going to miss the plane!'

'I know,' she replies matter-of-factly.

'What do you mean, you *know*?' I fire back. 'I've been waiting for you for over an hour, you promised you wouldn't be late—'

'I'm not late—'

'Amy, I'm not going to argue with you,' I snap. 'Where are you?'

'I'm with Shine.'

'Shine?' I exclaim. 'What are you doing with Shine?' For a split second I almost think she's going to tell me she's doing yoga.

'He's driving—' she begins, but I cut her off.

'But I thought Biju was driving you to the airport?' I'm standing on tiptoes, looking for her.

'I'm not coming, Rubes.'

'What?' My phone must be going funny, I must have misheard her. Snatching it away from my ear, I stare at it – no, it looks perfectly normal – then quickly press it back. 'What do you mean, you're not coming? You're late!'

'Rubes, you're not listening. I'm not getting on the flight.'

'But I don't understand . . .' Confusion is whirling.

'I'm not coming back to London.'

There's a pause as I'm momentarily lost for words. 'Have you gone mad?' I gasp, finding my voice.

'No, I'm not mad . . . I'm in love!' Her words come out in a sudden rush.

'In love!' I echo in disbelief. 'With who?'

'Shine,' she gushes, her voice bursting with excitement.

The surprises are coming thick and fast. 'You mean the yoga instructor?' I say, astonished.

But no sooner has his name come out of my mouth than it's suddenly all falling into place: the way they were when I first saw them on the beach; the text messages on her phone; her excuses that she was always doing yoga. I suddenly feel like a complete idiot. Of course! How could I have been so blind?

'Amy, you're being ridiculous,' I snap back. 'You have to come home. OK, so I understand why you've fallen for him – I mean, who wouldn't? I'm sure every woman in his class is in love with him.' I'm trying hard to be the voice of reason. Well, someone has to be. I remember what it was like when I was on holiday in Greece aged seventeen and fell head-over-heels for the water-skiing instructor. I wouldn't listen to anyone. 'But this is just some holiday romance—'

'We're getting married.'

What the . . .?

For a moment, I can't speak. Amy has pulled some crazy

stunts before but . . . I pause, mid-thought. Of course! This is her idea of a joke!

'Oh, ha-ha, very clever,' I snap, glancing across departures. She's probably hiding behind a pillar, ready to jump out. 'Only this isn't funny, Amy, the plane's going to leave without us at this rate. Now will you stop joking around? I'm serious.'

'So am I Ruby. I'm perfectly serious.'

She never calls me Ruby. I get an icy feeling at the bottom of my spine.

'Shine and I are eloping and there's nothing you, or Mum and Dad, can do to stop us,' she continues determinedly.

Oh my God. *Mum and Dad.* At the mention of them I feel a sudden horror. They are going to kill her. *But not before they've killed me.* My whole life I've been told, 'Look after your little sister.' I can't let her run off in a foreign country and marry a man she's only just met.

'Amy!' I say sharply, trying to corral her back to reality. 'Stop being so selfish, think about Mum and Dad! How do you think they're going to feel?'

'You said I could never let them down,' she replies petulantly.

I flash back to our earlier conversation when I was packing. Of course, this is why she was so nervous; it had nothing to do with her new job.

'And what about the research centre?' I remind her. 'You've worked so hard for this opportunity, it's what you've always wanted . . .'

There's a pause and for a split second I sense a moment of hesitation, of regret.

'It's an amazing opportunity, Amy, you can't just throw it away. Mum and Dad were so proud, we were all so proud.'

At the other end of the line, I can almost feel her wavering.

'I'm getting married,' she repeats more firmly, as if to convince both herself and me.

I feel myself explode. 'Amy, stop being so stupid and pig-headed,' I cry with frustration. 'You're being crazy, you can't get married!'

'Why not?'

'Because it's ludicrous! You've only known him a couple of weeks.'

'Love isn't measured by time,' she retorts. 'You should know. That's a line from one of your books.'

'But that's fiction,' I almost yell down the phone, 'this is real life!'

'It can happen in real life too,' she argues.

I catch my breath. She sounds so convinced, so sure, so certain, she reminds me of myself. Of how I used to be. I pause as my mind flicks back . . . Once upon a time I shared her conviction. I believed in love at first sight, in marriage, in happy-ever-afters . . . but now I've grown up, I remind myself sharply, and I don't believe in fairy tales any more.

'He feels the same way,' her voice interrupts my thoughts. 'He's in love with me too.'

Suddenly I have a flashback. To a few days ago. Going for the massage and getting lost down a side street. 'Amy, there's something you should know,' I say urgently. 'Shine's not being honest with you, I saw him . . .' I pause, briefly, wondering how I can tell her, then blurt it out. 'He was with another woman, ask him—'

But she doesn't let me finish.

'I knew you'd be like this,' she accuses angrily, 'that's why I didn't want to tell you!'

'Like what?'

'Not every guy is like Sam, you know.'

The mention of his name is like a raw nerve. 'This isn't about Sam,' I protest hotly.

'Yes it is! It's got everything to do with him!' she cries. 'Just because Sam turned out to be a cheat, and broke your heart, doesn't mean you have to write every guy off.'

Our voices are growing louder and louder.

'I am not writing every guy off,' I fire back, feeling stung. 'I just don't want you to make the same mistake I did!'

'And what mistake's that?' she demands, 'Falling in love?'

'No, it's believing in love,' I yell back.

As the words fly out of my mouth, there's silence on the other end of the line, and in the middle of arguing we both break off, breathless. Emotions are swirling around us and for a moment neither of us speaks. Until, after a pause, she says quietly, 'Tell Mum and Dad I'm sorry I'll miss their wedding anniversary and not to worry. I'll call in a few days.'

'Look, can't we just talk about this?'

'There's nothing to talk about, I've made up my mind,' she says stubbornly.

'Listen to me, he's seeing someone else,' I say urgently. '*I saw him!*'

'You're lying. Shine loves me!'

That's what Sam told me, I think desperately, my mind flashing back.

'Amy, please, I'm not lying—'

'And I'm not listening,' she says resolutely. 'Rubes, I know you're my big sister, but I know what I'm doing and I can look after myself.'

'It didn't seem like that when you were borrowing money,' I remind her peevishly, before I can stop myself.

'I'll pay you back every penny,' she replies stiffly. 'You don't have to worry.'

'Like I'm worried about the money!' I burst out. 'I just care about you, I don't want you getting hurt—'

'Look, I have to go.'

'*Amy, wait . . .*'

But it's no good. She's already gone.

Shocked, I stare at my silent phone, my mind whirling, my heart thumping.

What on earth am I going to do now?

9

I remember once seeing one of those life coaches being interviewed on some daytime chat show. I can't remember the programme, but I do remember him. He was one of the Dr Phil types, with grey hair and friendly eyes, and he was talking about how if you can't make a decision about something, you have to break it down into simple options. Like, for example, it's a multiple choice question.

In which case, if this was a multiple choice question, it would go something like this:

1) You are at the airport in India about to get a flight back to London, when your little sister tells you she's eloping with the yoga instructor. Do you:

A. Panic

B. Think sod it, she's old enough to make her own mistakes and get on the plane without her

Or C. Miss the flight and try to stop her

'Hurry! The flight is closing!'

I snap back to the check-in attendant who's frantically gesturing for me, a stricken expression on her face. An alarm sounds in my head. I need to make a decision. I need to make a choice.

And fast.

'Miss, if you don't come now, the plane will leave without you,' she instructs sternly.

My mind is running through a million different scenarios, seeing the consequences of every action, the domino-style effect it's going to have on everything . . .

If I get on the plane, I'll be leaving Amy to run off and make a terrible mistake. It's lust, not love. She can't *marry* him, she barely knows him. And what about the fact I saw him with another woman? Who was she? It could be innocent and yet . . . oh god, who am I kidding? It didn't look innocent and, moreover, why would he lie? Why would he pretend he was on his own? In which case, how long's it been going on? And what if she's not the only one? What if, god forbid, he's cheating on Amy with lots of women?

There are so many unanswered questions, but Amy's so impulsive, so headstrong, *so naive*. She thinks she knows everything, but she doesn't know anything. She still believes in happy-ever-afters, but this isn't a fairy tale, it's real life, and I can't just stand back and watch her throwing away her heart, her career and her life on a man she's just met and knows hardly anything about. Gambling everything on love.

And yet, on the flip side, if I don't get on the plane, it means I'm not going home. I'm not going back to my life in London, I'm staying here in India and for who knows how long . . . I suddenly think about work, about Heathcliff, about the reality of the situation . . . No, it's impossible, I have to get on that flight, I have to go back. I have responsibilities. I have a deadline to meet, a dog to look after, a pile of bills to pay. Not to mention Mum and Dad's wedding anniversary.

I feel a wave of anxiety. God, it's like *Sliding Doors*. Only in this case, there's no Gwyneth Paltrow, just an irate check-in attendant. I flinch, catching her eye, and feeling the knot in my stomach twist even harder.

I need to make a decision.

'*Miss!*' The attendant's unflappable calm suddenly disintegrates and she rushes over in a frenzy, almost rugby tackling

me to the ground in an attempt to grab my wheelie suitcase.
'We need to check this in!'

'No, stop,' I yell, holding on to it for dear life. '*Stop!*'

In mid-tussle she freezes, her hand on the suitcase handle,
and seeming to remember herself, stands upright.

As do I. And I suddenly realise:

I've made my decision, and it's C.

'I'm not coming,' I announce, my mind racing. 'I'm not
getting on that flight, I'm not going back to London . . .'

Well, what else could I do? She's my little sister, I have no
choice. I've looked after her my whole life, I can't just abandon her now.

'I've got to stop my sister from getting married,' I say,
reaching for my suitcase.

The check-in attendant stares at me in astonishment. 'But
weddings are wonderful,' she exclaims in confusion, 'you
can't stop a wedding!'

'I'm not stopping a wedding,' I reply.

'But . . . ?'

Leaving the attendant staring after me in confusion, I set
off towards the exit. And, under my breath, I add quietly and
determinedly to myself, 'I'm stopping her from getting hurt.'

In which case, I need to get a bloody move on.

Breaking into a sprint with my suitcase, I set off on a
hundred-metre dash across the terminal. Big Sister to the
rescue! I feel like I should go into a telephone box and change
into a cape and a pair of tights.

God, I just hope I'm not too late. I know Amy's impulsive,
but surely she's not that stupid. Oh, who am I kidding? This
is Amy, remember. The girl who once ran away to join the
fair at five years old. OK, so she only got as far as next-door's
garden, but still. My little sister is capable of anything.

I race outside through the automatic doors and grab the

first thing I can find that has wheels – a brightly painted tuk-tuk whose driver looks about fifteen – to take me back to the guesthouse.

What a difference a week makes. Whereas before whenever a stray chicken or goat wandered across the road, or we overtook into the path of an oncoming lorry, I'd bury my face in my hands. Now it's all I can do not to lean over and stick my hand on the horn myself.

'Please, can you hurry?' I plead as we rumble along dusty, potholed roads.

'You want me to step on it?' The driver turns down the radio, which is blasting out Bollywood music, and glances at me in his cracked rear-view mirror, his boyish face lighting up with delight. 'Like in the movies?'

'Yes, like in the movies,' I nod, swallowing hard. I daren't even *think* about what I'm letting myself in for. I just need to concentrate on finding Amy.

'Okey-dokey,' he grins, crunching the gears loudly and accelerating hard so the engine sounds as though it's about to explode.

Then again, I'm not going to be much good at finding Amy if I'm dead, am I?

Thrown around on the back seat, I cling onto the side handle like my mum does whenever my dad is driving, something which causes no end of amusement for me and Amy. I wouldn't mind, but they live in a tiny village in the Yorkshire Dales, where no one ever goes over thirty miles an hour and still she grips onto that handle shrieking, 'Slow down Roger, slow down!' I swear, you'd think Dad was Michael Schumacher, not the careful owner of a fifteen-year-old Peugeot.

As the tuk-tuk driver suddenly swerves violently to avoid a bicycle-rickshaw, I have a sudden image of Mum in this tuk-tuk. Actually, I'm not sure her nerves would stand it. Even with her smelling salts, which she carries everywhere with her in her handbag, I think she'd pass out.

Which is probably not a bad idea, I wince, as, with a twisting, crunching sound of metal, we lose a wing mirror to an oncoming bus.

Oh. My. God.

I've never been one for believing in miracles, but as we skid to a halt outside Rising Bliss twenty minutes later, I've completely changed my mind. Miracles do happen! Look! Lord behold! I'm still alive!

Pushing a fistful of rupees into my driver's hands, I abandon my suitcase on the front steps and run into reception. Well, I say 'run', but it's more a case of 'trip and stumble', as I'm wearing a pair of woven leather sandals I bought on one of my many shopping expeditions; although they *look* lovely, there's a bit of a design fault as they keep falling off my feet . . .

Narrowly missing twisting my ankle, I stagger across the tiled floor. A haven of calm and tranquillity greets me. The scent of burning incense perfumes the air. Soft, chiming music is playing. Frangipani flowers are floating in a gently trickling fountain.

And then there's me: a big sweaty stress ball hurtling through it all.

'Miss Ruby!' As I reach the front desk, Biju looks up and beams at me widely. 'Back again so soon!'

'Have you seen Amy?' I gasp, trying to catch my breath.

His face clouds. 'I'm very sorry, I'm afraid you've missed her,' he says gravely, his head jiggling from side to side. 'She's gone back to London with her sister.'

'I'm her sister!'

'I know,' he beams, his smile popping back onto his face.

I can feel my frustration about to bubble over, like boiling milk in a pan. 'Look, this is very important,' I insist, feeling stressed.

Beetling his eyebrows together, Biju calmly observes me. 'You seem very anxious, this is not good,' he tuts, shaking his head with disapproval.

Oh god, this is hopeless. I need to try a different tack. 'Where's Shine?' I ask, taking a deep breath to try and calm myself down.

'Ah . . . now I understand . . .' he says, nodding deeply. 'You want to do yoga.' Closing his eyes, he clamps a finger on one nostril and starts inhaling deeply.

'No. Biju. You've got it wrong—'

'*Ommmmmmmmmm . . .*'

I stare at him incredulously. This cannot be happening.

'*Ommmmmmmmmm . . .*' In the middle of omming, he snaps open one eye and observes me. 'You are not joining me in chanting,' he says, looking offended and directing my gaze sideways at the little shrine on the side of his desk. It's a statue of Buddha, decorated with a garland of marigolds and two sticks of burning incense.

I feel a flush of embarrassment. Oh crikey, I don't want to be disrespectful. 'Oh yes, of course,' I nod dutifully.

'In the Hindu belief, *Om* is the sound that was made when the whole universe was created,' he continues solemnly. 'Chanting has a very powerful effect on the person chanting and the rest of the world. It connects us to our deepest sense of being.'

'Wow . . . yes, I know,' I nod, remembering the one yoga class I attended. 'It's just that I'm trying to find Amy,' I begin again tentatively.

'*Ommmmmmmmmm . . .*'

As he fixes me with his gaze, I give up and close my mouth . . . then open it again . . . '*Ommmmmmmmmm . . .*'

Together we chant; Biju's low tones resonating around reception, mine sounding like a shriller, nervier descant. On and on and on *and on* . . . I close my eyes and try to focus on the great *Om*, but it's impossible. I can't stop thinking about Amy, about what's happening, about where she is.

Shooting an apologetic glance at Buddha, I sneak a peek at my watch.

'Now, do you feel better?'

I snap back to see Biju beaming at me.

'Um . . . yes, much better,' I smile nervously.

'Splendid!' Reaching into the little bowl of fennel seeds and sugar that is used as a mouth freshener, he takes a handful and begins to chew them energetically.

'But there's just one other thing,' I say, only more cautiously this time as I don't want to trigger any more of Biju's helpful suggestions. 'I'm . . . er . . . still looking for Amy,' I remind him.

'Ah yes, Amy,' he nods, beaming happily.

'Apparently she's with Shine,' I prompt.

'This is good.' He nods, and smiles even more broadly.

So he knows! I wait expectantly for him to say something more, except he doesn't. He doesn't say anything. He just stands there beaming at me.

Honestly, is there anything more frustrating when you're in a right old panic about something, than someone just standing there calmly, not doing or saying anything?

'She told me they're eloping,' I blurt finally in desperation.

Biju looks at me in confusion. 'Eloping?' he repeats, frowning. 'What is this . . . *eloping*?'

'Running away to get married!' I cry in frustration.

Biju's head stops jiggling and he stares at me, frozen, like a rabbit in headlights. 'But this cannot be true,' he explodes after a moment's pause.

'Yes, it is! It's true!' Now I'm the one jiggling my head up and down emphatically. 'They've run away together!'

'No! Shine told me he was going to visit his relatives . . .'

He throws his hands in the air. 'This is what he said to me. This is why he asked to take some time off from teaching yoga. He needed to go away for a few days, maybe longer . . .'

'So they're not here?' I demand.

The whites of Biju's eyes grow saucer wide. 'I would never lie to you,' he cries, shaking his head and beating his chest as if it's a drum. 'I only speak the truth! Ever since I was a little boy, this is a lesson that I learned from my father.'

He looks so tortured, I feel a stab of guilt. 'I believe you,' I reassure him quickly.

'You do?' He looks relieved.

'Absolutely,' I nod, 'but it's very important that I find her . . .' I break off, my mind racing. 'Do you have an address for Shine's relatives? Or maybe a telephone number?'

But now Biju is all of a fluster and beads of perspiration are starting to run down his face. Stricken with panic, he's still wordlessly shaking his head.

Suddenly I have an idea. 'I know! Can I look in her room?'

Pulling out a neatly folded handkerchief from his top pocket, he starts blotting his brow like he's mopping up spilled milk. 'Yes, yes of course,' he nods, finally finding his voice, 'please, follow me.'

I follow him as he hurries from behind the desk, his short legs propelling him with surprising speed down the corridor, his large bunch of keys hanging from his waist, jangling loudly. Until reaching Amy's old room he unlocks the door and, flinging it open, dramatically presses his body up against it, like a knife-thrower's assistant, so that I can get past.

The room is empty, but for a bed and a small wardrobe.

'See! She is not here,' he declares, as if I think he's been hiding her.

It's also suspiciously tidy. There's no overflowing bin, unmade bed or wet towels on the floor. 'Are you sure this is Amy's room?' I ask dubiously. At home Mum has been known to threaten to ring the fire brigade to gain access to Amy's bedroom.

'One hundred per cent,' he exclaims, blotting his face with his handkerchief. 'It has already been cleaned for the next guests.'

Oh well, that explains things.

'Right . . . yes, of course . . .' I nod, but inside I feel a pang of disappointment. I'm not sure what I was hoping to find, but there are no clues here to her whereabouts. 'OK, well thanks Biju, I really appreciate your help.'

'I am so sorry, Miss Ruby. If there is anything more I can do . . .'

Deflated, I turn to leave, and I am just walking out of the door when I spot something fluttering underneath the bed.

'Hang on, what's that?' Bending down, I scrabble for it. It's a scrap of paper on which is scribbled the word *Raja* and a number. I peer at it. It's Amy's handwriting. She always crosses the number seven like that.

I thrust it excitedly at Biju. 'Do you know this number?'

He squints at it myopically, then shakes his head. 'But don't worry, I will ring it,' he says decisively. Pulling his mobile phone out of the holster he has clipped onto his shorts, he dials the number with great deliberateness. We both wait on tenterhooks, my mind whirring around and around like the fan above our heads.

'No one is answering,' he says finally after a few minutes.

Of course not. Why did I think with Amy it would be that easy? I let out a loud groan of frustration, which startles Biju.

'What about this *Raja*?' I say desperately, 'Is this a person? Do you know him?'

Shaking his head, he grabs his handkerchief and buries himself underneath it.

So that's it. I've hit a dead end.

'Only Rajasthan,' he muffles, from underneath the cotton square.

'Who?' I can't quite catch what he's saying.

'Raja could be short for Rajasthan,' he repeats, his voice clearer as he emerges from beneath his handkerchief. '*Raja* means king, and Rajasthan is known as the land of the kings. It is a most beautiful area . . .' He breaks off, then adds excitedly, 'Now I remember, this is where Shine's family is from!'

Finally. I've got a lead.

'How do I get there?' I've heard of Rajasthan, but I don't know where it is on the map. I remember seeing it listed in the big guidebooks on India, but I only bought the smaller one for Southern India. Well, there didn't seem much point buying the bigger book, did there? I was only supposed to be going to Goa for a week.

Seriously. I am so going to kill Amy.

'Oh, that is no problem.' Biju's face emerges from beneath his handkerchief, damp but ebullient. 'You can get the train to Delhi.'

'A train?' I feel myself perk up.

'Yes, a train, and from there you can catch a local train or bus into Rajasthan,' he beams, looking as thrilled as I feel.

Because not only am I one step closer to finding Amy, I've suddenly got an image of one of those 'palaces on wheels' you see in glossy brochures. I can picture it now . . . luxurious cabins harking back to the bygone era when royal maharajas would travel in sumptuous style; dining cars filled with mahogany tables and starched white tablecloths; sitting drinking a gin and tonic and watching the colours of India go by . . .

Feeling my imagination running away, I sigh dreamily. It all seems so romantic, so enchanting—

So exciting! Suddenly, my frustration and annoyance at having to chase after Amy is replaced by a surge of exhilaration. It's going to be like *The Darjeeling Limited*. Only in real life! Oh my god, I *loved* that film! Maybe there'll even be an

Adrien Brody-type character on board too, I muse, feeling slightly giddy at the thought.

And yes, I know that's very immature at my age, having a crush on a movie star, but it's that Roman nose, it just sends me weak at the knees.

'Brilliant,' I hear myself saying. 'How do I get to the train station?'

'I will give you a lift in my car,' says Biju, looking very pleased with himself. 'If we go at once, you can catch the express. Please, come this way.'

'Great, thanks!'

Biju's already jangling down the corridor and I follow him through reception and outside, where he scoops up my suitcase and packs it neatly into the boot of his little blue car. Then, with a great show of chivalry, he opens the passenger door for me and, as I slide inside, he jumps in next to me, starts the engine, and with a little chug we're off.

See! This is going to be so much easier than I thought! I'll just find Amy, talk some sense into her, and I'll be catching a flight back to London and my normal life before I know it.

Smiling to myself, I gaze out of the window as we set off towards the station.

What was I so worried about?

Easy-peasy.

10

Er, I think there's been some mistake.

Standing on the hot, dusty platform, I hold tightly onto my suitcase and look uncertainly around me. This can't be right. There must be some mix-up. Biju took my credit card and sorted out my ticket, before cheerily waving goodbye and driving off in a cloud of dust and Bollywood music.

But he must have got it wrong when he told me where to go. This can't be where I catch the express train from. There must be a different platform, a special one, like in *Harry Potter* or something—

'*Baaaaaaaaahhhh!*'

Loud bleating behind me makes me almost jump out of my skin and I twirl around to see two scraggy, nervy goats being herded down the platform.

Despite being a small station, it's busy and crowded with a jumble of people. Several backpackers are flopped around, waiting with their rucksacks, a group of women, dressed in brightly coloured saris, like birds of paradise, are perched on metal seats, chattering loudly; a porter balancing plastic-wrapped suitcases on his head overtakes an old man pushing a wheelbarrow filled with cages of loud, squawking chickens, whilst a group of teenage schoolboys are staring curiously at me, their gazes unblinking . . .

Self-consciously I look away – hang on, and is that a *cow* just hanging out over there in the middle of everything? Undisturbed, it's chewing grass and swishing its tail and . . .

oh no, don't tell me it's going to do what I think it's going to do . . .

Oh yuck. Yes it is.

As a big, steaming pile of crap lands on the platform, I stare at it. I don't remember seeing that in all those glossy brochures about enchanting train journeys across India. I watch as the wheelbarrow man marches straight past the cow without batting an eyelid. He seems completely oblivious. As is everyone, I realise, looking around me and noticing that – apart from a few other tourists staring like me – everyone else is just carrying on as normal.

Because this is India, not King's Cross, I remind myself firmly. Come on Ruby, pull yourself together. Stop being so pathetic. OK, so it's a bit scary travelling on your own in a strange country that you're not used to, but it's all going to be fine. You just need to find the right platform, that's all.

'*Argh*!' I let out a shriek as a cockroach or something runs over my foot. Oh my god, did anyone see the size of that thing? It was massive! As big as a rat! As I turn to see it scurrying away, my blood suddenly runs cold. *It* was *a rat!*

OK, I'm pathetic! I don't care! I'm pathetic!

Snatching up my suitcase, I head back inside to try and find Tourist Information. I know this is India, and I know it's this amazing, incredible country, but I don't think I'm cut out for this. I'm not some brave, adventurous, independent traveller.

I'm the girl who's terrified of insects (including daddy-longlegs, which even my three-year-old goddaughter isn't scared of), who gets nervous in crowds and seasick on boats and for whom travelling consists of the Eurostar to Paris and package holidays to Europe. I mean, it's hardly Bear Grylls is it?

I'm distracted by the sound of brakes screeching and hissing, and I look up as a train pulls in alongside the platform.

At least I assume it's a train, but you can barely see the actual thing itself for people hanging off the sides, piled onto the roof and clinging to the bars on the windows.

And I thought the Central Line at rush hour was bad. This makes a packed commuter carriage look positively roomy, I realise, glimpsing the people crammed inside the sweltering carriages.

Spotting an information office, I quickly weave my way towards it through the surge of passengers waiting to board, and find the door ajar. Peering inside its shadowy depths, I spot a uniformed official smoking a cigarette and sitting behind a desk, studying some ginormous ledger. A small plastic white fan is whirring futilely on the filing cabinet next to him.

'Ahem, excuse me,' I say politely, tripping inside. Those damn sandals.

He looks up and observes me with interest. 'Can I help you?'

'Actually yes,' I reply, putting on what I call my 'best' voice. It's the posh one I use on my voicemail and sounds absolutely nothing like me. In fact friends have been known to hang up, thinking they've got the wrong number.

'I'm trying to find the express train.' I wave my ticket like a white flag.

Stubbing out his cigarette into an overflowing ashtray, he leans forward and stares at the ticket for a moment before opening a drawer in his desk and pulling out one of the longest fax print-outs I've ever seen. Page after page appears from his drawer, like a magician pulling handkerchiefs out of a top hat.

Methodically he starts going through each page, tracing each name with a nicotined finger, until finally he nods satisfactorily to himself.

'*Roobeee* Miller,' he says after a few minutes, tapping his finger on a page. I crick my neck upside down and, sure enough, buried amongst hundreds of Indian names, wedged in tightly between Sanjeev Chopra and Rupinda Malik, on a smudged fax print-out in a tiny, sweltering, smoke-filled office, in a train station in Southern India, there I am.

'Oh wow, yes, that's me,' I nod. It feels slightly surreal that in amongst all this disorder, there could be efficiency. A list. With my name on it. I'm impressed. It doesn't seem possible somehow.

But India, I'm learning fast, is full of surprises.

'That is your train,' he gestures to the platform behind me.

'Oh . . . great,' I smile. Well, that's a result, it must have just pulled in, I think happily. I turn around with anticipation—

Er, hang on. That's the same train as before, I realise, expecting to see a different one, but no; it's still the same train that's got dozens of people dangling from it, like a heavily decorated Christmas tree. 'I'm sorry, but I think there must be some mistake,' I say, turning back.

'No mistake.' The official shakes his head, and lights up another cigarette. 'That is the express train to Delhi.'

That is the express train?

My imagination, which has been whooshing along, suddenly screeches to a juddering halt. What happened to the luxurious cabins? Dining cars where I get to sip a gin and tonic? Romance and splendour evoking the bygone era when royal maharajas would travel across India in sumptuous style?

What happened to The Darjeeling Limited *and Adrien Brody?*

I suddenly feel like a prize idiot. What was I thinking? Those trips cost squillions and are just for wealthy tourists on five-star holidays. This is real train travel in India, not some glossy Hollywood version of it.

And I don't want it to be, I suddenly realise, as I turn to
see a family of six climbing on board, and for a moment I
watch them with a mixture of awe, disbelief and fascination.
Carrying two huge suitcases, a ten-foot-long rug and what
looks like part of a car engine, they're determinedly shoe-
horning themselves inside, the huge-bellied father squeezing
himself in through the door like an expanded cork trying to
fit back into the bottle.

It's like one of those record-breaking attempts at how
many people you can fit inside a Mini and, sure enough, they
manage it and all disappear inside. Apart from the little boy
who reappears on the stoop and peeps his head out, glancing
around the station with the feverish excitement of any small
boy on a train journey. He catches me looking and – despite
my predicament – I can't help smiling. Suddenly shy, he pops
back inside.

The sound of someone chuckling causes me to turn
around to find the official is watching me with unconcealed
amusement. No doubt he's used to lily-livered Western tourists unaccustomed to Indian train travel.

'It is a very popular train,' he grins, 'there are many people
travelling today.'

'Yes, I can see that,' I nod, feeling a flutter of nerves as I
wonder how on earth me and my huge suitcase are going to
squeeze aboard. Not for the first time do I regret buying all
those pashminas.

'You are very lucky . . .'

Well, I wouldn't go that far. I could be watching an in-flight
movie and making the most of the free bar as I wing my way
back home.

'You have a reservation in AC2.'

I look at him, nonplussed. 'What's AC2?'

'It is a carriage near the front of the train with air conditioning and your own individual bunk for sleeping.'

Hang on a minute, did he just say 'air conditioning' and 'individual bunk'?

In the stifling heat of his tiny office, I feel a sudden beat of joy. 'You mean that isn't my carriage?' I ask, motioning outside.

The official looks at me in astonishment.

'I mean, not that there's anything wrong with that carriage,' I add quickly. 'It looks a perfectly fine way to travel. It's just, well, it looks a little full and I was a bit worried how I was going to fit on there.'

He suddenly bursts out laughing. He seems to find this hilarious.

'Not that I haven't travelled on a busy train before – you should see the London Underground at rush hour, there's never anywhere to sit, and it can get really claustrophobic—'

'Miss Miller!' he interrupts. 'There is nothing to worry about.'

I fall silent.

'Except that if you don't hurry, you are going to miss your train.'

I glance at the clock on the wall. The minute hand is nearly on the hour. 'Oh bloody hell . . .' I gasp, suddenly realising the time, then clamp my hand over my mouth. 'Oh gosh, sorry . . . thank you so very much, you've been so very helpful!'

The official smiles and lights up another cigarette. 'Your ticket,' he reminds me.

It's still lying on the desk, and I snatch it up. I have a train to catch and a sister to rescue. And, grabbing my suitcase, I leg it out of his office.

By some miracle I manage to find the right carriage and as I slide open the door and the air conditioning hits my skin, a delicious shiver runs up my spine. Gosh, I never thought I'd be so happy to be in the cold. At home I'm always freezing but, after the sweltering temperatures outside, this is wonderful.

I start looking for my seat reservation. My eyes sweep down the fluorescent-lit corridor and the rows of metal berths. On one side, they're laid out in single file above the window with two seats underneath, and on the other side of the aisle they're arranged like vinyl bunk beds into compartments, each separated by a curtain. At the bottom of each berth is a sheet, pillow and a blanket placed in a tidy pile.

I'm pleasantly surprised. It's basic, but it's clean and there's plenty of room. Compared to the packed carriages I spied earlier, this is sheer luxury. The official was right, I'm very lucky. In fact, it's much better than British Rail. There the seats barely recline, even in first class, whereas here I have my own bunk bed with a pillow and everything!

Though what is *slightly* worrying is that there appear to be four berths in each compartment. Two up, two down, on each side. Which means you're sharing with three total strangers. *Men* and women, I realise, as a very large Indian man appears from the toilet and plonks himself on the bottom berth opposite. He starts shelling pistachio nuts whilst staring at me unblinkingly.

I'm fast realising foreigners are an object of curiosity and I give him a polite smile but he doesn't look away. Instead he continues to stare at me, transfixed, a little pile of shells beginning to pile up around him. Still, it's not like that's a big deal. I'm only on here for a few hours, I remind myself, happily sitting down opposite. I'll just read a bit of my guidebook, have a bit of a snooze, and I'll be there.

'Excuse me.'

I've just laid out my blanket and am getting all comfy, when I hear a voice. It's male and, by the sounds of it, its owner is American.

'Um, yes?'

I look up from my book and see there's a man standing at the end of my berth. Only his top half is hidden by the berth on top, and I can only see a pair of faded khaki shorts, tanned, hairy calves, and bare feet in flip-flops. I have a thing about feet, and I can't help noticing his are very nice.

'I think you're in my seat.'

I frown. All nice thoughts about this stranger's toes quickly evaporate. 'No, I don't think I am,' I say, to the feet.

'This is number eighteen. This is my seat,' he says, a lot more firmly.

I feel my hackles rise. Here I am, reading a book and minding my own business, and this faceless person has to come and disturb me.

'Well I'm sorry to disappoint you,' I bristle, 'but you're wrong. Eighteen is my seat.'

Seriously, what was I thinking? He's got dreadful feet. His little toes are all wonky.

'No, *you're* wrong,' he says flatly.

What? I'm startled by his reaction. Honestly, what is his problem?

'Look, I don't want to have an argument—' I begin, but he cuts me off.

'There is no argument. You obviously haven't learned how to read numbers properly.'

I'm aghast. Talk about rude!

'No, you're the one who can't read numbers,' I retort, peevishly. Well, if he wants to act like a child, two can play at that game. 'Now, if you don't mind—'

There's a pause. Good. That must have done the trick. He'll go away now.

I give a startled jump as a face suddenly appears underneath the berth.

'Are you always this stubborn?'

He's got hazel eyes, the whites of which look really bright against his tan, and appears to be around my age, with short, dark messy hair, and stubble. I notice he's wearing some kind of beads strung on a piece of leather around his neck and an old straw fedora.

Oh God, he looks like one of those really annoying traveller types. I bet you anything he's carrying a drum and a copy of *Shantaram*.

'I think you should check your reservation,' I say tightly, and with as much as authority as I can muster. Honestly, the ego on some men.

'I've checked it. That's my seat you're sitting in, lady.'

Lady? I feel myself physically bristle at the way he says it. God, he's so patronising!

And he's not budging, I realise, as his horrible feet stay planted to the floor and his face remains inches away from mine.

Right! That's it.

Irritated, I close my guidebook and reach for my bag. I start digging around for my ticket. I'll show this jumped-up ... annoying ... rude ... sexist ...

'See!' I declare triumphantly, thrusting it at him like a fencer in a dual. 'Eighteen!'

Ha! See what you have to say about that.

I wait for the realisation, the embarrassment, the grovelling apology—

'That's a thirteen,' he replies matter-of-factly.

What?

'A little smudged maybe, but it's still thirteen.'

As he hands me back the ticket, I stare at it incredulously. I feel a sickening thud as I realise he's right. The number's all smudged. I read it wrong. It's not 18 at all. It's 13.

'Unlucky for some,' I hear him say, and look up to see the

corners of his mouth turning up slightly, in the most irritatingly superior smile.

I have to grit my teeth. 'Right. OK,' I say, in a staccato voice. 'Sorry.'

'I think that's you over there.' He motions to the other side of the carriage where, underneath a fixed upper berth, there appears to be two single seats opposite each other. One of them is occupied by a young Indian guy wearing badly fitting earphones, out of which is blasting tinny music. 'You've got the lower berth. Kind of a bummer, as you can't go to sleep until he wants to.'

I look back at him in confusion.

'The side berths are different to the rest. They're narrower, so the bottom two seats are only converted into the lower berth at night, which is when he climbs on top . . .' He breaks off and I swear I see a flash of amusement in his eyes. 'I meant, onto the top berth, of course.'

'Of course,' I reply hotly, my face burning. Gathering up my things, I start pushing them roughly into my bag and get up from the berth. 'Excuse me,' I say sharply, not waiting for him to stand aside so I can get by.

'Hey!' he cries, as I wheel my suitcase over his foot.

Purely by accident, of course.

'I might be a lady but it's pretty obvious you're no gentleman,' I mutter, stalking past him.

'It's been a long day, I need to sleep,' he says unapologetically, moving swiftly into my berth without the merest hint of shame at turfing me out.

And to even *think* at one point I was envisaging thoughts of an ice-cold gin and tonic and Adrien Brody.

'Any decent man wouldn't make a girl move, they'd just swap seats,' I retort, plonking myself down on my hard plastic seat as he makes a big show of stretching out fully *on my blanket*.

'Are you kidding me?' he says, punching the pillow.

God, I hate how men do that. Why do they always feel the need to beat up defenceless pillows?

Ignoring him, I stare resolutely out of my tinted window.

'You want me to give up my seat for thirty-one hours? Are you serious?'

Er, hang on. What did he just say?

Propped uncomfortably upright, in a seat that does not recline, I swivel my gaze sharply across at him.

'What are you talking about?' I demand.

'The ride to Delhi,' he replies, folding his arms lazily behind his head. 'Over a thousand kilometres, and thirty-one hours . . . didn't you read that in your guidebook?' He motions to it lying on the side.

'It only covers Goa,' I reply hotly.

'Shame,' he shrugs.

I look away, determined to ignore him. He's just trying to wind me up and annoy me, that's all. But I can feel anxiety starting to prickle. 'I don't understand, I thought this was an express train,' I say, stiffly turning back to him.

'It is. This is India,' he says, looking at me as if I'm stupid.

Suddenly it hits me. *It's not a wind-up.*

My thoughts start spiralling. Oh my god, this cannot be happening. This *cannot* be happening.

'If I was you I'd get some sleep,' he yawns and tapping the brim of his old fedora, pushes it down over his eyes.

I stare at him speechlessly, the horror of his words slowly sinking in, then suddenly I hear a slight snoring and realise he's fallen asleep.

Asleep! While I'm sitting here, bolt upright!

I'm distracted by a blast of jangly music and turn back to see my travelling companion turning up the volume so it blasts out of his headphones. After the stress of the day I almost feel like crying. How did my relaxing week's holiday turn into this? One minute I was lazing on a beach, drinking out of coconuts with a straw, and now I'm trapped on this train for thirty-one hours.

I shift in my seat, trying to get comfy, then give up. Oh god, it's hopeless. And turning to look out of the window, I watch the station disappearing into the distance as the train slowly creaks its way on its long journey northwards.

11

Saying that, thirty-one hours isn't *that* long.

As the station gives way to the outskirts of the city and we move into the open countryside, I do a few calculations in my head. After all, let's face it, it's easy to kill time, isn't it? I only have to pop into Zara and an hour disappears. Or turn on the telly and *whoosh*, a whole evening has gone, just like that.

And I can't even *look* at a DVD boxed-set of *Downton Abbey* without losing an entire day. In fact, on a recent trip to Mum and Dad's, an entire weekend vanished into thin air because I discovered they had series two and three. Seriously, David Blaine's got nothing on Cousin Matthew when it comes to magic tricks.

In which case this journey isn't going to be a problem at all. There's lots I can do to pass the time – like, for example, I need to give myself a manicure, I realise, looking down at my fingernails and noticing what a mess they are.

And that's only for starters . . .

Feeling all cheered up, I dig out my nail file and get to work. At this rate I'll be in Delhi before I know it!

I had no idea how much fun killing time was.

After finishing my manicure – in which I get to apply two careful coats, not my usual rushed one – *and* let them dry properly, instead of smudging them as I'm too impatient to wait, I send my sister a few texts telling her I'm on the train (to which she doesn't reply, but then I'm not surprised; just because she's eloping, why should she change the habit of a lifetime?), order some food from a man who comes round with a small list, all of which is in Hindi, and none of which I understand, and spend ages sorting out all the junk in my wallet.

Honestly, I have no idea who half these business cards belong to, I muse, rifling through a huge stack of various colours and fonts. I stare at 'Deborah Seymour, *Conservatories Are Us*' in Times New Roman and wrack my brain for some recognition. Nope, nothing.

I screw up Deborah. I'm sure she's a really nice person. I probably met her at a party and thought ooh, she's lovely, and she gave me her card and I promised to ring.

And now here I am, scrunching her up like an old chocolate wrapper.

Feeling a twinge of guilt, I'm distracted by a baby's giggling laughter and glance across the aisle where a large, boisterous family has spilled out of their compartment. Sitting cross-legged in the corridor, three generations are passing around food, playing cards, and jiggling a baby who looks like a beautiful, kohl-eyed doll on their knees. I watch as she reaches out a chubby, gold-bangled fist, trying to eat a pistachio shell that has scattered from the large mound on the berth next door.

'How old is she?' I ask, breaking into a smile. Babies have a wonderful way of doing that to people, whatever the circumstances.

'Nearly one year,' the mum replies proudly, her face lighting up.

'She's very beautiful,' I nod, pulling a silly face as her daughter stares back at me with huge brown eyes, framed with the kind of eyelashes no lash-building mascara could ever hope to achieve. She smiles at me shyly, then buries her head in the bright blue folds of her mother's sari.

'She is very shy,' laughs the mum, jiggling her daughter encouragingly.

She glances at me from underneath her eyelashes and I pretend to hide behind my hands, then reappear. She giggles loudly, then buries her face again, and together we play peek-a-boo, me hiding behind my hands, her hiding inside her mother's sari, both lost in the game until it's time for her to be fed.

As she's passed to her grandmother to be given her bottle, I turn back to gaze out of the window. I wonder what time it is? It's probably getting really late. I must have been on the train for hours already.

I glance at my watch.

What?

Quarter to? *That's all?*

I've been on here for . . . I do a quick calculation . . .

Forty-five minutes?

I stare at my watch in disbelief, then look around me. A lot of people have already fallen asleep. Opposite me, the young Indian guy has fallen asleep in his seat, mouth open, headphones blasting, whilst across the aisle the man shelling pistachio nuts is snoring loudly.

And then there's *him*.

The American.

Sleeping like a baby on my berth.

Irritation stabs. OK, so I know it's not *really* my berth, but everyone knows possession is nine-tenths of the law, I think crossly.

Feeling myself shooting little envious darts towards him, I force myself to look away. I need to just ignore him. Rise above it. Who cares about a silly man, or some silly berth? It's not important. *He's* not important.

Closing my eyes, I listen to the rhythmic clack-clacking of the train as it trundles along the rail tracks and feel the gentle side-to-side rocking of the carriage. It's been a long day and it's only now the exhaustion hits me and I realise how tired I am. I let out a yawn, feeling the tension inside of me beginning to unwind.

And as I start to relax and grow more sleepy, I feel my annoyance fading away . . . feel the romantic dreamer inside of me slip past the practical realist who stands guard on my daydreams, like a jailer jangling his keys . . . and feel myself escaping out into my imagination . . .

Who doesn't dream about going on a train journey across India? Travelling across one of the most mystical countries in the world? Experiencing the sights, the scenery, *the magic*. It's the stuff of countless movies and novels. The subject of TV documentaries that I've watched from the comfortable mundanity of my living room sofa, whilst cradling a mug of tea in my hands and thinking 'one day'.

But then 'one day' becomes another day, and another, and busy life takes over, and it's not until you're sitting on an overcrowded bus, or pushing a trolley around a supermarket, or brushing your teeth late at night that your mind drifts off.

Like letting go of a balloon, it floats away from careers and relationships and responsibilities, from the everyday thoughts of paying bills, meeting deadlines and what you're going to have for dinner. And for the briefest, most fleeting of moments you have a fantasy of going on an adventure, of escaping normal life and leaving behind the daily routine.

Of seeing a different world, where no one knows you who are and where you can be anyone you ever wanted to be. Of forgetting the past and losing yourself in new experiences and endless possibilities. Of feeling like you're really living and not just flatlining through life.

Just for a moment. Who doesn't ever dream of that?

I must have dozed off for a little while, and when I wake up I'm stiff and cold. I give a little shiver. Gosh, that air conditioning is rather strong, isn't it? It felt lovely and cool before, but now I'm actually a bit chilly. Reaching for the blanket that was folded up on my chair, I try and snuggle underneath it, but I just can't get warm. In fact, I've even got goose bumps, I realise, glancing at my arms underneath my sweatshirt.

I give up. It's hopeless. I need to stretch my legs and warm up.

Abandoning the blanket, I get up and make my way along the corridor, stepping over various arms and legs, until I reach the end of the carriage where I slide open the door.

A burst of hot air hits me. It's like walking into an oven. Several men are standing outside in the space between the two carriages, smoking cigarettes, chatting in Hindi, or just hanging out, watching the world go by.

I join them. Leaning by the open door, my hair flaps around my face, blown about by the sweltering breeze. Tying it into a ponytail, I turn to gaze at the receding landscape. At the verdant, lush rice fields, bright shiny palm trees, makeshift houses painted in multi-colours, and half-naked children who run alongside the train, waving and laughing, trying to keep up and falling behind, huge smiles breaking across their faces as I wave back.

As I capture the sight of the children's faces, their smiles blurring into one as I pass by, it's like being dipped in melted happiness.

This is what it's all about. This is what they mean when they talk about train travel in India being magical. It's not about luxury cabins and being served gin and tonics. It's about those random moments when our lives touch other people's, however briefly. About a fleeting moment in time when a bunch of village children wave to a stranger on a train and she waves back, and for a split second their lives cross over.

And now they've uncrossed again, I muse, watching as

they recede away into the distance and wondering if I'll remember them, if they'll remember me. If in years to come I'll be somewhere, doing something, and I'll think again of the moment when I was once on a train, playing peek-a-boo with a baby and waving at children, while travelling across India . . .

I'm not sure how long I stand there, all thoughts of killing time long forgotten as the hot wind rushes over me, the rhythmic clatter of the train providing a hypnotic backing track, before I'm finally distracted by hair whipping into my eyes as my ponytail comes loose, the hairband falling onto the floor.

Quickly, I bend down to grab it. But I'm too late. As I fumble for it, a gust of wind grabs hold of it, and just when I think it's going to be blown away, another hand reaches for it. I look up and come face to face with the young boy with the headphones who's been sitting opposite me. Wordlessly he holds it out to me.

'Oh . . . thank you,' I say loudly above the clatter of the train.

His headphones are now slung around his neck and I notice he's smoking a cigarette.

As I take the hairband from him, his face breaks into a shy smile. 'Hello, I am Vijay, what is your good name?' he asks in quaintly old-fashioned English.

'Ruby,' I smile back.

'Where are you from?' he continues politely.

'England.' Scraping my hair back with my hands, I tie it tightly.

'Oh, jolly good,' he replies cheerfully.

I smile at his use of the phrase. It reminds me of something my Great-Uncle Harold would say, not a teenager smoking a cigarette.

'This is your first time in India?'

'Yes,' I nod. 'I'm travelling to Delhi.'

'Are you married?'

His last question takes me by surprise. As pleasantries go, I wasn't expecting this one. 'Um, no,' I shake my head.

He looks shocked. 'Why not?'

I'm not sure whether to be offended or amused by all these questions, but I don't have time to be taken aback as Sam leaps into my mind and for a moment I falter, blindsided by the emotions that follow. 'Because I haven't met the right person,' I reply, roughly shoving him and those emotions out again. It's become my stock answer. Well, isn't it every single girl's?

But if I think this is going to appease Vijay, I'm mistaken.

'How old are you?' he frowns, his dark eyes looking troubled.

'Older than you,' I smile, disarmed by his charm and honesty. Vijay, I realise, is genuinely curious, and it actually makes a refreshing change from when you meet a stranger in London and politely chit-chat about the weather and Tube delays. Neither of which either of you really cares about.

'I am nineteen and a half,' he replies defensively, puffing out his rail-thin chest.

'Not much older than me then,' I tease.

But he doesn't get the joke and instead replies solemnly, 'If you want to find a good husband I have many friends.'

I feel a flush of embarrassment creeping up my cheeks. First my agent and now Vijay. Do I really look that desperate?

OK, don't answer that, Ruby.

'No, thank you, I'm fine,' I say hastily.

'That is good,' he nods, breaking into a dazzling smile.

'So – are *you* married?' I ask, turning the conversation around to him. He seems too young to be married, but he's so interested in the subject, I'm intrigued.

'No,' he shakes his head and, putting out his cigarette,

reaches into his pocket and produces a mobile phone. 'But I am in love.' Angling the screen he shows me a photograph of a pretty Indian girl laughing into the camera. 'Her name is Suhana.'

'She's very beautiful,' I smile.

'Yes, I know,' he nods, and gazes lovingly at the screen.

'You make a great couple,' I add, charmed by the way he's cradling his phone in his hands and staring at the photograph, like a lovesick puppy. 'How did you meet?'

'She was in my class at school. I remember when I first saw her, I was just a boy and she was the most beautiful thing I had ever seen, she was like a princess . . .' He breaks off smiling as I listen, fascinated, to his story. 'I could not believe it when one day she came to talk to me! Little Vijay, with his brother's trousers that were too big and no front teeth.'

I laugh as he does a comical impression of a gawky, toothless little boy.

'I was so shy and she was so kind to me. As children we played together, we were childhood sweethearts, but then we grew up . . .'

I wait for him to continue, but he falls silent. 'And?' I cajole, wanting to know the rest of the story. 'What happened?'

'Her father sent her away to stay with relatives; we do not see each other any more . . .' He trails off sadly.

It's not the ending either of us was hoping for and I feel a crash of disappointment. 'But why?' I ask, confused. Now I'm the one asking all the questions.

'I am not a rich man,' he shrugs resignedly, his shoulders sagging in his thin cotton shirt.

'So what?' I protest. 'That shouldn't matter.'

'He wants the best for his daughter,' he replies with the kind of obedience I've never seen from a nineteen year old in London.

'But you are the best!' I protest, jumping to his defence.

OK, so I've only known Vijay for five minutes, and admittedly all I know is that he likes to play loud jangly music on full volume, but after listening to his story I just know he's a good guy. I can tell. Like you can tell a good apple.

'That is very kind of you, Ruby, but Suhana is very special . . . the most special woman that any of the gods could create . . .' He looks back at the photograph and sighs deeply.

'Do you know where Suhana is?'

'No,' Vijay shakes his head. 'And I know she will not disobey her father and contact me. She is a good daughter.'

'What about her father, have you tried to speak to him?'

'Many times,' he nods. 'But I know that I can never win Suhana's hand. He was very angry when he discovered we were in love . . . he is a very powerful man.'

'But maybe if you try again, maybe he will listen,' I suggest, but Vijay shakes his head.

'He is a wise man,' he says respectfully, rendering me silent. 'But I would like to be able to speak to her, to hear her voice, to know she is safe . . .'

I watch as he looks back at the photograph on his phone and strokes the screen gently with his thumb, before slipping it back into his breast pocket.

'That is all I want . . . to know that she is safe and happy in her new life.'

12

Vijay and I talk for ages about life and love, and then he asks whether we can be friends on Facebook, with such formality and politeness I have to stifle a smile. Finally, leaving him to smoke another cigarette, I make my way back inside the air-conditioned carriage.

As I find my seat I'm greeted by a man with a large metal urn selling what looks like hot milky tea, only it smells much more fragrant than my usual builder's brew back home.

'Chai?' he asks, gesturing to me.

Up until now my only experience of chai tea has been a latte from Starbucks, but this looks like the real deal. 'Ooh, yes please,' I smile.

For only a few rupees I buy a small plastic cup and take a sip. It's delicious. Like drinking a hot, sweet, spicy milkshake. No wonder it's so popular, I notice, glancing around the carriage and seeing everyone hugging their little plastic cups.

'Holy Moly.'

There's a loud groan from the bunk opposite and I see the American stirring underneath his blanket, like the Loch Ness monster. Stretching out his arms, he's yawning noisily and making a real show of waking up. Like he's just woken from a really deep sleep.

I feel a beat of irritation. Rub it in, why don't you?

Glancing sharply away, I ignore him and keep sipping my tea.

'Whoa . . . I was totally wiped out.'

I will be calm and serene and not even aware of his presence.

'Boy, I'm starving . . .'

Unfortunately his voice is like an irritating bluebottle buzzing around my head. Who is he talking to? Himself? I steadfastly stare ahead as if I can't hear anything. Rather like Sam used to do when he was watching TV and I was trying to talk to him about our wedding plans. Apparently it's all about men needing to retreat into their 'cave'. Though in Sam's case it turned out to be more to do with him wanting to retreat into Miriam-from-Marketing's 'cave'.

'Hey, is that chai?'

Think cave. Think silent. Think *I can't hear you*.

'Excuse me?'

Except I can. Loud and clear.

'Yes?' I swing around in my seat, like one of the judges on *The Voice*. Only, in my case, it's not because I'm liking what I'm hearing. Quite the opposite.

'Did I miss the *chai wallah*?'

Rubbing his sleepy eyes, he looks at me. His hair's stuck up all over and for a moment he looks almost sweet, like you could imagine him as a little boy waking up in his bunk bed.

If he wasn't such a rude, selfish pinhead, of course.

'Sorry?'

'The guy selling chai tea,' he explains.

From where I'm sitting I get a clear view of the corridor, at the far end of which I can see the man with his large silver pot of steaming hot chai. He's about to make his way into the next carriage.

Unless, of course, someone calls out and stops him.

''Fraid so,' I reply, turning away.

I know. I'm a terrible, terrible person.

'Darn.'

'Yup, shame,' I nod, nonchalantly taking a sip of my sweet tea. I make a little slurping sound.

Not on purpose, of course.

We continue on late into the evening, trundling through stations, stopping every so often. As we do, various vendors get on, selling all different kinds of soft drinks and exotic-looking snacks.

'Mmm, what are they?' I ask, peering at a tray of delicious fried things being offered to me by a lady with intricately hennaed hands. 'Are they samosas?'

'You know, I wouldn't eat anything from the vendors,' warns a voice.

I don't even have to turn around to know who it belongs to.

'Nobody was talking to you,' I mutter under my breath.

'Maybe not, but I'm just saying,' he replies.

At least I thought it was under my breath.

Feeling a hot blush creep over my cheeks, I try to focus on the lady with the hennaed hands, but her tray has been commandeered by the man with the pistachio nuts.

'It would seem not everyone shares your view,' I can't resist replying, as I watch pistachio man buying up half a dozen of her snacks.

'There's always gonna be someone who will swim in shark-infested waters.'

Rule number one. Never engage. It's like when you come home on the night bus and there's always some weirdo drunk guy trying to talk to you. It's the golden rule. And I've just broken it.

'I wouldn't exactly put samosas in the same category as sharks,' I bite back.

Well, sod it. In for a penny, in for a pound.

'I'm sure they're totally fine, but there've been a couple of reports of people being drugged and their stuff stolen,' continues Mr Know-It-All. 'When you're travelling alone, it doesn't hurt to be on the safe side—'

'I have travelled before, you know,' I say, hotly. OK, so a mini-break to Paris with a girlfriend isn't really the same as a train journey across India by myself, but still. I don't want him thinking I'm completely green.

'It's best to just stick with the food they give you on the train,' he nods, motioning to a uniformed employer who appears through the sliding doors with a trolley piled high with tinfoil trays.

As he enters I'm hit by a strong whiff of spices. I watch as he starts moving down the carriage, handing them out, and I suddenly realise I'm starving. With everything that's been happening, I'd forgotten to eat, but now my stomach has remembered and it starts complaining loudly.

As he hands out the food, I haven't a clue what I ordered, and I peel back the foil lid with a mixture of hunger and apprehension. After my run-in with the masala omelette I've learned that, although I love Indian food, *real* Indian food doesn't love me. My local Indian restaurant in London prepares its dishes with Western taste buds in mind, but here everything is much more authentic, and much, *much* spicier.

I feel a tug of relief. Boiled rice, OK, that seems pretty safe . . . I turn to the next tray which reveals some kind of innocent looking dhal . . . and that looks fine too . . .

I tentatively dip in a fork.

As soon as it touches my tongue, it's as if my taste buds are on fire. There's hot and then there's incendiary. Almost choking, I reach for a bottle of water and glug it back, but my mouth is still burning.

'Can't take the heat, huh?'

I hear a chuckle across from me and almost swallow the water down the wrong way. Coughing and spluttering, I turn to see the American tucking into his food like it's the blandest thing he's ever tasted.

Is it just me, or is this man deliberately annoying?

He waves a fork cheerfully.

'I'm actually not that hungry,' I fib.

'Well if you don't want it, hand it over,' he speaks through a mouthful of curry.

Nope. Definitely, 100 per cent annoying.

As the evening gives way to night, Vijay reappears and climbs onto the top bunk so I'm finally able to put down both seats and make a bed for myself. I probably should have asked him earlier, I'm sure he wouldn't have minded, but I'm not sure of the etiquette. And I don't want to offend anyone, I decide, gathering up my pillow and climbing underneath my blanket. Stretching out my legs, I let out a deep sigh of relief. Only when you've been sitting cooped up in a chair for nearly twelve hours do you realise just how wonderful it is to be horizontal.

The rest of the carriage has fallen quiet. Most of the curtains have been drawn, including my own, but through the small gap between them I can see the Indian family, the mother curled up around her sleeping baby, the white-haired grandmother, mouth wide open and emitting a rattling snore, two pairs of well-worn feet dangling from the top bunk belonging to the father and brother.

I stifle a yawn. It's been a long day. I'm tired, and hungry.

Propping myself up on my elbow, I rifle though my holdall for something to eat and find a couple of fruit gums, both covered in fluff. They're gone in two seconds. How on earth do those explorers who get stuck up mountains for weeks survive on half a packet of Polos?

I have another dig around in my bag, but there's nothing else to eat. Not even some chewing gum. I'll just have to try and go to sleep. Ignore it. There's nothing else for it, I decide, shoving my bag underneath my seat and closing my eyes.

But my stomach has other ideas and growls unhappily. God, there's nothing worse than trying to go to sleep on an empty stomach, is there? Well, actually, there are plenty of things a lot worse, like world famine. Or war. Or men who wear beaded necklaces, I muse, trying not to get annoyed by the thought of the American who's sound asleep on a full stomach.

I feel the train slowing down as we pull into a station. Opening my eyes, I absently turn to gaze out of the window, watching as people get on and get off, a whole hive of activity. Vendors hold baskets up against windows, others jump on board, dodging the rail staff, chancing their luck for a few rupees.

A small boy, not more than ten years old, appears in the carriage like an extra from *Oliver!* Barefoot, with ragged dirty trousers flapping around his shins and a grubby smile on his face, he works the carriage with a confidence beyond his years that is as engaging as it is heartbreaking. From the viewpoint of my bed, I watch through the gap in my curtain as he's wafted away by sleepy passengers, before closing my eyes and concentrating on trying to go to sleep.

'Coca-Cola, crisps, chocolate!'

It's right by my ear. Hang on, did I hear the words—

'*Chocolate!*'

I snap my eyes wide open and pull back my curtain. The little boy is beside me, his dirty face and gap-toothed smile by my pillow. He has my attention and he knows it, his eager eyes are shining and he launches into his well-rehearsed pitch.

'Chocolate. Real chocolate. Tasty chocolate, look, see.' He reaches into his basket, amongst the packets of masala-flavoured crisps and cans of Coca-Cola, pulls out several bars and thrusts them at me.

I look at them and immediately my mouth starts watering. Oh my god, *real chocolate*. After the kind of day I've had . . .

'How many you want?'

I can hear the American's warning, but temptation is whispering loudly in my ear: *Chocolate. Real chocolate. Tasty chocolate* . . .

'Miss, how many?'

The little boy knows he's got me.

I hesitate.

But seriously, how can anything bad ever happen with chocolate? Chocolate has got me through some of the roughest times in my whole life. It's comforted me after every failed romance, rescued me from bad exam results and never fails to cheer me up at that time every month. Milk, plain or white, chocolate has always been there for me.

'Two bars, please.'

Chocolate is my friend.

13

Eurgghhhh.

Where am I?

The next thing I know I'm vaguely aware of a clamouring around me, only it's as if my ears are stuffed with cotton wool and everything is all muffled and fuzzy. What *is* that noise? It must be the radio alarm, only it doesn't sound like Capital . . . and my bed feels funny . . . I only bought this mattress last year, the salesman in John Lewis convinced me to pay extra for a pillow-top, but now it feels all hard . . . damn, I'm going to have to return it . . .

What's that wailing? It's like a siren . . . and is that someone shouting? No, that's definitely not Capital . . . I feel really weird . . . where's my duvet gone? I've just got this blanket, it's all itchy . . . Oh god, my head hurts. Where am I?

Slowly I peel open my eyes. Everything swims before me.

I'm on a train . . . Oh yes, of course, I remember now, I'm on a train in India, I'm going to find Amy . . .

I blink a few times, trying to focus, but everything is bleary and in some kind of fog. Like a bad 1980s music video. God, I'm so groggy. I must have fallen into the deepest of sleeps. I shift my head on the pillow and a wave of nausea hits me. I swallow hard, fighting back bile. And now a hammering has started inside my skull, like there's someone in there beating a drum, only it's my brain.

Whoa, what's going on? I feel as if I've got the worst hangover. Yet that's impossible. I only drank chai tea.

I force myself up on my elbows, pull back the wafer-thin curtain and peer groggily out of the tinted window. It's daylight. Already! And we're in a station. A very big station by the looks of things, I realise, my vision focusing in on the swarming platform filled with chaos and noise. Gingerly turning my head, I look around the carriage. It's nearly all empty. Hang on, where is everybody? The Indian family has gone. So have Vijay and pistachio man. I glance at the trail of shells left behind, then across at the American. Only he's not there. His bunk is empty. The blanket folded neatly, with the pillow on top.

I feel surprise and, unexpectedly, an odd twinge of disappointment. He was annoying, but he'd become strangely familiar.

Still, I'm so glad he's gone. I really couldn't cope with any more of his . . . his annoying *know-it-all-ness*. I'm not even sure if that's a word, but if it's not, it should be. Now at least I can spend the rest of the journey in peace.

Swinging my feet over the edge, I stumble out of the berth. A guard is rushing his way past, and with a superhuman effort I manage to find my voice. 'Excuse me, where are we?' It comes out in a croak.

He stops, and turns.

'Delhi,' he says, peering at me as if I'm not quite right in the head, then continues hurrying on.

Delhi? Already? My disorientation turns into astonishment. Which turns into delight.

Wow, that killing time thing really worked, didn't it? I'm impressed.

Even if I do still feel all dazed and confused, I note, realising my balance is off.

Staggering slightly, I reach underneath for my luggage.

Except it's not there.

Huh? I fumble around with my hand for a moment, groping

around blindly, expecting my fingers to land on something large and nylon-y, but . . . nothing. Frowning, I crouch down and tip my head upside down – something that I was trying to avoid as, sure enough, the whole carriage starts spinning like a fairground ride – and peer into the shadowy darkness. An empty space stares back.

No, I'm wrong. I'm all confused and groggy. I've got mixed up, I must have put it on my bunk. Yes, that's it, it must be hidden underneath this blanket.

I pounce confidently on the woollen pile at the end of the bunk – it deflates like a soufflé.

Abruptly, the prickling anxiety that I've been steadfastly ignoring grabs me by the throat with sharp, pincer fingers.

My bag! It's not there! It's gone!

A horrible wave of ice-cold fear washes over me. The fear you get when something you don't want to imagine can be true really is true. Worst-case-scenario fear.

It's been stolen.

As the stark truth hits home, my mind starts to race . . . It must have happened in the night when I was asleep. But how? Who did it? And how come I didn't wake up? I'm usually such a light sleeper, at home I have to sleep with earplugs and an eye mask and even then I wake up at the slightest thing, so I don't understand . . .

Out of the corner of my eye I spot the glint of a chocolate wrapper and the domino-line of questions comes to an abrupt halt.

The chocolate.

Right on cue I hear the American's warning, loud and clear in my head, almost like it's being replayed through a Tannoy system.

'*There've been a couple of reports of people being drugged, and their stuff stolen.*'

Suddenly it all makes sense. Oh my god, I can't believe

it, I've been betrayed! Chocolate is not my friend! It was the enemy! It was drugged and now everything has been stolen! Everything has gone!

I'm thinking in exclamation marks, and my heart is hammering in my chest like a pneumatic drill. Thudding so hard that any minute now I feel as if it's going to actually leap through my skin like something from *Alien*.

I force myself to swallow hard. I need to calm down and think straight. Take some deep breaths like I'm in yoga.

But you're crap at yoga! reminds a shrill voice in my head. *You did one class! And you were so awful you never went back! You went shopping instead for too many pashminas and sandals that fall off your feet ...*

The shrill, panicky voice in my head is getting higher and higher, almost hysterical.

Shut up.

Shut up!

Another Westerner, a big-boned German girl wearing a backpack the size of a house, who's making her way towards the exit, turns to stare at me. 'Are you talking to me?' she demands, in a voice like Arnold Schwarzenegger.

Oh crikey, did I say that out loud?

'No, I'm just um . . . talking to myself,' I fluster. That's all I need. To get into an argument with Fräulein Terminator.

She gives me a scary look then turns and continues bumping and thumping down the corridor. Phew. That was a close call. Having my bags stolen is bad enough.

I feel a stab of relief. For, like, a second, until what's happened hits me round the head again like a cast-iron frying pan.

My bag has been stolen! They've taken everything! *Thwack*, it hits me again. My passport! Oh my god, they've got my passport! I'm in a foreign country, miles away from home, and I don't have my passport!

Or any money! I suddenly realise with a thunderclap of

horror. As the enormity registers I'm hit by another thwack, even bigger this time. Shit! They've got my wallet *and* all my credit cards . . . What else?

I'm scrambling madly about in my brain, trying desperately to remember. Now I know how those contestants used to feel in *The Generation Game*, when they used to have to recall the objects on the conveyor belt in order to win a holiday. Only this time the stakes are so much higher. It's not a food mixer and a giant cuddly toy, it's all my clothes . . . shoes . . . toiletries . . .

An item jumps into my mind and I'm almost too terrified to acknowledge it.

My phone.

I feel a vice-like grip around my chest and slump dizzyingly against the bunk. Fuck. If that's been stolen I'm doomed. Without it I'll never find Amy. I won't be able to contact her and she won't be able to contact me. Everything is replaceable, but not my phone. Not because it's some new-fangled smart phone – in fact, I'm probably the only person left who still uses an old Nokia that can't pick up emails. But because even if I could buy a new one – which of course I can't as I have no money or credit cards – *I don't know her number*.

In fact, I have a confession: I don't know *anyone's*.

The thing is, I've never had to. I just rely on my phone to store them all and never bother learning any. Which has always worked just fine.

Until now.

Now it's not fine. Now it's a complete and total utter fucking disaster – *unless* . . . In one final desperate effort I scrabble around in my pockets for the scrap of paper that has the Rajasthan number on it . . . But of course, it's futile. I must have lost it along with everything else . . . *Oh God.*

OK, calm down. Don't panic.

Swallowing hard, I put the brakes on my nervous

breakdown and step back from the ledge. This isn't as bad as it first looks. Things like this happen all the time. I was once pickpocketed on the Tube and they took everything, including my house keys, and I had to climb in through my bathroom window. I coped then. I'll cope now.

With superhuman effort I gather myself up and somehow manage to get myself off the train and onto the platform. It's filled with frenzied activity and a cacophony of noise and I find myself caught up in a huge swarming crowd. It's like swimming upstream, but I manage to make it out the other side and collapse onto a bench.

Taking a few deep breaths, I glance around me at the unfamiliar surroundings, trying to hang on to my resolve. But I can feel the reality of my situation fast sinking in, like a red wine stain on a stranger's white sofa. I'm alone. In India. Surrounded by total strangers. With no passport, money, or phone.

Plus, it's also freezing, I realise, suddenly noticing the marked drop in temperature from the south. And I have no warm clothes, except for this old grey hoody. Shivering, I untie it from around my waist and pull it over my head.

Right, well, I'm right about one thing: this isn't as bad as it first looks. It's worse. Much, much worse.

But I'm wrong about the other: *I really think I should start panicking.*

What am I going to do?

I mean, seriously, *What the fuck am I going to do?*

Then I see him.

Far ahead in the hazy distance, amid the moving sea of people, a head and shoulders standing tall above the rest. A battered old straw fedora bobbing up and down above the waves of shiny black hair and kaleidoscope of headscarves.

The American.

Like a drowning man spotting a lifeboat, my heart leaps.

Jumping to my feet, I begin to race after him. Shit, why didn't I ask him his name? I'm going to lose him in this crowd. I want to call out to him, but what do I yell? *Oi, you, the annoying American!* OK, no, maybe not.

I rush down the platform, trying to beat a path through the mass of people, 'Sorry . . . excuse me . . . I'm so sorry . . . If I could just get through . . . I'm sorry.' A man with a donkey blocks my view and I reach up on tiptoes trying to see. Oh no, now he's disappeared!

A fresh wave of panic propels me forwards and, abandoning my English politeness, I push past, bobbing and weaving from side to side, trying to spot a glimpse through the gaps in the crowd.

Oh, there he is! For a few seconds I catch sight of the hat, then it disappears from view again. Frustration bites. Along with panic, which is yapping at my heels like a crazed Jack Russell.

He's my only hope! I can't lose him. I just can't lose him.

My sandal slips off my foot and I go flying. Argh, these fucking sandals!

I throw out my hands to break my fall, grabbing onto the person nearest to me.

'Holy Moly!'

I'm not sure which happens first. Hearing his voice. Or realising my hands have gripped onto his chest. Either way, I'm too relieved to be mortified.

'It's you!' He does a double take.

As I lock eyes with the American it strikes me that I don't think I've ever been this happy to see someone. And especially someone who – a few moments ago – I never wanted to see again.

'Oh thank god . . . thank god,' I pant, trying to catch my breath. 'I was scared I was going to lose you . . . I don't know what I'd have done.' I'm babbling, the shock and the panic and the relief all merging into one big messy ball of emotion.

'I made that great an impression, huh?' His eyes flash with amusement. 'And there was me thinking you didn't like me—'

I come up short. 'No, not like that!' I snap. Suddenly realising my hands are still clutching his chest, I snatch them back as if I've been stung. 'I've been robbed!'

'Robbed?' His amusement is replaced by shock.

'Everything's been stolen! My passport, my money, all my credit cards, my phone . . . everything . . .' A lump forms in my throat; unable to hold it together any longer, I suddenly burst into tears.

For a moment he just stands there, watching me, then he lets out a groan. 'Oh c'mon, don't cry, I hate it when girls cry.' Digging into his pockets, he pulls out a wad of toilet roll. 'For the bathrooms,' he explains, peeling off a few sheets and handing them to me. 'Don't worry, it's clean.'

Fighting back tears I take the paper from him gratefully. 'Thanks,' I sniffle, roughly wiping my eyes. 'I just feel like such an idiot.'

Putting his hand on my shoulder, he manoeuvres me to one side where it's a bit quieter and puts down his backpack.

'So what happened?' he asks gravely.

Blowing my nose like a trumpet, I give a little shrug. 'I just woke up a few minutes ago on the train and it had all gone.'

'What? Whilst you were asleep?'

'Yeah, it must have been,' I nod, dabbing my eyes, which I can feel welling up again.

'Wow, that's terrible.' He shakes his head, his brow creased with concern.

I feel a surge of affection. Maybe I misjudged him. Maybe underneath he's really nice after all. I take another piece of loo roll.

'I know,' I sniff, 'I think they must have drugged the chocolate.'

There's a pause, and then . . .

'*Chocolate?*'

It's like the sound of a minor key chord on a piano.

'What chocolate?' he repeats, only the concern in his voice seems to have suddenly disappeared and is replaced by something that sounds a lot like accusation.

Feeling myself stiffen, I try to explain. 'Um . . . well, I was really hungry, and I couldn't eat my meal as it was too spicy – although I love Indian food, it doesn't love me – and then this little boy got on and he was really cute, and he had all this chocolate . . .' I feel my face growing red with agitation.

'You're kidding me.'

'What? No. I couldn't believe it either, he had such a selection, all different kinds—'

'I'm not talking about the chocolate,' he admonishes, 'I'm talking about you eating it!'

I fall silent at his rebuke.

On second thoughts, maybe I should stick with first impressions.

'After everything I said. I warned you about that happening,' he continues reprimanding me, as if I'm a small child. 'Were you not listening?'

'OK, you don't need to rub it in,' I reply. I can feel my tears drying up as quickly as they had appeared.

'Jeez,' he shakes his head. 'What's wrong with you?'

And suddenly, I feel myself snap. 'What's wrong with me is that I've had everything stolen!' I explode, 'and I already know I'm a complete moron for not being more careful and I don't need you telling me . . .'

He looks at me, not saying anything, but his silence only adds to my fury.

'And on top of that I feel like some stupid idiot tourist! I mean, just look at me, I've always dreamed of coming to India and here I am and I'm rubbish at everything! I'm useless at yoga, I can't find the right seat on a train, I can't eat the spicy food . . .'

But it's fury at myself, because suddenly it's all coming spilling out of my mouth. All my frustrations and disappointments and anger at myself from the past few days are pouring out in one big torrent, and now I've started, I can't stop.

'I can't even haggle!' Grabbing one of my sandals I take it off and waggle it at him. 'Have you any idea how much I paid for these stupid sandals? *Have you?* They'd have cost less at Nine West! *And* I wouldn't mind but they don't even stay on my feet!'

As I thrust it at him menacingly, he shrinks back.

'And I've only gone and weed all over them as I can't even squat properly in the loos without dribbling all over my feet!'

His eyes grow wider and he looks at me aghast. I know, I can't believe I said that either, but it's like a censor has been removed from my mouth and everything is spewing out.

'And not only that but I'm scared of everything! I'm like some big pathetic wuss! I'm scared of the roads, the stray dogs, the insects . . . look at all these mosquito bites.' I roll up my sleeve and shove my arm at him, which is covered in lots of angry red marks. 'I cover myself in repellent and they still get me!'

As if to prove my point I scratch them viciously.

'And I wish I'd just stayed at home in my flat because none of this would ever have happened, but I didn't, because I needed a break . . . and my sister sent me this postcard . . . and I just wanted to do something adventurous and impulsive and not sit on the sofa like I've done every night since Sam and I . . .'

I break off. Tears well up in my eyes again, but I brush them roughly away.

'And now I'm in a total mess and I don't know what to

do and the only person I can ask for help is a know-it-all American who prefers to stand here lecturing me about what a complete and total idiot I've been, instead of trying to help me . . .'

I break off breathlessly and I'm suddenly aware he hasn't said a word for the last five minutes and he's just looking at me, somewhat shocked by my outburst.

He's not the only one. Where did all that come from?

There's a pause, as I get my breath back. 'So are you going to help me, or what?' I finish finally.

He tips back his hat to wipe his brow, then studies me for a moment as if weighing me up.

'Only if you promise not to be a pain in the ass,' he replies.

Well you'd know all about that, I fire back in my head, but I bite my tongue. No answering back, Ruby; he's your only hope, remember.

'Thanks,' I nod, composing myself. 'I really appreciate it.'

'Well, I don't have much choice do I – after all that.'

I feel a flush of embarrassment. 'I was a just a bit upset, that's all,' I say stiffly.

'Understandably,' he nods.

I feel myself soften slightly towards him.

'And, for the record, I don't think you're pathetic. India can be a bit of a shock at first, it just takes a while to get used to,' he says evenly, 'and, once you do, you'll fall madly in love with it.' He holds out his hand. 'I'm Jack by the way.'

'I'm Ruby,' I reply, and we shake hands awkwardly.

It feels like a truce. For now, anyway.

14

'OK, let's go.'

Introductions over, Jack hoists his giant backpack over his shoulder and promptly sets off towards the exit.

'Go? Go where?' Plunging back into the crowds, I hurry to keep up alongside him. He has a very big stride.

'Well, the first thing you need to do is report it to the cops.' He pulls out a bottle of water and proceeds to glug down its contents. He drinks like my parents' Red Setter, water going everywhere.

'Right, yes,' I nod, making a mental list. 'Where's the police station?'

He shakes his head, coming up for air. 'Now that I can't tell you. I've been to Delhi before, but I've never needed a police station . . .' He shoots me a look.

I ignore it. 'Oh hang on, I've got a guidebook in my bag,' I remember triumphantly.

'Would that be the bag you just had stolen?' He raises his eyebrows.

I feel two spots of colour burning on my cheeks.

'And I thought it only covered Goa, anyway?'

The two spots merge into one great big blotch.

'Now I see why you need my help,' he mutters, and takes another swig of water.

I bite my tongue. He's my only hope, remember?

'Want some?' He offers me the bottle. There's only a dribble left.

'Do you have any aspirin?'

'Are you always this demanding?' He shoots me a look.

'Are you always so unfriendly?' I shoot one back.

'Hey, I'm helping you, aren't I?'

'I'm sorry, I just have a blinding headache.' Taking the bottle from him, I wipe the neck with my sleeve and take a thirsty glug.

'You won't catch anything, you know.'

'It's a habit,' I reply. 'You can never be too careful.'

'Shame you didn't think that about the chocolate,' he counters.

I hand him back his water bottle. *Only hope. Remember Ruby, he's your only hope.*

Repeat on a loop.

As we walk out of the station, a fanfare of traffic horns heralds our arrival and Delhi greets us like a pushy relative, enveloping us in a choking hug that almost knocks the breath out of me.

Despite everything I've heard before, all the travel programmes I've seen, the crazy stories I've listened to, the coffee-table books filled with photographs I've flicked through, nothing could have prepared me for the sensory overload that is Delhi. The sheer scale of people and traffic, the explosion of brightly coloured saris, the melee of honking taxis, the pungent smell of diesel oil and exhaust fumes mingled with incense and spices.

It's seriously loud. And polluted. And utterly chaotic.

And Goa suddenly seems a long, long way away, I realise, as we're immediately immersed into a crush of touts, beggars and tuk-tuk drivers, who tug at our clothes and stretch out their hands. Forget swaying palm trees, pristine white beaches and a sea breeze wafting over you as you recline lazily in a hammock. This is the real India and it's louder, brighter and faster than anything I could have ever imagined.

'We can ask my driver to take us to the nearest police station.'

Jack's voice interrupts my thoughts and I turn to look at him. 'Driver?' I repeat in astonishment. '*You* have a driver?'

'Yeah, why? What's wrong with that?'

Suddenly my opinion of Jack is turned upside down. He's a backpacker *with his own driver?*

'Erm, nothing. I just . . . I thought . . .' I trail off. Surprises are coming thick and fast and my head is still all groggy, like it's stuffed full of cotton wool. I can barely think straight, let alone make character judgements.

I look at him more closely, only this time I notice a few tiny flecks of grey in his dark stubble and realise he's older than I first thought. And is that an expensive watch he's wearing? I catch a flash of the gold strap as he pulls on a dark grey sweater. Which looks suspiciously like cashmere, I realise.

'Don't be fooled by the beaded necklace,' he says, meeting my eyes. 'I'm not some hippy, backpacking around India.'

'What beaded necklace?' I reply, forcing an innocent voice. 'Oh . . . that one . . .' I direct my eyes to just below his Adam's apple, more to avoid his gaze than anything else. His skin is smooth and tanned and I notice his pulse beating slowly.

'The car rental company said he'd be waiting for me,' he says, turning away and scanning the crowds.

I realise I'm staring and look quickly away. 'Who?' I feel all flustered. Like I've been caught stealing.

'The driver,' he replies and looks at me as if I'm stupid.

'Oh, I see.'

'Wish I did,' he frowns. 'I found the company on the Internet and we exchanged a few emails. We arranged for the driver to meet me here, but I can't see him.'

'What does he look like?'

'Good question.'

Together we stand on the side of the dusty road, surrounded by mayhem. I don't have a clue what I'm looking for, but I make a show of standing on tiptoe, my eyes passing over hundreds of faces. 'Will he have a sign?' I ask after a moment.

'Another very good question.'

'But if he doesn't have a sign and you don't know what he looks like, how on earth will you recognise him amongst all these people?'

Dumping his backpack on the dusty ground, he eases his haunches down onto it and leisurely pulls out a packet of chewing gum. I watch as he proceeds to take out a stick, unwrap the silver foil, and concertina it into his mouth. 'Just relax.'

'*Relax*?' I gasp in frustration. 'I have a stinking headache, I've lost my sister, and I've had my bag stolen. How can I relax?'

'You lost your sister *as well* as your bag?' Mid-stretch he shakes his head and lets out a low whistle. 'What did you eat *that* time?'

I shoot him a look. 'You're not funny.'

'Oh c'mon, that was kind of funny,' he says, his eyes meeting mine. The corners of his mouth curl up with amusement.

He's laughing at me. He thinks this is just one big joke.

I grit my teeth and ignore him. I can feel the uneasy truce is in danger of being broken already. Oh please hurry up, driver. I just want to get to the police station. Then this Jack person and I can go our separate ways and I'll never have to see him again.

He pulls out his iPhone and as he starts checking his emails I glance away again and stare out into the dusty distance. My mind starts to wander and I think about Amy . . . I feel the familiar prickling of worry that always surrounds the thought of my little sister, like the prickly casing covering a shiny conker, and I'm reminded again of why I'm here. God, I hope she's OK, and hasn't done anything stupid. Well, not more stupid than she's done already.

Vaguely I'm aware of a jostle of taxis, elbowing each other out of the way as they swerve in and out, picking up and dropping off fares. Absently I watch as one pulls out, leaving behind a cloud of dust that slowly clears, revealing a little white car.

Suddenly. Right here. Directly in front of us.

Abruptly I zone back in. That's weird. I never saw it pull up. It just appeared out of nowhere. Like magic.

I stare at it, curiously. It looks distinctly old-fashioned, with its rounded contours and shiny silver wheels, and I blink again. It seems out of place in the madness that swirls around it, almost as if it isn't there, and for a moment I think I'm seeing things. But no, it's there. Sitting quietly in the chaos of modern-day Delhi, with its 1950s classic lines and quiet elegance, it's like something from another era, a bygone world.

Or, to put it another way, it's a bit like spotting Grace Kelly in the middle of your local Starbucks.

I peer closer, trying to catch a glimpse of who's behind the wheel, but shafts of the late afternoon sun are reflecting against the windows, making it impossible to see inside.

And yet . . .

'I think that's your driver,' I blurt. Even as I hear myself say it out loud, I don't know why, but I feel sure that it's him. The moment I saw the car, I just had this feeling.

'Huh?' Jack stops fiddling with his iPhone, and looks up, squinting as he tips his face towards me. 'What? Where?'

'Over there.' I point to where the white car is parked as he stands, tipping his hat to shield his face from the sunlight.

'You mean the Ambassador?'

'The what?'

But he's already striding towards the car. 'Wait here with my backpack,' he instructs, 'I'll go ask . . .'

Being a head taller and twice as broad as everyone around him, he stands out above the swarms of people and I watch as he reaches the car, then rests a hand on the roof and stoops down to talk through the window. I can't see or hear what's said, but after a few moments he stands upright and gives me the thumbs-up.

'Yup, it's our ride,' he says, returning and picking up his backpack. 'I thought it was going to be more like a Jeep or a four-wheel drive, but whatever, this is cool—'

I quickly follow him, zigzagging through the bustle of people. Standing next to the car is an older, portly Indian gentleman. Bald but for two tufts of snow-white hair behind each ear and with his eyes hidden behind a pair of dark-tinted spectacles, he's smartly dressed in a grey Nehru jacket. With his shoulders firmly back and his chin held aloft, he bows his head ceremoniously as we reach him.

'It is a most pleasure to meet you,' he says very formally, 'I am your driver and guide.'

'Please, call me Jack,' smiles Jack affably.

'Yes, boss,' nods the driver with a poker face.

'And I'm Ruby,' I introduce myself, going to shake his hand.

He gives another bow of his head. 'My name is Mr Rukminesh Singh . . . Rocky for short.'

Shaking my hand, a look passes between us and for the first time I notice that, behind his glasses, he has the most incredible, piercing blue eyes. Out of nowhere a shiver suddenly scurries up my spine and goosebumps prickle on my arms.

What the . . . ?

'How do you open the trunk?'

Jack's voice snaps me back and I turn to see him at the rear of the car, fiddling with the boot.

'Please, boss, I will do it,' replies Rocky, and as I glance back at him it's as if the light behind his eyes has vanished as quickly as it appeared.

Or was it even there in the first place? I ask myself, feeling doubtful, and faintly ridiculous. Honestly. I'm hallucinating. His eyes look perfectly ordinary. And they're brown, not blue, I realise, as his glasses drop slightly down his nose. It's probably just the after-effects of whatever drugs were in that chocolate I ate. Or my imagination. Or something.

I watch as he walks stiffly to the rear of the car where he opens the boot with all the grandness of opening a treasure chest. 'I will take your luggage.' He gestures to Jack, who's twice his size and probably less than half his age.

Jack smiles. 'Oh, no worries,' and sort of reverses towards the back of the car as he swings the backpack off his shoulder.

He's almost rugby-tackled by Rocky. 'No, I insist,' he grunts, grabbing hold of it and with a strength that belies his age, lifts it into the boot. 'Miss?' He gestures to me.

'She doesn't have any luggage,' asserts Jack.

'No luggage?' Rocky looks perplexed and I feel my cheeks go hot.

'We don't talk about it,' says Jack, shaking his head and pulling a face as he gets into the car.

Rocky's expression relaxes, like a scrunched-up piece of paper being smoothed out. 'OK boss,' he nods and, without further questions, closes the boot and opens the passenger door.

'Please, get in,' he urges, 'we have a long journey ahead.'

Dipping my head, I slide onto the back seat next to Jack and, closing the door firmly behind us, Rocky climbs into the driver's seat.

'A very long journey,' he repeats, turning the ignition and, as the engine springs into life, he manoeuvres the little white car out into the traffic.

15

The police station is on the outskirts of town. After I file a report the thickness of the *Yellow Pages*, call my insurance company and contact my bank to cancel all my cards, Rocky drives me first to a bank where my credit card company has arranged for me to pick up some emergency cash, and then to the British consulate where several hours, dozens of forms and lots of official stamps later I'm issued with an emergency travel document.

'Which is valid for seven days,' instructs the grey-haired bureaucrat behind the window. 'So you must make arrangements to leave India by the end of the week.'

'Thanks so much,' I smile gratefully, scooping my hand into the tray underneath the window to retrieve the document.

'I hope you enjoy the rest of your time here in India.'

I feel myself sag with relief. Finally, it's all sorted.

'With no more surprises,' he adds, raising one eyebrow.

'Absolutely,' I agree, holding tight onto my travel document and clutching it to my chest. 'I couldn't agree more. Absolutely, definitely, one hundred per cent, *no more surprises*.'

As I walk back outside I discover darkness has fallen. Across the street, I spot the little white car parked up against the side of the dusty road. It's even colder now; pulling up my hoody, I hurry over. I can't see anyone inside, but as I walk around the side I find Rocky sitting on the wheel arch. He quickly stands to attention when he sees me.

'Miss Ruby,' he nods, with a quick flick of his head. 'Everything is good?'

'Yes, everything is good,' I smile, 'and thank you so much for waiting for me. I'm sorry it took so long.'

'It is the very least I can do. I am very sorry to hear what happened,' he continues solemnly. 'In India we have a saying, *Athithi Devo Bhava*, "the guest is god". We are very honoured to have you in our home. These are just a few bad people.'

'Thank you,' I smile, touched by his words. 'But please, don't feel bad, it can happen anywhere. I got my bag nicked on the Tube once.'

Rocky looks at me blankly.

'I had my bag stolen on a train in London,' I translate.

'You are from England?' he asks, his face brightening up.

'Yes, why? Have you been?'

'I have been to many places in my sixty-some years, but only in here,' he smiles and taps the side of his head. 'I like to watch movies and read books and talk to many different people, because this way I get to travel all over the world . . .' He breaks off, his smile broadening. 'Is the boss from England as well?'

'No, he's American,' I reply, smiling. Speaking of whom . . . 'Where is Jack?' I ask, glancing inside the car. All his things are on the back seat and for a split second I feel relieved. Which is a bit silly. It's not like I thought he'd run away and left me. And even if he had, so what? It doesn't matter now. I've sorted everything out.

Well, apart from Amy, of course.

'There you are.' I hear a familiar American accent, and look up to see Jack appearing from out of the shadows. 'I thought you guys could do with some of this.' He's balancing three steaming polystyrene cups between his hands.

'Chai,' beams Rocky, looking delighted.

'Thought it might warm us all up,' he says, passing them around.

I feel suddenly guilty as I remember the man selling chai on the train. 'Thanks, that's really kind,' I smile gratefully, as he passes me mine.

'Well, I did kick you out of bed.' He gives me a small smile.

Rocky glances between us, his brow furrowed.

'It's a joke,' I quickly explain. 'I was in the wrong bunk . . . there was a mix-up . . .'

'We just met on the train,' adds Jack.

'So you are not . . . ?' Rocky waggles his finger back and forth between us like a metronome.

Abruptly I get the implication. 'God, no way!' I gasp loudly, a bit too loudly probably, but I don't want Rocky getting the wrong idea. Or Jack for that matter, I think, getting a flashback to me clutching onto his chest at the train station. 'He's not my boyfriend! Not in a million years!' I exclaim, with a snort of derisive laughter.

However, there's not giving someone the wrong idea, and then there's torpedoing someone out of the water.

For a split second, I think I see an injured look flash across Jack's face, but then it's gone again. 'Just in case you were in any doubt,' he raises his eyebrows at Rocky.

'I'm sorry, I didn't mean, that just came out . . .'

'No worries,' he says evenly, 'you're not my type either.'

I laugh, but now I'm the one feeling a bit offended. Which I know is ridiculous. Who cares if I'm not his type, he's not mine. Saying that, I'm not even sure what my type is any more. I mean, can 'men-who-cheat-on-you-and-break-your-heart' be a type?

'So, everything's sorted?'

'Yes,' I nod, glad to be changing the subject. 'I've got my travel document and some emergency cash from my credit card company.'

'Thank god for American Express,' he smiles.

'Well, actually it's Visa,' I smile, 'but yes. And thank god for you saving me at the station, I really appreciate it. I wouldn't have known what to do without you.'

'Oh, it was nothing,' he says casually, shrugging it off. 'Damsel in distress and all that.'

'Well, thanks anyway,' I say, grateful to him for not making too big a deal of it.

'So what are your plans now?'

'I think I'll just stay the night in Delhi and get the first flight back to London,' I reply, taking a sip of hot chai. 'Probably the most sensible option, under the circumstances.'

I'd made my decision earlier. Without my phone, the chances of finding Amy would be impossible. I'd thought about emailing a few of her friends for her number (obviously I can't ask Mum and Dad), but even then it's no guarantee I'll ever find her. I don't even know for sure if she's in Rajasthan. She could be anywhere.

Because now I've had time to think about it rationally, I've realised this was a mad idea. OK, so I found a note in her room, and Shine's family are from Rajasthan, but that doesn't prove anything. I was so panicked and worried, I wasn't thinking straight. I just jumped to conclusions and jumped on a train.

Plus, who's to say she's still going ahead with the wedding? It wouldn't be the first time Amy's changed her mind by now. Dad's nickname for her is 'hokey-cokey', as she's forever putting one foot in and then taking it back out.

In fact, the more I think about it, the more I think that maybe what happened is an omen. I'm not superstitious, but even my sensible self can't help but see this as a sign that maybe I should give up now before I get myself into any more trouble, and go home. Back to London. Back to the life that's waiting for me . . .

Only now, saying it out loud, I feel a twinge of disappointment. So that's it. The adventure is over. Back to my normal routine.

'So, do you want a ride to our hotel? Maybe they have an extra room.'

'That would be great,' I nod, as Rocky opens the doors and we all climb inside.

As we pull out into the teeming traffic of Delhi's inner-city roads, I stare out of the window, trying to take it all in. After Goa's quiet sleepiness, the city feels both strange and exhilarating.

'What about you?' I say, turning to Jack. As I ask, I realise I know nothing about him. I have no idea why he's even in India. I've been so consumed with other things, I've never thought to ask him. 'What are your plans?'

He opens his mouth to answer, then suddenly cocks his head. 'Did you hear that?'

'What?'

'A beep. Sounded like a text or something.' He scrambles in his pockets for his iPhone. 'Nope, it's not me.'

'Well it can't be me,' I shrug. 'Rocky?'

'Not me, boss,' he says solemnly, shaking his head.

'You must be hearing things,' I conclude.

'Huh . . .' Jack furrows his brow. 'I guess so.'

Beep.

This time we all hear it.

'What is this?' frowns Rocky.

'It came from you,' accuses Jack, turning to me.

'But that's impossible.' Shaking my head I start patting down my combat trousers. 'See, there's nothing in them . . . my phone was stolen . . .' There're tons of pockets and I futilely run my hands up and down my legs. I feel like I'm a security officer at the airport. I mean, it's not like I'm going to find it, am I?

Er, hang on a minute. Lower down my leg, my fingers suddenly touch on something hard and flat. Stuffing my hand inside one of the pockets I'd forgotten about, I grab hold of . . .

'My mobile!' I exclaim, pulling it out and thrusting it at Jack. 'Look!'

'Wow, that's great.'

'I know, isn't it?' I say excitedly. 'I can't believe it!' In the same pocket is the scrap of paper with the number on it that I found in Amy's room. I feel a rush of relief.

'You sure you haven't got anything else in there?' he continues. 'You know, like your passport? Or your wallet, maybe? Or even some luggage?'

Realising he's being sarcastic, I throw him a look. 'I did check, you know,' I say tightly. 'I must have forgotten about this one.'

'That's understandable. I mean pockets are pretty obscure places to look.'

'What's it like to be perfect?' I scowl, feeling my earlier gratefulness fast disappearing.

'Well, now you mention it—'

'What did your message say?' interrupts Rocky, wading in between us like a referee.

'Oh, yes, of course . . .' Feeling a rush of anticipation, I quickly check it. It might be from Amy. 'Oh . . . it's just one of those promotional messages from T-Mobile,' I murmur, feeling a crush of disappointment. 'Nothing important.'

'But I heard two beeps,' he continues. 'You must have another message.'

I look again. Sure enough, there is another text.

'It's from my sister!' I say excitedly.

'The one you've lost?' counters Jack, but I'm quickly reading:

Hope you get back to London OK. I've gone to Rajasthan to get married. Tell Mum and Dad not to worry. Amy x

I suddenly have two thoughts.

She never got my texts from the train.

Followed by:

Oh my god she is there and she's really going ahead with it.

'She's in Rajasthan,' I announce, looking up from my phone. 'She's run away to get married . . . I have to find her. I have to stop her.'

My voice is suddenly drowned out as we turn into a narrow side street and slap, bang, into the middle of some kind of procession.

'Everyone is getting married!' hollers Rocky, honking his horn and trying to negotiate the little white car through the crowds swarming around us. 'It's wedding season!'

'*Wedding season?*' I repeat in astonishment, as we're engulfed by dozens of flame-torch-carrying revellers and a full marching band.

'Yes!' nods Rocky happily. 'Now is the most auspicious time in India to get married! It is in the heavens. It is written in the stars!' He slams his hand hard on his horn and the whole car reverberates. 'In India many people are very superstitious,' he continues, shouting to make himself heard above the loud beating of drums. 'Astrologers spend many, many hours studying charts to work out when is the luckiest time for couples to have their weddings, and now is the season!' Letting go of the steering wheel, Rocky throws his hands in the air. 'There are weddings everywhere!'

Sitting on the back seat, I'm listening to this information with a mixture of fascination and horrified disbelief. I mean, WTF? Here I am, jilted, jaded and single, *and I'm in the middle of fricking wedding season?*

'Even better is when there is a full moon,' continues Rocky excitedly. 'Then will be the most luckiest day! Then there will be *so* many marriage celebrations! It will be one big wedding!'

The irony isn't lost on me. Is this someone's idea of a joke? Well, is it? I mean, seriously, you couldn't make this up. With my own wedding plans still a painful memory, this is the last place I want to be.

Yet I have no choice, I have to find Amy.

If only so I can kill her for doing this to me, I tell myself, as I turn to peer out of the window at the excited faces and extravagant costumes. It's an explosion of dazzling lights and colour in the darkness and revellers start hammering jubilantly on the car as we inch our way forwards.

'Woah, some party,' whistles Jack, winding down the window so that the blasting music increases ten-fold and suddenly we're no longer spectators, we're part of it.

And all at once I feel my reservations drowned out by the buzz of energy and celebration. Hands appear, and faces, and excitement so tangible you can almost reach out and touch it.

'Look!' exclaims Rocky. 'Look, see the groom!' He points ahead into the crowd where a white horse has appeared, embellished in coloured plumage and a bejewelled saddle on which is seated a man, dressed all in white but for a flaming red turban. He's holding a little boy, who's dressed identically, like a mini-me.

Jack pulls out his camera and starts taking pictures. And now a coach has appeared heading in the opposite direction, forcing us to back up. Into the path of a fantastically decorated elephant, I marvel, spotting it majestically towering above the crowd. I feel a rush of adrenaline. I can't believe this is real! It's crazy. I feel like I'm in the opening scene of an Indiana Jones movie. I feel like . . .

Like I'm alive, I suddenly realise. That's how I feel. *Alive*.

Finally, after making our way through the procession, we park up outside a small, modern hotel and make our way inside the starkly lit foyer. Luckily they have a spare room and, dumping my things on the counter, I start filling in the check-in form.

'So tell me, what have you got against a wedding?' asks Jack, eying me curiously. 'I thought all you women wanted the church, the ring, the big white dress.'

'Not all women,' I reply, a little huffily. Let it be on the record that mine and Sam's was never going to be a big white wedding. It was going to be small and understated and I was going to wear a pale yellow shift dress and carry a bunch of daisies that Dad was going to pick from his allotment as a bouquet – I feel a lump in my throat as I remember. 'Anyway,' I say, brushing the thought quickly away, 'I don't have anything against weddings, just my sister's.'

'But why?'

'Because she's making a big mistake,' I reply flatly.

'How do you know?'

God, he's so persistent. 'Because I just do.'

'But how?'

I look up from filling in the form and our eyes meet. How do you begin to explain the relationship between two sisters? The lifetime of emotions and experiences you've both shared? The history? The love? The broken heart you hope she will never share. There are a hundred different reasons, so I just go with the simplest one. 'How about I saw the guy she wants to marry with another woman?' I reply. 'Is that a good enough reason?'

Rocky, who's carrying in the few bits of luggage left on the back seat, gives a sharp intake of breath. 'This is not good, this is terrible!' he thunders. 'This is a bad man!'

'Rajasthan's a big place,' cautions Jack. 'You'll never find her.'

'Well, I'll have to,' I say, with a new wave of determination. 'And I've got until the end of the week,' I add, remembering the words of the official when he gave me my emergency passport.

'So you're not going back to London?'

'Not without my sister,' I shake my head. My mind's made up. There's no way I can go home now. Not when I've come this far. Taking my key from the receptionist, I turn to Jack. 'Well, it's been nice meeting you. Thanks for everything.' I go to shake his hand.

'It's been fun,' he nods.

'That's one way of putting it,' I agree, then turn to Rocky. 'You too.'

'It has been my pleasure,' replies Rocky, holding my hand for just a little too long.

For a moment there's an awkward pause, nobody knowing what to say. 'Well, goodnight,' I say finally and, leaving them standing in the foyer, I turn towards the lift.

Waiting for it to arrive, I hear them talking together in low voices, and then . . .

'Hey, Ruby.'

I hear Jack's voice and turn around.

'I'm going as far as Udaipur, in Rajasthan.' He pauses and I hear Rocky loudly clearing his throat. A look flashes between them and I swear I just saw Rocky elbowing him in the ribs. 'If you need a ride,' he adds, gruffly.

Jack's offer takes me by surprise. I'm not sure what to say. We've known each other for forty-eight hours and we haven't exactly hit it off. We nearly killed each other on the train ride – correction: *I nearly killed him* – and when we're not arguing, we're hardly getting along like a house on fire. Quite frankly, the thought of a long car journey doesn't bode well.

And yet, I do need to try and find Amy and I have no clue where to start looking. Udaipur sounds as good a place as any. Plus, though I hate to admit it, I'm a little scared of travelling on my own. As much as I like to think I'm this strong, independent woman who can take care of herself, so far I haven't exactly done a great job of this travelling-solo business, have I?

'Well if you're sure you don't mind—'

'It is better you are not travelling alone,' interrupts Rocky gravely. 'It is not safe for a woman, it is better this way—'

I glance at Jack. He looks as reluctant as I feel. This is definitely Rocky's idea.

'That would be great, thanks,' I say decisively.

'So that's agreed then,' says Jack, in a business-like tone. 'I'll see you tomorrow morning at six a.m. We want to make an early start.'

'OK . . . right . . . six a.m.,' I nod hastily, still taking in this sudden turn of events as the lift arrives and the doors slide open. I step inside, then turn. 'By the way, I never did get to find out why you're here in India.'

Under his frayed fedora, Jack's hazel eyes meet mine, and for a moment he pauses, as if deciding how to answer. 'I'm here to keep a promise,' he replies finally.

I look at him, intrigued. A promise? *What promise?* Why is he being so evasive?

I open my mouth to say something, but before I can ask any more questions, the doors of the lift slide closed between us. Still, that's probably a good thing, I decide. I've got enough to think about without wondering what Jack is up to. Plus, who cares? It's none of my business. He's just some American guy I'm sharing a car with. After we get to Udaipur, I'm never going to see him again.

And pressing the number for my floor, I rattle upwards in the tiny elevator.

16

I'm woken at what feels like the crack of dawn by the alarm on my phone. It's still dark, and for a moment I lie in my strange bed, in my strange room, listening to the strange sounds from the street outside my window, wondering where on earth I am. Before suddenly I remember: I'm in Delhi. Trying to find my sister. About to set off on a journey across India to Udaipur, a place I've never heard of before, know nothing about and have no clue where it is, with two men I barely know.

Bit different from my usual morning coffee and slippers routine then.

I quickly get dressed, then hurry into the foyer to use the computer to check my emails. I scan through my inbox. There's a couple of emails from Harriet detailing another dating disaster, and a link Rachel has forwarded to a cheery article on how every woman in her thirties is freezing something, whether it's her forehead or her eggs. She's added the postscript: 'Sod this, the only frozen thing I want is a margarita. When are you free to get hideously drunk?'

But there's nothing from Amy.

I feel a clunk of disappointment. It was a long shot, but still. I pause for a moment, anxiety drum-rolling, then pull myself together. I don't have time to worry right now, I need to email Mum and Dad. I've been putting off contacting them as I was hoping for a miracle, plus I didn't want to bother them while they were caravanning in France, but they'll be heading back now. I can't put it off any longer. I start typing:

Having such a fantastic time, we've decided to extend our trip a few more days, Amy sends her love!

Crossing my fingers, I press send. I hate lying to them, but I can hardly tell them the truth, can I? Mum gets into a panic if she can't find her Tesco Clubcard, so telling her Amy's eloped to Rajasthan with a yoga instructor would probably give her a heart attack.

I also call Mrs Flannegan. It's after midnight in London but I know she likes to stay up into the early hours. She picks up immediately, and after a somewhat confusing few moments trying to explain that no, I wasn't ringing from next door and couldn't just pop over because I was in Delhi ('Deli? What you doing in a deli at this time of night? If you're hungry I can make you a sandwich, I've got some lovely cheese and pickle'), I finally manage to explain and ask if she could look after Heathcliff a little longer.

'Why of course dear, you should have just said,' she chastises. 'Heathcliff and Snoopy are getting on just wonderfully . . .' Her voice is drowned out by a burst of barking and blood-curling miaows. 'Oh, they do like to play,' she chuckles, her laugh turning into a hacking cough, which adds to the mayhem.

Poor Heathcliff, I wince. I'll make it up to you, I promise.

Feeling like a very bad mother, I hang up, then call both Amy and the number I found in her room. There's no answer on either. I'm resigned, more than disappointed. Like I said, she never answers her phone in normal circumstances, so it's hardly a surprise.

I leave a voicemail, telling her I'm in Delhi and to call me. There's nothing else for it, I'll just have to keep trying, I tell myself, hanging up and waiting for Jack and Rocky to appear. Which they do – Jack looking dishevelled with heavy bags under his eyes, striding down the corridor and yawning – and Rocky, immaculately dressed and ramrod straight, standing next to the little white car, which appears outside in the darkness like a ghost.

'Morning,' mumbles Jack, as he bundles himself onto the back seat.

'Morning,' I nod, sliding in next to him. It's a lot smaller in the back than I remember, and as our thighs press up against each other we spring apart awkwardly.

'Oops, sorry,' I fluster, trying to rearrange myself into the corner. It feels suddenly very cosy on the back seat.

'Actually, I think I'll get in the front,' says Jack, reaching for the door handle.

'I'm afraid that will not be possible,' says Rocky firmly from the driver's seat. 'Passengers must sit in the back.'

Ignoring him, Jack pushes on the door, but it won't open.

'It is for your own safety, boss,' he continues solemnly.

'Hang on, is this door locked?' Jack rattles the handle.

'It is better that you both travel in the back together. This way is much more comfortable and you will be happier. And if you are happy, I am happy.'

Jack mumbles something unintelligible under his breath, then slumps back against the seat. 'Whatever you say,' he surrenders, pushing his fedora down over his eyes. 'Just wake me when it's time for lunch.'

'Yes, boss,' says Rocky, beaming widely, and winking as he catches my eye in the rear-view mirror.

Hang on a minute, did I miss something? What was all that about? I peer at him doubtfully, but he's already turned the ignition and is shifting gears.

So this is it. We're off. As we pull out into the darkened street, I suddenly feel a clutch of trepidation. I've never done anything like this in my life. I hope I'm going to be OK. I get a flashback to my childhood and my parents telling me never to get into strange cars with strange men and feel a wave of panic. Oh fuck, it doesn't get much stranger than this. No one knows where I am or who I'm with . . . wait a minute . . . *I* don't really know where I am or who I'm with.

What if something happens to me? I know I need to find Amy, but still. I'm someone who likes to play it safe, and this is anything *but* safe. In fact, this is probably the most dangerous thing I've ever done in my whole, entire life!

It's also, I realise, with a flutter in my stomach, the most bloody exciting.

I must have fallen asleep because the next thing I know, it's daylight. Sunlight is streaming in through the window and I have to shield my eyes as I wind it down, letting in a blast of pollution and heat as I look out at the chaotic, traffic-choked roads.

'Um, where are we?' I ask, stretching myself out and tugging off my sweatshirt. I look across at Jack. He's still fast asleep. At least, I think he is. I can't see his face, it's still hidden underneath his fedora, but I can hear faint snores.

'Agra,' announces Rocky, rather grandly.

'Agra?' I repeat in confusion. 'But I thought we were going to Udaipur.'

'Udaipur is our final destination, yes,' nods Rocky, 'but it is very far and now it is time for eating.'

'Who mentioned eating?' Jack suddenly jerks upright like a jack-in-a-box, dislodging his fedora, which tumbles onto his lap. He glances at me, and does a double take.

'What?' I say defensively, at his expression.

'Um . . . nothing.'

He's a terrible liar.

'What?' I say again. 'Have I got something on my face?'

'No, it's not that . . . you just look a little different.'

Leaning across him, I angle myself towards the rear-view mirror to try and get a look at my reflection. And get the shock of my life. It had been dark this morning when I got up, and without any of my things I'd had to make do with washing my face with soap, brushing my teeth with the toothbrush I found in my hotel welcome pack, and that was it.

But now, seeing myself in broad daylight, I realise three things:

1. Never underestimate the power of a toiletry bag.

2. There is nothing I wouldn't do right now for a lash-lengthening mascara.

3. I would kill for Angelina Jolie's cheekbones. Or anyone's, for that matter.

'I . . . er . . . just did my hair differently,' I reply, quickly scraping it up into a pineapple on the top of my head. 'It makes me look . . . different.' Not for the first time in my life do I wish I was one of those natural beauties who look fabulous without a scrap of make-up and hair that's been left to dry naturally. Not someone who needs a good hour in the bathroom with an industrial-sized hairdryer and the entire contents of Selfridges' cosmetics hall at their disposal.

'Huh,' shrugs Jack, furrowing his brow as he peers at me, 'no kidding.'

I smile uncertainly. This is one of those times when I don't know whether to feel pleased or offended he's agreeing with me.

'Anyway, it's lunchtime,' I say, quickly changing the subject and making a show of checking my watch.

Fortunately that wasn't stolen, but then it's only a cheap little Timex I've had for years. I don't own expensive jewellery. Well, unless you count my diamond engagement ring that I still keep in my sock drawer. I tried to give it back but Sam didn't want it. He said he'd bought it for me and it was mine to keep. I half thought about selling it, I even took it to my local jeweller's for a valuation, but something stopped me. Maybe it was sentimentality, or the fact that it wouldn't be worth much second-hand, anyway.

Or maybe it was because sometimes I do something that I've never told even my closest friends. Sometimes, secretly, I take it out and slip it back on and for those few moments when the diamond sparkles softly on my finger, I pretend everything is perfect again.

I know. I really am pathetic, aren't I?

'Great, I'm starving.' Having woken up, Jack makes an attempt to stretch out his long limbs in the small confines of the back seat, arching his back and making loud groaning noises whilst sticking his fingers into his tufts of flattened hair. I watch him scraping them back and forth so vigorously, it's almost like he's trying to scrape ice off a windscreen.

God, he can be so annoying. Why can't he wake up like a normal person? I grimace, being splashed with water as he unscrews a bottle and begins drinking thirstily.

'I know an excellent place,' nods Rocky, indicating left at the traffic lights. A rather futile gesture, as no one else on the road appears to pay a blind bit of notice and there's nearly a pile-up as cars, tuk-tuks, mopeds and pedestrians converge upon us.

'What kind of food does it serve?' I ask, a little nervously.

'Italian,' replies Jack, resurfacing from his water bottle.

'Ooh, really?' I feel a flicker of happiness at the thought of a nice plate of pasta. Since the train I've only had a packet of crisps and a couple of bananas.

'No, of course not,' he laughs, shaking his head at me. 'We're in India, not Italy!'

'Oh.' My face falls. Feeling like a complete idiot, I quickly try to hide my disappointment. 'Right, yes, *durr* . . .'

His brow furrows. 'Hey, I was only joking,' he says, his voice softening. 'You're not really disappointed, are you?'

'Me? Gosh, no!' I lie and shake my head vigorously. 'I love Indian food!'

'But Indian food doesn't love you, right? Of course, now I remember that little speech you gave.'

My cheeks flame at the memory of my outburst. I'm still embarrassed about that. 'It's fine, I'm not that hungry.' My stomach betrays me by gurgling loudly. 'I think my stomach's still a little upset.'

'Your stomach, not you?' he frowns.

'No, not at all!' I protest, shaking my head. 'I'm fine, honestly.' I feel myself warm towards him. He can actually be quite sweet when he wants to be.

'Good,' he nods, looking satisfied. 'Because I know we didn't get off on the best foot.'

'Oh, I wouldn't say that,' I fib, trying to be all nice and polite.

Unlike Jack, who pulls a face and laughs. 'I would. You looked like you wanted to murder me on that train.'

Well, in that case . . . 'OK, you're right. I did,' I admit sheepishly.

'It's cool, I didn't like you much either,' he continues cheerfully.

I feel unexpectedly miffed. 'You didn't?'

'Talk about uptight.'

'*Uptight?*' I echo.

'Yeah, totally,' he grins. 'I was like, "Holy Moly, this girl's got a stick up her ass."'

I stare at him in disbelief, all thoughts of being nice and polite evaporating. 'You think I have a stick up my ass?' I demand indignantly. What on earth was I doing thinking he was sweet? He's not sweet! My first impressions were right: he's a rude, arrogant pinhead.

'I did,' he nods, seeming not to notice the outrage in my voice, 'but not now.'

'Oh really? Well that's nice to hear.'

'Now I've got to know you a little bit better, I like you.'

The conversation, which a moment ago was careering along Highway Arsehole towards Major Bust-Up, does a sudden U-turn. I stare at him, taken aback. 'You do?' His statement disarms me, pricking the anger I felt like a balloon.

'Yeah,' he replies, looking at me thoughtfully. 'I like you a lot, Ruby.'

There's a heavy pause. I want to stay angry at him, I really do, but it's as if all the anger has disappeared somewhere and instead I'm . . . I'm . . . Flailing around, I glance quickly away, trying to catch the tail of my thoughts. 'You do?' I say again, only this time it's much less of a question. Is it me, or has it got really quiet in this car?

'Yeah,' he nods, 'and now we're going to be spending all this time together, I really want us to be friends.'

Abruptly, I snap to. '*Friends?*' I repeat, feeling wrong-footed.

'I know we're totally different but I really want us to get along.'

'Right, yes, absolutely,' I nod vigorously, the sound of the honking traffic loud in my ears again.

'Good,' he nods, looking pleased.

'Great,' I enthuse, giving him a bright smile.

God, what was I thinking? I almost thought . . . Anyway, whatever. It's not like I'm disappointed. I'm not looking for love, I'm looking for Amy, remember? I mean, phew, for a moment there I was actually a bit worried about what he was going to say.

We pull into a long driveway and the car shudders to a halt in some pretty landscaped gardens.

'Grub is up,' chortles Rocky, delighted by his vernacular.

'Awesome,' cheers Jack.

'Brilliant.' I keep smiling. No, I'm not disappointed at all.

And as Rocky opens my door I clamber outside and race ahead into the restaurant.

After a bland and cautious lunch of plain rice and plain naan for me, and a delicious-looking, exotic meal of tandoori this and spicy that for Jack, we pile back into the car to continue our journey. Only Rocky has other ideas.

'You cannot leave Agra without visiting the Taj Mahal,' he insists.

'The Taj Mahal?' I reply, my interest piqued.

'Fraid we don't have time for any sightseeing,' replies Jack, checking his watch. 'In fact, are you sure this is the way to Udaipur?' Digging out a crumpled map, he peers at it, frowning. 'Judging by this map, we've gone completely out of our way.'

'There are many ways,' replies Rocky, waving his hand dismissively.

'Well, we need to hit the road,' he says firmly.

'True,' I nod, thinking about my search for Amy.

'But boss, it is one of the Seven Wonders of the World.'

'There's always a next time,' Jack placates him, settling himself back on the seat in preparation for a long drive. He looks annoyed.

But Rocky is insistent. 'It is the greatest symbol of eternal love!'

'Not for Princess Diana,' I interject. 'Don't you remember that famous photograph of her sitting there alone on that bench when she was still married to Prince Charles?'

Jack shoots me a sideways look across the back seat.

'Well, don't you?' I persist. 'It was heartbreaking, she looked so sad.'

'No, no, no, it is the most romantic thing in the world!' cries Rocky, gesticulating wildly with his head.

'Romance, *showmance*,' I say, rolling my eyes.

Jack raises his eyebrows. 'You don't like romance?'

He catches me off guard. 'I'm just a realist, that's all,' I say, shifting uncomfortably under his gaze.

'And romance isn't real?'

Like a piece of elastic, my mind snaps back to Sam and the moment he proposed. At the time I thought it was so romantic; I thought it was for real. But now . . . 'No,' I shake my head. 'It's all show, it doesn't mean anything,' I say defiantly. 'Romance isn't real love, it's just gestures.'

There's a pause as he looks at me thoughtfully, and for a moment I think he's going to say something.

Suddenly we're both distracted by the car pulling in at the side of the road.

'Five minutes walking,' announces Rocky, abruptly turning off the engine.

'Huh?' we both say in stereo, turning to look at Rocky, who's already jumped out of the driver's seat.

'What going on?' asks Jack.

'I cannot go any further, you must do self-service,' he says firmly, opening the doors and shooing us out of the car.

We exchange bemused glances, and for a moment I think Jack's going to argue, but then he seems to think better of it and obediently gets out of the car. I do the same and together, under Rocky's watchful eye, we set off, following the small pathway that lies in front of us. Past tourists laden down with cameras, a herd of goats, Indian children playing, a couple of stray dogs. We have no idea where we're going and for a few minutes we keep walking until unexpectedly we reach a river.

We both stop dead.

It's almost like a mirage. Across the water, rising majestically from its banks and shimmering in the afternoon haze, is the Taj Mahal.

It literally takes my breath away.

'Wow,' I utter, awestruck.

Standing next to me, Jack lets out a low whistle. 'Now that,' he says, shooting me a sideways glance, 'is what you call a fucking big gesture.'

17

'Rabindranath Tagore described it as a "teardrop on the cheek of eternity", Rudyard Kipling as the "embodiment of all things pure", while its creator, Emperor Shah Jahan, said it made the "sun and the moon shed tears from their eyes".'

Listening to our tour guide, I gaze through the shadowy archway, which perfectly frames the vision beyond. Made of white, almost translucent marble, it glows in the sunlight, and I nearly have to pinch myself. It's a Monday afternoon and usually I'd be sitting at my desk, staring at my laptop. But instead I'm standing here, staring at the Taj Mahal. I feel as if I've stepped out of one world and into another.

After queuing for ages, along with dozens of other tourists, Jack and I finally got our tickets and made it inside the grounds of the Taj Mahal. It was inevitable. Gazing at it from across the river was like catching sight of the most beautiful human being you've ever seen across the room at a party, and desperately wanting to get closer. It was impossible to resist. There was more chance of Jack and me flying to the moon than of getting back in the car and driving away. From the moment we saw it, in all its white marble splendour, we were hooked.

Which, of course, is exactly what Rocky knew only too well would happen when he made us walk down to the river.

'In 1631, the Mughal emperor Shah Jahan's favourite wife,

Mumtaz Mahal, died while giving birth to their fourteenth child. On her deathbed, her dying wish to him was for a symbol of their love. The result was the Taj Mahal . . .'

As we slowly shuffle down the steps and begin making our way along the marble pathways, I get a sense of wonderment that I haven't felt since I was a child. Never in a million years did I think I could be this moved by a building, but there's something magical about the Taj Mahal. Something you don't get from looking at a photograph, or seeing it on TV. Something that surpasses all your expectations; something that makes it more than just a beautiful building.

'According to legend, the death of Mumtaz left the emperor so heartbroken that his hair is said to have turned white virtually overnight . . .'

'Wow, he really loved her,' I sigh wistfully, fascinated by the story.

'So, you still don't believe in romance?' challenges Jack.

I zone back in to see him looking at me, amused.

'Well, of course I'll make an exception for the Taj Mahal,' I reply tightly.

'And that's it?' he replies, raising an eyebrow.

'Well, it's not like this any more, is it?'

'What isn't?'

'Love,' I say simply.

He frowns. 'Why do you say that?'

'Because love stories like this only exist in the pages of history books. The stuff of myth and legend.' Over his shoulder I see the bench that Princess Diana sat on, surrounded by people taking pictures. 'I mean, look what happens to our modern-day fairy tales,' I say, gesturing towards it.

He glances over and his brow suddenly clears. 'Are you still going on about that bench?'

'You know what I mean,' I say huffily.

'What is with you Brits and Princess Diana?'

'Now if you want to follow me, we will take a closer look at what is considered to be the most beautiful building in the world,' the guide continues.

I throw Jack a stern look. 'Sshh,' I hiss and, ignoring him, I turn back to the tour guide.

'. . . a memorial to a love so powerful, that it has lasted hundred of years . . .'

As the guide speaks, I glance at the faces of the people around me – the couple from Japan, two old bearded men from Afghanistan, a bunch of young Italian boys, a family of Canadians. They're not here because it's a beautiful building, or because it's hundreds of years old, but because of what it represents: the power of love. A love so great it could create all of this. Could attract all these people, from all over the world. Could stand the test of time.

That's the something that gives this place its magic, I suddenly realise. *Love.*

Only you won't find this kind of love in today's world, I reflect, with a moment of sadness. It doesn't exist. Forget love lasting centuries, these days you're lucky if it lasts six months. And I'm not just talking about Sam and me. *No one* stays together any more. Celebrities change partners faster than I change my bedding. I only have to flick through a magazine to read about another newlywed couple breaking up once the honeymoon period is over. It's just depressing. It makes you want to give up before you've even started.

Not that I'm thinking of starting again, I remind myself sharply. Been there, done that, bought the T-shirt. Or rather, in my case, the wedding dress. Which, to add insult to injury, I'm still paying off on my credit card. Honestly, modern-day love sucks. I'm happy to be single. Perfectly, one hundred per cent happy, thank you very much.

'The Taj Mahal took twenty-three years and several thousand master craftsmen from all over the world to create. A gruesome legend exists that afterwards these craftsmen had their hands chopped off to prevent them from building anything so beautiful again. Fortunately, there is no historical evidence for this story . . .'

I feel a tap on my shoulder and turn sideways to see Jack waving at me with just a stump, the sleeve of his sweatshirt flapping away where his hand should be.

'Ha, ha, very funny,' I whisper, pulling a face.

'Oh, c'mon,' he smiles, revealing the hand he'd hidden up his sweatshirt. 'That wasn't bad.'

'No, it was terrible,' I hiss, rolling my eyes. 'Now will you stop fooling around, I want to listen, this is really interesting.'

'Now, if you look closer at the ornamental gardens, you will see that they are laid out in a square which is divided into quarters by watercourses, each one offering a beautiful reflection . . .'

There's a murmur of approval from the assembled group of people.

'Classic Mughal design,' nods Jack.

I glance at him in astonishment. 'How do you know that?'

'I know a little bit about buildings,' he shrugs modestly.

'What else do you know?' I ask curiously.

He pauses to scratch the stubble on his chin. 'Well, see the vaulted arch and the minarets on either side,' he begins, pointing them out.

'Uh-huh,' I nod, my attention now fully caught.

'These are repeated on each of the four faces of the building,' he explains, 'and each one is identical, so that wherever you stand your view will never change, which all adds to the feeling of timelessness.'

Listening to him, I'm taken aback by how knowledgeable he is. Just the way he's talking, how he's moving his hands, the way he's so earnest and animated, I can't believe this is the same Jack who always seems so flippant and dismissive about everything.

'And not only is it perfectly symmetrical, but it's built on a platform, so that the backdrop is only sky which, from a design point of view, is total genius—' He suddenly breaks off, blushing. 'Sorry, am I boring you?'

'No, not at all.'

'I can get a bit carried away, you should have told me to shut up.'

'No, seriously, it's fascinating,' I reassure him, 'though I thought you said you only knew a bit?'

He smiles ruefully. 'OK, I've been busted. I'm an architect.'

'Unfair advantage!' I exclaim.

He bursts out laughing. 'Well, the hand thing didn't work, and I had to do something to get your attention.'

My attention?

'Well, you certainly got it,' I laugh, but out of nowhere, I feel my stomach flutter.

'I did?' he asks, his eyes meeting mine.

I suddenly realise he's stopped laughing. 'Absolutely,' I reply cheerfully, trying to appear normal. 'Talk about being full of surprises!' God, what's wrong with me? Why do I feel so nervous all of a sudden?

'Do you like surprises?'

Is it me or has he just moved a hair's breadth closer?

'Erm . . . yes . . . I do . . .' I nod vigorously, 'though only if they're good ones, of course.'

'And am I a good one?'

My breath quickens. Is he flirting with me?

'Oh look, we're losing the group,' I say briskly, pointing to the crowd of people and suddenly noticing they've moved on ahead of us.

'So what do you reckon, shall we make a break for it?' He raises an eyebrow, smiling.

Feeling all flustered, I hesitate, now suddenly at a loss how to respond. 'Actually, um . . . I think I need to use the loo,' I blurt out.

Good one, Ruby. As always, I can be totally relied on to completely ruin a moment.

'Oh, OK,' he nods, his smile slipping slightly. 'All that water you've been drinking, huh?' He gestures to the bottle of water I was given along with my ticket.

At the same time we both notice it's unopened.

'Well, see you in a minute.' I quickly turn away and set off towards the toilets.

'Hey, you forgot something.'

I turn to see him pull out a few sheets of toilet paper from his backpack and waggle them at me.

I stop dead in my tracks. In the last couple of days there have been so many shocks and surprises, so many new experiences and emotions, it's not so much a steep learning curve that I'm on, it's a bloody rollercoaster. Yet still, it has to be one of the most curious, and quite frankly, amazing things about life, that within just 48 hours you can go from complete strangers on a train, to sharing loo roll.

Talk about a whole new meaning to the words 'comfort zone'.

'Thanks,' I say gratefully, running back and taking it from him.

'Don't mention it,' he nods. 'Oh, and Ruby?'

'Yes?'

'Try not to pee on your feet,' he adds, his eyes flashing with amusement.

Oh god. There's a comfort zone and then there's me and

my big mouth. I cringe, feeling a hot flush of embarrassment, and hurry off to seek refuge in the toilets.

I had to do something to get your attention.

Washing my hands five minutes later, I stare at myself in the mirror and roll the phrase around in my head. What does that *mean* exactly? It's so vague and ambiguous. OK, so I know what it means literally. But *why* was he trying to get my attention? And what kind of attention are we talking about? The purely *platonic* kind of attention? Or could it be he was meaning a *different* kind of attention?

Well, obviously it was the first one, I think hurriedly, as we had that whole conversation in the car about just being friends. Except . . . I feel a nagging doubt. Except, in that case, what was happening out there then? Did I imagine it? Has it been so long I can't even read the signals any more? In fact, were there any signals in the first place?

And, more importantly, what on earth am I doing wasting time even thinking about this? Letting out a gasp of frustration, I turn off the taps. The toilet attendant in the corner glances at me and I smile self-consciously and quickly hand her a few rupees for a paper towel. Honestly, what on earth's got into me? I swear, it's all the Taj Mahal's fault. However hard you try to resist all this love stuff, it rubs off. Being here makes you think all kinds of crazy romantic things.

Like, for example, that Jack might fancy me and I might secretly want him to—

I catch myself. See! Totally bonkers. Forget mutual attraction, the only thing Jack and I share is loo roll.

Finishing drying my hands, I try to freshen up a bit. Thankfully I look slightly better than I did earlier and, in the absence of any make-up, I turn my attentions to my hair.

Hmmm, now shall I leave it up or put it down? I wonder which Jack prefers—

Argh! I'm doing it again! Bloody Taj Mahal!

Leaving the toilets, I go back outside and head over to where I left Jack. Only the grounds have got even busier and for a moment it's impossible to see him amongst the hundreds of tourists. Finally, after a few minutes, I spot our guide with his umbrella over by the fountains and I start making my way towards them . . . only, that's funny, I can't see Jack amongst the rest of the group. I scan the heads for his old fedora . . . Where is he?

A loud shriek of laughter pierces my thoughts, disturbing the respectful hush of the Taj Mahal, and I twirl around to see where it's coming from. Then I spot her. Just a few feet away. A tall, skinny blonde with big boobs, laughing and joking as she poses for a photograph. A small crowd of tourists are staring. Not just because she's obnoxiously loud, but because she's also stunningly good-looking. *And she knows it.*

Wearing an old straw hat, white T-shirt and a gorgeous sparkly Indian skirt that shows off her tiny waist, she's flashing a million-dollar smile and tossing her hair around like she's in a shampoo advert. Automatically, I look to see who's taking the picture. It's probably her equally good-looking boyfriend.

My eyes land on a man, his face obscured behind one of those big, black swanky cameras.

Hang on a minute. Isn't that . . . ?

'Oh, hey, Ruby!'

I stare open-mouthed as a familiar tousled head reappears grinning from behind the huge zoom lens.

'*Jack?*'

'Lemme see, lemme see,' interrupts the blonde in a loud American accent, bounding across like an overexcited puppy.

It's like watching Pamela Anderson in slow-mo. Transfixed, I watch as she slips a long, slim arm around Jack's shoulder, presses her ample chest up against his back and reaches for the camera around his neck. Flicking a button, she peers into the viewfinder.

'It's awesome! You're so super-smart!' she coos.

'Oh please, I just pointed and pressed the button,' he shrugs.

'Nonsense! You're way too modest,' she scolds teasingly, planting a kiss on his cheek.

Honestly, I've never seen such a display of blatant flirting, I think indignantly, looking at Jack, who's no doubt totally embarrassed by this stranger's antics.

Except, wait a minute. *Is he blushing?*

'Um . . . Cindy, this is my friend Ruby . . .' He tries to extricate himself.

The blonde reluctantly unlocks her lips from his stubble and swivels her eyes towards me. 'Oh, hi,' she says tightly, noticing me for the first time. She doesn't look best pleased to see me. In fact, I've seen cats happier to see dogs.

'Hi,' I smile, feeling her eyes running up and down me like laser beams. I shift uncomfortably in my unflattering outfit of combat trousers and ancient grey hoody from Gap. Up until this moment, I hadn't given much thought to what I'm wearing, primarily because this is the only outfit I have, and since arriving in Delhi my mind's been focused on other things.

Until now.

Now, seeing myself through Cindy's eyes, I'm suddenly brought up short. What must I look like? For the last forty-eight hours I've been sleeping and travelling in these clothes. I glance down at my trousers, they're all crumpled, my hoody has an unidentifiable stain, and – god forbid – I look down at my feet and feel my toes literally curl.

What was I thinking? OK, so my feet were cold, but still. It's like I've had a total style lobotomy. I don't care how frozen my feet were. Even if they had frostbite. There is never, *ever*, a good enough excuse to wear socks with sandals.

'Cindy's from LA,' Jack begins explaining for my benefit. 'She asked me if I'd take her photograph.'

'Well, you can always trust a fellow American to know what they're doing,' she teases.

'Cool,' I nod, glancing up from my red, striped woolly toes to take in Cindy, who not only looks even more stunning up close, but is effortlessly put together. I've never been able to do accessories; I always end up feeling like a badly decorated Christmas tree. But she makes it look so easy, with silver jewellery, strings of beads, embroidered scarves, even that straw hat . . .

Hang on.

I suddenly realise she's wearing Jack's fedora and do a double take. I feel a curious stab of possessiveness. I've never seen him without that fedora. He never takes it off. Not for anyone.

Still, I'm being ridiculous. Who cares about a silly old hat, for goodness' sake?

'You know there's a self-timer,' I can't help adding peevishly.

Cindy's smile freezes slightly. 'Yes, but it is so much easier to ask someone,' she says, smiling coyly at Jack, 'especially awesome photographers like this guy.'

'Aw, please,' he protests.

Yup, he's definitely blushing.

'Seriously, you're better than some of the professional photographers I work with,' she flirts.

'Why, are you an actress?' I blurt, before I can stop myself.

She gives a little tinkly laugh, as if that's the funniest thing in the world. 'No,' she says, casually shaking out her hair. 'I'm a bikini model.'

For a split second I feel myself reel. *She's. A. Bikini. Model.*

'That's nice,' I nod, without missing a beat.

I see Jack's jaw drop.

He catches me looking at him. 'Um . . . Cindy's travelling with her parents,' he proffers, quickly pulling himself together.

'I don't usually travel with my folks,' she adds hurriedly, 'but they're getting a little older now, and although I had a crazy schedule I said to myself, "No, Cindy, they've looked after you, now it's your turn to look after them," and so I cancelled everything. Like, literally everything,' she says, turning to Jack, her expression serious. 'Yoga, acupuncture, therapy, even a colonic!'

'*A colonic?*' I repeat.

'I know, right?' she nods earnestly, seemingly misinterpreting my incredulity, 'but when it comes to my folks, my health comes second. It was way more important for me to be a good daughter. I just *had* to come along to make sure they're OK.' She turns to Jack and smiles bravely.

'That's really nice of you,' he nods.

I glance at Jack in disbelief. I can't believe he's falling for this stuff.

'Well, I think it's really important to be selfless and do things for others, put them first, don't you?'

Oh please. Next she'll be saying she wants world peace.

'We're on a tour of the Golden Triangle, but they went back to the hotel early. Sightseeing can get very tiring for them.'

'We're actually just in the middle of a tour ourselves, aren't we, Jack?' I say pointedly, gesturing towards our guide.

'Yeah, right, we should get going,' nods Jack, snapping out of some kind of daze. Unlooping the camera from around his neck, he passes it back to her.

'Well, if you feel like meeting for a drink later, we're staying in town,' she says, handing him back his hat, 'and my parents like to go to bed early,' she adds pointedly.

'A drink sounds great,' grins Jack, replacing his fedora.

'But we have to get on the road,' I remind him with a regretful smile.

Which is a shame, as obviously I would have loved to have met Cindy and her big boobs for a nightcap.

'Yeah, Ruby's right,' he nods, 'we have to get going.'

'Oh, OK. Well if you change your mind, give me a call,' she shrugs, brazenly grabbing his iPhone out of his pocket and punching in her number. Then, giving a little wave, she tosses her blonde mane over her shoulder and trots off down the path, hair bouncing, sparkly skirt swishing, like a supermodel on a catwalk.

Then it's just the two of us again.

'She was very pretty,' I note, trying to sound all nonchalant. Well, I don't want him thinking I'm *bothered* or anything.

'Was she?' he feigns surprise. 'I hadn't noticed.'

We turn to each other and as Jack looks at me, I look back at him.

And suddenly, out of the blue, it's like we've crossed some invisible line. Something's changed between us. I've looked at Jack hundreds of times before, only this time he seems different.

Or is it me that's different?

'Come on,' he says, gesturing towards the tour, 'let's go.'

I hesitate, thrown off-balance.

'You OK?'

'Yeah, fine,' I manage, my heart thumping.

Quickly gathering myself together, we set off towards the tour guide.

But I'm not fine. I feel unsettled. Nervous, almost. Like pushing a heavy door that's been closed for a long time, something inside me has shifted to reveal long-forgotten emotions. As if the Taj Mahal has somehow opened a chink in my heart. Not much, just enough to let something, *or someone*, in.

Or, to put it another, much less poetic, way.

I suddenly fancy the pants off Jack.

18

So now not only have I lost my sister and all my belongings, I've also completely lost my mind. *Me? Have the hots for Jack?* I don't even *like* Jack that much. And yet for the rest of the tour he's all I can think about.

It's completely insane. It's like he's hijacked my brain.

How did I not notice his arms before? I wonder in amazement, unable to take my eyes off his flexing biceps as he folds them and thereby missing a very important ancient carving. Or the way his bum looks in those faded jeans? I ask myself, hanging back to check it out as we walk down the marble steps and I nearly go flying as I miss a step.

At one point, when the guide is talking about the fountains, I even find myself gazing at the sprinkling water and imagining the two of us in the shower together.

Naked. Wet. Soaping each other up—

Oh my god, what has *happened* to me? I've turned into some kind of raging nympho! In my defence, it's been a while, but even so, I'm acting like some kind of hormonal teenager. I need to get a grip. I'm here at one of the Seven Wonders of the World. I should be consumed with highbrow, intellectual thoughts about history and culture and architecture, not fixated by thoughts of Jack with no clothes on.

I mean, just look at this amazing view!

I lean against the balcony and stare out at the stunning scenery. It's incredible. Really incredible.

On the terrace below me, Jack walks across my eye-line and starts taking photographs. My eyes remain studiously fixed on the view. *I'm not going to look at him. I am not going to look him. I am not—*

I look at him. Correction: *I stare at him.* In fact, I cannot take my eyes off him. I take in his broad shoulders, the strength of his back beneath his flimsy T-shirt, the way his body narrows in a V-shape to his hips . . .

My breath quickens. It's like a switch has been flicked inside me and every part of my physical being has suddenly sprung to life. Including bits I'd completely forgotten about, I realise, feeling my groin ache. God, it's been *so* long. It's like that part of me has been asleep and now, unexpectedly, it's woken up and my mind is suddenly filled with fantasies about having sex with Jack.

And not soft-lighting-and-scented-candle sex, but rough-and-ready, throw-you-over-the kitchen-table-and-rip-your-clothes-off sex.

My legs wobble beneath me and, closing my eyes, I place my hand on the cool marble to steady myself.

'Are you OK?'

Hearing Jack's voice behind me, I come to. I turn around quickly to see him standing on the balcony, looking at me curiously. 'Um . . . yes,' I nod, all hot and flustered.

'You looked flushed.'

As he speaks I stare at his mouth and think about kissing him. 'Is it me, or is it really hot in here?' Hastily, I start fanning myself with my leaflet.

'I'm actually a bit chilly,' he says, frowning. 'I hope you're not coming down with something.'

Did he just say going down on someone?

'Yes . . . um . . . I mean no,' I manage, my voice coming out all weird and strangled.

Oh god, this is awful. It's like my brain is turning everything into some kind of sexual innuendo. Like watching the news with X-rated subtitles.

'Are you sure you're OK?'

'Absolutely,' I nod vigorously. I know. I'll just focus on the most unsexy things I can think of, that'll do the trick. Right, yes. Good idea.

He regards me for a second, then checks his watch. 'Good,' he nods. 'Because I came to tell you we should go. It's getting late.'

My old maths teacher. Frozen peas. Cutting your toenails. Watching someone on the Tube pick their nose.

See? It really works. As we reach the car, I'm feeling so much better. On the walk back I haven't had one sexual fantasy about Jack whatsoever. I feel almost normal again.

Brussels sprouts. Flesh-coloured tights. Cleaning the loo. Watching someone on the Tube eat whatever they've just picked out of their nose.

I just have to keep focusing on things that are so unsexy that it's physically impossible to think sexy thoughts.

Bad breath. Combovers. My big, comfy 'period' knickers (so-called because they remain hidden in my drawer and only come out once a month. I have several well-worn pairs, each with perished elastic, and each so baggy I look like I'm wearing a nappy. In fact, they are so ugly and unsexy that if anyone ever saw them I would have to kill them to ensure the shameful secret never got out. *That's* how unsexy they are).

'What are period knickers?'

'Excuse me?' Startled, I look at Jack.

'You just murmured something about "period knickers"?'

I did?

Fuck. That's a habit of mine. Talking to myself. It comes with being a writer; I spend all day by myself, walking around having conversations with characters in my head.

At least, I *think* they're in my head, but Mrs Flannegan once waved at me in the street and asked me who I was talking to. I had to pretend I had one of those Bluetooth earpieces in and was on the phone, so she didn't think I'd gone totally loopy.

Like Jack does, I realise, looking at him and wondering how on earth I'm going to get out of this one. Somehow I don't think the Bluetooth thing is going to work this time.

'Boss! Miss Ruby! You are back!'

Oh, thank god. Saved by Rocky.

As his familiar figure springs from the car, I feel a rush of relief.

'Was it not the most romantic place you have ever been in the whole wide world?' he asks, a broad grin on his face.

'It was awesome.'

'Incredible.'

Both nodding enthusiastically, we shuffle onto the back seat whilst Rocky climbs back into the front. 'I have heard from my passengers that Paris in France is also very romantic and in Italy there is the most beautiful place called Venice with boats like in Alleppey in Southern India . . .' Starting the engine, he pulls out into the traffic.

'They're called gondolas,' I reply helpfully.

'And in England there is Birmingham . . .'

Birmingham?

'This is also very romantic, yes?' he asks, glancing at me in the rear-view mirror.

'Um, well . . . I'm not sure it's *particularly* famous for that,' I say uncertainly.

'But even so, I cannot believe there is anything like the Taj Mahal,' he continues, unfazed, flicking his eyes back to the road. 'It is a very special place.'

'Yes, very,' I nod.

'You cannot go there and not be touched by the hand of

love, no, you cannot.' Rocky gives a firm shake of his head. 'Even American presidents, like your Mr Bill Clinton.'

'Really?' Jack raises his eyebrows.

'Yes indeed,' he says, nodding vigorously. 'He said that there were two kinds of people in the world. Those who have seen the Taj Mahal and love it and those who have not seen it and love it.'

Jack smiles. 'Well, our former president's never wrong.'

'Miss Ruby, do you agree?' prompts Rocky.

'Um, yes,' I nod again. Gosh, he's very persistent, isn't he?

'I have taken many, many people here and when they go they are friends and when they return they are to be married . . .' There's a heavy pause as Rocky breaks off and looks pointedly at both me and Jack in the rear-view mirror.

Suddenly the penny drops with a loud thud.

Oh god, of course. *He's trying to match-make.* That explains why he insisted on us sitting together on the back seat and going to see the Taj Mahal. My cheeks flame and beside me I feel Jack shift awkwardly. Oh, how embarrassing. Could he *be* more obvious?

'So, what route are we taking?' asks Jack gruffly, not-so-subtly changing the subject.

'It is already dusk. Soon it will be dark and I'm afraid it is too dangerous to drive in the dark, boss.'

'It is?' I feel a stab of alarm. Up until now I've been doing pretty well with the driving. Make no mistake, the roads are still terrifying, but I've felt quite safe with Rocky at the wheel. But now my anxiety comes back with a vengeance. If a driver with over twenty years' experience says it's dangerous . . . Automatically, I reach for my seatbelt, but it's wedged underneath the seat and, when I tug on it, it comes free and I realise it's not attached to anything . . . Well, let's just say I'm out of my comfort zone.

'Many drivers take drugs to stay awake, there are many

bad accidents, many crashes,' he says gravely, pointing out a mangled bus in a ditch at the side of the road. Its front is completely smashed in and the windows are broken. I give a little shudder.

'So what are you saying? That we need to stay here tonight?' Jack frowns.

'Yes, boss. It is much safer this way.'

There's a moment's silence as Jack takes this on board and thinks about it, then he gives a shrug. 'OK, well if you think that's better.'

'There is a saying in India, it is much better to be safe than sorry,' replies Rocky gravely.

'We have that saying in England too,' I smile.

'You do? Splendid,' he beams widely. 'Then we are all in agreement. We will stay the night here in Agra and leave in the morning.'

Fortunately Rocky knows a good, cheap place to stay in town. For a budget traveller in England, that would mean a bland room at a motel, but here nothing is bland. Nothing is ordinary. Everything, I'm fast learning, is extraordinary.

As he takes us to a gorgeous old *haveli*, which used to be a private mansion but has now been turned into a hotel, it's like stepping back in time. We're greeted by ornately carved doors, antique furniture and beautiful hand-painted frescos on the walls and, after checking in, we make our way through the courtyard to our separate rooms. However, Jack's mood seems to have changed. On the drive here he didn't say much and kept looking at his iPhone as if he was distracted. I wonder what's wrong?

'Well, at least I get to take a shower,' I say, making an attempt at small talk as we climb the stairs.

'You mean a *cold* shower.' Turning to me, he raises his eyebrows pointedly.

Alone with him in the dimly lit corridor, I feel my chest tighten. *He's telling me I need to take a cold shower?*

I'm suddenly gripped with paranoia. Oh god, has he realised I fancy him? Is that what this is all about? My mind starts to race. That must be why he's gone all quiet. I must have made it really obvious. Embarrassment sweeps over me. I know, I'll just deny it.

'No . . . I don't think so . . . not at all,' I croak, shaking my head vigorously.

'Really?' Jack looks surprised.

I feel a twinge of indignation. OK, so he's sexy, but it's a tiny bit arrogant to think I can't resist him. I do have some self-control. 'Absolutely not,' I continue, emboldened.

'Wow, you're pretty optimistic,' he replies as we reach our rooms.

'I wouldn't say I'm optimistic,' I bristle.

'I would,' he shrugs. Unlocking his door he pushes it open and walks inside.

Watching him disappear into his room, I feel my pride rush to the surface. Right, that's it; I need to clear this up. Enough of this schoolgirl-crush business, I need to be grown-up about this.

Still standing in the doorway, I screw up my courage. 'Look Jack, I think we need to talk,' I begin, my voice all forced and wavery. God, this is excruciating. *We need to talk?* That's far too heavy. It's like asking 'where do we stand?' after a first date. I need to be more casual. More relaxed.

I start again. 'Please let me assure you a cold shower is not necessary.' Oh god, and now I sound like Mr Carson in *Downton Abbey.* Why don't I just add 'm'lord' and be done with it?

Swallowing hard, I blunder on. 'What I mean is, you're perfectly safe; just because I find you really attractive, it doesn't mean I'm going to try and jump your bones—'

'I can never get any hot water, can you?' he says, his head reappearing around the door.

I stare at him blankly. What's he doing talking about hot water? Hasn't he been listening to a word I've just said?

'Those water heaters in the bathroom never work, it always runs freezing after about two minutes, so I've been having to take cold showers . . .' He trails off and pulls a face. 'I really hope you're right about there being a hot shower. I haven't had one since I arrived.'

Oh god. I am *such* an idiot.

'Sorry, what were you saying about being safe?'

I completely got the wrong end of the stick. 'Oh . . . um, nothing . . .' Waves of mortification are washing over me. How much of my speech did he hear? Any of it? *All of it?* 'Right, well, I'll leave you to your . . . er shower,' I say, turning and bashing my toe against the doorframe.

Fuck. These stupid sandals. It throbs painfully as I start trying to unlock the door. Oh god, and now the key won't go in.

'Need a hand?'

'No, I'm fine!' I protest shrilly, jangling it around desperately. Finally it turns. Flinging open the door, I charge inside and close it behind me.

Then slump thankfully against it.

Who knew fancying someone could be so *stressful?* I should have stuck with my resolve of swearing off men. My heart's racing, my head's all over the place, I'm all jumpy. I'm like a nervous wreck.

I'm distracted by sounds on the other side of the paper-thin wall of a shower being turned on. An image of Jack, naked, flashes through my head. I feel a tug of desire and frustration. Oh my god, there I go again.

Seriously, I can't cope with all these *feelings!*

19

As it turns out, I get my cold shower anyway.

Correction: nearly die of hypothermia.

This region of India might have the most beautiful palaces and lavish fortresses, amazingly colourful cities and gorgeous *havelis*, glittering tribal costumes and stunning jewellery of anywhere in the world.

Constant hot water, however, is proving a little trickier to find.

For ten minutes I stand shivering in my towel, waiting for the water to warm up and deliberating over whether or not my hair really does need washing. Which is something of a rhetorical question, considering there's less grease on a fish-and-chip wrapper. Every so often I stick my hand underneath the icy spray and try not to scream.

There's cold, and then there's *cold*. I'm not kidding, even those swimmers you see on New Year's Day, jumping in frozen seas in bathing suits, would balk at getting under that shower.

Because it's not just the temperature of the water. It's a combination of the temperature outside, which plunges down to freezing once the sun goes down, and the marble floors of these old *havelis*, which were designed to keep guests cool in the heat of the summer, but are like ice cubes underfoot in the winter.

Hopping on one foot, then another, I briefly wonder whether I can take a shower in my woolly socks. Fashion faux pas or no fashion faux pas, I'm not sure I can bear to take them off. I have goose bumps the size of *marbles*.

And, of course, the *haveli* being over two hundred years old, there's no such thing as central heating here. Instead of radiators, there are beautiful old tapestries on the walls. Which are stunning, truly they are.

It's just hard to admire them when my teeth are chattering.

In the end I screw up all my courage and dive underneath the shower and for a brief, glorious moment I'm rewarded by a hot jet of water. Oh the joy. Watching myself turning a lovely shade of lobster pink, I feel like I've died and gone to heaven. There are only a few things in life that can feel this good: 1) An ice-cold gin and tonic on a hot summer's day 2) finding those shoes you've really wanted marked down to 50 per cent off in the sale and there's one pair left in your size, and 3) a paparazzi shot of a supermodel in a bikini with what looks *distinctly* like cellulite.

But a hot shower when you're tired, dirty and cold has to come tops.

Conversely, there are only a few things that can feel as bad as a shower suddenly turning freezing cold when you've only been in it for a few minutes.

I shriek loudly, and leap out again.

Especially when you realise you've still got to rinse the shampoo out of your hair.

Oh fuck.

It takes until the time I'm dressed for the feeling to start returning to my head. Still, at least I finally have clean hair, I console myself, wincing as my frozen scalp starts to thaw. Finishing towelling it dry, I pull it into a damp ponytail. And there's something about having clean hair that makes you feel loads better. All I need now are some clean clothes, I muse, reluctantly pulling on my hoody. I've managed to get the stain out, but still. First thing tomorrow, I must try and buy something else to wear.

Locking up my room, I go to knock on Jack's door to see if he wants to eat dinner, only there's no answer. He must have gone out. Feeling disappointed, I turn to leave, then pause. On second thoughts, maybe he's fallen asleep. I hang back to see if I can hear any faint snoring coming from inside. No, nothing. Oh, wait . . . I think I can hear a voice.

'I'm really sorry . . . yes . . . it was unavoidable.'

It's Jack and it sounds as if he's on the phone. His voice is slightly muffled and he's saying something about being delayed in Agra and missing an appointment. What appointment? I feel my curiosity piqued. I wonder who he's talking to?

Anyway, whoever it is, I'd best not interrupt him. That's probably why he seemed so distracted earlier, I decide, turning away.

But not before I hear, 'Ruby . . .'

I turn back. Hang on. Did he just say my name?

For a moment I stand frozen in the corridor, my head cocked, straining to hear. Is he talking about me? And if so, what's he saying? I feel a hopeful flutter. *Is it something nice?* I wait, my curiosity ratcheting up a notch, but of course now I can't hear a bloody thing. Maybe if I press my ear up against the door? . . . Nope. Still muffled. I know, there's a glass in my room, maybe if I use that—

Oh my god, *what am I doing?*

All at once my common sense slaps me round the head. What is it about fancying someone that turns normal, sane women into secret agents? When we're not Googling them and searching for them on LinkedIn, we're snooping through pictures on their Facebook page.

And why stop there?

Why not just take complete leave of your senses and go into full stalker-mode and loiter outside their hotel room, eavesdropping on their personal conversations, huh?

Huh?

Quickly snatching my ear away from the door, I take stock of the situation. Who knows what Jack was saying, but if I carry on like this, the only thing he'll be saying about me is that I'm bat-shit crazy! I mean seriously, there might as well be a policeman with a megaphone in my ear, blasting, 'Put down your crush and step away from the door, Ruby.'

I give myself a shake. Right, come on, pull yourself together. It's time to stop all this nonsense and behave like a normal person.

Squaring my shoulders, I lift my chin and set off purposefully down the corridor.

Quickly. Before I completely lose the plot.

I go downstairs and walk through the courtyard towards reception. It's very quiet and there's hardly anyone around, just an older couple sitting on a sofa having a drink. I'm almost tempted to join them. I haven't had an alcoholic drink since I left Goa and I could really do with one right now, though on second thoughts perhaps that's not such a great idea. In my experience, alcohol + unrequited lust = making a complete fool of yourself. I've done quite enough of that already *and I'm sober*.

I keep walking. Ahead are the two large wooden doors leading out onto the street, and as I get closer I can hear music. Lifting the iron latch, I step outside and see the white Ambassador parked in a row of cars and Rocky leaning against the bonnet, talking to another driver.

'Miss Ruby,' he smiles, standing to attention.

'Please, it's Ruby,' I insist, even though I know it's futile. 'What's happening?' I ask, gesturing towards the music drifting from the building opposite.

'A wedding,' he replies matter-of-factly.

Ah yes, of course. I should have guessed.

'Much dancing,' he grins, relaxing his stance and giving a little wiggle of his hips.

He looks so comical, I can't help but start laughing.

He stops wiggling and looks at me thoughtfully. 'You should laugh more,' he says decisively, 'it is good to laugh.'

'Yes,' I nod in agreement. 'Only there just hasn't been much to laugh about recently,' I can't help confessing.

'But that is the beauty,' he replies, his eyes shining. 'Laughter doesn't need a reason. It just feels good to laugh, like a scratch feels good.' As if to prove his point, he gives his head a good scratch.

'Does that feel good?' I smile in amusement.

'Yes, you should try it!' he exclaims, and lets out a roar of laughter. 'I laugh when I am sad. I laugh when I am angry. Because let me tell you,' leaning closer, he lowers his voice as if sharing a secret, 'it tricks the gods into thinking you are happy, and when you are happy, good things happen.'

Despite the cold night air I feel an unexpected warmth inside me. He makes it sound so simple, doesn't he? And maybe it is, I reflect, turning the thought over in my head. Because somehow, being here right now, it feels like it could be that simple. It's just back in my life in London, things seem a lot more complicated.

'You should try it,' he nods, with a grin.

'Maybe I will,' I smile, feeling a sudden bond between us. I really like Rocky. There's a lot more to him than just a driver and tour guide. Underneath the smart clothes and polite demeanour, he's got a wickedly mischievous sense of humour and his habit of giving sage advice, which at first I thought was amusing, has an awful lot of truth behind it.

'So, you are by yourself?' he's asking now.

'Yes, Jack's on the telephone . . .' I begin, then break off. I feel embarrassed just talking about it. 'I mean, I think he is,

I'm not sure.'

'Are you hungry? Do you want me to drive you to a restaurant in the town?'

'Oh, no thank you, I don't want to put you to any trouble,' I say quickly. 'I'm sure I can eat something here.'

'It is no trouble,' he protests. 'It is my pleasure.'

'No, really.' Shaking my head, I glance back inside the courtyard. The couple that were drinking cocktails are now sharing a romantic candlelit meal together.

Actually, on second thoughts . . .

'Are *you* hungry?' I ask, glancing at Rocky.

'A little,' he nods, looking uncertain as to where this line of questioning is going. 'But I am happy to drive you to a restaurant before I go to eat.'

'Where do you have dinner?'

'It is just a little place in the town,' he replies dismissively.

'Is it OK if I come with you?'

'You want to eat with me?' He looks astonished.

'Yes. I mean . . . if you don't mind,' I add quickly.

'No, not at all,' he says hastily, 'it would be a pleasure, except . . .' he pauses, then looks abashed ' . . . except I am afraid this is not a fancy place; it is where all the local people eat.'

'It sounds great,' I say enthusiastically.

Rocky's face breaks into a huge smile. 'Excellent. In that case, I am honoured for you to be my guest.'

20

Together we zigzag through the intricate maze of dusty roads, dodging cars and motorcycles, stray dogs and street hawkers. Darkness has fallen, but the town is still very much alive and I follow Rocky away from the busy tourist restaurants to a street corner on which there's a man with a vast frying pan, filled to the brim with bubbling oil. He's cooking something that smells delicious, but before I've got time to ask what it is, Rocky dives up a staircase next to a fabric shop.

Where on earth are we going? Doubtfully, I follow him, wondering if perhaps I should have stuck with the safer option of gate-crashing the romantic-meal-for-two at the *haveli*, when abruptly I'm led out into a large open-sided café. A wall of chatter hits me. Bright and noisy, with strip lighting and vivid blue painted walls, it's crammed with long tables and benches, canteen-style, and packed with people.

All at once everyone turns in my direction, and I get lots of overtly curious looks, before the diners obviously decide that, actually, I'm not that interesting, and turn back to their food.

'Gosh, it's so busy,' I gasp, taking in the scene. 'We'll never get a seat.'

'It is always like this; there are always many people,' nods Rocky, seemingly unfazed. He signals to a waiter who whisks us through the crowds and shows us to a a table.

At first I assume there's been some mistake: the table is completely full, there's no way we can fit on there. But without a word of complaint, just lots of friendly smiles, everyone shifts up and two spaces appear.

'See, no problem,' Rocky beams, as we sit down.

I think about the restaurants in London, with their subdued lighting, dress codes and credit-card reservations. It's funny, but whereas before they appeared so fashionable, now they just seem pretentious and unappealing, and I'm so glad I'm here instead.

'I'm afraid there is no alcohol served,' apologises Rocky as the waiter brings us water.

'I'm fine with just water,' I smile, glancing around for the food menus. It's been a long time since lunch and I'm hungry.

'Do you need anything?' Rocky's brow furrows.

'Oh, I'm just looking for a menu,' I smile, amused at how overprotective he's being. 'Will they bring us some?'

'There is the menu,' says Rocky, gesturing towards the blackboard on the wall.

I look at it. Everything is in Hindi, of course.

'Don't worry, I will order,' smiles Rocky at my expression and, beckoning the waiter, proceeds to reel off a string of dishes. When he's finished he turns to me and his expression falls solemn. 'So, you have not found your sister yet?'

The familiar knot of worry tugs in my stomach. 'No, not yet,' I shake my head. 'I keep ringing her phone, but there's no answer. I just hope she's OK.'

'Do not worry,' he says calmly. 'She will be fine.'

'I hope you're right,' I say with a grateful smile. I've been trying to push my fears to the back of my mind, but now they come back with a vengeance. As each day passes I'm getting more and more worried.

'I know this,' he says, waggling his finger authoritatively. 'Everything is going to end well.'

'But how can you be sure?' I counter.

'Show me your right hand,' he says evenly.

I look at him uncertainly, then hesitantly reach my hand across the table. Slowly he turns it over, stretching it out in his smooth fingers, studying it.

'Do you read palms?' I ask, looking at Rocky with surprise.

He nods solemnly. 'My grandfather taught me many years ago. I come from a long line of palm readers, we all have the gift of foresight.'

'Gosh, really?' I reply, intrigued. Though, to tell the truth, I don't really believe in this stuff. The last person to read my palm was a fortune-teller at the local fair when I was fifteen. She said I'd be married at twenty to a man called Malcolm, have five sons and move to Papua New Guinea.

Some fortune that was. More of a *mis*fortune.

Saying that, I'm in a different, more mystical part of the world, where time-old traditions are passed through generations, I remind myself. Having my palm read in India is a bit different to having it read in a muddy field in Yorkshire, by a woman sporting a headscarf, a pair of wellies and a broad Manchester accent.

Staring at my palm, Rocky nods gravely. 'You are very lucky . . . very, very lucky indeed . . .'

It's all still a lot of silly nonsense though.

'You are going to live a very long life.'

I mean honestly. Next he'll be saying I'm going to meet a tall, dark handsome stranger – my mind suddenly throws up an image of Jack; actually, thinking about it, I *have* met a tall dark handsome stranger.

'But first I will tell you a little of your past, so you will believe me when I share with you your future,' he continues solemnly.

Doubt niggles. In fairness, the woman in Yorkshire with the headscarf never said that.

'You fell in love with a man but he broke your heart . . .'

I feel a jolt. 'Well yes, that's true,' I reply, trying to be all normal and matter-of-fact. After all, what girl hasn't had her heart broken by a man? It's not exactly specific.

'He had hair the colour of copper.'

I suddenly get goose bumps. Sam's hair is red. He hated it and used to shave it off, but I thought it was sexy, like Damian Lewis from *Homeland*.

My heart starts thudding loudly in my ears, but I try to ignore it. Coincidence, that's all it is. Beginner's luck.

'You will meet another man,' he traces his finger down my love line, 'but there will be some problem – look, see how the line breaks here?'

I peer at my hand. Gosh, he's right, I've never noticed that before.

'A break in this line signifies a setback, a difficulty to be overcome.'

'What kind of difficulty?'

'You have said no to him once.'

'I have?' I stare at him, agog.

'Yes,' nods Rocky, 'most, very definitely.'

I wrack my brains. Who can it be? I haven't exactly had men queuing up to ask me out recently. There was the guy at Tesco's last summer who tried to chat me up over the cherry tomatoes . . . he was actually quite sweet, until he asked if he could take a picture of my feet. Apparently he found my 'high arches very attractive.'

Oh god, I hope it's not him.

Then again, the only other person I can think of is the rollerblader in the park who stopped to tell me I was wearing cute jeans. Though when I'd later told Rachel at the pub, her response had been, 'Do you know what's the hardest part about rollerblading for men?' Fixing me with that steely lawyer gaze of hers, she'd replied drily, 'Telling their parents they're gay.'

'I see a lion . . . a big lion . . .'

'*A lion?*' I zone back in with a jolt. Oh crap, they don't have lions in India, do they? I suddenly have an image of being eaten by a lion . . . no, I'm being stupid, they only have tigers. *I think.*

'But this lion is red.'

'Huh?' What *on earth* is he talking about?

Screwing up his forehead, Rocky stares long and hard at my palm. 'There is a connection between this lion and the man you are meant to be with,' he says after a few moments.

Don't tell me he's a lion tamer and I'm going to finally run away and join a circus.

'I don't understand,' I frown, shaking my head in confusion.

'Sometimes it is difficult to understand now, but everything will make sense one day,' he says calmly.

I look at Rocky, trying to untangle it all in my brain, and abruptly I get a dose of realism. Oh please, what am I doing? This is nonsense. I can't believe I'm nearly falling for this stuff.

'Can you give me a name?' I challenge. That's the thing with psychics and fortune-tellers, they're always so vague, their predictions could apply to anything or anyone.

'A name?' Rocky frowns.

'Yes, his name,' I repeat, only a little more insistently.

He pinches the bridge of his nose as if he's thinking hard. There's a long pause, and then:

'Simon,' he suddenly announces.

Only one of the most common names on the planet.

'You don't believe me,' he says, at my expression.

'No, no, it's not that,' I say quickly, crossing the fingers of my left hand under the table. I don't want to offend him. 'I'm just a little sceptical, that's all . . .'

'The lines on our palms are destiny's imprint,' he says firmly. 'They are formed in our mother's belly before we are born, there is no way to change them; this was always your journey.'

'What? To come to India?' I can't help scoffing a little.

He fixes me with his steadfast gaze. 'You are in India to find something,' he continues, not letting go of my hand.

'Well, yes, my sister,' I nod, meeting his eyes. 'I told you.'

Gosh, that's so odd, but in this light I'd swear his eyes were blue.

'No.' He shakes his head. 'It is something else.' Leaning closer he holds my palm tighter, and suddenly, out of nowhere, I get that weird sensation, the same one as when I first met him at the railway station in Delhi.

'It will all become clear one day. Until then, you must have faith, Ruby.'

And it's as though everything seems to recede away, the noise of the restaurant fading into the background, like someone has just turned the volume down low on the TV. All I can hear is Rocky's voice, soothing, chanting, hypnotising.

'Faith, Ruby, you must have faith. You must trust in the universe . . .'

I feel light-headed, almost as if I'm going to faint. Everything is starting to spin. I close my eyes.

'Please, be careful, the food is very hot.'

Abruptly I snap to and realise Rocky has let go of my hand. An array of dishes has arrived on the table.

'How do you say in England? Tuck in!' he beams.

It's as if someone has just turned the volume back up. The noise is back. The dizziness has disappeared. Everything is back to normal. What on earth just happened? I glance at Rocky and notice the blue walls reflecting in his glasses. All at once I feel a bit silly. Honestly, Ruby, nothing happened, of course. It's just my mind playing tricks on me. Reaching for my glass, I take a large sip of water. Next I'll be believing Rocky really can read my palm.

21

'So what do you think of the food?'

Fifteen minutes later, even more dishes have arrived and Rocky is tucking in hungrily. I glance at the silver plates filled with lots of different ingredients in rich, colourful sauces. There's so much of it!

'Gosh, yes, it all looks delicious,' I reply.

And very spicy.

I look back at my own plate, on which there are just a few untouched spoonfuls. Apprehension knots inside me. These dishes haven't been cooked with namby-pamby Western taste buds in mind, they've been cooked for the locals.

'You are not hungry?' Looking up from his half-empty plate, Rocky glances at mine and raises his eyebrows.

'No, it's not that . . .' Oh dear, I don't know what I was thinking. It never crossed my mind to say anything when Rocky was ordering, I just presumed I'd be able to eat something, but now, sitting here, I realise I'm a world away from my bland lunch of plain white rice and a naan bread.

'The thing is . . .' I trail off. God, this is so embarrassing.

'Is something wrong?' Rocky frowns. 'Do you not like this place?'

'No, no, I love it here,' I reassure him hastily, 'it's just . . .' I hesitate, trying to think of how I can put it without offending him, what excuses I can make. Oh, what's the point, I might as well just tell the truth. I can't keep moving my food around my plate forever. 'I'm really sorry but I can't eat any of this food,' I blurt out.

Rocky looks at me, confounded. 'I'm afraid I do not understand.'

'It's completely my fault,' I apologise. 'I should have said something when you were ordering. You see, I'm not an adventurous eater, I can't eat spicy Indian food.' I can hear myself gabbling as I try to explain. Oh god, this is awful. Rocky has been kind enough to bring me to his local restaurant, I don't want him to think I'm being rude. 'I'm so sorry, I'm really rubbish, maybe I can order some plain rice instead?'

'Nonsense,' he shakes his head.

'No really.'

'Of course you can eat Indian food,' he says firmly, 'I will teach you.'

I stop protesting and stare at him. '*Teach me?*'

Until this moment it's never occurred to me that I could *learn* how to eat Indian food, in the same way you can learn how to swim, or speak French.

'This is *paneer*,' he says, pointing to the first dish, which contains small, bite-sized cubes in a rich sauce. 'It is a kind of cheese.'

'Cheese?' I look at him in surprise. I would never have guessed. Somehow it seems suddenly less scary.

'Yes, and we use this in *Malai Kofta*,' he points to another dish, which looks like meatballs. 'Please, repeat after me.'

'*Malai . . . Kofta*,' I stumble over the pronunciation, feeling self-conscious. Actually, it reminds me a lot of trying to learn French. My accent was always horrible.

'This is vegetables and the paneer, deep-fried, it is very good,' he smiles, patting his tiny pot belly. '*Chana Masala*,' he says, pointing to another dish.

'*Chana . . . Masala*,' I repeat clumsily, only this time I

secretly enjoy the sensation of hearing myself trying to say the unfamiliar words.

'This is chickpeas with onions, tomatoes, dried mango root and spices . . .'

'Oh, but you see, that's my problem, it's the spices—' I begin vocalising my fears, but he won't let me finish.

'And here is dhal, my favourite. It is made of lentils and it is *very* spicy . . .'

I open my mouth in protestation, but he waggles his finger sternly, silencing me.

'And so you must eat it with the raita.' He points to a bowl of creamy-looking yoghurt, then to pile of flatbread, 'and the chapatti.'

I nod, captivated by my lesson.

'Now watch.'

Spooning various dishes onto his large silver plate, Rocky proceeds to mix it together with his fingers. I watch, fascinated, and it's then I realise no one is using cutlery to eat. 'Use only your right hand,' he says, crushing and mashing the mixture together, before scooping it up and pushing into his mouth, using his thumb. 'Now your turn,' he instructs.

I peer at the slivers of bright red chilli, glistening in the spicy dhal, and blanch.

'Don't be afraid,' he cajoles, 'eat a little with the raita.'

I take a deep breath and do as he says, spooning a little of the dhal on my plate and mixing it with the creamy yoghurt.

'It is very important to eat both together,' he nods. 'This is the secret.'

Gingerly I scoop up the mixture with my fingers and place it in my mouth, bracing myself for the familiar fiery burning.

'It's good?'

As the different spices converge in my mouth, tingling all my different taste buds, I feel a split second of regret. That 'oh-no-what-I-have-done?' feeling you get when you know you've just made a big mistake. It was very sweet of Rocky to try and teach me how to eat spicy Indian food, and for a moment I almost believed he could, he seemed so sure, so insistent. But I can't change just like that, I'm a lost cause, it's impossible.

But hang on a minute.

Abruptly I realise: there's no burning. No watering eyes. No desperate grab for my glass of water. Just lots of delicate spices and the combination of sweet and savoury flavours melting in my mouth.

'Oh wow, it's delicious!' I gasp, still with my mouth full. 'Oops, sorry,' I quickly mumble, covering my mouth.

Rocky bursts out laughing. 'See! What did I tell you?' he beams, tearing off a piece of chapatti and passing it to me.

I take it from him and tear off a piece myself, using it to scoop up another mouthful. It tastes even more amazing the second time.

'More?' Rocky offers me the dhal, only this time I'm not scared and, taking a large scoop, I add the raita.

'Thanks,' I smile, and as Rocky turns back to his food I take a moment to glance around me and take in my surroundings. Here I am, sitting in a crowded restaurant, eating Indian food with my hands. Who would ever have thought it? Talk about a whole new experience. I never would have done this in London.

Only I'm not in London now. I'm in India, and everything is totally different.

Tearing off a piece of a chapatti, I eagerly scoop up another mouthful.

Me included.

Afterwards, it's with a full belly and a sense of satisfaction that I walk back to the *haveli* with Rocky. After thanking him profusely, he bids me goodnight and I head happily into the courtyard to look for Jack, bursting with my news. I've had such a great evening, I can't wait to tell him all about it. He won't be able to believe it!

Ahead I can see a few more people sitting having drinks, and imagine Jack and me doing the same. Over a couple of cold Kingfisher beers I can regale him with stories of how I braved the spicy dhal and won. Or the *Chana Masala* and how delicious it was. Or how I know all the different types of bread. For example, here are just a few off the top of my head: chapatti, parathas, *pooris* . . . I feel a flush of pride. Seriously, he's going to be *so* impressed.

Eagerly, I turn to head upstairs to knock on his door and invite him for a drink, when I see a flash of straw in the corner of my eye. Hang on, is that Jack's fedora? I glance sideways, trying to see past a large potted fern to one of the big leather sofas. He's got his back to me, but yes, that's definitely him, I realise, unable to stop the big smile breaking across my face. I *cannot* wait to see his face when I tell him.

I start to hurry over, then stop dead.

He's not alone.

Having moved a few steps, the fronds of the potted plant have shifted to one side and suddenly I get a clear view of the attractive blonde sitting next to him. *Cindy.*

For a brief moment I stand there, watching them, all the anticipation, excitement and happiness of the evening trickling away like sand through an hourglass. Deep in conversation, their heads bent low; their body language says it all. All at once I feel crushed. He must have called her. Old insecurities come rushing back and hit me in the solar plexus. And there was me thinking he'd be interested in hearing about my evening.

God, I'm such a fool.

And quickly turning away before either of them spots me, I hurry up to my room.

22

Anyway, whatever, I don't care. It's better this way.

Five minutes later I'm sitting cross-legged on my four-poster bed, wrapped up in a blanket and brandishing my mobile. I need to focus on finding my sister, not fantasising about Jack. Unfolding the piece of paper I found in Amy's room, I determinedly dial the number. Things are complicated enough without adding some ridiculous infatuation to the mix. As if I don't have enough problems.

I wait for the call to connect.

I mean, honestly. Me and Jack? It was a stupid idea. Even if anything had happened, *which it wouldn't have done*, it would have only ended in disaster.

On the other end of the line, the phone starts ringing.

No, it's much better that he gets together with Cindy. Much better.

I let the phone ring for a good five minutes, before I finally give up. Hanging up, I lean back against my pillow. The room is quiet, and glancing around me I take in the unfamiliar surroundings, feeling a weariness descend upon me.

What am I doing here? I mean, seriously, *what am I doing here?*

As I ask myself the question, every single nagging doubt and fear that I've been trying to ignore over the last few days rises to the surface. Let's face it, I'm never going to find Amy at this rate. It's just hopeless. I don't have a clue what I'm doing. I'm a novelist, I spend my days sitting at home at my laptop in my fluffy slippers, drinking cold coffee and procrastinating. I don't go gallivanting off across India on a whim, losing sisters and falling for handsome strangers. I *write* about stuff like that, I don't do it!

As the floodgates open, I feel suddenly overwhelmed. I'm completely out of my depth here. It's one thing daydreaming about having an adventure when you're sitting safely on your sofa, but it's quite another when you're plunged into the middle of one without even a spare pair of knickers. Nothing is going right. I used to be this tidy, organised, sensible person who made lists and had a routine. And now look at me! I'm a complete mess. My sister's still missing. I've had all my stuff stolen. I'm lying to my parents. Everything is a disaster.

And just to add the icing to this cake of calamity, I'm having wildly inappropriate thoughts about Jack and making a total fool of myself.

Trust me, adventures are totally overrated.

Filled with gloom, I stare at the ceiling fan, watching it whirr around and around, along with the thoughts in my head. All the earlier joy I'd felt at eating Indian food with Rocky has worn off and reality is biting. Coming here was a big mistake. I want my old life back. OK, so it might not have turned out exactly how I'd hoped in the love department, but it's safe and predictable *and* I have a whole drawer full of clean underwear. I should just admit defeat and go home.

As the thought strikes, I greet it with a feeling of inevitability. I'll tell Jack tomorrow morning. I'll get a train or a bus back to Delhi and from there I can get a flight back to London. As for Amy . . . well, I did my best. My best just wasn't good enough.

For a few moments I lie there, until my thoughts are distracted by the sounds of faint burbling. What's that? I feel a vibration underneath my thigh and suddenly realise I'm sitting on my phone. Oh my god! It's ringing! Stirred from my stupor, I start frantically rummaging underneath the blanket. I snatch it up. Please god let it be Amy!

'So how was India?'

It's Diana, my agent.

Disappointment stabs the hope in my chest like a balloon, and the air escapes from my lungs with a heavy sigh. Where do I begin? 'Well . . .'

'Oh my god, I've always wanted to go there,' she continues her rapid-fire dialogue. Diana is famous for her ruthless editing and she approaches telephone conversations like manuscripts, striking through polite introductions and hesitant answers with a verbal marker pen. 'Was it just totally amazing?'

I can hear Diana walking down the street, her stiletto heels hitting the concrete pavement, the bustling, urban sounds of twenty-first century New York in the background. It's so surreal. Sitting here on my antique four-poster bed, wrapped up in a hand-embroidered blanket and the still quietness of a 300-year-old *haveli*, I don't just feel like I'm in a different country, I feel like I've travelled back in time. 'Yes, it's amazing,' I agree.

'So when did you get back?'

'Well that's the thing . . .' I reply. 'I'm not . . . *Back*, that is.'

There's a loud honking of horns. 'Hey! Watch where you're driving, mister! It's my right of way!' yells Diane above the din. 'I swear, one of these days me and that crosstown bus are gonna come to blows. Every time I leave the goddam office it's . . . Wait – what do you mean you're not back? Where are you?'

'I'm still in India,' I shout, holding the phone away from my ear slightly so I'm not deafened.

'What are you doing still in India?' she exclaims. 'I told you to take a vacation, not move there!' She breaks off and

I hear her take a sharp intake of breath. For a split second I think there's been an accident with that crosstown bus, then, 'Oh Jeez, you haven't gone all *Eat, Pray, Love* on me, have you?'

Despite everything, I can't stop myself smiling. I can almost see her shuddering on East 56th and Lexington. 'No, don't worry,' I reassure her quickly. 'It's just a bit complicated.'

'Oh my god, that means you've met a guy!'

'*What?* No!' I protest hurriedly. I haven't had a chance to tell her about Amy yet, or what happened to me on the train, or anything. I don't even want to mention Jack. He's not important.

'Seriously? There's no guy?'

I don't think I've heard her sound this disappointed since she lost out in a bidding war for an erotic bonkbuster about a female vampire and a wizard. Apparently the sadomasochistic sex scenes involving a giant head of garlic and a magic wand were quite something.

'Well, yes, there is,' I admit reluctantly, 'but it's not about that—'

'It's always about a guy,' she counters.

'No, it's about my little sister,' I correct her firmly. 'I was with her in Goa, you see, and she met this yoga instructor and they eloped to Rajasthan, so I ran after her. Well, I didn't run, I got on a train . . .' As I start running through everything that's happened in the last couple of days, I suddenly realise it's more than I've done in the last twelve months. 'But I had all my things stolen, so this American guy said I could hitch a ride with him, which is why I've been in a car for two days, travelling across India trying to find her.'

'So what's he like?'

I stare at my phone in disbelief. Is she not listening to a word I've been saying? 'Look, I don't want to talk about Jack—'

'Great name,' she says approvingly.

'You think so?' I reply, distracted for a moment to reflect upon it, before suddenly catching myself. 'Honestly, I really don't want to talk about him—'

'Oh my god, this is great!' she exclaims, ignoring my pleas. 'You like someone!'

'I don't like him, *like* him,' I correct, quickly putting her straight. 'I fancy him, it's different.'

'Is it?' she replies dubiously.

'Absolutely,' I say firmly.

'How so?' she demands. 'Please explain, I'm American, we don't do this *fancying* business.'

'I'm attracted to him but I don't want a relationship with him,' I say simply. 'It's purely a physical thing. This isn't about his personality; in fact I don't even *like* his personality most of the time. And I'm not remotely interested in getting to know him and spending time with him—'

'Didn't you just say you've spent two days in a car with him?' she points out.

'You know what I mean,' I bristle. 'There's no romance.'

'I don't know. Travelling across India with a dark handsome stranger sounds pretty romantic from where I'm standing,' she says archly.

'It's lust. Not love,' I say firmly. 'Like I said, I don't believe in all that.'

'Well, in that case, you need to get yourself some lust,' she says decisively.

'I can't do that!' I gasp.

'Why not?'

'I'm not that kind of girl,' I protest, albeit a little hypocritically, considering I've been having sexual fantasies about Jack all day. Still, having fantasies are one thing, doing something about them is entirely different.

'When was the last time you had sex?'

I balk. I have a very close relationship with my agent – in fact, to be honest, it's more personal than professional. Even so, this is a little *too* personal. 'It's been a while,' I say vaguely.

'A while!' she snorts. 'There must be cobwebs down there!'

I recoil in shock. I've always loved Diana's honesty, but there's honesty and . . . *cobwebs*? 'Eww,' I cringe, burying my face in my blanket.

'Well seriously, you need to use it or lose it!'

Worry pricks. I venture gingerly out from the safety of my blanket. 'You can't lose it . . . *can you*?'

'Muscles atrophy,' she warns me darkly.

There's a pause as I digest this information. Then:

'I still can't,' I say resolutely.

'This is the twenty-first century, of course you can!' she cries. 'There's nothing wrong with having no-strings-attached sex. Think of it like going to the gym. You're just exercising different muscles.'

'No, you don't understand, he's with a girl.'

'What girl?' she demands.

'Another tourist we met. He's sitting with her in the bar downstairs.'

'So what?' she snorts dismissively. 'You get yourself down there!'

'She's a bikini model.'

There's dead silence on the other end of the line. All I can hear is traffic honking in the background, though to be honest it might as well be tumbleweed blowing. For the first time ever, my unflappable agent has been rendered speechless.

'*A bikini model?*' she repeats finally in a hushed voice.

It would appear these are three words that will strike fear into any woman. Even my scary agent Diana.

'Plus-size?' she adds hopefully.

''Fraid not,' I reply flatly.

'Well, you'll just have to dazzle him with your sparkling wit and personality,' she encourages, quickly recovering.

'Thanks Diana,' I say gratefully.

'Either that or get him completely drunk and pounce on him.'

I raise a smile underneath my blanket.

'That's what I did with Eric, my first husband. It took three whisky sours and a *very* dirty martini . . .' She breaks off and laughs throatily. Diana has one of the filthiest laughs I've ever heard. 'I'm not kidding, what have you got to lose?'

'My self-respect?'

'Totally overrated,' she fires back.

I raise another smile.

'OK, well look sweetie, I've got to go into a meeting, but remember I'm your agent, you need to do as I say.'

It crosses my mind to point out that doing just that got me into this mess in the first place, but she's already saying her goodbyes.

'And just remember, she might be a bikini model, but we can eat cupcakes!' she reminds me cheerfully, and hangs up.

Except I don't think there are any cupcakes in Agra. Well, I haven't seen any. If there were I'd probably sit in my room consoling myself with a dozen red velvets and be done with it. After all, not a lot comes close to a freshly baked cupcake topped with rich buttercream frosting. Not even sex.

I hold that thought, for like a second.

Oh, who I am kidding? Of course cupcakes aren't better than sex with Jack!

Jumping determinedly out from underneath my blanket, I shake out my hair and give my teeth a quick brush. Diana is right, I tell myself firmly. I'm not going to hide away in my room because of some bikini model. So what if she has cellulite-free thighs and big boobs? I'm not going to be intimidated! I write books! (My last one even got a five-star review on Amazon, and no, it wasn't from my mum. *At least I don't think so.*) I can tell a good joke! (Or an even better one, depending on how much wine I've consumed.) And I've never, *ever* been beaten at Scrabble!

Filled with resolve, I reach for the door, then take one last look in the mirror. Saying that, it wouldn't hurt to sex it up a little. I mean, personality only goes *so* far. I unzip my hoody to show a bit of cleavage, then experiment with folding my arms to give myself an extra bit of *oomph*. Standing back, I survey the results. Oh god, I look ridiculous. Especially next to Cindy, who has cleavage like the Grand Canyon. Plus it's freezing.

And, firmly zipping myself back up, I flick off the light and go downstairs.

Jack spots me first. 'Hey, there you are!'

'Oh, hi,' I smile, trying to sound all casual and surprised, as if I've just happened across them. 'Fancy seeing you here.'

'I couldn't stay away,' quips Cindy, who's dressed as if she's in Aspen, in a designer fur-trimmed jacket and boots. She flashes a lip-glossed smile at Jack and flicks her hair in a way that says *hands off, he's mine*.

For a brief moment my resolve wobbles, but Diana's warning about cobwebs is still ringing in my ears, and I hold firm.

'We were just having a beer, want one?' Jack invites.

'Yes, please, that would be great.' I smile broadly and, ignoring Cindy's glares, plop myself down between them.

'So where have you been? I knocked on your door but you weren't there,' continues Jack.

'I went to a local restaurant with Rocky; he taught me how to eat Indian food.'

'*You ate local food?*' gasps Cindy. '*Are you insane?* You know they won't have washed anything in purified water and, let

me tell you, if you had ice in your drink, you're screwed.'
Giving a large shudder, she pulls out a huge bottle of hand
sanitiser and starts vigorously squirting it on her hands, as if
she might catch something by just talking about it. 'I packed
my own food. I mean, seriously, thank god for power bars
and protein shakes!'

'What did you eat?' Jack asks me, looking impressed.

'*Chana Masala . . . Malai Kofta . . .*' I clumsily try repeating the names.

'I'm impressed!' He grins.

I smile modestly, but inside I feel a flutter of pride. 'It was
all delicious.'

'What did I tell you? India just takes a little while to get
used to, and once you do—'

'You'll fall in love with it,' I finish.

There's a pause as our eyes meet and, just for a moment,
I could swear—

'I was just going to show Jack some photos of my trip,'
interrupts Cindy, brandishing her camera.

Well, whatever it was, it's gone now, I reflect, trying not to
feel disappointed as we both turn to her.

'Oh my gawd, you've *so* got to see this one,' she gasps,
thrusting the camera under both our noses. 'The hotel
in Delhi was awesome – the infinity pool on the roof was
a-ma-zing.'

It's a picture of Cindy in a string bikini, by the pool.

'I mean, just look at the view!'

She starts zooming in and we're suddenly given a close-up
of her impressive chest.

'Oops,' she laughs, before scrolling upwards to the skyline.

'Nice,' I murmur politely, not looking at Jack. My earlier
confidence is fast waning. Trust me, it's going to take a lot
more than being able to get a seven-letter word at Scrabble
to compete with *that.*

'And what about this one?'

Needing no encouragement, she starts flicking through the photos on her camera. There's Cindy posing with a cocktail, Cindy posing with a monkey, Cindy posing at the Taj Mahal . . . basically, lots of close-ups of Cindy. In fact, India seems to be there only as an afterthought.

'Oh and wait, Jack, you just *have* to see me on the elephant,' she exclaims, leaning in towards him so he can get a closer look at the screen.

And her cleavage. She went for the unzipping thing, only with a lot more success, I observe, although thankfully Jack doesn't seem to have noticed.

'Where was this taken?' he asks, peering at the screen.

Cindy doesn't look best pleased that he's not focusing in on her. 'Oh, that's just some old castle-y thing in Jaipur,' she says dismissively.

'You mean the Amber Fort,' he says knowledgeably. 'One of the finest examples of Rajput architecture.'

'Whatever,' she shrugs. 'It was kinda boring, to be honest, but the elephant ride up there was fun. Well, apart from the fact my folks were on one elephant, so I had to share with this girl who was kind of a downer . . .'

'What's so special about it?' I ask, turning to Jack. I'm genuinely curious.

'Well, it's most famous for its amazing mirrored hall. It's designed in such a way to refract light, so that you only need two candles, one at each end, to light the whole palace.' He passes over the camera as Cindy keeps talking.

'She'd had some fight with her boyfriend about something, she was pretty upset . . . He was the one who took the photo – really cute guy, body to die for – but I said to her, "Honey, listen, they're just not worth it".'

Holding the camera, I take a look at the photograph. My breath catches in the back of my throat.

'Impressive, huh?' says Jack.

I can see the fort in the background but I'm focused on the foreground. There's Cindy on an elephant, and sitting next to her is a girl . . .

I zoom in, but I didn't have to. I recognised her immediately. *Amy.*

23

Fast-forward to early the next morning, and I'm already dressed and waiting in reception for Jack to surface. I'm eager to leave. I couldn't sleep at all last night for thinking about Amy. After the radio silence of the last few days, seeing a photograph of her is a relief. It's alleviated my scary worst-case-scenario worries: she's not lying dead in a ditch; she's sitting on an elephant in a T-shirt and a sarong, looking tanned and healthy.

And upset.

Because of that, the photograph has also managed to inflame my fears. If only she'd listened to me. I said it would all end in tears! What have they been rowing about? What's happened? Is she all right? A million questions are racing through my head. I hate to think of Amy upset. She can be headstrong and stubborn and totally bloody selfish sometimes, but she's still my little sister and I'm worried about her. If anything bad happened to her, I'd never forgive myself.

Which is why seeing that photograph has made me more determined than ever to find her. The picture was taken in Jaipur, which isn't that far from here, and apparently Amy mentioned something about heading on to a town called Pushkar. At least Cindy thought so. Trying to get details out of Cindy was like asking a goldfish to remember what happened yesterday. Actually, I'd probably get more sense out of the goldfish.

Saying that, the one thing Cindy was 100 per cent sure

about was that Amy wasn't married yet. 'I can spot a rock a mile away and there was nothing on her finger,' she'd said categorically. 'Trust me, girlfriend, he ain't put a ring on it yet.'

'There you are.' I hear a voice and look up to see Jack walking in through the front gates. 'I was just coming to wake you.'

'Oh, I thought you were still in your room,' I say, looking at him in surprise. Discovering the photograph had got my mind racing and I'd turned in soon after, leaving Jack and Cindy together. 'I presumed you would have stayed up late drinking and still be asleep.'

'No, I was outside talking to Rocky,' he replies, his breath making little white clouds in the cold morning air.

'Oh . . . well, I wanted to ask you a favour,' I say, in the most business-like voice I can muster.

Jack raises his eyebrows.

'I think my sister might be in Pushkar. I'm not certain; it's hard to get information out of Cindy.' I stop myself. Jack likes Cindy, he invited her for a drink last night, remember? 'But anyway, I think it's worth a shot. So I was wondering . . . I know you're going to Udaipur, and you've been really kind to give me a lift this far.' I can hear myself starting to ramble ' . . . and I don't want to put you out.' *Get to the point Ruby, get to the point,* ' . . . but well, is there any chance . . .'

'It's on the way,' he says evenly.

I stop talking and look at him in surprise. 'It is?'

'Well, I don't have a map to hand, but I'm pretty sure,' he nods.

'Oh . . . wow,' I smile, broadly. 'That's great. I really appreciate it, you've saved my life.'

'What, again?' His eyes flash with amusement.

Reminded of the train, I feel my cheeks go hot despite the chill. I'm never going to live that down. 'So, are you ready to leave?' I ask, briskly standing up.

'Well actually, that's why I was coming to find you,' he says, his face falling serious. 'There's a bit of a problem.'

'Problem?' I feel a clutch of anxiety. It's like my body's on a flight-or-fight response the whole time, just bracing itself for the next disaster. 'What problem?'

'Something's wrong with the car. Rocky says we won't be able to leave for a couple of hours.'

'Oh. OK.' I feel a flash of disappointment. I'm eager to get on the road. Still, at least it's nothing major.

'So I was thinking of doing a spot of sightseeing and going to the fort here in Agra, seeing as there won't be time to visit the one in Jaipur,' he adds in explanation. 'Apparently it opens at sunrise, so if you fancy coming along . . .'

With the events of last night, my feelings for Jack have taken a back seat, but now they rear their head again. 'That sounds interesting,' I reply casually, my disappointment at not leaving replaced by a flicker of excitement.

'OK great,' smiles Jack. 'I told Cindy we'd leave in about five minutes—'

'Cindy?'

At that precise moment I hear a door slam closed and look up onto the balcony to see her emerging from Jack's room. I feel like I've been kicked in the stomach. They must have spent the night together.

Well, what did I expect? *Of course* they spent the night together, Ruby. Did you really expect they wouldn't? Did you really think you stood a chance?

As I watch Cindy bouncing towards us like a Victoria's Secrets Angel, I swallow hard, pushing down my feelings of rejection. I can't let Jack see I'm hurt and upset. I have to act normally.

'Hi, handsome!' she beams, planting a large kiss on his cheek. 'Oh, and hi, Ruby,' she adds, spotting me. 'You look great.'

'Er, thanks,' I reply, taken aback by her compliment.

'There's nothing like having a favourite outfit,' she smiles sweetly.

I flinch slightly but don't react.

'So, we all ready? I'm so excited!' she whoops. 'This is going to be awesome!'

'Actually, on second thoughts, I've just remembered something I need to do,' I fib quickly. 'Damn! Silly me, head like a sieve.' I make a show of slapping my head, but Jack doesn't look convinced.

'What have you got to do?' he asks, his brow furrowing.

'Erm . . . just a few errands,' I say vaguely. I desperately need to find some new clothes, but I'm not saying that in front of Cindy and giving her the satisfaction of knowing I'm well aware of what a state I look. 'You two go ahead without me.'

'OK,' beams Cindy, without the need for any further persuasion. Looking thrilled, she loops a long slender arm through Jack's.

He frowns. 'But if it's only a few errands, it won't take long,' he reasons. 'We can wait, can't we, Cindy?'

Cindy gives a lip-glossed pout. 'Well, I suppose so,' she says reluctantly, 'but it does get really busy – we should go early to avoid the crowds.'

I bite my tongue. Isn't this is the same person who thought the famous Amber Fort was a 'kinda boring old castle-y thingy'?

'You should go.' I force a bright smile. 'I can always catch up with you,' I add, with absolutely no intention of doing so.

'Well OK, as long as you're sure,' says Jack uncertainly, after a pause.

'Absolutely,' I nod, glancing at Cindy, who's holding on to Jack in the same way women clutch on to their designer handbags, as if someone's going to try and steal him away from her.

'Bye, have fun,' she trills, in a tinkly, singsong voice.

'Yes, you too,' I say, waving them off with a cheery smile, which collapses like a soufflé as soon as they disappear out of sight. Still, it's my own fault for being so naive and foolish. I should never have listened to Diana; she was just being loyal. And anyway, so what if he slept with Cindy? As I said, it's not as if I *like* him. It's just my pride that's hurt, I tell myself firmly, not my feelings.

Yet, for some reason, that doesn't make me feel any better.

For a moment I stand there, feeling deflated, then glance at my watch. It's still early; they won't be back for a while. What am I going to do for a couple of hours?

Exactly what I was going to do, I decide. Go buy some clothes.

And not just because I urgently need some. But because it doesn't matter where in the world you are, or how different things are, there are some things in life that will always remain the same. When you need cheering up, there's only one thing for it.

Shopping.

I've heard about the famous local bazaar and so, armed with a map from reception, I go off to explore. Despite it still being early, Agra is awake and already bustling with activity. Whoever said New York is the city that never sleeps has obviously never been to India, I muse, as I walk around the narrow, dusty streets, teeming with people and rickshaws.

It's funny how quickly I've become acclimatised to the noise and mayhem of India. Like the dust underneath my fingernails, I no longer notice it. It's almost hard now to recollect that initial shock to the senses when I first arrived. It's as if India gives you a new set of eyes, allowing you to see through the dust and the pollution, past the mayhem and the poverty, to the true beauty and magic beyond.

I pause for a few moments to watch a group of boys playing a makeshift game of cricket at the side of the road. Using sticks as improvised stumps and a piece of wood as a bat, their faces are filled with concentration as they bowl and bat, their shrieks of frustration and jubilation filling the air as one team bowls the other out.

One boy sees me watching and waves, his smile lighting up his face, and I wave back, wishing I had a camera so I could take a picture, yet at the same time knowing I don't need a photograph. I won't forget that face, or that smile.

Leaving them to their game of cricket, I continue walking, and it's not long before I come across the labyrinth of lanes overflowing with dozens of markets that make up one great big bazaar. Forget the famous Portobello Road market in London, this place puts it to shame, selling everything from exotic spices to pashminas to electrical goods to intricately carved marble work.

Turning a corner, I leave one market selling only spices and enter yet another filled with row upon row of stalls selling nothing but clothing. I feel a wave of happy relief. I've spent years wailing 'I have nothing to wear,' but now I really *don't* have anything to wear. I've spent the last two nights hand-washing my underwear.

Eagerly, I pounce on the first stall. OK, so I need socks, underwear, a change of clothes, ooh, and look at that jacket . . .

Reaching for it, I quickly take it off the coat hanger and try it on. Wow, it's so lovely and warm!

'Welcome.' The stallholder appears from the back of the shop. A big man, he has an even bigger beard. 'Can I help you?'

'Hi, yes,' I smile broadly. 'How much is this jacket?'

Taking a calculator, he punches in some numbers and passes it to me. I look at the display. OK, so that's . . . I do a quick calculation in my head . . . '*How much?*'

'It is a very fine jacket,' says the stallholder gravely.

'Um . . . yes, I know,' I nod hastily, not wanting to offend him, 'it just seems rather expensive . . .' I break off.

Of course! I'm such a dummy, I nearly forgot. I'm supposed to haggle!

Haggling, I've learned, is a way of life in India, but until now I haven't been bold enough to try it. I haven't got the skills or the confidence and so in Goa I just paid the asking price. But I've decided: if I can learn to eat Indian food, I can try my hand at haggling. So I did a quick bit of reading up on it before I set off. According to the guidebook I found in reception, all I need to do is follow a few simple rules:

Rule number one: Never make it too obvious you like something.

I catch sight of myself in the jacket in the stallholder's mirror. Oh dear, I don't think I've got off to a very good start. Does actually wearing the item class as making it too obvious?

Rule number two: Don't buy the first thing you see. You can often find the same or similar items on other stalls. Look around and check out the prices.

Right OK, I can do that.

'Thank you, but I'm going to think about it,' I say politely, hanging the jacket back up.

'You don't like it?' he frowns.

Oh no, I've insulted him. 'Yes,' I say hastily, before quickly remembering. 'I mean, *maybe*,' I correct myself. Actually, this isn't as easy as it sounds. 'But I'm going to take a wander around,' I add, doing my best to sound nonchalant.

Throwing him what I hope is a confident smile, I slowly mosey over to the stall next door, only I can see immediately that they don't have any jackets like that one. That jacket was really nice.

'How much do you want to pay?' demands the stallholder, following me with the jacket. He thrusts it at me with a flourish. 'Give me a good price.'

Rule number three: Begin by offering half the asking price. The seller will not accept this but it's a good starting point.

I gesture to his calculator and as he hands it to me, I hesitate. I'm not sure I've got the nerve for this. I look at the stallholder. He strokes his beard and stares back at me. I stare back nervously. It's a Mexican stand-off, India stallholder-style. Plucking up courage, I punch in a number and hand it back to him.

There's a loud explosion as he snorts violently. 'No, this is impossible,' he thunders, throwing his hands in the air.

Startled, I jump a mile. Oh god, this was a terrible idea, I'm not cut out for this. I'm a chicken.

Plus, I really like that jacket.

Rule number four: Be prepared to walk away. You'll find that most sellers will lower their final price if you're prepared to leave empty-handed.

'Goodbye Mohamed,' I smile, giving the stallholder a wave.

'Goodbye Ruby,' he beams, tucking my wad of rupees in his pocket.

Fifteen minutes and two cups of chai later, I've learned all about Mohamed's family, met his lovely wife, and seen pictures of all his ten children, who go down in size like Russian dolls. And we've struck a deal for the jacket. OK, so it wasn't anywhere near half price and no doubt I could find one a lot cheaper somewhere else later on, but you know what? I don't care. I can't haggle, I'm rubbish at it.

Plus, when I realised the few rupees I was haggling over were the equivalent of the cost of a cappuccino at Starbucks, it all seemed a bit ridiculous.

'You look very good,' nods Mohamed approvingly. 'It is an excellent jacket, it will keep you very warm.'

'Thanks. I love it,' I smile broadly. 'And thank you for the tea.'

'It is my most double welcome,' he nods cheerfully, giving

the end of his beard a twirl. 'Come back soon and drink tea with me again.'

Smiling happily, I leave my new friend and continue on through the maze of stalls. The sprawling bazaar has everything you could possibly need, be it new clothes or your sandals fixing by a little man with a sewing machine, who deftly and quickly stitches the straps tighter to stop them slipping off my feet. I soon find myself loaded down with much-needed basics such as underwear and toiletries, a pair of jeans and trainers – which have neither the designer label or the price tag, and the only T-shirt I can find that doesn't have a picture of the Taj Mahal on the front.

I even manage to find a stall selling make-up, around which are clustered dozens of Indian women, in the exact same way their British counterparts cluster around the cosmetics counters at Selfridges, where I buy a lipstick and some kohl for my eyes.

And I would probably have bought a whole lot more if I hadn't been distracted by the most gorgeous fragrance. Following my nostrils, I find an old man with dozens of glass decanters filled with perfumed oils. Musk. Sandalwood. Amber. He patiently dabs them on my wrist, each one more divine than the next.

I leave with several little bottles and, feeling much more cheered up with all my purchases, glance at my watch. I should probably start heading back now, I decide, turning around to find my path blocked by a pair of hands.

'*Mehndi*,' urges a woman, her palms outstretched.

'I'm sorry?' I reply, not understanding.

'Henna,' she says, gesturing to her hands.

I glance down at them, and it's then I notice she has the most amazingly decorated hands. Elaborate swirls and intricate designs of dots and flowers form a beautiful pattern all over her palms and fingers. 'Henna,' she repeats, reaching for mine. She holds out a small bottle.

'Oh, no thank you,' I smile, shaking my head, 'I have to go.'

'Very pretty,' she continues, still holding my hands in hers.

Caught, I take another look at them. They *are* gorgeous. 'OK,' I nod, before I can stop myself, and as she ushers me to sit down, I feel a flutter of anticipation and excitement. I'm never going to have a bikini body, but I am going to have beautiful hands.

An hour or so later, I arrive back at the *haveli* to find Jack waiting by the car with Rocky, who's under the bonnet.

'Perfect timing,' Jack smiles, 'I just got back from the fort.'

'How was it?' I ask casually. Now the initial shock has worn off, I'm totally cool about everything.

'Pretty impressive,' he nods, 'it's one of the finest Mughal forts in India. It's a shame you couldn't come.'

I try to look regretful. 'I know, what a pity, but I had to do a few errands.'

'Like shopping?' He raises his eyebrows at the bulging assortment of bags I'm carrying in the crooks of my elbows.

'Oh, these?' I say with surprise, as if I didn't know how they'd got there. 'It's just a few basics,' I shrug dismissively. Why is it women always feel they have to fib to men about how much they've bought?

'What happened to your hands?' he frowns.

'Henna,' I reply, holding up my palms and showing them off proudly. Painted in an intricate pattern, they're still covered in the henna paste. 'I just have to wait for it to dry. Apparently it takes a few hours, but then you wash it off and underneath you have this gorgeous design.'

Thwack.

The car bonnet suddenly slams shut and we both turn to see Rocky revealed. 'OK boss,' he nods, wiping his hands on an oily rag. 'Let's go.'

'We're leaving right now?' I ask, feeling a rattle of

excitement and anticipation. Suddenly the idea of finding Amy seems much closer to a reality.

'Yes, we are leaving,' smiles Rocky.

'Great,' smiles Jack, then turns to me. 'You got everything?'

I hesitate. Damn. I really wanted to get changed into some clean clothes before we set off but I can't, as my hands haven't dried yet. 'Um, yes. Thanks,' I smile, as he helps unhook my purchases from my arms and deposit them in the boot. At least there's one advantage of having your bags stolen: no packing.

'Cool,' he nods, slamming it shut and sliding onto the back seat.

I slide in next to him. 'So, er, has Cindy gone?' I ask nonchalantly.

I said I was cool with it, I didn't say I wasn't human.

'Yeah, she left on her tour,' he replies, equally nonchalantly.

As Rocky starts up the engine, we both turn to look out of our windows.

'Why do you ask?' says Jack, glancing across at me.

'Oh, um . . . no reason,' I say casually.

He gives me a long hard look, then shrugs. 'All right,' he says, glancing away again.

After a few seconds, Jack puts in his earphones and starts listening to music and I turn back to gaze out of my window. The car rumbles out onto the open road and, as the outskirts of town give way to countryside, I feel a sudden sense of optimism. Of moving forwards and leaving things behind.

Finally, I feel as though things are starting to go right.

24

The next thing I know, I'm being woken by the sound of a door slamming. 'Uh . . . what . . . where are we . . . ?' I say groggily, peering out of the window. City walls, painted a bright flamingo pink, swim before me and I try lifting my head. Ow. I've got a crick in my neck from the way I've been sleeping.

'Jaipur, the capital city of Rajasthan.'

It's Rocky's voice. Blearily I open my eyes to see the car is parked up at the side of the road, and Rocky is in the front seat, a newspaper spread out over the steering wheel. Slowly turning my head, I glance sideways. The back seat is empty. 'Where's Jack?' I ask, letting out a yawn.

'He had to go to the men's room,' he says, still engrossed in his paper.

At the mention of the toilet, I feel my bladder twinge. I need to go too. I hesitate, struck by a thought: damn, we only have one loo roll and Jack will have taken it. Followed by another one: how on earth could Diana think this car journey was even *remotely* romantic. Followed by: oh no, look, it's here!

Discovering our shared loo roll wedged down the side of the seat, I pull it out triumphantly. Brilliant. That's a relief. Though it's also a bit odd, I wonder why he left it? I stop that train of thought before it goes any further. I really don't need to go there.

'I'm just going to go to the ladies' room,' I tell Rocky,

spotting a petrol station across the road. The twinge has now intensified. How is it that you can switch from not needing to go, to suddenly bursting? Wincing, I quickly reach for the door handle.

'Do you need me to accompany you?' he offers, looking up from the paper, but I'm already out of the door.

'No, thanks,' I say quickly, 'I won't be a mo—'

By the time I've made it across the road I'm ready to burst. Thankfully there is a toilet and it's empty. I dash inside. It's a tiny cubicle and the light's broken, but it's a real loo and they even have paper. Oh, I'm so happy. I can sit down and everything. I feel a beat of relief . . . and amazement at how in just over a week, things I've taken for granted my whole life now feel like such a luxury. Which makes me wonder . . . if such a little thing as loo paper can seem like a luxury, just how many other things do I take for granted?

A few minutes later, I head back outside. After the smaller towns we've driven through, Jaipur feels like a city. Fast and furious, it's a melting pot of old and new. Neon signs hang from ancient buildings. Women in traditional saris and headscarves mingle with girls in skinny jeans and designer sunglasses. Old men on bicycle-rickshaws share the road with shiny, expensive four-wheel drives driven by men with mobile phones glued to their ears.

On the way back to the car, I stop to buy a few things for the journey from a little hole-in-the-wall, which has a sign pinned up declaring proudly, 'Small Shop, But Many Things'. It's not wrong. Every available inch is piled high with a million different items; in fact, everything I'll probably ever need is in that tiny shop.

So it feels like a bit of a shame to just ask for a bottle of water and a packet of biscuits.

'Is that all?' asks the vendor, looking disappointed. 'I have many things.'

I smile apologetically and add a couple more packets of biscuits to try and make it up to him, before turning to cross back to the car.

Which is when I see Jack.

He's much further along the road and for a moment I'm not sure if it's him or not, but no, it's definitely him. He's standing outside a shop, shaking the hand of a smartly dressed man. I pause to watch him, curious. What's he doing? I thought he'd gone to the men's room? I try to read the sign above the store, but the sun is shining in my eyes and without my sunglasses or a free hand to shade them, it's difficult to make it out. I squint in the brightness until finally I manage to decipher the letters:

JAIPUR FINE JEWELLERY

What's he doing in a jeweller's? As the thought strikes, it's as if the audio-tape in my head rewinds back to the phone conversation I overheard last night and someone presses 'play'. He was talking about missing an appointment in Jaipur, about rescheduling, it was just before he mentioned me . . . Abruptly my train of thought stalls.

Ruby.

I feel a flash of embarrassment.

Of course. Jaipur is famous for its incredible jewels. Jack wasn't talking about me at all; that wasn't my name he mentioned. He was talking about *a* ruby, the gemstone.

Suddenly it dawns on me that I know very little about Jack. OK, so he told me he was an architect, but that's about it. When I asked him why he was in India, he just said something about a promise. I watch as he shakes hands with the man in the business suit, my curiosity piqued.

Thinking about it now, there's a lot that doesn't add up.

Why would he be travelling alone in India? Something tells me he's not on holiday, and with his expensive gold watch and cashmere jumper, he's not just some backpacker. And what was he doing on the train? If he can afford his own driver, he can afford an internal flight, so why wouldn't he just fly to Delhi? The train journey was over thirty hours, plus he seems to be in a rush to get to Udaipur. Which begs the question, why? What's in Udaipur? Why does he need to go there?

No sooner have these questions flashed through my mind, than my imagination starts running wild. Oh my god, what if he's some kind of jewel smuggler? What if he's trading in precious gemstones and that's why he was on the train, as he can't go through airport security? What if he's involved in some kind of international crime ring and now I'm implicated as an accomplice because I'm travelling with him? What if—

Oh for god's sake, Ruby, you've watched too many thrillers.

Sharply, I grab hold of my imagination by the scruff of its neck. Calm down and don't be so ridiculous. You're getting completely carried away. There has to be a perfectly rational explanation.

And I'm sure as hell going to find out.

'Buy anything nice?'

A few minutes later Jack opens the car door and slides onto the back seat next to me.

'Sorry?' He looks at me blankly.

'I saw you coming out of the jeweller's.'

Well, there's no point beating about the bush, is there?

'You did?' There's a moment's silence as he seems to absorb this. 'It's my mom's birthday. I wanted to buy her some earrings,' he says, after a pause.

Which is a perfectly good reason to be in a jeweller's.

So why do I think he's not telling the truth?

'That's nice,' I smile, and then something inside me can't resist asking, 'Can I see them?'

Jack seems to stiffen. 'No, I'm, er, getting them shipped directly,' he says quickly, 'it's much easier that way.'

I knew it. He's definitely lying.

Taking a deep breath, I swallow hard. Right, that's it. I'm just going to have it out with him. I might have an over-active imagination, but I'm not going to end up in some Indian jail as his unwitting accomplice. I've seen *Midnight Express*! OK, I know, so that's Turkey and drug smuggling, but still, if Jack's doing something illegal, I want to know about it.

Squaring my shoulders, I turn my whole body towards him so we're face-to-face.

'Now, look, Jack,' I begin gravely.

'Holy Moly!' he gasps. 'What happened to your face?'

Oh please. Like I'm going to fall for such an obvious attempt at changing the subject. 'Why, what's wrong with my face?' I ask drily. Folding my arms, I challenge him with a look. I know my beauty routine is off, but I can't look *that* bad, as earlier I put on a bit of eyeliner and some of that new moisturiser I bought at the market.

'Maybe you should take a look in the mirror,' suggests Jack.

I roll my eyes impatiently. 'Honestly, this is so ridiculous.' Angling my body, I take a look in the rear-view mirror.

And get the shock of my life.

'Oh my god,' I gasp with horror. One side of my face is completely covered by a huge black swirly pattern.

'You look like you've had a tattoo,' quips Jack.

I shoot him a scowl. How can he joke at a time like this? 'But how . . . ?' I gasp, then catch sight of my hands, covered in henna, and all at once it falls into place – waking up to find myself leaning against the window, my chin resting on my elbow, my face all smushed up against the palm of my hand . . .

'Miss Ruby, why do you have henna on your face?' Hearing the commotion, Rocky has looked up from his newspaper and turned around in his driver's seat. He stares at me, aghast.

'I'm sure it will wash off,' I say hastily, trying to reassure both him and myself.

'No, I am afraid this is impossible,' warns Rocky, shaking his head feverishly. He looks almost scared.

'Really?' I look to Jack for reassurance, but I can tell he's finding this extremely amusing.

'You gotta be kidding,' he says, shaking his head, 'that stuff stains for days.'

What? I clutch my face in alarm. It's all gone horribly wrong. After the whole Cindy episode, I just wanted to give myself a boost and look pretty and nice and now . . . *now I look like I've had a facial tattoo?* I feel like bursting into tears. 'No, really, I'm sure,' I fluster, digging around frantically in my pockets, 'I just need a tissue.'

'Here.' Jack passes me the shared loo roll.

'Don't you dare laugh,' I admonish, 'this isn't funny.'

'I'm not laughing,' he protests, struggling to keep a straight face. 'Look, it could be worse.'

'How it could be worse?' I demand, frantically scrubbing at my cheek. I feel upset and furious with myself, and everyone. '*Tell me! How*?'

'I'm not sure, but I'll try and think of something,' he tries to reassure me.

Which only makes me even more annoyed.

'Don't bother!' I snap, wishing I could flounce off and leave him and Rocky and everything behind. But I can't. We're on a road trip together. I'm stuck. *We're* stuck. So I'm just going to have to be mature and grown-up about this, I tell myself firmly.

'Just pretend I'm not here,' I huff and, turning away from him, I stare determinedly out of the window.

Or just be childish and ignore him. Whichever works best.

25

As it turns out, Jack doesn't have to tell me how things can get worse.

I find out all by myself.

Having arrived late into Pushkar, we head straight to bed, and the next morning I wake up, all fired up and ready to find my sister. After a quick shower I get dressed in my lovely new clothes. Boy, what a difference wearing something fresh and clean makes! Buoyed up, I put on a bit of make-up and reach for my phone. Which is when it all takes a bit of a turn: I discover my phone is about to die. And I don't have a charger.

Fuck. Alerted by the sound of the battery beeping, I look at my screen and let out a groan of dismay. This can't happen now. Not when I've got so close.

'What's wrong?'

I glance up to see Jack sitting in the hotel lobby on his iPhone. No doubt checking emails from his jewel-smuggling crime ring, I think testily, or flirty texts from Cindy. 'Nothing,' I stay stiffly, handing my key in to reception.

'You can't fool me with that one, I know what women mean when they say "nothing".'

'Oh, really,' I say, distractedly. The last thing I need right now is to be treated to evidence of Jack's wealth of experience with the female sex.

'It means something's definitely up.'

I feel like an idiot for ever having fancied Jack. What was I thinking? It was being at the Taj Mahal; it was so romantic

I got totally seduced by it all. It was almost like I fell under some kind of spell. A spell that is now broken, I tell myself firmly, ignoring him and thanking the receptionist, before turning towards the exit.

'Where are you going?'

I'm really tempted to just walk right past him – after all, he'll probably find this new predicament of mine even more hilarious than the last one – but my manners get the better of me.

'My phone's died. I'm going to walk into town to buy a charger so I can try and call my sister.'

'Wait, I'll come with you—'

'No, there's really no need to bother,' I say hastily, hoping he'll get the hint.

He doesn't. I swear sometimes I think the part of his brain that deals with sensitivity is Teflon-coated.

'It's no bother, I need to stretch my legs,' he says, getting up from his chair before I can stop him.

'Oh, OK,' I say reluctantly as he joins me. What a difference thirty-six hours make. Before, I would have been thrilled to spend time with him, but now everything's turned 180 degrees.

'By the way, you were right.'

I look at him blankly.

'The henna washed off.' He gestures to my face. 'That was lucky.'

'Oh, right. Yes,' I nod, though if the truth be told it's not so much down to luck as the hour spent at the bathroom sink, scrubbing my face with a flannel until it was red raw. I probably took off about three layers of skin. Though of course I'm not going to tell *him* that. In fact, from now on, I'm not going to tell Jack anything very much at all. If he wants to be secretive, two can play at that game.

'Very lucky,' I say tightly and, without waiting for him, I stride off ahead.

★ ★ ★

Some people say you shouldn't go by first impressions, and in some cases that's very true, but not when it comes to Pushkar. The moment I step out of the guesthouse, I can tell immediately that this is a very special place.

Maybe it's because of the religious energy. As Rocky explained, this small town, which curls around a holy lake, is actually one of the most sacred Hindu towns in India. Or maybe it's because of the enchanting, almost mystical feeling that comes from being right on the edge of the desert. From the borders of the town, the sand stretches far away into the distance and, as we start walking into town, camels saunter by. An actual real caravan of camels!

I gaze at them wide-eyed in amazement, feeling as though I've been transported to another world. If London felt a million miles away before, now it's hard to imagine it even exists.

Still, whatever the reason, Pushkar has a feeling quite unlike anywhere else I've been. There's both an energy and a timelessness to it, and I can quite imagine whiling away days and weeks here. Apparently a lot of backpackers who arrive here do just that, I realise, glancing at the hippy tourists who drift by in their tie-dye T-shirts and baggy harem pants.

As we head into town, we're instantly greeted by swarms of local children. They run up to us with outstretched hands and infectious smiles, and we empty our pockets of sweets and coins. Yet my eye is caught by a little girl sitting cross-legged on the ground. She can't be more than three years old and is with her family, who are selling strings of wooden beads at the side of the road, along with lots of other hawkers. With her hair cut into a short bob and large, chocolate-drop eyes, she's waving randomly at passers-by and squealing delightedly whenever anyone waves back.

There are other children around her, playing – her brothers and sisters most likely – but there's something about her. She's like a magnet. A bundle of energy. As she sees me looking, I wave back and she waves more furiously, with both hands this time, and beckons me over.

'Later,' I shout, smiling, 'I'll come back later.'

The main street is one long bazaar lined with shops and stalls, selling everything a tourist could want, and more. Mirrored bags and rainbow-coloured pashminas that I've seen for twenty times the price in chichi shops in Notting Hill; silvery jewellery, embroidered Rajasthani wall-hangings and billowing silk scarves.

In amongst them are a couple of shops selling electrical goods where I find several phone chargers, but none of them are the right kind – much to my disappointment and that of the shopkeepers, who almost turn their shops upside down in their determination to find one that fits.

'Why haven't you got an iPhone?' frowns Jack, as we leave yet another shop empty-handed. 'You could have used my charger, then.'

'Because I don't,' I say, for the umpteenth time.

'But that thing's ancient,' he grumbles, 'you can't even get emails on it.'

'That's why I like it,' I say loyally. 'I don't want to be online all the time, like some people,' I say, shooting him a look. 'I like being able to switch off.'

'Well, you've definitely achieved your aim then,' he quips sarcastically.

We both glower at each other, our tempers fraying fast.

'Look, I'm getting kinda hungry: how about we go in there and get some breakfast?' he suggests, gesturing to a rooftop café filled with coloured umbrellas fluttering in the breeze.

It looks sorely tempting. The cold morning air has melted

away in the sun and the temperature has risen steeply. I'm hot, thirsty and hungry. I could kill for a banana pancake and a lassi. But I can't.

I shake my head. 'Sorry, but my sister's more important. I *have* to find a charger.'

'Oh c'mon, can't it wait?' replies Jack frustratedly. 'I don't see your sister dying to get hold of you. She hasn't answered any of your calls or texts so far. What difference is another couple of hours going to make?'

I feel myself bristle. 'No, it can't wait,' I say defensively, 'and anyway, I need to try the number that I found in her room again. Maybe it belongs to someone in this town, maybe that's where she is—'

'Give me the number,' he instructs me.

'What?'

'Give. Me. The. Number.'

His expression is stern and I hesitate, then wordlessly unfold the piece of paper and pass it to him. He glances at it and punches the digits into his iPhone.

'It went straight to voicemail,' he says matter-of-factly. Handing back the number, he slips his phone into the breast pocket of his jacket. 'Now can we go eat?'

'You can't just do that,' I cry.

'Do what?' he frowns.

'Ring once, then give up,' I gasp. 'You need to keep trying!'

He looks at me, then lets out an impatient sigh. 'Look, I hate to be the one who says this, but don't you think it might be time *to* give up?'

I stare at him, open-mouthed. 'No, I don't!' I gasp, shocked by his suggestion.

'All I'm saying is, I don't think she wants to be found.'

'Well, of course not,' I reply tightly. 'People who elope usually don't.'

'Well in that case, just forget about her.'

'Forget about her? I can't do that!'

'Why not?'

'Because she's my little sister, I can't just abandon her!'

'Like she abandoned you at the airport?' he reasons, and I feel my cheeks flush. I'd told Rocky about that over dinner in Agra; he must have told Jack. So much for my resolution not to tell him my secrets.

'It wasn't like that,' I say protectively. 'She didn't mean to . . .'

'You sure about that?' He raises an eyebrow. 'She sounds pretty selfish to me.'

I feel my hackles rise. Everyone knows the golden rule that only you can criticise your family, and Jack just broke it. 'She's not selfish, she's headstrong,' I retaliate, jumping to her defence. 'She thinks she's in love.'

'Maybe she is,' he argues.

'You don't know what you're talking about,' I retort.

'Who says?' he counters. 'Have you ever stopped to think she might actually love this guy?'

I stare at him, taken aback. Suddenly, somehow, the conversation has taken a new turn and is now hurtling in a completely different direction. And one I don't want to go in.

'I'm not getting into this with you, Jack,' I cut him off.

'Why not?'

'Because I'm standing here in the middle of the street discussing something that's private,' I hiss, gesturing to the people standing nearby, several of whom are now glancing over.

But Jack ignores them and carries on, regardless. 'You know, you might like to try opening up to someone; it might not kill you,' he tuts loudly.

'Oh? Like you opened up to Cindy?' I retort, then wish I hadn't. I don't want him to think I care. Correction: *cared*.

'What's this got to do with Cindy?'

'You tell me, you're the one with all the secrets,' I reply, before I can stop myself.

'Oh yeah?' he challenges. 'Somehow I don't think so.'

His accusation catches me by surprise. 'Meaning?' I demand.

'Why are you so down on love?' he cries, losing his temper. 'You don't like weddings, you don't believe in romance . . . What the hell's wrong with you?'

I feel myself reel. All the hurt, all the disappointment, all the emotions that I've pushed down deep inside of me come suddenly rushing back and I squeeze my fists tight, digging my fingernails hard into the palms of my hands to block out the pain.

'I don't have to listen to this,' I say tightly.

Jack snorts loudly. 'Don't you feel anything? Don't you *have* a heart?'

It's like a boxer's jab. Sharp and hard, it inflicts the most pain.

'Get lost, Jack.'

His jaw sets hard. 'Fine,' he says angrily. 'I've had it with you.' And throwing his arms up in the air, he turns his back on me and walks away.

26

Watching Jack's figure striding away, I resist the urge to chase after him. I feel angry and upset. I don't want to row with Jack; I don't know what just happened. One minute I was trying to find a stupid charger, and the next everything was unravelling into insults and anger.

I pause, caught between wanting to run away from him and run after him. I can't bear to be near him, and yet, now, standing here on my own, in this busy marketplace, I can't bear not to be. Tears prickle on my eyelashes and I rub them roughly away. What the hell is wrong with me?

For a few minutes I don't move. I can't. I just stand there, motionless, in the busy street, emotions and activity swirling around me. I feel all shaken up and turned upside down, like one of those figures in a snow globe. Until gradually my breathing returns to normal, my heart stops thudding loudly in my ears, and the outside world filters back in again.

Vaguely, I become aware of Bollywood music floating from across the street and, glancing over, I see a café on the corner. A large sign reads, 'We have coffee and Internet', and it's filled with backpackers bent over their screens. India may be a wildly fascinating and exhilarating country – in one town alone there might be four hundred temples to visit and holy waters to be blessed in – but sometimes it would appear it can't hope to compete with the lure of a latte and Facebook.

It's the smell of fresh espresso that gets me. I haven't had a decent coffee since I arrived in India. Chai tea might be delicious, but sometimes nothing quite hits the spot like a strong coffee and, boy, could I do with one now, I muse, feeling tempted. I give in to the urge and walk across; I'm immediately swooped upon by a waiter in a tight T-shirt and even tighter jeans, who's bopping backwards and forwards between the tables, serving up cappuccinos and dance moves.

'Hi beautiful, what can I get you?' he says, flashing me a smile.

Still feeling tearful about the fight with Jack, I can only manage a small smile in return. 'Just a cappuccino, thanks,' I say, perching on the one empty stool at the counter, as all the tables are taken.

'OK, beautiful,' he winks and shimmies over to the espresso machine, where he begins grinding beans and frothing milk, his hips still gyrating as if there's an invisible Hula Hoop around him.

As someone who's never had any rhythm, I watch in fascination as he dips and bops, swiftly moving from one Bollywood dance move to another, the beat of the music flowing right through him. It's as if he cannot stand still.

'Here you are,' he says, putting the cup down in front of me, and I notice he's drawn a love heart in the foam. 'For you,' he smiles, before exclaiming, 'I love this one!' and quickly turning up the volume.

A catchy Bollywood tune blasts out loudly and, despite feeling upset, his exuberance makes me smile. Seeing my expression he boogies over. 'You want to dance?' he grins, holding out his hand.

'Oh, no . . . no,' I protest, hurriedly making excuses. 'I have two left feet.'

'No way! I have two right feet!' he declares with mock-seriousness, 'so together we make a perfect pair!'

I laugh and his face explodes into a grin. 'I'm Billy,' he says, stretching out his hand.

'Ruby,' I smile, shaking it. 'Is Billy your real name?' I ask curiously.

'No,' he laughs, 'but my real name is very difficult for tourists to pronounce.'

'Try me,' I challenge him. After my success with the names of Indian food, I'm feeling a lot braver.

'Really?' he asks.

'Really,' I nod confidently, folding my arms.

'OK, well it's . . .' and then he proceeds to rattle off the longest string of vowels and consonants I've ever heard.

Actually, on second thoughts . . .

'I think I'll stick with Billy,' I say with an apologetic smile, and he laughs delightedly.

'So is this your first time on holiday in Pushkar?' he asks, turning the music back down so we can have a conversation without yelling.

'Yes, I arrived last night,' I nod, 'though I'm not really on holiday.' I break off as I realise that if anyone is going to have seen Amy in Pushkar, it's going to be Billy, as the place is teeming with tourists. 'You haven't seen a girl with blonde hair, about this tall, skinny as a rail . . . ?' I ask hopefully, trying to describe her.

'Is she with a handsome Indian man, a yoga instructor?'

My heart leaps. 'Oh my god, yes, that's her!' I exclaim, excitedly. 'Where is she?'

'I don't know,' he shakes his head. 'I have not seen her.'

'But . . .' I say confusedly, my smile collapsing.

'I only know this, because you are the second person to ask.'

'I *am?*' I feel a jerk of surprise.

'Yes,' he nods, 'a woman came in earlier, asking questions about them. She said it was very important that she find them, she said it was urgent.'

The news that someone else is trying to find Amy and

Shine is as unexpected as it's alarming. 'Who was she?' I ask urgently.

'She didn't say,' he shrugs, shaking his head, 'but she wasn't from around here. She was wearing city clothes and in a very expensive car. A dark grey Mercedes with tinted windows.'

Dark grey Mercedes? I'm suddenly transported back to the small back street in Goa where I saw Shine and that woman . . . she was in a dark grey Mercedes. It must be the same person. I quickly reel off a description of her and Billy nods his head vigorously.

'Yes, yes that's her,' he says, adamantly. 'Why? Who is she?'

'I don't know,' I say, shaking my head in bewilderment. Unless of course, she's the wronged girlfriend and has found out he's eloped with Amy and is trying to stop the wedding. Or, even worse, what if she's the wronged wife?

Newspaper headlines flash across my brain:

WIFE KILLS CHEATING HUSBAND . . . WOMAN ARRESTED AFTER MURDERING PARTNER AND NEW GIRLFRIEND . . . NO FURY LIKE A WOMAN SCORNED: TRAGEDY AFTER THE DISCOVERY OF AFFAIR WITH MISTRESS.

Fuck. Women who find out their partners are unfaithful do all kinds of crazy things. Well, unless you're me, of course, I think grimly. I was so sensible – the craziest thing I did was cancel his subscription to *Cycling Weekly*. The least I could have done is cut off some shirtsleeves, or stuff frozen prawns up his exhaust pipe, or *something*. God, I really am a total wuss.

'But you know the blonde girl?' asks Billy, his voice interrupting my thoughts.

'Yes, she's my sister,' I explain, a knot of anxiety twisting in my stomach. Now it's not just about me finding Amy, it's about me finding her *first*.

Seeing my worried expression, he pats my arm reassuringly. 'Have you got a photograph?' he suggests helpfully. 'Maybe if I showed my friends, someone will have seen her.'

Which is a great idea, except—

'Only on my phone, and the battery is dead,' I say glumly, waving it at him, 'and I can't find anywhere that sells a charger.'

'Let me see it.' He gestures for my phone.

'It's hopeless, no one has one, I've tried everywhere,' I continue as I pass it to him, futilely.

Unexpectedly, his face brightens. 'It's the same as mine, look!' he exclaims, pulling out his own phone from the pocket of his jeans and waving it at me excitedly. It's a perfect match. 'You can use my charger!'

'Oh wow, really?' What a total stroke of luck.

'Yes, one hundred per cent! I'll go get it, I live close to here.'

'Are you sure? I don't want to be any trouble,' I begin to protest, but he bats away my objections with delighted exuberance.

'No, of course, it's no problem, beautiful,' he grins. 'Wait here, I'll be back in a few minutes,' and before I can protest further, he dashes off through the café, jumps on a battered old moped parked outside and disappears in a high-pitched roar and cloud of dust.

Leaving me sitting here with my coffee. I take a sip of the hot, frothy liquid – god, it's delicious – and glance idly around me. The café is still packed and my eyes drift from person to person. I love people-watching; it's one of my favourite pastimes, only this time there's not much to watch as everyone is focused on their computer screens.

Call me a philistine, but I just don't get all this social networking. For starters it's hardly social, is it? Glancing around at everyone, I can't help noticing that no one is speaking to each other; instead they're all busy tweeting, IM'ing, and Facebooking. I joined Facebook when it started, but to be honest I barely use my account. I've never understood why people put their whole lives on there. Or why, instead of posting status updates telling people what an amazing time they're having, they aren't out there *living* that amazing time.

But then I guess it must just be me. I mean, Amy was obsessed with Facebook. She's forever updating her page, posting photos, tagging – I freeze, mid-thought. Of course! How can I have been so stupid?

Urgently, I look around me. Most people are on their own iPads and laptops, but there are a couple of communal desktop computers . . . and someone's leaving! I leap off my stool and jump on it with such speed the person vacating mumbles something about me 'jumping in his grave'. I mutter my apologies and grab the mouse. Facebook is already open from the previous user and I quickly enter my login details.

I don't know why I didn't think of this before. Amy might be ignoring me, but there's no way she'll be able to ignore her beloved Facebook. There's a good chance she'll have posted something about her whereabouts.

As my page loads, I'm about to flick onto Amy's when I see I have a couple of messages. Like I said, I rarely go on here, and I quickly click on them. The first is a friend request from Vijay, the guy with the headphones whom I met on the train. I hit confirm, then open the next one. It's a message telling me I've been tagged in a picture. What picture? As it opens up, I gasp out loud. It's the photograph Amy took of me in my Elton John-style sunglasses! I feel an immediate sense of outrage. I can't believe it; she promised! Though she's right, I do look bloody terrible . . . I click to comment and start typing. *Amy! Where the bloody hell are—*

Suddenly the screen goes black.

What the . . . ?

I jab at the keyboard and am about to check the power cord when I hear a loud groan from the shaven-headed guy sitting at the desktop next to me.

'Bloody power cut,' he swears from behind his computer screen.

'Excuse me?' I frown, but he's already gathered his things and is heading out of the café.

It's then I realise the radio has fallen silent. Frustration bites. I can't believe my bad luck.

The loud buzzing of a moped distracts me and I glance over to see Billy is back.

'I have it!' he announces as he bounds towards me, waving his charger in the air like a trophy, a triumphant smile on his face.

'It's no good, the power's out,' I smile ruefully.

His forehead creases up and he glances at his watch. 'It's that time already?'

I look at him for an explanation and he shrugs. 'The generator has been switched off, it happens twice a day for two hours.'

'Really?'

'Yes. In winter it is OK, but in the summer when it is fifty degrees and the fans stop working . . .' He rolls his eyes. 'It gets very hot, especially for the children and old people.'

'Gosh, yes,' I nod, trying to imagine being in fifty degrees without even a fan, but not succeeding. 'So what will you do now?' I gesture towards the espresso machine, now standing defunct. 'You can't make coffee . . . and if the Internet connection is down . . .'

Around us, I notice the tables are quickly vacating.

'I close the café and show my new friend around town,' he says and, holding out his arm to link with mine, he flashes me the biggest smile. 'Come, let me show you the real Pushkar.'

27

Imagine visiting a stately home and going on the official tour. Shuffling around with all the other tourists, taking pictures of all the same things, visiting only the rooms that are open to the public, listening to the authorised history . . .

Now imagine being able to go behind the scenes with someone who was actually born and lives there. Exploring all the secret passages and places, discovering things that other tourists never get to see, getting to hear the real lowdown – an enthralling mix of insider knowledge, fascinating personal experiences and hilarious anecdotes . . .

That's what it's like being with Billy.

For the next couple of hours, he takes it upon himself to be my personal tour guide and throws himself into the role with more enthusiasm and delight than I've ever experienced from a stranger. And yet, almost instantly, Billy feels nothing like a stranger. He feels like someone I've known for years and hope to know for many more.

He has an amazing ability, as a few special people do, of being able to take me completely out of myself, and for the next few hours I get to forget all about being upset and angry, about trying to find Amy and fighting with Jack, and instead get to totally immerse myself in a whole new set of experiences.

'Legend has it that the lake appeared when the god Lord Brahma dropped a lotus flower from the sky,' he explains, as he takes me down to the holy lake. '*Push* means lotus flower, and *kar* means hand.' Pausing at the top of the steps to take in the view, he stretches out his hand before him. 'Look how the lake is surrounded by over fifty ghats; this is where people come to bathe and offer prayers.'

I nod wordlessly. It really is beautiful here, and the air hums with the distant sounds of temple bells ringing and prayers being chanted.

'Come, follow me.'

It's teeming with a colourful mix of Pushkar locals, Western tourists and Hindu pilgrims, but he finds a quiet spot and, instructing me to take off my shoes so we can get closer, we sit together on the smooth stone steps, gazing out across the water.

There, with solemn reverence, he explains all about the performing of *puja* (prayers) at the lake. Billy, like so many Indian people I've met on my trip, is both deeply spiritual and respectful of age-old traditions, whilst at the same time fully embracing everything modern contemporary life has to offer.

They seem at odds, but somehow he manages to find a place for it all to coexist quite happily. Switching his mobile phone to silent and tucking it into the pocket of his skinny jeans, he enthuses about his daily ritual of offering blessings, before warning me to be careful of the bogus priests who target the tourists for money.

'They will offer to do *puja* for your family and in return you will receive your Pushkar passport,' he says, 'but be careful as they will try to trick you into paying for a prayer for each member of your family.'

'What's a Pushkar passport?' I ask curiously.

'A piece of red thread that they tie around your wrist,' he says, showing me his, 'and look, I have more,' he grins, pulling several pieces of red thread out of his pockets. 'Here, let me tie one around your wrist too, and then they won't bother you; they will see it and leave you alone.'

I laugh, but shake my head in refusal. 'That's faking it,' I smile, 'it wouldn't feel right. I want to do it properly.'

'Really?' He looks both surprised and delighted.

'Absolutely,' I nod, then glancing around the lake, point towards an old man wearing robes and a large turban. He looks just how I imagine a devout priest to look. 'What about him?' I say, pointing towards him. 'Will he do *puja* for me?'

Billy falls about laughing. 'Oh no, Ruby,' he exclaims, shaking his head, 'he's the local pot-head!'

'*He is?*' I whisper, wide-eyed. I've obviously still got an awful lot to learn.

After vetting several would-be priests, he finally declares someone suitable and, in exchange for a few rupees, I'm taken down to the water's edge by a gently spoken man who recites prayers for my family, floats flowers on the water and duly presents me with my Pushkar passport.

It's a moving experience. I'm not religious; the nearest I've got to it is a brief brush with Sunday school as a child, taking Mrs Flannegan to Midnight Mass on Christmas Eve and a turbulent flight to New York when I clung onto the stranger next to me and recited the Lord's Prayer. But there's something here that draws me in.

Next, we visit a temple. But not the one in the town at which all the other tourists are congregating with their guidebooks and cameras. Instead, Billy takes me on a trek up to a small, isolated hilltop temple, perched high above the town, which offers incredible views and is well worth the climb up hundreds of steep steps that we take to get there.

Afterwards we make our way back into town. Tired and hungry, Billy takes me to his friend's rooftop restaurant overlooking the lake and we order lots of delicious vegetarian food. Local custom enforces a strict no meat, no eggs, no alcohol diet, but there are all kinds of imaginative things on the menu and, after my lesson with Rocky, I'm feeling a lot more confident about trying different dishes.

'So, tell me, where did you learn to dance?' I ask, sampling a plate of sizzling aubergine.

'From my mother . . . and watching a lot of movies,' he grins, taking a sip of his freshly blended lassi. 'Now I teach Bollywood dancing to children at school.'

'Wow, really?' I smile.

'Yes, every week,' he nods, 'and for weddings too.'

'As well as running the café?'

'I'm a busy man,' he laughs, reclining back in his chair and letting out a sigh. 'Amazing view, hey?'

I follow his gaze across the whitewashed rooftops and out across the lake.

'Yes,' I murmur, drinking it all in, 'it's amazing.'

'I bring my son up here to fly kites. He loves it.'

'You have a son?' I say in surprise.

'Yes, he's three years old, and I have a daughter who's just a baby.'

I look at him in wonder: he doesn't look old enough to have children, though I guess he is. I mean, if we're talking from a biological point of view, I'm old enough to have a teenager – something that my mother is always fond of telling me, for some reason known only to her. 'I had no idea you were married.'

'I'm not,' he replies, shaking his head.

'Oh, I see,' I fluster, suddenly feeling foolish that I'd jumped to conclusions. I should have known Billy wouldn't necessarily follow the traditional route of an arranged marriage. 'I'm sorry, I didn't mean . . . I just assumed . . . not that it matters, of course, I mean, lots of people live with their partners and have children; in fact I know tons of couples who aren't married—'

'We don't live together. My girlfriend ran away and left me with the children,' he says matter-of-factly.

'Left you?' However, I wasn't expecting this.

'She said she was too young, she didn't want to be tied down,' he says, his ever-present smile slipping. 'She lives in Mumbai, where we met. She didn't like it here.' He breaks off, and looks out across the middle distance. 'How can she not like it here? It's beautiful.'

'Oh Billy, I'm so sorry,' I say, giving his arm a squeeze.

'It's OK,' he nods. 'My mum helps me with the children while I am at work.'

I feel indignant for him. 'Well, your ex is a fool,' I say supportively.

'It's not her fault,' he shrugs. 'She's young.'

This, from a man who can't be more than in his early twenties. I feel a sense of admiration for how he's handling all this; it can't be easy.

'I still believe in love,' he adds after a pause.

'You do?'

'Of course,' he says and flashes me his trademark smile. 'There are so many, many things to love . . . I love this view, I love my family, I love that we are spending these wonderful hours together . . .'

As he throws me a wink, I can't help smiling. There's something about Billy, his irrepressible good humour is infectious.

'Yes, it's true, she stole my heart and broke it. But, you know, every time your heart is broken it gets stronger.'

I suddenly feel ashamed. Sam leaving me suddenly seems trivial compared to what happened to Billy, and he's not bitter or jaded – on the contrary.

'The heart is also a muscle,' he continues, and changing the mood he starts comically flexing one of his large biceps, 'and it is very important to exercise it.' Jumping up from his chair he launches into one of his Bollywood dance moves, sticking out his chest and making a heart-shape with his fingers.

I laugh with delight as he pretends to make it beat from his chest.

'Hey, watch out.' He suddenly stops dancing.

'What?' I frown, and turn just in time to see a giant monkey swing down from the corrugated iron roof and grab my food from the table. Startled, I jump and let out a shriek.

Which makes Billy laugh even harder. 'You are so funny, beautiful,' he cries, shaking his head with amusement. 'We have to be careful of the monkeys here, they steal everything!' We both watch the monkey scampering away before, turning to me, Billy flashes me a smile. 'But never our hearts!'

Afterwards, it's with the biggest hug that Billy bids me good-bye. 'I will miss you, beautiful,' he grins, squeezing me tightly.

'You too,' I smile, then as we break apart he hands me something.

'This is for you.'

It's the charger for his phone.

'No, I can't,' I protest, trying to hand it back, but he's insistent.

'No, please,' he protests, before adding with a wink, 'now you have to return to Pushkar, so you can bring it back.'

Laughing, I leave him practising his dance moves in the street, a big goofy smile on his face, and start walking back slowly through the town towards the hotel. It's early after-noon but already the temperature is starting to drop and, thankful for my warm jacket which I've had tied around my waist, I put it on. Absently I make my way down the main street, letting my gaze drift past the rows of shops and cafés until, on the outskirts of town, I happen to notice the little girl again, still sitting at the side of the road with her family.

She spots me immediately, her face lighting up with recognition, and this time I go over to say hello.

'Hi ... hi ...' I smile and nod politely as her family welcomes me warmly, making room for me to sit down and join them under the tent-like canopy they've erected, whilst the little girl shrieks with delight. Clambering all over me, she claps her hands excitedly, almost in disbelief, as if to say *hey, that waving thing really works!*

'Chai?' offers a teenage girl, who I think is one of the sisters. She holds out a small plastic cup of steaming tea and I accept their hospitality gratefully.

'Thank you,' I smile, taking a sip. It's grown even colder and I'm glad of the hot sweet liquid to warm me up. Their mother, a slim, fine-boned woman in a pale green sari, is busy cooking chapattis on a small stove in the corner. Seeing me glance over, she smiles shyly – unlike her children, who dive on top of me, curious to see who this new visitor is.

This is where they must live, I realise, noticing a washing line of rainbow-coloured clothes strung across the wall behind the tent, next to which lies a pile of blankets. Earlier I saw some other families camping on the side of the road, and Billy explained they were travellers who come for a few months to sell their wares before returning to their villages in the mountains when the weather becomes too hot.

But now it's cold and the temperature can easily drop to freezing at night. I think of my own family with our central heating and warm beds, our jumpers and duvet coats, and look at the children in their thin clothes.

'Here,' I motion to the little girl, impulsively taking off my warm jacket and wrapping it around her shoulders. Thrilled to be playing dress-up, she slips it on jubilantly. It completely drowns her. 'It suits you,' I cheer and her family laugh and clap as she dances around in it, tripping over the hem, sticking her hands in the far-too long sleeves and waggling them.

My intention had only been to say hello but I end up drinking chai tea with the parents and their teenage daughter, playing with the little girl and her two brothers – identical twins with wild mops of hair and smiles that would lift your soul. I've written about love at first sight but always as a romantic love, never as an instant overwhelming love you can feel for an entire family. The Taj Mahal might have opened a chink in my heart, but this family blows it wide open.

As I leave I try to buy a few strings of beads, but they push them on me as gifts and, humbled, I thank them all one by one, politely shaking each one's hand as they line up to bid me a formal farewell. It's only then I realise that, apart from the odd word, we haven't spoken to each other the whole time. I don't speak Hindi and they don't speak English. I don't know anything about them and they don't know anything about me, and yet it's not important. Sometimes it's just not about words.

They wave me off, the little girl still proudly wearing my jacket, and I wave back until my wrist hurts, before turning away to set off back to the hotel. When suddenly I'm aware of someone's eyes on me and I glance over into a shop doorway across the street. I see a figure watching me.

It's Jack.

For a moment I pause. I've been so absorbed by the little girl and her family, I'd completely forgotten about our row, but now seeing him again I'm suddenly reminded. I brace myself, but as he walks towards me I can see the anger has gone from his face. Instead, without saying a word, he takes off his jacket and puts it around my shoulders. I reach my eyes up to his and a look passes between us. Neither of us has to say anything. Silently, we start walking and after a few steps he reaches his hand across me. As his fingers brush against my chest I feel the breath catch in the back of my throat and for a split second I almost think—

Slipping his hand inside the breast pocket of the jacket, he pulls out his phone.

'What are you doing?' I ask as he hits redial.

'Calling that number,' he replies, putting it to his ear.

'Look, it's OK, I'm sorry—'

'No, I'm sorry,' he says firmly, 'I was wrong.' His eyes meet mine and for the first time it's as if the tables have turned and I see a newfound respect. I'm not some silly tourist any more. 'I should never have said those things, I should never have doubted you,' he continues quietly. 'Your heart's wide open.'

We've stopped walking and are standing close together, our bodies almost touching, and I can feel an energy field between us, an anticipation—

Then something happens that neither of us expected.

Someone answers the phone.

28

Less than an hour later we're in the white Ambassador, heading to Udaipur. At first, Rocky had been reluctant to leave. The late afternoon sun was already fading and it would be nightfall by the time we arrived, but he agreed once Jack explained the urgency.

It had been a woman who'd answered. Her name was Mrs Gupta and she was the owner of a bridal shop in Udaipur. It was actually the shop we'd been calling, but she'd been so busy with the wedding season, her phone was ringing off the hook and her answering machine was full of messages from frantic brides. One of which, it transpired, was my sister Amy, 'the pretty blonde English girl', who was due to pick up her sari tomorrow.

'But what time?' asks Rocky, from behind the wheel.

'I don't know, she couldn't say,' I reply, 'she was doing last-minute alterations.'

'Which is why we need to get there tonight,' adds Jack, 'so Ruby can go to the store first thing tomorrow morning, as soon as it opens—'

'So I'll be sure to be there when Amy arrives,' I finish.

I feel both relieved and excited. And a little scared about how she's going to react. She's not going to take too kindly to her big sister showing up. Over the years I've lost count of the times I've turned up at late-night parties, illegal raves and a particularly dodgy ex-boyfriend's house – the big bad wolf come to spoil the fun. But I just want to talk to her.

Even if I can't stop her, I just want to see her and make sure she's OK.

I look at Jack across the back seat. 'Thanks,' I mouth.

He frowns. 'For what?' he mouths back.

I pause, my mind flicking back through a photo album of mental images from the past few days since he rescued me at the railway station. 'Everything,' I mouth back.

I turn back to look out of the window. I feel buoyed up and hopeful that I'm coming to the end of my journey, yet there's also a part of me that doesn't want this to ever end. I've travelled before, but the travelling part was just a means to an end. An inconvenience. A necessary evil to be got through as quickly as possible with the aid of high-speed trains and aeroplanes, so that I could reach my destination. My whole life it's been about the destination, never the journey.

But now I realise I've never experienced the true magic of travel. Being stripped of all the things that usually occupy my everyday thoughts has left me open to serendipity and adventures, to new people and experiences. Casting my mind back to London, I try to remember the last time I struck up a conversation with a total stranger on a train. Or, on a whim, accepted an invitation to explore a new town and learn about new things.

I can't, because I haven't. I've walked around wearing headphones and listening to my iPod. I've sat on the Tube and read my Kindle. I've ridden up escalators with millions of other people and never once made eye-contact. And yet here, in India, I've sat on the ground and drunk tea with an entire family.

Outside the window, the desert landscape passes by. A dusty, sandy countryside, dotted with small tribal villages, stretching as far as the eye can see, all the way to the horizon. The road stretches hypnotically away into the wide-open distance, empty but for the occasional herd of camels. I feel a sense of liberation. I'm in the middle of nowhere, in an exotic land, far, far away from London and the parameters of my life. Far away from the ghosts of my past.

And, for the first time in my life, I feel something I've never felt before.

I feel free.

An hour passes. We continue rumbling along the open road, the needle on the speedometer never going above thirty miles an hour. Jack has dozed off. Rocky is listening to the radio, which is playing softly in the background, one hand on the wheel. It's quiet. A truck appears over the horizon. Absently I watch it heading towards us on the opposite side of the road, a part of my brain thinking how it's too far over into the middle, how it needs to get over—

'*Beeeeeeeeep!*' Blasting his horn, Rocky swerves to avoid it.

I feel my heart shoot into my mouth as I'm thrown about in the back seat.

'What the hell?' Jack wakes up as the truck thunders by, narrowly avoiding us.

'Talk about a near miss!' I gasp, relief exploding.

But it's short lived. Suddenly there's a hard jolt and the car rocks to one side.

'What's that noise?' I cry in alarm.

'Sounds like a tyre just blew,' says Jack, as there's a loud rattling noise.

'Oh goodness me, oh goodness, goodness me,' exclaims Rocky, his voice in a high falsetto. There's a screeching of brakes as he slams them on, but he loses control and the car veers off the road.

'*Ayeeee!*'

It all happens so fast. Suddenly we're hurtling into the undergrowth, bushes are scratching and scraping the doors, we're being thrown around like rag dolls, stones fly up, chipping the windscreen, the car tips on its side—

'*Ayeeeeeeeeeeeee!*'

And now we've stopped. As the car grinds to a halt in a big cloud of dust, everything falls quiet. Except for the sound of someone shrieking. For a moment I think it's coming from me. Until I realise that, in fact, it's coming from Rocky. He sounds like a stuck pig.

'Rocky,' says Jack, shaking his shoulder, but it's no good. 'Rocky!' he shouts louder.

'Huh?' He falls silent, as if snapping out of a trance.

Heaving open the passenger door, which has got wedged against a bush, Jack climbs out. With lots of coughing, we both follow suit.

'As I thought. A flat,' says Jack, his face grim.

I glance at the deflated tyre and then at Rocky, who's hopping up and down from one foot to another as if he's on hot coals.

'This is not good,' he's saying, looking at the car with dismay. 'This is not good at all.'

'Don't worry, it's not as bad as it looks,' reassures Jack, trying to placate our driver who looks like he's about to faint at the state of his car. 'All we need to do is change the tyre.'

'Yes boss,' Rocky nods dutifully. He looks relieved that someone else is taking charge of the situation. But he doesn't move.

'I trust you've got a jack and a spare?'

Rocky looks at him blankly. 'But you are Jack?'

'A jack, to lift up the car,' explains Jack, doing hand actions.

'Oh, yes, yes,' nods Rocky, snapping to and scurrying over to the boot. Flicking it open, he rummages inside and produces a small foot-jack.

'Great,' nods Jack. 'Now, let's have a look at your spare tyre.'

Up until this moment I'd been feeling comforted. Yes, OK, after the near miss with the truck and now this, we've cheated death twice, but fortunately we're all in one piece. It won't take long to change a tyre and then we'll be on our way.

At least that was the thinking before I saw the expression on Rocky's face. And heard the loud groan from Jack.

'Er, is there a problem?' I ask tentatively.

'You could say that,' says Jack, his jaw set hard.

'It is not so much a problem as a misfortune,' corrects Rocky, with all the diplomacy of a politician.

A look flashes between Rocky and Jack. I'm not sure how to describe it but, put it this way, it's not a look of love.

'Call it what you want but . . .' Lifting a tyre out of the boot, Jack drops it with a thud onto the ground. A cloud of dust rises up as he pokes the rubber with his foot. It's all squidgy.

Now, I don't know much about cars and flats and spare tyres. I live in London. I spend my life on the Tube and the number nine bus and only drive when I go to see my parents. But even I know that's not a good sign.

'Erm, it looks flat.'

'As a pancake,' agrees Jack.

'So what do we do now?'

'You tell me.'

We both turn to look at Rocky, who's wearing a frozen expression. Eyes open wide, mouth agape, hands clutching at the side of his face, he looks as if he's doing his impression of Macaulay Culkin from that iconic *Home Alone* poster.

'Rocky?' I prompt.

He snaps back. 'Yes, Miss Ruby?' He smiles broadly, as if nothing is the matter and it's perfectly normal to stand in a ditch, in the middle of the desert, next to a car with a flat tyre and pass the time of day.

'What are we going to do?' I can feel panic beginning to

creep in around the edges. This is not a case of just calling the
AA and waiting for the nice man in the tow truck to arrive.
Or hailing a taxi. Or pulling out my Oyster card. We're in the
middle of a goddam desert!

Oh god. I'm panicking.

'That is an excellent question,' he beams.

I wait expectantly for him to elaborate. He just continues
smiling. It begins to dawn on me that, actually, Rocky has
absolutely no clue whatsoever what we're going to do.

'Unfortunately, I don't have an answer. Just yet,' he confirms.

'But it's going to get dark soon!' I wail.

'Look, there's got to be a way out of here,' Jack reassures
us firmly. 'We'll just have to hitch a ride into town—'

'There is no town.' Rocky shakes his head.

'What do you mean, no town? There must be.' Jack is
getting impatient now.

'We are in the middle of the desert. The nearest town is
many, many kilometres away . . .'

As the reality of the situation begins to sink in fast, we all
look at each other, no one speaking.

'We could start walking,' I suggest, after a pause.

'It's too far and too dangerous,' sighs Jack. 'The sun's
going to start setting soon.'

I glance over towards the horizon, to the sun that's already
starting to sink. He's right, it would be too dangerous – hang
on, what's that? Did something move? I shield my eyes, trying
to make out shapes in the far distance. It's a camel. No, two
camels. And with them I can see the figure of a man.

'Look!' I exclaim, pointing towards them.

As Rocky and Jack twirl around, Rocky lets out a yelp of
excitement.

'He'll never see us,' begins Jack, but Rocky has already
started running towards him, waving and hollering, clouds
of dust flying up from his feet.

The man stops and turns.

'He's seen him,' I gasp.

'Holy Moly,' murmurs Jack.

As the two men reach each other, we see Rocky gesticulating wildly and pointing over to us. This seems to go on for a few minutes. We both wait, wondering what's happening, until finally Rocky comes scampering back towards us.

His face says it all. 'Everything is wonderful,' he cries. 'We have an answer, Miss Ruby!'

What a relief. I feel the tension from my body drain away.

'Awesome,' says Jack, who looks more relieved than I would have thought. I hadn't realised he'd been that worried.

'Yes, it is very awesome,' nods Rocky, excitedly.

'So, what is it?' I prompt.

Throwing his arms wide, he proclaims triumphantly, 'We will stay the night in the desert!'

There's silence as this announcement sinks in and then . . .

'*The desert?*' repeats Jack dubiously.

'Yes, we can go on camels, you will see the sunset, it will be like going on a desert safari,' smiles Rocky, looking very pleased with himself.

'But we have to get to Udaipur tonight,' I remind him anxiously.

'We will leave first thing tomorrow morning. My new friend Mohan says there is a small village nearby and knows of people who can fix the car. He will send a boy with a new tyre. This way we can leave at sunrise and you will be there before the shop has even opened!' He beams happily.

Jack and I look at each other doubtfully. I'm relieved that we can get the car fixed (for a scary moment there the situation looked hopeless) but it's this sleeping-in-the-desert business I'm worried about.

'There is a saying in India, "We can't change the direction

of the wind, but we can change the sails",' continues Rocky, 'and camels are ships of the desert, are they not?'

You know, I'm not really sure about all these sayings.

'Stay in the desert where, exactly?' asks Jack, taking charge of the situation. 'It gets very cold at night and we don't have any camping equipment.'

'This is no problem. My friend has tents!' says Rocky cheerfully. 'You can sleep underneath the stars!'

We both turn to look at Mohan who's standing, waiting, in the distance. With his elaborate red turban, curly moustache and white tunic, he looks very much the part.

'I guess that could be kinda fun,' says Jack, turning towards me.

'True . . .' I nod, feeling my objections fading. He's right. After all, who hasn't looked at those glossy pictures of rolling sand dunes and incredible sunsets and thought, wow, that looks amazing?

'Trust me, it will be very romantic!' beams Rocky.

Uh-oh.

Suddenly I get where this is going and feel a flicker of panic. The last time Rocky said those words we were at the Taj Mahal, and we all know how *that* turned out, don't we? When I wasn't lusting after Jack, I was making a total fool of myself. I daren't risk a repeat performance. Last time I only escaped by the skin of my teeth.

'Come! Tonight will be a night you will never forget!'

I can't look at Jack. Instead I swallow hard and force a bright smile as we set off to join Mohan and his camels.

That's *exactly* what I'm worried about.

29

I needn't have worried.

There are lots of words to describe what I am experiencing right now, but none of those words is 'romantic'. Try torturous. Or scary. Or my-arse-is-fucking-killing-me.

Sorry, that's six words.

OK, so I know a desert safari might sound wonderful *in theory*. But seriously, have you ever *been* on a camel? Trust me, there is nothing romantic about riding a four-legged hump.

Ten minutes later and I'm about twenty foot up in the air, clinging on for dear life. On the camel in front is Jack.

'Are you OK back there?' he asks, turning his head slightly so I can hear him above the weird roaring noise the camel is making.

'Um . . . yes, fine thanks,' I say in my chirpiest voice as I jig along uncomfortably, my bottom thwacking itself, up and down, up and down, up and *ouch!* 'You?' I smile, through gritted teeth.

'Yeah, awesome,' he enthuses, going all American on me, 'it's pretty amazing, huh?'

Oh god, I hate it when people do that. I feel the pressure to agree, like when Mum's neighbours had a baby and everyone was cooing over it and saying how adorable it was, and I swear it looked *just* like Benjamin Button when he's an old man. All crinkly-faced and bald as a coot.

'Er yeah, amazing,' I mutter, burrowing my nose in my

sleeve as I suddenly catch a whiff of something foul-smelling. I have no idea which end of the camel that came out of, but neither can be good.

'You've been on a camel before, right?'

Why of course! I live in London, I'm always hopping on and off camels with my Oyster card – *not*. But of course I'm not going to admit that to Mr Worldwide Traveller over there. 'Oh yeah, heaps of times,' I reply nonchalantly, 'I'm just a little rusty, that's all.'

Ha. Rusty. Good one, Ruby.

'Cool, for a moment I was a little worried there,' he laughs.

'Ha ha, yeah right,' I laugh back.

Oh god.

Thing is, I fell off before I'd even got on. It was *beyond* embarrassing.

The problem started when I was instructed to put one leg in the stirrup and throw my other leg over the hump 'in one vigorous move'. In my defence, it was a big hump, and I have little legs. Plus, as proved during my recent attempt at yoga, I have the flexibility of an ironing board.

Now, normally it doesn't bother me. In fact, when I'm not in a yoga class, there are only a couple of moments in my life that I can recollect wishing I was more bendy. One was at primary school, when Julie Higgins did the splits in the Wendy House and showed all the boys her knickers; and the other time was twenty years later when I ended up in bed with a man who was keen to perform sexual gymnastics.

And there's now. Trying to mount a camel.

Believe me, lots of grunting and groaning had ensued. Adding to this humiliating experience, it had taken two pairs of hands – belonging to Mohan the camel owner and Rocky – to push my backside over the top. Even worse (and, trust me, at this point I didn't think it could *get* much worse), they both made such a palaver of huffing and puffing, as if I'm a total heifer. To call it mortifying doesn't even *begin* to come close.

Jack was already on his camel, of course. He'd jumped – *nay, leaped* – up there like a professional gymnast vaulting over a horse. I eventually followed, legs akimbo with my bottom in the air, to make it onto the funny little stool-like saddle. With my face all flushed and hair all over the place, I tried hard not to look at Jack. Well, it's not exactly the entrance you want to make, is it?

But anyway, I seem to be getting the hang of it now.

'Come on, giddy up,' I instruct, quickly banging my heels against the camel's sides to try and gee him on.

See! Now I'm up here, all those pony classes are fast coming back to me. This is going to be a doddle.

'Are you sure that's a good idea?' asks Jack, glancing back at me with concern.

'Absolutely,' I nod confidently. 'I'm just getting him into a rising trot.'

'Rising trot?' repeats Jack, shooting me a quizzical look.

'Oh, don't you know the rising trot?' I try to keep the smugness out of my voice, but I can't help it. Finally, something I know more about than him. 'There are two beats to the trot, so on the first you rise up out of the horse's saddle and on the second you sit in the saddle. To keep a rhythm you count one-two, rising to one and sitting to two.'

'Actually, I think a camel is a bit different to a horse—'

'Nonsense,' I dismiss. 'So it's one-two, one-two, one-two . . .' I keep jabbing the camel with my heels – gosh, it's really being stubborn. It gives a loud belch and keeps plodding along.

'Ruby, look, I really think you should be careful . . .'

I tut loudly. 'Oh, you Americans, you're always so careful about everything. We English are practically *born* in the saddle.'

Well OK, perhaps that's only true of the royal family. Personally I was born in the local infirmary, but still.

The camel continues bumping along with its weird gait and I continue bumping along with it. Not for the first time do I wish I was wearing a sports bra. Wincing, I have a flashback to me at my first (and last) gymkhana and my teacher telling me to take control of my pony. I remember, I had a right little madam called Snowflake, who refused all the jumps and tried to throw me off into the sandpit. I was gutted. I really, *really* wanted one of those shiny satin rosettes.

I feel a stirring of old 'I'll show you' determination. I feel as if I'm on Snowflake all over again. Right, OK. Gathering strength in my thighs, I throw the scarf I bought from the market around my face, Bedouin-style, and with all the force I can muster, dig in my heels.

Lawrence of Arabia, eat your heart out!

Suddenly the camel lets out a loud shrieking growl and bolts. Only, it's a bit more than the rising trot. It's more like a gallop.

Oh my god!

Thrown around on the small stool, I nearly go flying and have to frantically cling onto the reins as I'm propelled forwards. *Oh my god, oh my god, OH MY GOD!*

'Ruby?' shouts Jack, as I go thundering past him, hooves flying.

'Jack!' I scream at the top of my lungs, my voice being whipped away by the wind. '*Jack!*'

But it's hopeless. As I go tearing over the scrubland, I glance back and see a whole caravan of people behind me. Mohan is yelling and chasing after me in his long white robe and bright red turban. Rocky is following. And then there's Jack. All seeming to blur into the distance.

Oh Crikey Moses, this is a whole world away from Snowflake and the local gymkhana . . . I turn forwards again to see a steep sand dune looming up ahead, and feel the camel accelerate.

Argh!

Abandoning the reins, I throw my arms around the camel's neck and squeeze my eyes tightly shut. At least this way I won't see the ground as I hit it . . .

And then, as suddenly as the camel bolted, it stops dead. Gingerly, I open my eyes and see we're at the top of the dune, I'm still on the camel, and I'm in one piece.

Oh thank you, thank you, thank you.

'Miss Ruby!' I hear Rocky's voice and a few moments later he appears, scrabbling over the top of the dune, panting heavily. 'Thank gracious me!'

Next, the bright red turban comes into view and Mohan appears, leading the other camel, followed by a straw fedora, and Jack.

'Are you all right?' Perched up high on his camel, Jack looks at me with concern.

'Erm yes, fine . . . fine, thanks,' I reply, trying to steady my breathing. Oh lord, how embarrassing. Now I'm safe, my fear has been replaced by waves of humiliation.

'So that was the rising trot, hey?' He raises his eyebrows and I can see the flicker of a smile playing on the corners of his lips.

'Just thought we'd have a little gallop there, didn't we?' I pat the flank of the camel, and it belches loudly. 'It was, er, invigorating,' I add, averting my eyes and glancing at Mohan, who's surveying me.

'Um, great camel you have here,' I smile.

He doesn't reply, just continues to gaze at me steadily.

'Just as long as you are safe,' nods Rocky, 'that is all that matters.'

'Oh yes, thanks, I'm perfectly fine, it was all under control,' I smile, trying to be all breezy and nonchalant. 'In fact, I could tell the camel was really responding to my commands . . .' I falter as I realise everyone is now staring at me. ' The, er, relationship between man and beast is quite something, isn't it, Mohan?'

No reply. He just keeps staring at me. I blunder on.

'It's almost symbiotic . . . a mutual respect . . . a sort of master and servant . . .'

'Ruby.'

Jack's voice penetrates and abruptly I stop talking. 'Yes?'

Slowly, he raises his hand and points behind me. 'Look.'

'Huh?' Frowning in confusion, I turn around and look in the other direction.

And then I see it.

On the horizon is the most amazing sunset I think I've ever seen. A blazing kaleidoscope of reds and oranges. It's as if the sky is on fire.

Wow.

All thoughts of my sore bottom vanish as the breath catches in the back of my throat and I gaze at it, mesmerised by the colours and intensity. It's incredible. Far into the distance, I can see other camels silhouetted against the glowing sky, their black, stick-like figures moving slowly across the horizon. I watch them with awe and wonderment. It's so beautiful. *It's so romantic.*

Uh-oh.

India has gone and done it again. Because, as hard as I try to resist, I can't. It oozes romance out of its pores without even trying. And there's not a damn thing I can do about it . . .

30

An hour later and we're sitting out in the middle of the desert, a campfire burning. Food has been brought from the nearby village, along with tents, and after we've feasted on the most delicious *thali*, a woman appears in traditional tribal dress. Accompanied by two men playing instruments, she proceeds to perform a desert gypsy dance. It's as haunting as it is thrilling.

With nothing but the flames of the fire to illuminate her and the flash of coins on her veil, she leaps and swirls her mirrored skirts in the sand to the seductive sounds of beating drums and wailing voices. Her hands, her hips, her head, all move in a frantic feverish rhythm that becomes faster and faster, until she's whipped into a trance-like ecstasy, as she spins around and around and around.

Afterwards we remain around the campfire, listening to the crackle of the flames and Mohan's low, hypnotic voice as he tells us mesmerising stories of mysticism, astrology and reincarnation.

'What is taking place on earth is nothing but a mirror to what is happening in the heavens. We are on a wheel of life, like the universe itself. This is not our first life and this is not the first universe. There have been many, more than even the grains of sand in this desert . . .'

He pauses and gestures at the space all around us. 'How long does one single universe last?' He turns to me, his dark eyes shining in the light from the flames.

'I don't know,' I answer quietly, shaking my head.

His lined face breaks into a smile and I catch the perfumed scent of his tobacco as he exhales. 'It is more than we can dream of . . . the universe is created by Lord Brahma, preserved by Lord Vishnu and destroyed by Lord Shiva. One day and night to Lord Brahma is more than four billion years to us, and it is only when he has lived a lifetime, that the universe is destroyed so that it can again be recreated . . .'

I listen, trying to grapple with the timescale, but he's right. It's too mind-blowing to comprehend; it's beyond even my imagination.

'And so this great cycle of life goes on, like the breath in our bodies and the stars above us in the sky, we are all forever dying and being reborn . . .' He pauses to glance around at each of us. 'There is an amazing harmony in the universe, the stars, the planets, mankind, we are all as one. But what is most wonderful of all is that everything is perfectly timed, more so than even the most expensive watch you can find on the wrist of a rich man . . .'

Mohan falls silent and, after a few moments, bids us goodnight and goes to tend to his camels. Rocky accompanies him, and for a little while Jack and I sit quietly, our bellies full, our minds filled with his powerful words.

'It's pretty amazing here, isn't it?' says Jack after a few moments.

I turn to him and suddenly I'm aware that it's just the two of us. I feel a familiar prickle on my skin, a fluttering in my stomach. I swallow hard. 'Yeah . . . it's nice,' I add, trying to make my voice sound casual, like it's no big deal. When, of course, the opposite is true.

If I was intoxicated by India before, all these tales of heavens and the stars and being as one have seduced me even further. Try as you might, India will work its magic on even the hardest cynic. If it's not the wedding season, or the Taj Mahal, it's the dazzling colours and seductive scenery.

But I'm determined not to have a repeat performance of what happened at the Taj Mahal. No siree. I'm not going to fall under the influence and go gaga after Jack. Not this time. And certainly not after Cindy, I remind myself firmly. I mean, if Jack thinks I'm going to be another notch on his bedpost, he's got another think coming.

'I mean, have you seen these stars?' Flopping onto his back, Jack stares up at the glittering canopy above our heads. Despite the glow of the moon, the sky is awash with constellations.

I nod dumbly, using every ounce of self-will not to gasp in wonderment. Out here in the desert, it feels as if we're the only two people in the entire universe.

'Look, there's Orion,' he says, tracing the constellation.

'Hmmm,' I say, noncommittally. This is all getting a bit too dangerously romantic for my liking. I have to do something, and quick.

'You don't think they're amazing?' He turns to me, and I can see the flames of the fire casting a flickering light on his dumbfounded expression.

They're incredible, truly incredible, I think silently, but I need to change the mood.

'Yes, but all the stars are dead, aren't they?' I force myself to reply, 'So in actual fact we're looking at dead things.'

Jack turns to look at me and shakes his head. 'You know, you really are a total contradiction. You never cease to amaze me – I still can't work you out.'

I smile awkwardly. If only he knew, I'm actually pretty simple.

'So tomorrow we'll be in Udaipur,' he says, giving up and changing the topic, 'the end of our road trip.'

'Yes,' I nod, feeling a sense of relief. But it's also tinged with disappointment.

'What will you do?' I ask. 'I mean, after I've gone to meet my sister?'

'Oh, there's a few things I need to sort out,' he says vaguely, looking back at the flames.

I hesitate, then, 'Jack,' I say boldly, 'can I ask you a question?'
'Sure.'

With it poised on my tongue, I hesitate again, nervously. 'You're not a jewel smuggler, are you?' I finally blurt.

Jack looks at me and suddenly lets out a roar of laughter. His mouth opens crocodile-wide, showing off rows of white American teeth. 'That has to be the funniest thing I've ever heard,' he says when he finally stops laughing.

My cheeks flame. 'It's just that I don't know anything about you, or why you're here,' I begin trying to explain, 'and you were in the jeweller's in Jaipur and I, well—'

'Just put two and two together and came up with a million?' he grins.

I feel suddenly foolish. But still curious. 'Well, are you?' I persist.

'No, though I almost wish I was – it sounds kind of exciting.'

I shake my head. 'I just don't know anything about you.'

'Yes you do,' he disagrees, 'I'm an architect. I have a terrible line in jokes . . . and I wear this crazy old hat.' He tips his fedora at me, and flashes me a smile.

'So why were you on that train if you can afford to fly?' I challenge.

'You really want to know?'

'Yes,' I say, emboldened.

'OK, well . . . I'm terrified of flying,' he confesses. 'There, I've said it.'

I look at him in shock. 'You? Scared of flying? But you're not scared of anything!'

'And I was in Goa overseeing the building of a new school; I do some work for a charity.'

The surprises are coming thick and fast.

'Anything else?' He turns to me, his eyebrows raised.

I hesitate, about to say no, nothing, and yet . . .

'Why are you going to Udaipur?' My words come out in a rush. 'You said it was to keep a promise?'

There's a pause, as he seems to absorb the question. 'That's a little more complicated,' he says finally.

'Complicated, how?'

'Life's just complicated, that's all,' he shrugs, and as he turns away towards the dying flames, it's obvious he doesn't want to talk about it any more. 'The fire's going out, I think it's time to go to bed.'

I was right. Whatever it is he's not telling me, the subject is most definitely closed.

Bed is a tent. And one that Jack and I are sharing, I suddenly realise as, getting up from the fire, he folds back the heavy tarpaulin and motions me to follow.

'Mohan and Rocky are in the one over there,' he says, pointing to the other tent, pitched a few hundred yards away. 'This one's ours.'

I don't know why this hadn't crossed my mind earlier, considering there are only two tents, and four people. But then maths has never been my strongest subject.

'Um, great,' I smile, suddenly feeling ridiculously nervous.

'What's wrong?' Jack catches my expression.

'Oh – um, nothing,' I say hastily. 'I'm just a bit scared of creepy crawlies.'

Which is true. The last time I found a spider in the shower I had to call Mrs Flannegan over to get it out. Now *that's* what I call scared. Getting your elderly neighbour, who uses a walking stick, to come and rescue you, isn't just scary, it's pretty horrifying.

'Don't worry, I've got a flashlight, I'll check for scorpions.'

'*Scorpions?*' I gasp. Shit. And I thought spiders were scary. '*There are scorpions?*'

'None that are deadly, as far as I know,' he nods, digging out a torch from the pocket of the small daypack he always carries around with him. Switching it on, he shines an illuminated beam into the pitch darkness inside the tent. 'OK, let's have a look . . .'

Suddenly I'm so very happy to be sharing a tent with Jack. Relieved, actually.

Flicking the torchlight into corners and lifting up blankets like a man who knows what he's doing, he soon declares the tent scorpion free. 'Nothing's going to bite you tonight,' he says, turning the beam towards me.

I laugh weakly.

'So, which is your side?'

'Um, sorry?'

'The bed,' he says, motioning towards the layers of mattress rolls laid out on the ground sheet, on which are piled thick blankets and cushions.

'Oh . . . either, I don't mind,' I say, trying to act all cool and casual, but inside I feel absurdly nervous. As if I'm about to sleep with someone for the first time. Which, I suppose technically I am, in a way, except—

'OK, cool, well I'll have this side then,' he shrugs and, putting the torch between his teeth, kicks off his boots and starts unbuttoning his trousers.

Oh my god, he's going to take them off!

I stare, frozen by his striptease, then snap to. 'Um yeah, sure,' I stammer, quickly turning around to face the other way before I see something I shouldn't. With my back to him, I slip off my trainers and quickly dive under the blankets fully clothed.

Behind me, I can hear Jack undressing, the sound of a belt buckle being undone, the soft thump of items of clothing landing on the ground. Then the blankets lift and he slips in next to me.

'Mmm, comfy,' he murmurs approvingly.

'Yes, isn't it?' I reply, trying to sound all cheery and not in any way freaked out by the situation.

And then we both fall silent. Neither of us speaks. There's just the sound of us both breathing. Except, that suddenly sounds really loud. In fact, even the slightest rustle of a blanket is deafening. Every noise seems amplified somehow, every movement exaggerated. I lie very still. I daren't move in case I touch Jack. I have no idea what clothes he's wearing. Or if he's wearing any clothes at all. I mean, what if he's naked?

Naked? Oh my god, why did I just think about Jack being naked? My stomach flutters and I try to steady my breathing. Do not think about that, Ruby; don't even think about that.

He turns over. I can feel his breath, warm against my cheek. Even though our bodies aren't touching, just the presence of him next to me is electrifying. I swallow hard. It sounds so loud in the quiet and I try to steady myself. I shouldn't be thinking like this. What about his one-night stand with Cindy? I try to focus, but all thoughts of Cindy have flown out of the window. It's as if she doesn't exist – no one else exists. It's just the two of us now: me and Jack and no one else.

My heart is hammering so loudly I'm sure Jack can hear it. It's been such a long time since I've shared my bed with a man, I feel like a tightly wound spring. We're here, together, alone, out in the desert, in the middle of Rajasthan . . . the setting is so wildly erotic, I feel like *something's* going to happen, I can tell he feels like something's going to happen—

'Ruby?' His voice is almost a whisper.

'Yes?' Mine is barely audible.

I'm aware of his body moving closer. Even though we're not touching, I'm heady with desire. I hold my breath; the air hangs, suspended in that moment before something happens . . .

Suddenly there's a commotion outside and a figure appears through the tent flap.

'Rocky?' I gasp, as he stands silhouetted by the moon in the doorway. 'Is that you?'

'Is everything OK?' Jack jerks himself up on his elbows.

'Yes, yes, everything is wonderful,' he beams happily, 'but I must ask you something . . .' He breaks off and I notice him sway unsteadily on his feet. 'There is no room in Mohan's tent . . . He has some local men who helped with the car . . .'

As we both realise where this is leading, there's a palpable sense of something sinking. I think it's both our hearts.

'Of course . . .'

'You must sleep here.'

We both speak at the same time, our words toppling over each other in our eagerness to make Rocky feel welcome. And our haste to show the other person there's no sense of disappointment; that there were never any thoughts entertained of any other kind, *whatsoever*.

'There are extra blankets,' Jack is saying now.

'And here's a cushion,' I add.

'Oh thank you . . . you are so kind . . . thank you.' Thanking us profusely, Rocky stumbles into the tent.

I listen to him staggering around, tripping over things. And I thought I was clumsy. I hear a loud hiccup and suddenly, without any warning, he lurches forwards and lands like a dead weight, slap bang in the middle of us.

I let out a gasp. 'What the—?'

'I think someone's had one too many beers,' says Jack, flicking on his torch and shining it on Rocky, who's lying flat on his back, completely passed out. I don't know about a match-maker, he's a total passion killer.

We look at each other, not knowing what to do, both

knowing there's nothing we *can* do. Apart from try to get some sleep. Jack shrugs then switches off the torch. We both settle back down.

At least it's quiet, I try to console myself, I'll be able to get some sleep.

For a few moments it's silent, then Rocky's breath starts to deepen, growing gradually louder and louder until – with one large inhale – there's a rattling snore.

Oh no. Please no.

I wait on tenterhooks as he exhales . . . then there's another rattling snore. Louder, this time than the last.

Argh. Grabbing my cushion, I pull it round my ears. It's going to be a long night and, sadly, I realise, not in the way I'd hoped.

31

Last night I had a sex dream.

Usually I just have ones about finding myself naked in the town centre, or sitting my exams without having done any swotting or, worst of all, the one where my teeth fall out. And not just fall out, but get stuck in sandwiches, or crumble away as I'm trying to talk and the whole time I'm valiantly trying to stuff them back in . . .

Apparently they're all classic anxiety dreams. I obviously have a lot of anxiety. Which isn't surprising. I mean, I don't need an expert in dream analysis to tell me that if I spend the whole night having my teeth fall out, I'm going to wake up feeling anxious.

But not this morning. This morning I wake up feeling vaguely excited and hover in that lovely woozy place between sleeping and being fully conscious. Images and feelings waft back to me. *Tangled sheets . . . naked limbs . . . desire . . .* A delicious shiver tingles up my spine as the emotions wash over me like waves. *Kissing . . . stroking . . . being spooned by a warm body behind me . . .*

Wait a minute.

That's not a dream. *I am* being spooned by a warm body behind me.

Stirred from slumber, my heart goes from nought to about sixty in less than a second. I feel a sudden thrill. And pleasure. It feels nice, *really* nice. I get a flashback of Jack last night taking off his clothes, and feel ridiculously horny.

I try to lie very still, I don't want to wake him, but it's hard to resist. Ever so slightly, I wiggle my bum into him a bit more. There, that's better, now I can feel his warm breath on my ear.

With his body next to mine, I stay like that for a moment, relishing the closeness. Then, without making a noise, and feeling like a child sneaking a peek at their Christmas presents, I surreptitiously peep over my shoulder . . .

And come face-to-face with Rocky, who's sound asleep.

Oh my god! I take a sharp intake of breath. I'm spooning Rocky! Or is he spooning me? And does it matter who is spooning whom?

We're all spooning each other!

With horror I look past Rocky's shoulder, and spot Jack, blissfully curled up behind him, his arms entwined around Rocky's waist.

'Jack! Wake up!' I bark, jumping upright out of bed.

Rocky rolls over and lets out a loud moan.

'Uh . . . wassup?' Blearily opening his eyes, Jack takes a moment to focus, and then when he does: 'Jesus! I thought that was you!'

'And I thought that was you!'

Jerking bolt upright, Jack stares at me in disbelief, then together we both swivel our eyes to look at Rocky, who's lying there, blissfully sleeping like a baby. Well, that is if babies have tufts of white hair, spectacles askew and mouths that hang wide open, drooling.

Jack digs Rocky roughly in the ribs and he lets out a loud snort that only serves to fire up the snoring again, rather like giving a motorbike a kick-start. He elbows him even harder.

'Huh?' Rocky's eyes flicker open, roll into the back of his head then, seeming to think better of it, come back again.

Finally they focus on us. 'Miss Ruby . . . Boss . . .' he croaks in a raspy voice.

'Do you think he's ill?' I whisper, shooting a panicked look at Jack.

'Ill?' frowns Jack. 'No, he's hungover!' He points at the empty whisky bottle on the side and gives him another shove with his elbow.

Rocky starts coughing loudly, clutching his head and rolling around.

'Oh god, he sounds terrible!' I gasp.

'And I'm sure he feels terrible,' says Jack, grimly.

'My head, my head,' Rocky moans, wobbling into an upright position of sorts and pressing the heels of his palms onto his forehead.

'Would you like some water?' I suggest, grabbing a spare bottle.

Rocky doesn't reply; instead he lets out a noise that sounds like a wounded animal, then flops back down onto the blankets.

'Oh dear.' I shoot Jack a look. 'What are we going to do?'

Climbing out of bed, Jack reaches for his clothes and I see he's only wearing shorts. I catch a flash of his body. Strong thighs. Muscular, tanned chest. Flexing biceps. I quickly avert my eyes.

'Rocky, listen, it's me. Jack.'

I look back to see he's crouched down next to him. His earlier annoyance has disappeared and there's a concerned expression on his face. 'Is there anything I can get you?'

There's silence, but for the sounds of faint moaning. 'A new head, boss,' Rocky groans, lifting his barely an inch off the cushion, before it collapses back down again.

''Fraid I can't get you one of those,' smiles Jack good-naturedly.

Rocky smiles weakly, then suddenly clutches his stomach.

'Oh no,' I gasp, recognising the warning signs, 'I think he's going to be—'

Too late. A loud retching noise fills the air as Rocky throws himself over the side of the mattress.

'I guess a bucket might have been more handy,' winces Jack.

Hand clamped across my mouth, I stare in horror. 'Poor Rocky, he's so ill,' I mumble, behind the parapet of my fingers. 'He's probably not used to drinking.'

'You can say that again,' nods Jack, raising his eyebrows.

As Rocky finishes being sick, he rolls back onto the mattress and closes his eyes. In the distance there's the sound of a cock crowing.

'What time is it?' asks Jack, turning to me.

I glance at my watch and see the time: five thirty a.m. 'We need to leave!' I cry, suddenly panicked. 'We need to get to Udaipur before the shop opens.'

We both turn to look at Rocky, who's now fallen fast asleep again.

'OK, well, first things first, let me find out if the tyre's fixed,' says Jack calmly, taking control of the situation. 'Wait here a minute, I'll be right back.'

He disappears out of the tent, and I pull a spare blanket around my shoulders to stave off the early morning cold, then busy myself trying to tidy up around Rocky. A few times I try to wake him to make him drink water, but apart from a few sips, he lies comatose.

Jack returns a few minutes later with a big thumbs-up. 'All fixed, you'll be pleased to know,' he grins.

'Oh, thank goodness.' I feel a rush of relief. For a moment there I thought we might get stuck in the desert after all.

'Yeah, the boys from the local village did a good job; the car's back on the road and ready to go.'

'Great,' I beam. 'And I'm all done in here,' I gesture to the folded blankets.

'Which leaves . . .' Trailing off, Jack motions towards a snoring Rocky.

'I don't think he's fit to drive,' I venture.

Jack grins, despite the situation. 'A slight understatement,' he nods, 'though I'm not sure you can get a DUI here . . . "Driving under the influence",' he explains, seeing my puzzled look.

'So what shall we do?' I ask.

'There's only one thing we can do.'

Fifteen minutes and lots of huffing and puffing later, Rocky is stretched out on the back seat of the Ambassador, still fast asleep.

'Phew, well, at least that bit's done,' says Jack, closing the passenger door.

I nod, still winded from having to lug Rocky out of the tent. Mohan had kindly offered to help, but to be honest he looked to be in the same fragile state as Rocky. 'Great,' I pant, catching my breath. 'The sun has risen but it's still early and if we get going now, we should be there before the shop opens.'

'OK, well let's go,' nods Jack.

Waving our thank-yous and goodbyes, we turn and reach for the door handle. And crash into each other.

'Wrong side, they drive on the left here,' I laugh. I feel a buzz of happiness. Finally, after all this time and all these setbacks, I've made it. I've found my sister, and in only a few hours I'll be with her in Udaipur. 'This is the passenger side.'

'Yeah, I know,' nods Jack.

I realise his fingers are still curled tightly around the door handle. How odd.

'The driver's side is that side,' I clarify. Well, it is early; he's obviously getting mixed up.

'I know,' he nods again.

All at once, I feel a doubt start to creep in around the edges.

'What do you mean, you know?' I ask, frowning, though for some reason I already know I'm not going to want the answer to this question.

'You're driving,' he replies.

I *knew* I wouldn't want the answer.

As his words register, I stare at him in disbelief. 'What do you mean I'm . . .' I break off. 'Oh ha-ha, this is one of your jokes,' I smile, suddenly getting it. 'You know how terrified I am of the roads, you thought you'd pull my leg.' Playfully shoving him away, I push the button on the handle to release the door and tug it open.

Only Jack doesn't move. In fact, he's still holding stubbornly onto the door handle. Actually, make that *hanging* on to the door handle.

'I don't drive a stick.'

I look at him blankly. '*A stick*?'

'I'm American,' he says simply. 'We drive automatics.'

'You mean, this isn't a joke?' Anxiety knots.

Jack shakes his head. 'Nope.'

'You don't know how to change gears?'

Jacks shakes his head again.

'Or use the clutch?'

And again.

I feel my mouth go dry. This is my worst nightmare. My biggest fear: *I'm going to have to drive*.

'Oh fuck.'

There's a famous book entitled *Feel the Fear and Do It Anyway*. It's an international bestseller and over twenty-five years has sold millions of copies, changing millions of people's lives. Personally I've never read it and now I will probably never need to as I'm feeling the fear and doing it anyway *and I'm absolutely terrified*.

Ten minutes later and we're on the road. Such an

innocuous phrase – 'we're on the road'. It sounds so casual and harmless, as if one should be having a jolly old time on a day trip down to the coast, driving along playing I-spy and eating sausage rolls. Not white-knuckling the steering wheel, rigid with fear, eyes staring straight ahead, dodging camels and trucks and rickshaws.

And stray dogs that run out in front of you, causing you to swerve, slam on the brakes and your heart to jump into your mouth as the gears crunch and scream.

'Argh, where's second?' I screech, along with the gears.

'Um . . . after first?' suggests Jack, from the safety of the passenger seat.

Well, I say safety, but judging by these roads and my driving, that's open to debate.

I shoot him a look. 'Listen, smarty-pants—'

'Look out!' he yells, as I take my eyes off the road for a second and a bus appears from nowhere.

I pull down sharply on the steering wheel and veer out of its path.

'*Argghh . . .*' we both shriek loudly as it hurtles past us, its horn blasting.

'Jeez, Ruby!' Clinging onto his seat, Jack turns to me, ashen-faced. 'The roads here are crazy, maybe you should try slowing down.'

'I can't slow down,' I say determinedly, above the whirr of the engine. 'I've got to get to Udaipur before the shop opens. There's no time to lose.'

I stare fixedly ahead at the road, my jaw clenched tightly. Out of the corner of my eye, I can feel Jack still looking at me. 'Great manoeuvre, by the way,' he nods approvingly, after a few moments.

'Thanks,' I shrug and, feeling a faint swell of pride, I press my foot back on the accelerator and we race on ahead.

But it's not just the roads; the car itself is also taking a bit of getting used to. Compared to driving my parent's zippy new Renault, the thirty-year-old Ambassador feels heavy and solid – apparently its nickname is 'The White Elephant' – but it's also surprisingly fast and powerful. In fact, the accelerator seems to have a mind of its own, as does the horn, which makes me jump out of my skin every time I have to use it. Oh my god, this is awful. My nerves are frayed. I don't know if I can do this.

And yet, as we speed along the highway, the engine roaring loudly, the desire to get to Udaipur to save my sister propelling me forwards, something odd starts to happen. It's as if a strange sort of transformation begins to come over me. Gradually my fears start to recede. I start feeling less jumpy. Not as scared. More in control. I feel my confidence growing . . .

Fast-forward to three hours later, and the terrified scaredy-cat who had to cover her eyes and clung to the back seat of the tuk-tuk on the ride from Goa Airport is long gone. Now I'm behind the wheel in the driver's seat, my eyes wide open and my hand permanently on the horn. Changing gears and revving hard, I'm swerving in and out of traffic, overtaking tuk-tuks and careering around cows like I've been doing this for years. Jenson Button, eat your heart out!

Finally, after several hours' driving, we arrive on the outskirts of Udaipur. As we race into town, the little white car negotiating the tiny streets, we catch our first glimpse of the shimmering lake that stretches out before us. After the long, dusty drive, it's like a mirage. Beautiful.

Wow.

But we don't have time to stop and take in the view; I have to find the shop and my sister and, armed with the address, we take off down a small side street.

'According to Google maps it should be first left,' instructs Jack, peering at his iPhone.

I swing a hard left and I hear a groan from the back seat as Rocky is thrown sideways. It's the first noise I've heard from him the whole journey, so I take it as a good sign, rather than a cause for concern, and keep driving.

We pass lots of little shops that are starting to open, shop-keepers sweeping steps, dusting off their awnings and putting out their wares. We slow down as we weave through the crooked maze of higgledy-piggledy streets and race across the bridge.

'OK, now take a right,' instructs Jack.

I do as I'm told. I have to say, we make rather a good team, him reading the map, me driving. It makes a nice change, this role reversal. Turning in to the small narrow street, I see the shop sign straight ahead.

'Bingo!' I exclaim, thrilled. I pull up quickly. 'Good job with the directions.'

'Good job driving,' says Jack, impressed.

Smiling, I turn off the engine and throw him the keys. 'I've done the driving, you can take care of him,' I gesture to the back seat. 'I'm going to get my sister.'

Leaving Jack to take care of Rocky in the car, I take the steps in one leap and push open the door. The shop is already open, and as I enter it's like walking into an Aladdin's cave of shimmering golds and reds, vibrant pinks, sapphire blues and luminous emerald greens. Walls are lined with roll upon roll of fabric, stacked from floor to ceiling in an array of dazzling colours, whilst hanging from racks are a glittering display of exquisitely embellished ready-made garments.

As someone who spends her whole life head-to-toe in boring old black leggings and T-shirts, I've never realised clothes could be this beautiful, and for a moment it stops me in my tracks.

'Hello, can I help you?'

I snap back to see a tiny middle-aged lady appear from the back of the shop. Dressed in a beautiful peacock green sari, with a glossy black plait reaching down her back that is almost the same length as she is tall, she looks at me enquiringly through a pair of gold-rimmed glasses.

'Mrs Gupta?' I ask hopefully.

'Yes, this is me,' she nods.

A smile of relief washes over me. 'Hi, I'm Ruby . . . I spoke to you yesterday on the telephone,' I begin hurriedly explaining, 'about my sister.'

The crease down her forehead disappears. 'Ah yes,' she says briskly, 'you are the older sister of Amy Miller.'

'Yes, that's me!' After all this time, just hearing someone say my sister's name feels like a massive breakthrough.

There's a pause as Mrs Gupta peers at me and I feel jittery with expectation.

'You don't look anything alike,' she observes, clicking her tongue.

'Um . . . yes, I know . . .' I nod, suddenly conscious that not only being heavier and darker, I'm a complete mess. Glancing down at my new clothes, I realise that after camping out in the desert they're covered in dust and dirt. Plus, the only mirror I've looked in today has been a rear-view, so I dread to think what kind of state my face and hair are in. I swear, trying to keep clean and look pretty on a road trip is just impossible.

'I'm more the tomboy of the family,' I say with a weak laugh.

Mrs Gupta nods, her lips pursed with disapproval. I have a feeling Mrs Gupta can actually be a bit scary.

'So you are here because you need a sari as well? I have lots of beautiful silks.' Walking across her shop floor, she starts pulling out rolls of the most beautiful material. 'Or perhaps something ready-made would be better because of the time . . . Here, see, we have wonderful embroidered *choli* and *lehenga*.' Plucking hangers off the rack, she begins briskly laying out gorgeous tops and matching skirts, 'Beautiful *salwaar kameez* . . .'

'Oh . . . no, no thank you,' I say hurriedly. 'I think there's been some misunderstanding.'

Mrs Gupta pauses and turns, her arms overflowing.

'I'm just here to see my sister,' I explain, 'when she comes to collect her bridal sari.'

She looks at me blankly. 'But your sister has already collected her sari.'

My heart suddenly freezes. 'Already?' I stammer. 'But I thought she was coming today.'

'She came very early, along with several other full-moon brides,' nods Mrs Gupta. 'I was almost still in my nightdress.' She gives a little chuckle.

I stare at her in horror, the shock and disappointment hitting me with full force.

'I tell you, it is always busy at this time of year, but never like this,' she continues chattering away, shaking her head. 'Udaipur has become the mecca for weddings. This full moon I know of one dozen ceremonies, here alone! It is incredible – my seamstresses have been up all day and all night, the phone is ringing off the hook . . .'

I've missed her, I can't believe it. I was so close and I've missed her.

'Are you all right?' I snap back to see Mrs Gupta looking at me, a concerned expression on her face.

'Yes, yes, I'm fine,' I mumble, but I can feel tears pricking on my eyelashes and I blink them away furiously. 'Did she leave an address perhaps, or a contact number?'

'One moment, let me see . . .' Dipping behind the counter, she pulls out a large ledger, almost as big as herself and, as she starts flicking through it, I cling onto the last bit of hope.

'Ah yes, I have her email address. If you want I can give that to you . . .'

But then it's gone. 'No, it's OK . . . but thank you so much . . . I'm sorry to have bothered you . . .'

'It is not a problem,' she replies, waving a hand behind her head as if batting away any problems that might have been lurking, 'and don't forget, if you change your mind about a sari' – plucking a card off the counter, she thrusts it at me – 'I am the best in town.'

32

Jack is leaning against the car, waiting for me, his face filled with expectation.

'So? When do I get to meet this sister of yours?' he says jokingly, but I can see the hope in his eyes.

For a moment I can't speak. I feel dazed by the turn in events. 'You won't,' I say quietly, shaking my head.

'What?' His smile slips.

'I've missed her. She's already been and gone,' I blurt out, and then unable to plug the dam a moment longer, I burst into floods of tears.

He looks at me, almost paralysed, then groans loudly. 'Oh god, I hate it when you do this.' Reaching inside the car, he pulls out the toilet roll and unravels it, until there's a long swathe of white tissue. He passes it to me and I take it gratefully.

'I'm sorry,' I sniffle, 'it's just . . .' I shake my head, my thoughts and emotions tumbling over each other. 'I just don't want her to get hurt, I don't want her making the same mistakes as I've made . . .' Everything's jumbling together into one big sorry mess inside my head and I gulp back a lump in my throat, trying to stop the tears that are still springing from my eyes. 'She's my little sister, I've always looked after her . . .'

'Look, don't worry, we'll find her,' he tries to soothe me.

I shake my head. 'It's too late.'

'It's never too late,' he says, but this time his voice is firm.

I glance up from the scrunched-up tissue in my hand and meet his gaze. I see a determination in his hazel eyes that I haven't seen before.

'What did the shopkeeper say exactly?' he asks.

I feel a prickle of frustration. I know he's only trying to help, but why can't men ever just listen and be sympathetic? Why do they always have to be practical and try and find a solution, when there isn't one? Try and fix things that can't be fixed?

'What does it matter?' I retort, 'I can't stop a wedding if I don't know where and when it's taking place.'

'You were saying . . . about Mrs Gupta?' he prompts again, ignoring my impatience.

I give in. 'Nothing much,' I shrug, 'just that Amy collected her sari really early this morning, along with a bunch of other full-moon brides—'

'What did she call them?' he interrupts.

'Who?' I frown. 'Oh, you mean the other customers?'

He nods, his brow creased as if deep in thought.

'Full-moon brides. Why?'

Jack's face floods with realisation. 'When's the full moon?'

'Tonight!' exclaims a voice from the car, and we both twirl around to see Rocky spring up from the back seat like a dead man come back to life. 'Remember what I told you? This is the most auspicious date in the astrological calendar!' he cries excitedly, waving his arms around in the air. 'Tonight all the planets will be in alignment! Tonight good fortune will fall on all the couples solemnising their marriage vows under these happy celestial skies! Tonight there will be so many weddings, *it will be one big wedding!*' He breaks off breathlessly and beams at us, wide-eyed.

'She must be getting married here in Udaipur,' says Jack, turning to me, his eyes flashing with success.

I feel a flash of hope, of elation, then: 'But we'll never find her,' I shake my head, thinking of all the obstacles in our way. 'We don't know where to start looking.'

'I do love a negative Brit,' he grins, and my cheeks colour.

'Look, Jack, you've done enough to help me already,' I protest, 'and I really appreciate it, but I'll be fine on my own now. And, anyway, I'm sure you've got plenty to do now we've arrived.'

'Well, that's where you're wrong,' he replies evenly. 'I don't have anything arranged until tomorrow.'

As he removes one obstacle, I reach for another. 'Mrs Gupta said there are over a dozen ceremonies taking place here in Udaipur alone.'

'Well, if you're not doing anything tonight, neither am I.' He looks at me, challengingly.

I feel a glimmer of possibility, and then: 'What? You mean . . . you and me . . .?'

He nods and flashes me a smile. 'Wedding crashers.'

Rocky seems to have made a remarkable and rather suspiciously fast recovery and now springs into the driving seat as we look for a place to stay. Only it's not that easy. Udaipur, we soon discover, is fully booked. It's not just wedding season, it's high season, and the city is buzzing with tourists.

Eventually we find a small guesthouse by the side of the lake. Tucked behind one of the luxury five-star hotels, it doesn't overlook the water but it's a fraction of the price.

'Don't worry, we have a magnificent view of Lake Pichola from our rooftop,' the pretty teenage receptionist informs us as she leads us through the small walled courtyard and up the marble staircase, 'and the world-famous Lake Palace Hotel. Did you know this is the setting for the James Bond movie, *Octopussy?*'

'Yeah, I heard,' nods Jack.

'I'm sure you've heard this many times already,' she laughs.

As her face breaks into a smile, I feel a flicker of recognition. Gosh, she looks really familiar. Have I met her before?

'Everywhere you go in Udaipur you will see posters saying "tonight's movie: *Octopussy*" . . .'

Don't be silly, of course I haven't met her.

' . . . but it is the same movie showing every night,' she continues animatedly.

And yet I still can't help looking at her a little more closely. I'm usually really good with faces. I really feel as if I've seen her before.

'But let me tell you a secret.' She turns to me, meeting my gaze and wrinkling up her small, thin nose. 'I never liked this movie.'

Jack laughs and says something but I don't catch it. I'm too distracted, rummaging through my memory, even though I know it's impossible. Dressed in skinny jeans and a T-shirt, she looks like a million other teenagers back home. She must just remind me of someone, that's all.

'Ruby?'

Jack's voice snaps me back and I see him looking at me, questioningly. 'You're quiet, you OK?'

'Yeah, fine . . . fine,' I nod hastily, shoving the thoughts out of my mind. 'Just a bit tired, that's all.'

'We drove from the desert,' adds Jack for the receptionist's benefit. 'We camped there last night.'

'Oh wow, how romantic,' she smiles, her eyes wide.

Jack and I exchange awkward glances. 'Well, not exactly,' I reply, having a flashback to me spooning Rocky – then really wishing I hadn't.

'So, this is your room.'

As she stops by a door and unlocks it, we follow her inside. It's perfect. Clean and light, there's a large window with shutters and a small bathroom attached. There's just one problem.

'There's only one bed,' I say, my eyes going immediately to it.

'Yes, is this not OK?' she smiles, looking between us.

'We'd prefer a room with twin beds,' replies Jack tactfully, saving my blushes.

'I'm afraid we don't have any rooms like this.' The receptionist shakes her head apologetically. 'Only rooms with one bed.'

'Well, in that case we'll take two rooms,' I say swiftly.

The receptionist's face falls. 'I'm sorry, but that's not possible. We only have one room left. It's very busy – there are many tourists here, and also it is the wedding season.'

'Yes, we know,' nods Jack, catching my eye. 'OK, well, no worries.' He smiles one of his disarming smiles and her face relaxes. 'This is great; thanks for all your help.'

'Are you sure?' The receptionist glances at me for reassurance.

'It's perfect,' I smile cheerfully.

'Oh, I am so glad,' she smiles, brightening, 'and if there is anything else, please don't hesitate to ask,' and, bidding us goodbye, she leaves to return to reception.

As soon as the door closes behind her, Jack turns to me. 'I'll sleep on the floor.'

'Don't be silly,' I say dismissively, as if the thought had never crossed my mind. 'We shared a bed in the desert, it will be fine.'

A split second memory of Jack and me, together in the darkness, fires across my brain, and I feel my chest tighten. It was many things, but fine certainly wasn't one of them.

'That was quite something; you, me and Rocky.' He raises an eyebrow and we both look at each other.

Nope, definitely not fine.

'We can sleep top to tail,' I suggest.

'Did you just say *top to tail*?' The corners of his mouth twitch with amusement and I feel myself blush.

'It's something Amy and I used to do when we were little,' I say hastily. Honestly, what am I? *Five?*

'OK,' he nods, 'but first you have to take off your clothes.'

'Excuse me?' I balk.

'I said take off your clothes,' he repeats, matter-of-factly. 'I'll get them laundered, we're both filthy.'

'Oh – right – yes, of course,' I fluster. Cheeks blazing, I charge off into the bathroom and peel off my grubby trousers and T-shirt. I can't give him my underwear; I'll wash that myself in the sink. I re-emerge wrapped in a towel the size of a postage stamp. Trying to tug it down over the backs of my thighs whilst clutching it tightly against my chest, I awkwardly pass him my clothes.

'Great, these should be ready in a couple of hours,' he says, adding them to the large pile in the middle of the bed. 'Anything else you need laundered? I'm taking the whole lot, it could all do with a good wash.' Having already changed into a pair of shorts, he pulls off his T-shirt and chucks it on top.

And then he just stands there, bare-chested, like it's perfectly normal.

Says me in a towel, I realise, quickly averting my eyes.

'Um, well . . . actually, in that case . . .' I end up giving him the rest of my things. I don't have very much, but everything I do have is all dusty and dirty from the travelling. 'Do you want me to come with you?' I offer as he scoops up the bundle of clothes into a sarong and ties it like a knapsack.

'In that towel?' he grins, and I redden. 'No, don't worry, chill out.'

I smile gratefully and open the door for him.

'You'll need your energy for all that dancing we're going to be doing later,' he adds, pausing in the doorway. Then he's gone, disappearing down the corridor.

33

Closing the door behind him, I flop down on the bed. So, I made it. I'm here. After going on a crazy, magical mystery tour across Rajasthan, filled with forts and palaces, wonderful people and amazing experiences, I'm finally in Udaipur.

I let out a long gratified sigh and gaze out of the window. If I crick my neck, I can just catch a glimpse of the Lake Palace hotel floating on the water. It's immediately recognisable from the Bond movie. I smile to myself. There was me thinking I'd never been here before when in actual fact I've spent many a Christmas Day in Udaipur, watching Roger Moore give chase around these twisting, colourful streets.

I yawn, a wave of tiredness washing over me. It was a long drive from the desert and I hardly slept last night. I close my eyes and am just thinking about the possibility of getting some sleep when there's a knock on the door. It's probably Jack; no doubt he's forgotten something, I decide, getting up.

'Don't tell me, you're missing a sock,' I quip, pulling open the door.

'I'm so sorry to bother you.'

Only it's not Jack, it's the young girl from reception.

'Oh, hi, sorry,' I smile, slightly flustered, 'I thought for a minute you were someone else . . .'

'Is this a bad time?' Her eyes fall to my towel. 'I can come back later.'

'Oh no,' I shake my head, and quickly tuck the towel in firmly around my chest. 'My clothes are at the laundry.'

'Because I wanted to ask you a question,' she begins, then swallows hard and I realise she's extremely nervous. 'I was looking at you when you first arrived, as I thought I recognised you from somewhere . . .'

'Oh my gosh, me too!' I exclaim. I knew it! I never forget a face.

'And I could not put my finger on it, but then when I went back downstairs it was quiet and so I started to read my book again, and I realised . . .' She breaks off and looks at me, her eyes shining with excitement, 'It's you!'

The whole time she's had her hands folded across something she's clutching to her chest and, as she holds it out to me, I realise it's a book.

My latest novel.

'Ruby Miller!' she continues, breaking into a smile as she points to my author photograph on the back cover. 'You are my most favourite author!'

'Oh . . . wow,' I smile, both delighted and confused. It's so great to meet one of my readers, and here in India! And yet that doesn't explain why she looks so familiar.

'I don't want to trouble you, but would you sign it?'

I snap back. 'Yes, yes of course,' I say readily, 'please, come in.'

'Thank you so much, Miss Miller—'

'Please, call me Ruby,' I insist.

'Ruby,' she nods, blushing, and follows me inside. I motion to a chair whilst I perch on the small ottoman at the foot of the bed. She smiles gratefully and, sitting down, passes me my book to sign.

It feels so strange to see it. Here, in this little room, in a guesthouse in Rajasthan. Holding the book in my hands, I let my thumb flick through the pages. The whole time I've been here in India I haven't thought of writing. For the first time in my life, I've been too busy living a plotline worthy of one of my own novels to want to escape into my imagination. But now sitting here, my writer's block seems like a thing of the past. I feel a renewed energy, I feel inspired again—

'Do you have a pen?'

I zone back in to see her looking at me expectantly.

'Oh, yes, somewhere,' I say hurriedly, getting up to look around the room. I always feel slightly embarrassed whenever I can't lay my hands on a pen. I mean, I'm a writer for goodness' sake – by rights I should have pens coming out of my ears.

'Your books make me so happy,' the girl continues, 'even when I am sad. They teach me to believe in true love, to believe that I will have a happy-ever-after . . .'

As she speaks I feel a stab of guilt. I suddenly feel like a fake. Here I am, writing about happy-ever-afters and true love, and look at me. I'm hardly a walking advertisement for it, am I?

' . . . but how can I ever live happily when I cannot be with the person I love? If all the time my heart is broken . . .'

I glance up from rummaging in a drawer and realise her eyes have welled up and a tear is spilling from her cheeks.

'I'm so sorry,' she sniffles, quickly wiping it away with her fingers.

'Oh please, don't be silly!' I admonish, impulsively reaching across and squeezing her hand. 'We've all had a broken heart.'

'Even you?' she looks at me, surprised.

'Yes, even me,' I nod, ruefully.

'So tell me, what do I do?' Expectantly, she looks at me for advice.

I can't help smiling at the irony. 'I don't know,' I confess with complete honesty, and see a flash of disappointment across her face.

'But you write about love,' she replies, her brow creasing.

'I write about love because it fascinates me, but I'm not an expert on love. No one is. No one knows all the answers, because there *are* no answers,' I say firmly. 'It's not called the mystery of love for nothing. In fact, the more I learn, the less I realise I actually know.'

I think back to how I felt just a few weeks ago – how I didn't believe in love, how I thought it was all bollocks, and now . . . 'But one thing I have learned is that even when you've lost faith and hope, love can surprise you.'

I look at the young girl sitting across from me and think about all the millions of people in the world, all of us looking for answers in one way or another.

'You've just got to hold on,' I add firmly. 'Don't ever let go.'

Our eyes meet and we share a moment of complete understanding. Because that's the thing about love: it doesn't care how old you are, where you live, what religion or culture you belong to. Deep down inside, it feels the same for every single one of us.

'Oh look, a pen.' Turning away, I spot one on the small table behind her and reach for it, then open the book and turn the page. 'Who shall I sign it for?'

'Suhana,' she replies, smiling gratefully.

With the nib of the pen already resting on the page, I feel myself stiffen. Hang on, that rings a bell. '*Suhana?*' I repeat, rolling the name around in my head.

'Yes, that's me,' she nods.

I have a flashback to the train from Goa: Vijay – the photo on his mobile phone.

'Do you know a boy called Vijay?' I ask, and no sooner has his name escaped my lips than I know I'm right. Her face says it all.

'*Vijay?*' she gasps, as if hardly daring to believe it. 'You know *Vijay?*'

'I met him on a train,' I nod. 'He told me all about you!'

'He did?' Her voice falls to almost a whisper. 'How was he?'

'In love with you,' I answer simply.

I see her breath catch inside her and for a moment it's as if she hardly dares exhale, as if holding it tight inside of her will keep my words forever suspended in the air around her. 'Please . . . tell me about him,' she asks finally, her voice trembling. Her dark eyes meet mine. 'Tell me about my Vijay.'

And so I tell her. I tell her everything. About how much he loves and misses her. About how he knows they can never be together because she would never disobey her father. About how he doesn't want her to, because he respects her father. 'All he wants is to know that you are happy,' I tell her. 'That's all he wanted to know.'

And Suhana listens, her eyes shining with tears of both happiness and sadness, and says it's a sign. And I can't help thinking maybe she's right. Love works in mysterious ways, and who's to say destiny didn't play a part in me catching the same train as Vijay? In that breath of wind that blew my hair loose and caused us to strike up a conversation about Suhana, the girl he was in love with. In the flat tyre that saw us arriving late into Udaipur and happening across this guesthouse because everywhere else was full. In me writing a novel that would be read by a young receptionist called Suhana who asked me to sign it . . . and me returning the favour by asking her to be my Facebook friend . . .

Well, actually, that's me giving destiny a little helping hand. Because maybe one day Suhana and Vijay will be looking through my friends list and see each other, and who knows what will happen? The rest is up to destiny.

After we've finished talking, Suhana hugs me goodbye and I'm just closing the door behind her when Jack reappears around the corner carrying two large bags.

'Do you want the good news or the bad news?' he asks, spotting me in the doorway.

Immediately I feel my heart sink. *Uh-oh.* What now?

'I'm a Brit; the bad news,' I say, without missing a beat.

He smiles. 'OK, well the bad news is all our clothes are ruined.'

'What?' I frown, looking at him in confusion. 'But how?'

Without saying a word he walks past me into the room and empties one of the bags onto the bed. A jumble of pink rags fall out onto the bedspread. At least I think they're rags, only on closer inspection I realise it's our clothes.

'Everything's pink,' I say, somewhat redundantly.

'Do you like pink?' He raises his eyebrows.

Picking up a T-shirt that is now a strange shade of bubblegum and stretched to twice its size, I stare at it in bewilderment. 'And what's the good news?' I ask tentatively.

'I got us both new outfits,' he says simply.

'You did?' I feel a flash of panic. Oh dear. This is not good. The last time a man surprised me by buying me an outfit, I ended up having to wear a revolting dress that was like something Bo-Peep would wear.

I watch nervously as he dumps the other bag on the small chair.

'You know, the pink isn't *actually* that bad,' I begin, then fall silent as Jack pulls out the most gorgeous length of sparkly bright blue sari material I've ever seen.

'Oh wow,' I gasp, mesmerised by the shimmering flashes of colour and glitter. 'But how . . .?'

'Mrs Gupta,' he says. 'I figured if we've got a whole night of weddings to crash, we should dress the part.' As he tugs out an elaborate golden silk tunic and holds it up to himself, I stare at him in amazement. 'And she does have the best deals in town,' he grins, flashing me her card.

For a moment I just stand there, wordlessly. Then,

breaking into a delighted smile, I pounce on the sari material and scoop it up into my hands. 'Wow, Jack, this is gorgeous!'

Pleasure flashes across his face, then he gets down to business. 'Come on, let's get ready, we've got a big night ahead of us,' he says, clapping his hands to hurry me along.

Reminded, I snap to and, clutching my new outfit to my chest, dash into the bathroom. Closing the door behind me, I tug off my towel, then pause, suddenly daunted by the evening ahead. I feel a clutch of nerves at the thought of chasing through the streets from wedding to wedding . . .

I also feel a thrill of excitement. Reaching for the swathe of sparkling silk, I start getting dressed. Forget 007, right now I feel like I'm in my own adventure movie.

34

Who's that girl?

Standing in front of the mirror, I gaze in disbelief at the reflection staring back at me. I almost don't recognise myself. Gone is the scruffy, dusty, hair-in-a-scrunchie tomboy who camped in the desert; in her place is a woman wearing the most exquisite cornflower blue silk sari, delicately embroidered with gold thread and sequins, that shimmers and sparkles as she moves. Freshly shampooed hair hangs in loose waves across her shoulders, her eyes are lined with dark kohl, and her intricately hennaed hands, which have now darkened properly, look amazing.

She's even wearing the most gorgeous jewelled bindi, I muse, touching it delicately. As I do so, the glittering stack of bracelets on my arms jangle and I can't help smiling.

'I feel like a real-life fairy princess,' I say, turning to Jack who's standing beside me dressed in a traditional Indian *achkan*, a knee-length jacket made from gold silk, and a pair of tight-fitting trousers.

'So what does that make me? Prince Charming?' he grins.

I laugh, but something inside me flips right over. Clean-shaven, his dark hair brushed back from his tanned face, and without a frayed fedora, pair of flip-flops or tatty old shorts in sight, Jack looks ridiculously handsome, like a hero in a Bollywood movie.

'So how do we look?' Turning back to the mirror, he asks my reflection.

'Um . . . not bad,' I say, trying to make my voice sound nonchalant. But instead I feel as if every nerve ending is alive.

Dressed in our traditional Indian outfits, we don't just look completely different, it's as if somehow we *are* completely different. We're not Jack and Ruby, two travellers thrown together on a road trip across India, with two completely different agendas. We're Jack and Ruby, a man and a woman, all dressed up and on their way to not just one wedding, but possibly a dozen of them.

Crikey. I feel a tremble of excitement and panic. Usually if you go to a wedding as a couple, it's a sign things are getting serious, *and we've got up to twelve to go to.*

But we're not a couple. Jack's just doing me a favour. We're only doing this together because he's helping me find Amy, I remind myself firmly. Before it's too late and she makes the biggest mistake of her life.

'You look gorgeous, Ruby.'

I turn to see Jack looking at me in a way he hasn't looked at me before.

'Um, thanks,' I say, my voice coming out high and squeaky. 'You, er, don't look too bad yourself,' I add, trying to be all jokey.

He remains looking at me for a moment, as if he might say something, then seems to think better of it. 'OK, let's go.' He holds out his arm.

Like I said, we're definitely not a couple. He's just doing me a favour. That's all.

And, threading my arm through his, I head out of the door with him.

Downstairs we encounter Suhana racing around reception. Balancing a large pile of post on top of several towels, she crashes blindly into us. 'Oh, I am so sorry, sir and madam,' she exclaims, then suddenly stops dead as she recognises us. 'Oh my goodness me! Ruby!'

'Hi Suhana,' I smile, as Jack flashes me a perplexed look, wondering how we're on first-name terms. I make a mental note to tell him all about it later.

'You look so . . . so different,' she gasps, goggling at us both.

'We've got a wedding or two to go to,' smiles Jack, scooping up several envelopes that have fallen to the floor and balancing them on top of her pile.

She shoots him a grateful smile. 'The whole town is going to a wedding!' she exclaims. 'I have my cousin's and I am so late!' She glances at the clock on the wall and lets out a little squeak of horror. 'Oh no, look at the time!'

'Well, we'd better not keep you,' I say, sensing the panic that only another female understands, of not having enough time to get ready.

'Maybe we'll see you later,' nods Jack as she dives behind the reception desk.

'Yes . . . please . . . you must come to the party afterwards,' she nods, hurriedly switching off various electronics. Popping her head back up from behind the parapet of files, she flashes us both an excited smile, 'There will be live music and lots of dancing! Look for the Royal Shiva, it is a five-star hotel on the lake . . .' Then she disappears under the desk again.

Exchanging hurried, and muffled, goodbyes, we leave the guesthouse and walk outside onto the front steps. The street is already crowded with people and noise and there's a carnival atmosphere. Dusk has fallen and the moon has risen in the sky, but the whole town is alive.

'You both look wonderful!'

Hearing a voice, I tip my head and see the little white car tucked into the smallest of spaces across the street, and Rocky leaning against it.

'Oh, hey!' waves Jack. 'I didn't see you there.'

'But I saw you,' he nods with a smile. 'You make a wonderful couple.'

I feel myself blush awkwardly. 'Thanks,' I smile, not looking at Jack.

'So my job is done,' he adds, as together Jack and I begin descending the steps to cross the street to him.

'Yes, well done for getting us safely to Udaipur,' grins Jack.

I glance at Rocky, and as he meets my eye I somehow get the feeling that isn't what he was referring to, but no sooner has that thought zipped across my mind, than we're distracted by the sound of a brass band, the buzz of energy and excitement, and then, from around the corner, a wedding procession appears.

It's led by a drummer, and he's followed by a dozen or so musicians – tuba players, trombonists, drummers, all in band uniforms of red jackets and gold buttons; there are boys carrying candelabras connected to generators, and crowds of revellers swarming behind. The whole effect is dazzling and chaotic and completely exhilarating.

'Rocky was right, everyone is getting married,' I gasp, as we're separated from him by the procession and lose him in the crowd.

'Mrs Gupta said she knew of at least twelve weddings, right?' asks Jack.

'Uh-huh,' I nod, mesmerised by the flashing lights and brightly coloured saris that are streaming past like a school of tropical fish.

'So where do you reckon we should start?'

'I have no idea!' I yell, above the clash of cymbals and trumpets.

'Well in that case . . .' Without further hesitation, Jack grabs me by the hand and together we dive into the procession.

Engulfed by noise and surrounded by people smiling and cheering, there's no time to wonder what to do, or worry about my sister, or feel nervous about what's going to happen. All we can do is surrender ourselves to the moment and allow the night to take us where it will.

And, laughing with delight, we join everyone else in raising our arms in the air. Let the great big wedding extravaganza begin.

I once read that life should not be about the number of breaths you take, but the number of moments that take your breath away. If that's true, then this one night in Udaipur is filled with a million of those moments. Just the colours are enough to set your heart racing. People talk about an 'explosion of colour', but you've never really experienced the true meaning of that phrase unless you've been to India, and never more so than at a wedding.

Canary yellows, dazzling pinks, emerald greens . . . and those are just the saris. Add to them flaming red turbans, showers of golden marigolds, brightly decorated horses, camels and elephants, and a blaze of fireworks lighting up the dark sky overhead and it's like suddenly seeing life in high definition. Believe me, if colour was an Olympic sport, India would win the gold medal every time.

Mine and Jack's first wedding experience finishes when we spot the groom on a white horse. Resplendent in a long white silk jacket, elaborately jewelled turban, and carrying a sword, he looks like a fairy-tale prince on a white charger. But he looks nothing like Shine. So reluctantly we duck out of that wedding.

And straight into another.

This procession is even bigger and louder than the last. Led majestically by an elaborately adorned elephant, fire-breathers entertain whilst crowds dance to Bollywood tunes blasting out from giant speakers.

'Come on, let's dance,' whoops Jack, grabbing hold of me and twirling me around.

'I can't dance,' I protest self-consciously, laughing in embarrassment, but he just twirls me harder.

'Just look around you,' he yells, above the music. 'It doesn't matter!'

And as I spin around, I glance at all the people around me and see he's right. It doesn't matter, no one is watching; everyone is too busy flinging their arms in the air, bumping and gyrating, leaping and clapping. Inhibitions have gone out of the window, for some more than others, I muse, catching sight of one man who's rocking out with a sort of jive crossed with head-banging routine.

It's true what they say: weddings, wherever they are in the world, bring out some crazy dance moves. I've seen some bad dancing at weddings, and I mean *really* bad dancing, but the best part of it is no one cares; everyone's too busy enjoying themselves. Plus here, thankfully, there isn't a handbag in sight to dance around.

'Woo-hoo!'

Caught up in the throng of revellers, I find myself dancing with a bunch of other tourists, some Dutch girls and several Italian guys, who really know the meaning of letting their hair down, whilst Jack is commandeered by a larger-than-life lady and her friends, who chuckle loudly in delight. And then for a few moments I lose him in the crowd as a swell of people push past and, hearing a loud honking, have to stand to the side to try and let a cab that's found itself caught up in all of this mayhem drive through.

Just like we did when we first arrived in Delhi. My mind flashes back. It seems so long ago, I feel like a different person, I muse, glancing in through the car window as it inches past.

And get a surprise. It's Cindy! Sitting alone on the back seat, she looks terrified.

'Hey!' I say, rapping on the window, which is open just an inch.

She shrieks and frantically winds it up, looking even more petrified.

'Cindy!' I say again, only louder this time. 'It's me, Ruby!'

She glances sideways, a puzzled expression on her face. '*Ruby?*' she mouths from behind the safety of the glass. 'Is that really you?' She looks me up and down in disbelief.

'Yes, it's me,' I laugh, amused by her reaction. 'Where are you going?'

Gingerly she winds down the window, looking left and right as if someone might reach in and pull her out at any minute. 'I'm trying to get to the airport but this traffic is just insane! It's worse than on the 405!' Shaking her head, she cricks her neck out of the window and peers down the street. 'I wish all these people would just go home! What are they doing?'

'It's wedding season,' I explain.

'Whatever,' she gasps bad-temperedly, 'I feel like I'm in the goddam riots!'

'Where are your parents?' I ask, peering inside the car and seeing it's empty except for Cindy and one very stressed-out cab driver.

'In LA. Where I'm gonna be as soon as I can get out of here!' Lunging forwards in her seat, she jabs the cab driver in the shoulder. 'Can't you go any faster? I'm gonna miss my flight!'

Dutifully he rests his hand on the horn, but to absolutely no avail. They've completely ground to a halt.

'LA?' I look at her in confusion.

'I lied,' she says simply, turning back to me. 'It was all bullshit. They were never here, I came on my own.'

'You did?' I stare at her, agog. 'But why?'

'Bad relationship, bad break-up . . .' She rolls her eyes and chews hard on her gum.

'Oh, I'm sorry.' I suddenly feel myself softening towards

her. So even stunning Californian bikini models can get their hearts broken.

'Yeah, well, I needed to get away, but the last thing I needed was a pity party,' she says briskly, 'so I said I was with my parents.'

'But why India?'

She pulls a dog-eared copy of *Eat, Pray, Love* out of the Louis Vuitton handbag sitting next to her on the back seat. 'Though coming here was a big mistake. I should have gone to Bali instead and found myself a sexy Javier Bardem type – instead all I got was Jack.'

At the mention of his name I feel myself stiffen.

'Not that he was even interested,' she tuts and, pulling out a compact, starts powdering her nose.

My emotions, which have caused my chest to tighten so I can barely breathe, suddenly relax their vice-like grip. 'What do you mean, he wasn't interested?' I barely dare ask.

'I got the impression he was already spoken for,' she shrugs, snapping the compact shut. 'Not that he ever said anything, but it was pretty obvious he was in love with someone else.'

My heart skips a beat. *In love with someone else?*

She turns to me and snorts loudly. 'What? You didn't think anything happened between us, did you?'

'Er . . .' I snap to, feeling myself fluster. My face must say it all. Of course I thought something had happened. I thought they'd slept together! 'Well, I thought maybe . . . with you staying the night . . .'

'Oh gawd, no!' Cindy rolls her eyes. 'I totally crashed out that night. I haven't been drinking alcohol as I've been on this cleanse, and god-only-knows what they put in those drinks! Anyway, he was a total gentleman,' she adds, then tuts loudly, 'more's the pity.'

But my mind is racing. I barely dare think it, or hope it – and yet: could there be a chance that the person he's in love

with . . . I stop myself, teetering on the edge of the thought . . .
could it be me?

No, that's nuts. Of course it's not me! I tell myself sharply.
Except, my mind flashes back to the way he looked at me
earlier; the feeling I got as we lay next to each other in the
tent in the desert; the moment he wordlessly gave me his
jacket. Like a stone skimming across a pond, my mind skips
from one memory to the next. There was something there, I
didn't imagine it, I know I didn't— I cut myself off briskly.
Stop it, Ruby. You can't think like this. You'll only get hurt.

'Anyway . . .' Cindy looks ahead at the traffic and gasps
loudly. Her taxi hasn't moved an inch. 'Jesus, this place is the
pits!' she gasps then, turning to me, demands, 'Seriously, how
can you love this place?'

I look around me, at the people, the colours, the magic.

'How can you not?' I ask simply.

She stares at me, uncomprehending, then unexpectedly a
space opens up and her cab lurches forwards. 'Finally!' she
whoops. 'I'm outta here!' And throwing her arm out of the
window, she waves as she moves off through the crowds.

I wave back, my bracelets jangling, and as I watch the
brake lights of the car receding into the distance, I suddenly
can't help feeling sorry for Cindy. And to think I used to be
envious of her.

Funny how things turn around, isn't it?

I keep waving until she disappears, swallowed up by the
crowd, and for the first time in a long time I feel truly happy
to be me. For so long my bruised heart has been a constant
reminder of everything I've lost, everything I've wanted to
change, but here, now, amid all this chaos and festivity, I feel
a sense of peace. Of coming home. As if I've come out of a
long dark tunnel and into the shiny dazzling light, to find my
old self waiting for me.

'There you are!'

I twirl around to see Jack, out of breath from all that dancing. 'I thought I'd lost you!'

'Me too,' I smile.

'Huh?' He looks at me in confusion, but before he can ask any questions, I grab his hand.

'Come on, Amy's not here. We need to keep looking.'

A shower of fireworks explodes down by the water's edge, and with no time to lose we hurry into a side street and race down towards the lake.

35

As the evening unfolds, Jack and I find ourselves plunging from one wedding to another, each overlapping the next like a cleverly edited movie montage. I've heard Indian weddings can go on for days, but we only have this one night, and our quest to find Amy turns into a breathless, giddy adventure that leads us from processions to parties, feasts to fireworks, and more dancing then I've done in my whole life.

'Ruby!'

As we finally reach the lake we see a string of hotels and restaurants and a girl dressed in a glittering pink sari, who starts waving madly at us. 'You came!' she cries excitedly, rushing over.

Suddenly I realise it's Suhana. And this must be the Royal Shiva, I realise, just as I spot the sign of the five-star luxury hotel.

'Well, actually, we're looking for my sister—' I begin, but she grabs hold of both of our arms and starts dragging us through the arched entrance.

'Please, come inside, the ceremony is about to begin.'

'Ceremony?' Jack shoots me a rather panicked look.

'My cousin lives in Los Angeles. He's a movie producer and he's marrying an American actress, the wedding is going to be Hollywood meets Bollywood!' she chatters along excitedly. 'He won't mind you being there at all; he's really cool like that.' She laughs happily at the use of the word cool, and shoots a shy glance at Jack.

'That's great,' he smiles evenly, 'but you see, we really need to be someplace else—'

'Where?' she demands.

'Um . . .' He stalls and glances across at me for an answer, but all I can do is throw my hands palms-upwards. 'See, that part's a bit tricky . . .'

'So, you must come!' she instructs. 'My family will be honoured!'

Jack and I exchange looks. Neither of us wants to be rude. And it would be amazing to go to an actual ceremony. Plus, I don't know about Jack, but I have to confess, I'd really like to see who this American actress is.

Except . . .

'But we haven't found Amy,' I whisper anxiously.

'Yet,' he replies reassuringly.

His steady eyes meet mine and I flash him a small grateful smile. Then, turning back to Suhana, who's peering at us both impatiently, I nod in agreement. 'OK, cool,' I grin, copying her turn of phrase, much to her delight. 'Let's go!'

When it comes to wedding ceremonies, I've sung the hymns, thrown the confetti and bought the hat. In my mid-twenties I'd only done this once or twice, but by my late twenties I was beginning to spend nearly every other weekend in an Irish castle or a church in the country, and since turning thirty there's been what I can only call a stampede up the aisle by all of my friends from school or university.

However, not one of those weddings was anything like this one, I muse, as the bride and groom make their grand entrance on lavishly bejewelled elephants and are taken to a stunningly decorated tent that has been erected by the side of the lake and filled with brightly coloured flowers and decorations. Part Hindu, part Hollywood, it's a mix of tradition and glamour and a whole world away from the stuffy white weddings I've had to sit through. Here, they place garlands of rose petals and marigolds around each other's necks and various rituals and ceremonies are performed, including one that involves the bride and groom taking seven steps together around the holy fire.

'This is the *Saptapadi*,' whispers Suhana in explanation, as they begin circling the flames. 'These are the seven promises to each other . . .'

I watch in fascination as the groom leads the bride by her little finger, the priest reciting the vows and the groom repeating them in English for the benefit of his American bride and her family.

'With the first step, let us share our food together . . . With the second step, let us vow to be strong together . . .'

I never cry at weddings; I mean, they're lovely and all that, but I'm usually the practical one providing the tissues. But now, sitting here, at the side of the lake, witnessing these vows, I suddenly feel myself tearing up

'With the seventh step, let us vow to be friends with each other.'

Of all the steps, I think that's my favourite. It's all very well to be in love with the person you're marrying when everything's wonderful and exciting and you're wearing a fabulous dress. But to promise to remain friends with each other, years down the line, when sometimes you won't actually *like* your partner, let alone feel like you love them – well, that's something else. That's what true love is actually all about.

'Now it's official! They're married!' whispers Suhana excitedly, as her cousin places a beautiful necklace around his bride's neck and they daub sandalwood paste on each other's foreheads. 'Time to party!'

And boy, do they know how to party.

Ten minutes later we're at the wedding reception and it's in full swing. Strobe lights and fire-breathers, magicians and street performers, a world-famous DJ spinning disco tunes and Bollywood hits, and a feast of Indian dishes prepared by the best chefs and served with cocktails mixed by bartenders flown in from the trendiest bars in LA.

'Wow, this is amazing,' cries Jack, sipping on a rainbow-coloured cocktail that has real gold leaf in it, apparently.

'I know, it's incredible,' I reply, doing the same. Oh wow, these are delicious.

'So do you recognise the bride?' he asks, pointing over to where the pretty blonde, dressed in a stunning red sari embroidered with millions of tiny glittering sequins, is having her photograph taken.

'Wasn't she in that movie with Ryan Gosling?' I suggest.

'Was she?' Jack pulls a face. 'I'm hopeless with celebrities, I never know who anyone is.' He breaks off, his jaw suddenly dropping. 'Hang on, isn't that . . .?' He gestures over to an older man sitting by the corner of the dance floor. Surrounded by a bevvy of beauties, he's smoking a cigar and wearing his trademark dark glasses.

'Oh my god, *yes*!' I gasp excitedly, and then something I once read in one of those celebrity magazines suddenly rings a bell. 'Actually, I think he might be the father of the bride!'

'No way!' he gasps, all goggly-eyed, and then we both look at each other and burst into giddy conspiratorial laughter.

Actually, I'm beginning to feel quite tipsy. These cocktails are really quite strong. I turn to watch the action on the dance floor. As always at a wedding, it's a hive of activity.

'Come on, let's dance,' cries Jack, draining the last of his cocktail.

'Hang on, I haven't finished my drink,' I stall, waving my glass in front of me as a sort of protective shield. Making an idiot of myself by dancing on the street is one thing, but on the dance floor at a big fancy wedding in front of *A-list Hollywood celebrities* is quite something else, thank you very much.

The music is really beginning to pump now, as a catchy song starts blasting out of the speakers. Is it me, or is it getting louder?

And then suddenly, dozens of dancers burst on to the huge stage above the dance floor and start performing a carefully choreographed routine, like something out of a Bollywood movie.

'Oh wow!' I gasp in delight. 'How amazing!'

'I know, look at all the kids,' grins Jack, pointing to the cutest children you've ever seen, bopping away in the front row. 'I wonder how they learned how to dance like that?'

And then I see him in the front row.

Billy.

I let out a shriek of elation and, handing my drink to a bewildered Jack, charge onto the dance floor. 'Billy!' I cry, waving madly as I rush towards the stage. 'It's me, Ruby!'

Hearing his name, I see him glance over mid-dance-move. 'Beautiful!' he exclaims, flashing a smile bigger than Texas as he spots me in the crowd. Reaching down, he holds out his hand. 'Come dance with me!'

For a split second I pause: he's wanting to pull me on stage – to dance – in front of all these people. *Are you kidding?*

No, I'm not kidding. I'm throwing out my hand and grabbing his fingers, and now suddenly I'm up here on stage with everyone, and he's showing me how to dance and the crowd are going mad and cheering, and I can see Jack clapping and laughing, and I know I'm going to remember this moment for the rest of my life: Bollywood dancing at an Indian wedding and feeling so happy I could burst.

Life, sure as hell, is full of surprises.

The party looks set to run all night but finally we manage to tear ourselves away and continue our search around the old walled city. Around every corner there's a groom resplendent on a white horse, a marching band of tuba players, or a procession of revellers, until Udaipur blurs into one big, fat, Indian wedding.

But still no Amy.

'I give up,' I admit finally, a few hours later. It's after midnight and we're both exhausted. 'We're never going to find her.'

Jack opens his mouth to protest, then thinks better of it. 'You sure?'

'Yeah,' I nod. I feel a bizarre mix of disappointment and elation. Disappointed that I couldn't find Amy, and yet elated by my experiences of the night. Another burst of fireworks explodes overhead and I pause to watch them light up the night sky. 'It does seem a shame to miss this, though.'

'True, but I am pretty beat,' admits Jack.

'I've got blisters,' I confess, smiling ruefully.

Jack pulls an 'ouch' face. 'How about we go back to the guesthouse and watch the fireworks from the roof?' he suggests.

'You mean I can sit down and take my shoes off?'

Jack nods.

Oh god. *Heaven.* 'That's the best idea you've had all night,' I grin.

We set off walking through the maze of backstreets to the guesthouse and, climbing the stairs, finally make it up onto the roof. It's much quieter up here; slipping off my sandals, I relish the cool tiles beneath the soles of my feet. Above us the moon seems much closer, as if you could almost reach out and touch it with your fingertips and, as I turn towards the lake, the view takes my breath away. Wow. Now I know why they call Udaipur one of the most romantic places on earth. It's amazing, magical even. I gaze at the Lake Palace Hotel, floating like a fairy-tale castle on the water, whilst in the background fireworks light up the sky, raining down like sparkling raindrops.

Leaning against the parapets, I take a deep breath, breathing it all in. To be honest, the whole night feels like a bit of a fairy tale.

'Who's Sam?'

Jack's voice behind me snaps me out of my reverie. 'What?' I twirl around, taken aback at the mention of his name.

Jack is looking at me intently. 'You mentioned him when we first met, that time at the railway station when you were upset.'

Reminded of my meltdown, I feel my cheeks redden.

'He was my fiancé. He cheated on me. We broke up,' I say simply. Talking about him, I suddenly realise I haven't thought about him for ages; in fact the thought of him now feels almost like an intrusion.

Realisation floods Jack's face. 'Oh I see. It all makes sense now.'

'What does?' I frown.

'All that stuff about weddings, the Taj Mahal, romance . . .' His voice trails off but his gaze is still fixed on me.

'I stopped believing,' I shrug, 'it all seemed like crap. It never worked out, not for me, not for anyone I know . . .' I pause as I think back over the years, not just to Sam but to all the disastrous dates and failed relationships I've known people go through, all the disappointment and heartbreak, all the evenings spent drinking wine, consoling friends and being consoled. 'But then I came to India and, well . . .' I trail off and turn back to the lake, to the moonlight reflecting on the water. 'Everything changed.'

'Yeah, India can do that to you,' nods Jack quietly, following my gaze.

And then for a moment we're both silent, staring out across the water, listening to the distant sound of music and celebrations. High above the rest of the world, I feel as if we're in our own little bubble, as if somehow up here we've managed to make time stand still.

'What about you?' I ask. All this time I've been asking everyone I meet about their love life: Rocky, Vijay, Billy, Suhana . . . and yet the one person I've never asked about it is Jack. 'What's your story?'

There's a pause as I wait for him to speak, and I feel my chest tighten. I want to know but I'm almost too scared to hear his answer.

'It's kinda complicated,' he shrugs.

Three words. That's all I get? Three words?

I got the feeling he was already taken. Cindy's words ricochet around in my head and I feel my heart freeze. Oh god, please don't let him have a girlfriend.

Quickly I look away so he can't see the expression on my face.

'We met at a fundraiser in New York.'

Hearing his voice, I glance back at him, but he's gazing into the distance. 'She was working for a charity based here in India, we got serious pretty quickly.' He turns to me. 'We talked about me moving here – my company's multinational, they have offices all over the world . . . I promised I'd try to get a transfer and come back, but then my dad got sick . . .' He trails off, as if retreating into the past, then smiles ruefully. 'There's a reason they say long-distance never works.'

'So what happened?' I ask quietly.

'My dad died. We broke up.'

'I'm sorry.'

He shrugs. 'Like I said, life's complicated.'

There's a pause and, as we both look at each other, something passes between us. An electricity, an energy, an anticipation.

'Things happen that you don't expect,' he continues quietly. 'Like I never expected to fall in love with you.'

It's as if we're suspended in time. Everything seems to

hold its breath. The world stops spinning. *Did he say what I think he just said?*

'I'm sorry we didn't find your sister,' he adds softly.

'Me too,' I murmur, managing to find my voice, and as I meet Jack's gaze I see the uncertainty in his hazel eyes and realise he's just as nervous and scared as I am. And with every drop of courage inside me, I finally admit it, to him and myself, 'But I found something else. Love.'

Then, with fireworks bursting over my head and inside my heart, Jack wraps his arms around me and does something I've wanted him to do for a very, very long time.

He kisses me.

36

The room is in pitch darkness but for a streak of pale moonlight, which pokes through a tiny gap in the shutters. It catches the glint of sequins. Clothes strewn on the floor.

A naked couple lying curled up in bed together, sleeping.

Me and Jack.

Something stirs me awake and for a few moments I do nothing but relish the feeling of lying here, not moving, my head resting on his chest, his arm around me. Everything is quiet but for the sounds of our breathing and his heartbeat beneath my cheek. Cocooned in a warm fuzziness, I feel a sense of peace and blissful contentment.

And a flutter of excitement.

My mind flashes back to earlier: kissing on the rooftop, on the stairs, in the corridor . . . Being in the room, Jack undressing me, his fingers brushing against my skin, his hot breath against my cheek. The urgency . . . the desire . . . his nakedness . . . both of us falling into bed, his mouth on mine, skin against skin, our limbs tangled together . . .

As a delicious shiver runs up my spine, a vague noise in the background creeps into my consciousness. I ignore it, enjoying the sensations flooding my body, but it's distracting. I listen, wondering if it's coming from outside. It's almost like a faint burbling . . .

Suddenly I recognise the sound – it's my phone.

Oh my god, it might be Amy!

Quickly I slide out from underneath the covers, carefully

moving Jack's arm so as not to wake him. Where is it? I can
hear the muffled ringtone but the room's in darkness apart
from the one shaft of moonlight, and I can't see anything.
I try to open the shutters but the bolts are too stiff. It's no
good, I'll just have to turn on the light. I go to flick on the
bedside lamp, but it doesn't work. Neither does the switch on
the wall. Shit. The generator must be down.

I can hear my phone still ringing and feel a rising panic.
It's going to ring off!

Then suddenly I have an idea. Jack's torch! He used it in
the desert. I remember him putting it in the little daypack
he carries everywhere. It must be here somewhere . . . I start
feeling my way around the room, fumbling around the bed,
through our clothes strewn on the floor, then finally trip over
it at the entrance of the bathroom.

Ouch. He's always leaving stuff everywhere: trust him
to leave it there, I think affectionately, rubbing my toe,
then smile at myself. Honestly, I don't think Jack could do
anything right now that wouldn't make me think of him
affectionately.

My phone falls silent. Still, there's no need to panic, I try
to tell myself reasonably. Whoever it was will either leave a
message or I can call them back, if I can just find it . . .

Grabbing the rucksack, I start rummaging inside the pockets for the torch. No, nothing. Oh, hang on . . . My fingers
curl around something small and hard.

What's this? I pull it out.

In the pale shaft of moonlight I can see it's a jewellery box.
These must be the earrings he bought for his mum. Though
that's odd, I thought he'd already shipped them to her?

Curiously, I flick open the lid. Only it's not a pair of
earrings. Nestled in the soft velvet is a ruby, glowing softly in
the moonlight. *It's a ring.*

Suddenly my insides turn to ice.

Every girl knows there's only one reason a man would have a ring. I mean, men don't carry rings around with them for any casual reason. And they certainly don't secretly carry them around India in backpacks.

Unless . . .

Carefully I pluck the gold band out of the velvet and hold it between my fingers. The ruby sits up high, shouldered by two delicate baguette diamonds.

Unless it's an engagement ring.

My heart starts thudding loudly in my ears and all at once I feel claustrophobic, as if the walls are closing in on me. I try and force myself to calm down. I'm jumping to conclusions. There's got to be some kind of simple explanation.

But what would Jack be doing with an engagement ring?

In India. In wedding season.

Abruptly someone presses 'play' on the recording in my head: *She was working for a charity here in India . . . I promised I'd try to get a transfer and come back . . .*

For a moment I feel numb. Then, like a ten-tonne truck, it hits me, and suddenly everything seems to crash into place. Him acting strangely. Never telling me why he was here in India. Why he needed to get to Udaipur . . .

Like a ghoul, a phrase jumps out at me. *I'm here to keep a promise.*

Oh my god. *Oh my god.* He's here to propose to his girl-friend, that's the promise he's here to keep. My mind is racing, I can feel myself spiralling. Anger stabs, yet my heart is breaking. How could he do this to me? Sleep with me? Tell me he loved me? When all the time—

My mind jerks back to Sam. He cheated on me with Miriam, now Jack's cheated on his girlfriend with me . . . I thought Jack was different. I trusted him. I *believed* in him. I believed in love, and now . . .

My whole body has started to shake as if I'm in shock. I

am in shock. A moment ago I was asleep in his arms and now everything has been turned upside down and I'm trapped in some kind of nightmare. He said he was in love with me, I try to reassure myself frantically. *He said he'd never expected to fall in love with you*, another voice inside my head reminds me, *that life was complicated.*

A wave of panic rushes over me and I shove the ring back in the box, snapping the lid closed. I can't look at it any more. Maybe if I put it back where I found it, I can make it all go away, pretend it never happened. With trembling fingers I begin fumbling with the rucksack. Yet, even as I'm trying to persuade myself, I know it's impossible. I know it even before the backpack slips from my fingers, scattering chewing gum, pens, a few coins, *a strip of photographs* . . .

It's one of those taken in a photo booth. The black-and-white pictures have been torn in half, leaving two small pictures of a couple smiling and laughing, their arms wrapped around each other. A beautiful young Indian woman and a man with longish hair.

I squint at it in the moonlight.

The breath catches in the back of my throat.

It's Jack. Jack when he was younger.

The room tilts on its axis and the floor gives way beneath me. Clamping my hands to my mouth, I feel like I'm going to be sick.

Suddenly, the sharp beeping sound of a text message pierces my consciousness, interrupting my spiralling thoughts, and I snap to. *My phone, I'd completely forgotten* . . . Dazed, I look around me and see a small flashing light, illuminated on the shelf. Pulling everything I've got together, I reach up and grab it.

Two missed calls from Amy and a text: I have one new voicemail. She must have left a message.

I hit call. It seems to take forever to connect. Muddled

thoughts are spinning around in my head. A few moments ago everything was perfect, and now . . .

I hear her voice.

'Rubes? Are you there? It's me, Amy.' There's a pause and I hear her voice breaking. 'I don't know what to do, it's all gone horribly wrong . . .' and with that, she suddenly bursts into tears.

37

I lean my cheek against the window of the bus as it rattles along the dusty roads. It's early. The sun has just risen, tinting everything in a weak sepia glow and, as we pass through towns and villages, I gaze absently through the glass. Looking, but not seeing. My mind spools backwards with every turn of the wheels, back to that hotel room in Udaipur, back to a few hours ago . . .

I'd dressed quickly, pulling on some of my ruined clothes without caring, and filling a bag with a few things, and quietly opened the door. It was as if my mind had gone into laser focus: *I had to get out of there. I had to go. Now.* But at the doorway I'd paused and, for the briefest of moments, let my eyes rest upon Jack's sleeping figure, at the space where only a few moments ago I'd been lying, the imprint of my body still on the sheets, before firmly closing the door behind me and slipping away into the night.

A passing cab had taken me to the local bus station. Once there I'd called Amy back. She'd answered immediately and, on hearing my voice, promptly burst into tears again. It turns out she hadn't got any of my messages until now. Partly because the mobile phone service can be so hopeless here, but mostly because the battery on her phone had died soon after our argument and she'd left it out of avoidance and laziness, until she'd finally charged it and made the shock discovery that I hadn't flown back to London, as she'd assumed, but was still in India looking for her. Furthermore, that I was here in Rajasthan.

'I'm so sorry, Rubes,' she'd sobbed down the phone, 'I had no idea you were looking for me,' but I'd quickly shushed her.

There was no need for apologies, justifications or explanations. None of that was important right now.

'Just as long as you're OK,' I'd told her firmly, 'that's all that matters.'

There was so much to say, on both our parts, but all of it could wait.

She was in Jodhpur, a few hundred kilometres away; as luck would have it, there'd been a bus leaving shortly that would get me there by noon. When I told her, I've never heard her sound so relieved.

'What would I do without you?' she'd said gratefully.

'I dread to think,' I'd replied, as I always did.

But what I didn't tell her, and what she couldn't know, is that I needed her as much as she needed me. If the truth be told, probably even more so.

This time Amy isn't late to meet me. As I pull into the bus station, she's already here, anxiously waiting, and I've barely disembarked before we're giving each other the biggest hug. It's so good to see her. It's been less than a week since we were together in Goa, yet it's felt like forever. So much has happened, to both of us. But there's an invisible bond between sisters that's unbreakable, and now, back together again, time does that thing of simply melting away, and it's as though we were never apart.

'Hang on, where's your suitcase?' she asks, as we finally break apart.

'It's a long story,' I reply, looking her up and down and feeling relieved that, apart from the puffy eyes, she doesn't seem any the worse for wear. 'More importantly, what's happened? Where's Shine?' Earlier on the phone she'd been so upset I hadn't wanted to press her, but now I was full of questions.

As usual my sister is full of surprises. 'He's back at the house,' she answers, her face clouding over.

'House?' I repeat in astonishment. 'What *house*?' Listening to her voicemail, I'd assumed they must have broken up. 'Amy, what's going on? I don't understand. You said on the phone it's all gone wrong—'

'We didn't get married,' she blurts, her eyes reddening. 'We couldn't . . .' She breaks off and I can see she's fighting back tears.

After all this time, I thought I'd be relieved, but all I feel is concern. 'Why? What happened?

'I discovered something terrible!'

Oh god, it must be because of the other woman. Amy must have found out. *That's* what must have happened. I suddenly feel fiercely protective.

'Hey, come on, it'll be all right,' I say, giving her arm a squeeze. 'You don't have to talk about it now, you can tell me all about it later, over a nice cup of chai.'

She gives me a small, grateful smile, then seems to pause, as if just noticing something. 'Ruby, why are you wearing pink clothes and a jewelled bindi?'

'Huh?' Quickly snatching my hand to my forehead, I feel my fingertips brush against it. 'I must have forgotten to take it off,' I murmur, my mind flashing back to last night's weddings, to Jack, to the ring—

It's like a door blasting open on an aeroplane. My stomach lurches as I start freefalling through my emotions: pain . . . disbelief . . . *betrayal* . . . Another man has lied and cheated on me . . . With sheer brute force, I slam it closed again. I don't want to go there. I *can't* go there.

Looking up, I meet Amy's gaze. She's staring at me. 'Looks like we've both got a lot to talk about,' she says quietly and, looping her arm through mine, leads me to the waiting taxi.

Set in the middle of the desert, Jodhpur has a timelessness that makes you feel as if nothing has changed here for hundreds of years. A magnificent fort cut out of the rock dominates the old walled city below, which is made up of a maze of winding back streets filled with textile shops, bazaars, and the indigo-painted houses that give Jodhpur its alternative name of the Blue City.

Driving through the ancient walls, we twist and turn along narrow streets, zigzagging back and forth, until the taxi pulls up outside a magnificient old *haveli*.

'Hang on, this is *the house*?' I ask, in bewilderment. I stare at it, feeling stunned.

'Yes, it belongs to Shine's uncle,' nods Amy, seemingly unfazed. 'Nice, isn't it?'

'Nice?' I gasp, staring at it, feeling slightly dumbfounded. And I haven't even *started* on the uncle bit.

As Amy pays the taxi driver, I climb out to get a better look, shielding my eyes from the strong midday sun. If I had questions for Amy before, now I've got even more. I stare at the imposing stone archway and huge studded doors that look like something you'd see on a castle, whilst thinking of our own uncle and his pebble-dashed bungalow. To say our family and Shine's come from two different worlds is something of an understatement. Now I think I know how Kate Middleton must have felt, meeting the in-laws.

Or nearly-in-laws, I remind myself, feeling thankful Amy didn't go through with the wedding. Followed by a flash of fury towards Shine. I don't exactly know what's been going on, but I'm more than ready to give him a piece of my mind. How dare he treat my little sister like this? Leading her on, getting her to elope, when all the time . . .

Indignation bursts inside me. I'm usually a pretty calm person, but seeing my sister so upset makes me furious. I'll show him! He might have been able to pull the wool over Amy's eyes with his sexy yoga teacher act, but now it's me he's dealing with!

Feeling fiercely protective, I turn towards Amy, who's waiting for me by the archway. Together we walk through and into the courtyard. It's stunningly beautiful, opening out into a large paved area with a fountain in the middle and a kind of terraced veranda filled with potted ferns, large velvet sofas, and walls hung with old sepia photographs of maharajas.

'There's Shine,' nods Amy, towards the fountain.

I glance across and at first I almost don't recognise him. He looks completely different. Gone are the white robes and bare feet; instead he's wearing jeans, a smart blue shirt and what look like a pair of polished brogues. Hearing our footsteps, he turns and I'm bracing myself for our greeting, when we're interrupted by the rumble of car tyres behind us and have to step to the side as a car sweeps past us. And not just any car, but one of those really expensive Mercedes.

Somewhere, deep inside me, an alarm bell starts ringing.

One of those really expensive Mercedes.

Hang on. Surely it can't be the same . . .

No sooner has that thought fired across my brain than the dark-tinted windows buzz down and the dark-grey door opens. One long, stiletto-clad leg appears, followed by another, and a woman emerges. Swishing back her curtain of glossy dark hair, I catch a glimpse of her face. She's wearing big black sunglasses, but there's no mistaking her. It's the same woman I saw Shine with in Goa!

'Oh my God, Amy,' I hiss, grabbing onto her sleeve and trying frantically to pull her back.

'Rubes?' Glancing at me, she looks taken aback at my panicked expression. 'What's wrong?'

'That's her!' I gasp, my mind racing in disbelief.

Fuck! What is she doing here? And what's going to happen when she sees Amy? I suddenly feel a beat of fear.

Well, one thing's for certain, I'm not going to stand around to find out.

'Who?' asks Amy, frowning impatiently. 'What are you going on about?'

'Quick, before she sees us!' I watch Shine walk over to greet her and feel a beat of indignation. Oh my god, he's so brazen!

'Rubes!' Amy sounds really quite cross now. 'What are you doing?'

'I'll explain later,' I hiss, trying to drag her in the other direction, but she's not budging.

'Ouch!' she yelps, 'you're hurting me.'

'Sssshh!' I hiss.

But it's too late. The woman's seen us. She's coming over. Oh, fuck!

'Amy, get back,' I instruct, stepping in front of her to act like a sort of human shield, but she sidesteps out from behind me with a loud tut.

'*Rubes!* Have you gone stark, staring mad?'

'No, you don't understand . . .' I break off as the woman bears down upon us.

'Amy, there you are!' Pushing her sunglasses onto the top of her head, she leans towards her and kisses her politely on both cheeks.

I stare in disbelief.

'And who is this?' she asks, turning towards me with a courteous smile.

'My sister, Ruby,' replies Amy, quickly introducing me. 'And Ruby, this is Aisha, Shine's sister.'

His sister?

'I wish he wouldn't use that silly nickname,' Aisha says, holding out her hand to shake mine. 'Hello, it's very nice to meet you. I've heard a lot about you.'

I don't react. I can't. I'm still trying to take it all in.

'Ruby, what's wrong?' Amy peers at me with a worried expression.

'I saw you with Shine . . . you were in a back street in Goa . . . I assumed . . .' I trail off. It's as if my mind has been lagging behind and has now only just caught up with this sudden turn in events.

Amy's face suddenly registers that the penny's dropped. 'Oh no, you didn't think . . .'

But she doesn't even have to finish. I blush beetroot. I suddenly feel very foolish.

'Well, how was I to know?' I protest weakly. 'I saw them together' – my mind flashes backwards – 'and they were arguing.'

'This is true,' nods Shine's sister, seemingly unfazed. 'I was holidaying in Goa, I had come to visit my baby brother, but when he confessed to me that he was in love with your sister and wanted to marry her, I was very much against it.'

As the nuggets of information are starting to drop into place like jigsaw pieces, Shine reappears, walking towards us. 'I'm sorry, I was just helping the driver park the car . . .' he begins apologetically then, seeing me, he hesitates slightly and bows his head. 'Hello Ruby,' he says politely.

'Hello Shine,' I nod, somewhat stiffly. OK, so I might have jumped to conclusions, but he still eloped with my sister. Plus, that still doesn't explain why he lied to me. 'Why didn't you tell me the truth?' I blurt, looking to him for an explanation. 'Why did you lie to me?'

Shine's handsome face puckers. 'I'm sorry, I don't understand.'

'That day I saw you in Goa, when I was lost in the back streets, you told me you weren't with anyone, that you were by yourself.'

As I enlighten him, his face floods with the memory. 'I didn't want you to tell Amy,' he says, after a moment's pause.

'I didn't want Amy knowing my sister was in town. If she knew, then she would have wanted to meet her, and that would have been impossible . . .' He trails off. 'It would have created many problems.'

'So you just ran away?' I reproach.

Well, I'm sorry, I can't help it. I've been worried sick.

'My brother has always been headstrong, even as a baby,' interrupts Aisha. 'I should have realised he would not listen. When I discovered he had run away to be married, I was very angry and upset.'

'Yes, me too,' I nod, remembering my phone call with Amy at the airport.

'I say to myself, he cannot go against years of tradition, he cannot marry some stranger he hardly knows, this is crazy!' she continues vehemently.

'Yes I know, it's crazy,' I agree, and yet deep down inside of me I unexpectedly feel a niggle of doubt.

'I knew I had to find him and stop him. I didn't want him to make a big mistake, something that he would regret for the rest of his life . . .'

I recognise those words – those are the same ones I'd used, I reflect, glancing across at Shine and Amy. They've moved closer together and his arm is wrapped protectively around her waist, whilst she's holding onto his hand. Except, seeing them now, somehow it's hard to imagine either of them as a mistake.

'The man who owns the retreat couldn't tell me anything,' she tuts, shaking her head and I have a vision of poor Biju, terrified into silence. 'I called friends, visited relatives, until finally, after travelling the whole length of the country looking for him, I find him here at our uncle's house,' she finishes, throwing her hands onto her hips and glaring at him.

I flinch slightly. Aisha's actually pretty scary.

'Our parents will be turning in their graves!'

'*Aisha*,' says Shine sternly, throwing her a look, before turning to me, his expression solemn. 'Please don't be angry with your sister, it was all my idea,' he says earnestly. 'I take all responsibility.'

I feel myself soften. 'Don't worry, I can never stay angry at her for long,' I smile ruefully. 'That said, I don't believe for a minute it was all your idea.' I glance across at Amy and she shifts uncomfortably. 'Her nickname at primary school wasn't Little Miss Trouble for nothing.'

She blanches. 'That was a bit unfair,' she protests indignantly.

'Tell that to the little boy you buried in the sandpit, or the girl whose hair you painted. *Literally*.'

Everyone smiles and I feel the atmosphere lightening.

'I'm just relieved you're OK,' I confess, 'I was really worried. Especially when I met someone who had a photo of you both on an elephant in Jaipur.' My mind flicks back to Cindy. 'She said you were upset—'

'Oh my god, not that crazy American girl!' gasps Amy incredulously.

'She wasn't *that* crazy,' I correct, feeling strangely protective.

'She was crazy,' repeats Amy, 'and an outrageous flirt. She was all over Shine like a rash!'

Having witnessed Cindy's flirting techniques first-hand, I don't doubt it, but still . . . 'She said you'd had a fight with your boyfriend,' I persist.

Amy's cheeks pinken. 'OK, so I admit, I got a bit jealous.'

'Now you're the one being crazy,' smiles Shine.

'And she told you he wasn't worth it.'

'Like I said, she was completely crazy,' nods Amy.

'But . . .' My mind is scrambling; as so often recently, it seems to have been another misunderstanding. 'But I've been really worried,' I gasp, finally.

'I told you not to worry,' objects Amy, but Shine shushes her.

'Big sisters always worry,' he says, putting his arm around her.

'It's true,' nods Aisha. 'I have spent my whole life looking after my little brother, making sure he doesn't get into trouble.'

'Me too,' I nod sympathetically, and a look passes between us.

'It is all my fault,' continues Shine, his expression falling serious. 'My love made me rash, impatient and thoughtless. And I love your sister forever, Ruby. I love her more than anything in the world.'

I look at them together. Whereas before I didn't believe it, now I don't doubt it.

Except . . .

'But then, I don't understand . . .' I begin, my mind turning. Because now everything has been explained, I'm more confused than ever. 'Why did Amy ring me, really upset? She said it had all gone horribly wrong.'

At once, both their faces cloud over.

'Well, seeing as you were both trying to stop us, you'll both be pleased to hear we can't get married,' says Amy, looking upset. 'It's bad luck. If we do, something terrible will happen.'

I stare at her in bewilderment. Like I said, my sister is full of surprises. 'What do you mean, something terrible will happen?'

'We were supposed to get married last night in Udaipur,' explains Shine. 'We had everything arranged, and then we had our charts read—'

'It was my idea,' interrupts Amy. 'When I found out it was traditional to consult with an astrologist before you get married, I thought it would be fun – you know me and my horoscopes . . .'

'I was against it from the beginning,' says Shine, shaking his head. 'This match-making of horoscopes is outdated nonsense. I should never have agreed. But Amy wanted to do it and I stupidly thought: where is the harm?'

'. . . and it turns out I'm a Manglik!'

I look at her blankly. 'A *what?*'

'It's to do with the position of Mars in your chart. It's called Mangal Dosha, and it will bring terrible luck to the marriage.' Her eyes well up and Shine holds her closer.

'Oh come on, you can't believe that superstitious nonsense,' I scoff, but even as I'm saying it, I'm remembering how my sister wouldn't let me put the umbrella up in my room in Goa.

'I told her not to worry,' reassures Shine, 'that he was a silly old man and we would be fine, but she wouldn't listen—'

'Vedic astrology is very important in our culture,' interrupts Aisha, reproving her brother. 'For a woman, to be a Manglik is very dangerous. Amy is right not to ignore this.'

'Hush, sister!' retorts Shine, crossly. 'You are scaring Amy. Plus there has never been any scientific evidence to support such claims. It's just superstition.'

'Maybe, but many believe it can bring troubles to a marriage. Some say it can lead to separation and divorce, or even worse.'

Hearing all this, I suddenly realise this is serious. This isn't just some silly superstition. My mind flashes back to the night in the desert, listening to Mohan talking about mysticism and the heavens. Whether you believe it or not, for Amy and Shine this is a real problem.

'Shine could even die,' whispers Amy, hugging him tighter.

Looking at her scared expression, I feel my mind working overtime. Up until this point I've been doing everything to stop this wedding, but now, seeing how much in love she and Shine are, I want to do everything to make it happen.

'We must help them,' I say to Aisha, firmly.

'What?' She looks at me, shocked.

'There must be a way to fix this, surely?'

'I cannot say. You would need to consult with a priest or an astrologer,' she says unhelpfully, and I get the distinct impression that even if she does know something, she isn't going to tell me. She doesn't want to help try and fix this; after all, she likes the fact that something is preventing her brother marrying my sister.

'What did the astrologer say?' I look at Shine, but he shakes his head.

'He wasn't a good astrologer. He didn't try to help us, only scare us.' He wraps his arm tighter around my sister. 'Amy was so upset we left Udaipur immediately. I didn't know where to go, so I brought her here to my uncle's house. It was here we met with Aisha—'

'But I don't understand,' interrupts Amy, frowning. 'I thought you'd be pleased we can't get married.'

'I was wrong,' I say simply.

'Wrong?' she echoes, in disbelief.

I can't help but smile ruefully. 'I know, it's hard for a big sister to admit to her little sister that she was wrong, but you were right . . .' I break off and think about Sam, about Jack and about everything that's happened. 'I thought happy-ever-afters were for fairy tales, that believing in love was a mistake, that you'd only get your heart broken, like I did, and I wanted to stop that from happening. I wanted to protect you. But then something happened . . .' I break off, thinking of this journey I've been on, of all the people and places I've seen, of all I've experienced and learned.

'What happened?' prompts Amy quietly.

'India,' I reply, and as I say it out loud for the first time, I realise it's true. 'I closed my heart to love but India forced it wide open again.'

My gaze flicks across the faces of Aisha, Shine and Amy, all listening to me intently; but instead of feeling self-conscious, I feel emboldened.

'Yes, it doesn't always work out, but you guys had the courage to go for it. To take the risk. Because in love there are no guarantees. There is no insurance that we won't get our hearts broken.' My mind flashes back to the hotel room in Udaipur, and I feel a sickening twist in my heart as I think about Jack. 'But we must never give up on love,' I say, quietly but firmly.

As I finish speaking, my eyes meet Amy's.

'Thank you,' she says quietly.

'What? For being a pain-in-the-ass big sister?' I smile and, grabbing my bag, I turn to leave.

'Where are you going?'

'I'm not sure yet, but I'll be back in a couple of hours.' And, feeling a wave of determination, I leave them staring after me and stride purposely across the courtyard and out into the city.

38

Saying that, I haven't a clue what I'm doing.

Plunged into the bustling maze of streets, I pause for a moment on a corner to try and gather my thoughts. Doubts start to mushroom. Actually, maybe I've been a bit impulsive. I mean, it's all very well wanting to save the day – big sister to the rescue and all that – but the truth of the matter is I don't know the first thing about astrology, Vedic or otherwise. Or having your charts read. Or horoscopes.

Other than that my star sign is Taurus and I always seem to be 'due for a surprise' near the date of my birthday, it's all a complete mystery to me.

A bit like love.

As the thought strikes, I feel a renewed hope. Because I suddenly realise it doesn't matter that I'm not an expert in astrology. What matters is love. The love between Amy and Shine. That's what fascinates me and drives me; that's what's important. Like I said, I'm a bit of a love detective because I'm always looking for answers. And there has to be an answer to the question of how Amy and Shine can be together, I think determinedly. There just *has* to be a way to solve this mystery.

First, however, I need a coffee.

Setting off in no particular direction, I head down one of the busy streets towards a large clock tower. I barely slept last night and it's all starting to catch up with me. I feel exhausted, both physically and emotionally. My mind trails off. Alone, memories of last night are starting to resurface and I have to force thoughts of Jack to the back of my mind. It's over, I remind myself sharply. It was over before it even began. I'm never going to see him, or think about him, ever again. I can't. *I won't.*

Across the street I spot a small, hand-painted sign advertising 'Real Espresso', hanging outside a small doorway. It's not Starbucks, but it'll do. Dodging the stream of rickshaws and mopeds, I make it to the other side and enter up a narrow staircase that opens out at the top into a small café. It's obviously a backpacker favourite, as there are quite a few lounging around inside and out on the wooden veranda, clutching their dog-eared guidebooks and drinking coffee, whilst in the corner is the requisite computer on which to check Facebook.

'Hi, I'd like a cappuccino please,' I say to the girl working behind the counter.

'Anything to eat?' she asks, passing me a menu.

I cast a dutiful eye over it, but I've no appetite. I haven't eaten for hours, but just the thought of food makes my stomach churn. 'No thanks, just the coffee.'

'OK, please take a seat, I'll bring it over,' she smiles.

There's a small rattan sofa near the window, and it's empty. I sit down gratefully and glance abstractedly around at the other tourists, at a couple sitting together in the corner, chatting and smiling, affectionate, *happy*. I watch them, feeling oddly detached. It's hard to imagine that I was so happy just a few hours ago. It's strange, but I don't even feel upset or angry any more, I'm just numb. Everything feels unreal. Like none of it really happened.

A stash of well-worn magazines is lying on the table and I pick one up and start flicking through. It's like an Indian version of *Grazia*, filled with lots of photographs of celebrities, most of whom I don't recognise. I glance absently at the pictures, whilst my mind focuses back on Amy. I don't have any bright ideas yet – to be honest I'm still trying to digest this whole new turn of events. Until a few moments ago I'd never even *heard* of Mangal Dosha or being a Manglik, and I still don't fully understand it. However, it does sound pretty scary, almost like some kind of curse.

In which case, there must be a way to lift it. I mean, maybe there's some kind of spell, or magic potion . . .

Er hello, Earth calling Ruby. What on earth are you talking about? *Spells and magic potions?* What is this, *Harry Potter?*

Feeling suddenly ridiculous, I glance around at the other customers and say a silent thank you that no one can actually read my mind. I've often thought that before, when I start daydreaming about all kinds of strange things whilst I'm sitting on the bus or the Tube, but this time people would think I really was completely gaga.

I try to focus back on my magazine, so at least I *look* normal, but I keep wracking my brains. There must be something we can do; there must be something—

I stop dead. I've been turning the pages on autopilot but now suddenly my eyes home in on the photograph of a stunningly beautiful Indian woman. Underneath the picture is a caption, out of which jumps a word. '*Manglik.*'

What the . . . ?

'I'm sorry for the wait.'

I'm interrupted by the waitress bringing me my cappuccino.

'Oh, no worries, thank you,' I fluster, looking up from the article, then add quickly, 'Excuse me, do you know who this is?'

The girl takes one glance at the photograph and laughs. 'Why, of course, she's a huge Bollywood star,' she nods. 'She married another very big Bollywood heartthrob.'

'She's married?' I gasp.

'Yes, the wedding was very famous here in India.' She breaks off and points to the magazine in my hands, 'That's a photograph from her wedding a couple of years ago. Look, see, there's her husband.'

I glance back at the photographs, skimming the article furiously to try and glean any information, but it's mostly about her film and charity work – though, hang on, it does mention that she got rid of this Mangal Dosha before her celebrated marriage. See! I knew there must a way to fix this.

I pause, furiously scanning the article for more information, only there isn't any.

But how? How did she do that? It doesn't say!

I feel a stab of frustration. Damn, how can I find out about this? Maybe there's some expert I can talk to, or an ancient book on astrology I can read, or a specialist I can find . . .

I catch sight of the computer sitting in the corner and have a brainwave. Of course! Why didn't I think of it before?

Google.

'Is there anything else you would like?'

I turn back to the waitress. 'Yes,' I nod, smiling. 'Is the computer free? I'd like to get on the Internet.'

Five minutes and a hundred rupees later, I'm sitting on a stool waiting for Internet Explorer to load. As the screen opens up, I quickly type in the actress's name, followed by 'Mangal Dosha, wedding, Manglik'. As I hit search, tons of stuff comes up. There are 973,000 entries for Manglik alone. I click on link after link, typing in various combinations, following different leads. Being a love detective isn't just about being good at Google, but it sure as hell helps.

From one website about the actress I glean that: '*Mangal Dosha was removed by performing Kumbh Vivah before the ceremony . . .*'

Kumbh Vivah? I feel a rustle of curiosity. Hang on, what's that? And so on I Google.

Quite frankly, it's absolutely fascinating, and for the next hour or so I'm completely absorbed. Before, I've always been slightly contemptuous of astrology. I mean, how can some middle-aged man with a bad taste in jumpers and a daily column in a newspaper tell me what's going to happen to me by reading my stars? But now I realise there's far more to astrology than just daily horoscopes.

As I follow the rabbit warren of links from one website to the next, I read about all the different belief systems and astronomical phenomena, about searching for meaning in this giant cosmos, and how just because science can't explain something, it doesn't mean it's not real.

Which I guess makes astrology a lot like love, I muse, reading on to the bit about Mangliks and Mangal Dosha. Aisha was telling the truth when she said it's viewed by many as a pretty big problem, but that doesn't mean it has to be insurmountable. I don't know about the astrologer being a silly old man, like Shine said, but he was obviously rubbish or lazy, maybe even both. Even worse, he scared Shine and Amy and made them believe all was lost. I click onto a new page and a smile bursts out across my face – and that's not true, look! There's a way to fix it!

All you need to do is first perform a ceremony called a Kumbh Vivah, in which the Manglik woman 'marries' a banana tree or a clay pot, which can then be broken before she ties the knot with her husband. By breaking the clay pot after this 'wedding', the bride effectively becomes a widow and the problem has been done away with. She is now free to marry her groom, and live happily ever after . . .

I feel a burst of happy relief. I should have known. One of the things that I've grown to love about India is that it doesn't matter what the problem is, whether it's spiritual, mystical, or astrological, there's always a practical solution for everything. No job is too big or too small. Everything can be fixed. Whether it's my sandals, or my sister's happy-ever-after.

Asking the waitress for a piece of paper and a pencil, I turn back to the computer screen. OK, here goes.

Things you will need.

Grabbing the pencil, I start writing a list . . .

An hour later I'm back at the 'house'. Amy rushes out to greet me.

'Rubes, where have you been?' she exclaims. 'I've been worried!'

I have to stifle a smile. 'I thought that was my job?' I say, giving her a hug.

She tuts loudly. 'OK, OK, point taken,' she pouts. 'So, where have you been?'

'Shopping,' I reply.

'Shopping?' She looks at me in surprise. 'That's why you rushed off so suddenly? To go *shopping?*'

'Uh-huh,' I nod, looking towards the entrance where a teenage boy has appeared with a wheelbarrow.

'Well, what did you buy?' she frowns, looking at my empty hands.

'Thanks very much,' I say, turning to the boy and passing him a tip as he unloads my purchase. 'It's like I said, never give up on love,' and at Amy's look of confusion, I throw out my arms and gesture to the large clay urn now resting on the floor courtyard. 'All you need is a clay pot . . .'

It's all arranged. A few hours later, I've showered and borrowed some of my sister's clothes. Well, it's not like she'll be needing them. I glance across at her. Amy looks beautiful in a stunning red wedding sari carefully hand-embroidered with golden silk, whilst Shine couldn't look more handsome, in a long silk brocade jacket that belonged to his father, and an ivory turban.

Only it's not him she's marrying. Not just yet, anyway . . .

As the priest who is going to perform the ritual takes his

position, Amy shoots me a nervous look and I give her the thumbs-up. Just like I used to do when I would watch her perform in school plays, only this is slightly different. My little sister's getting married!

I suddenly feel absurdly nervous. I think about Mum and Dad and how they're going to react when they find out. I did think about at least calling them up and telling them. But then I decided that, for once in my life, I'm going to leave that decision to Amy. It's hard not to treat her like my baby sister, but that's one lesson I've learned in all of this – I don't always know what's best. I've jumped to the wrong conclusions, made the wrong decisions, and there's actually a lot I can learn from my little sister, not just the other way around.

She's right, I reflect, looking across at her; she's all grown up now. Wiping away a tear, I watch with Aisha as the priest performs the ritual Kumbh Vivah. It's a short ceremony, and afterwards the clay pot is ceremoniously broken. I break into applause, much to the disapproval of Aisha, but I can't help it. Shine and Amy look so happy. Now they're free to marry!

Except . . .

'We've decided to wait,' announces Shine, holding Amy's hand tightly.

'What?' say both Aisha and I in stereo, looking at the happy couple in disbelief.

'You were both right,' continues Amy, 'what's the hurry? We've got the rest of our lives together, plus we want to get married properly, with our families.'

I stare at Amy. Like I said, she's certainly full of surprises. 'I'm glad,' I say, once I've got over the shock. 'I know Mum and Dad will want to be there. Any excuse for a new hat, you know Mum.'

'So will our uncle,' smiles Aisha, looking pleased. 'He is away on business and would have been very disappointed to miss his beloved nephew's wedding. It is he who has looked after us since our parents died when we were young,' she explains, turning to me. 'He paid for our education, for my brother to go to Cambridge, for everything.'

'You went to Cambridge?' I turn to Shine.

'Yes, I studied law,' he replies evenly.

'You're a lawyer?' When it comes to surprises, it seems he and Amy have more in common than I thought. Suddenly the earlier outfit of shiny brogues and Ralph Lauren shirt makes more sense.

'I only practised for a few years, it wasn't for me,' he replies, smiling at my reaction.

I feel myself blushing with embarrassment. And there was me thinking he was just a hippy-dippy yoga teacher.

'So do you guys have any more surprises?' I ask good-humouredly.

'Only that his uncle's a maharaja,' whispers Amy wide-eyed, sneaking a peek at Shine, who rolls his eyes in amusement.

'You're not serious?' I look back and forth at Aisha and Shine in disbelief. '*Your uncle is a maharajah?*'

I can't even begin to think what Mum's going to say. It's going to be round the local village faster than you can say, 'My daughter's marrying into royalty.'

Actually, hang on . . .

'Does that mean you're a prince?' I blurt out, and then immediately blush, feeling very uncool.

'I'm afraid not; I'm not his son,' smiles Shine.

'Though he might as well be, he treats him like one,' remarks Aisha, clicking her tongue. 'Our uncle never had a son and so he indulges my little brother terribly!'

Listening to everyone, I can't help breaking into the biggest smile.

'What?' asks Amy, looking at me. 'What is it?'

'Well, I guess this makes Shine your very own Prince Charming,' I remark and, despite everything that's happened, I feel the hopeless romantic rising up inside me once again. 'Who said fairy tales don't happen in real life?'

39

'OK, is that everything?' asks Shine, as he puts the last of the bags in the taxi.

'No,' smiles Amy ruefully.

Shutting the boot, he wraps his arms around her and gives her a kiss. 'I'll be with you in a few weeks, my darling, don't worry.'

It's the next morning and Amy and I are leaving to fly back to London. I couldn't leave it any longer because my emergency travel document is about to run out. Plus anyhow, Mrs Flannegan will be reporting me as a missing person if I'm not careful, and I have a book to write, and things to do and . . . well, every journey has to come to an end, doesn't it? It's time for me to go home.

Despite Amy's reluctance to leave Shine, she's happy to be heading back with me. 'Thanks to you, everything's sorted now,' she'd declared. Shine is due to fly out in a couple of weeks to meet Mum and Dad and officially ask for her hand in marriage. In the meantime she's eager to start her new job. 'The plan is for Shine to teach yoga in London for a few years, just until I finish my research fellowship, and then who knows where we'll live?' she'd explained excitedly.

'Bye . . . see you soon . . . it's been wonderful to meet you!' Saying my goodbyes to Shine and Aisha, I climb into the back seat of the taxi, followed by Amy. Then, before you know it, the driver is starting the engine and we're rumbling out of the courtyard, windows down, waving.

Having both missed our earlier flights, we needed to buy new tickets, but fortunately Shine had about a million air miles from all his trips back and forth when he was at Cambridge. We're flying from Delhi straight to London, so we're getting a connecting flight first, only there's just one flight a day from Jodhpur and it's fully booked. So instead we have to leave from the nearby airport in Udaipur.

Udaipur. My mind jumps back to the night of the full moon. To the breathless kaleidoscope of colour, music, excitement, lust . . . I try to drag it quickly away. I'm not going to go there, remember?

'So, do you want to talk about it?'

Amy's voice penetrates my thoughts and I turn sideways to see her looking at me. The last twenty-four hours have been such a whirlwind of people and arrangements that this is the first real chance we've had to be alone.

I hesitate. I promised myself I wouldn't talk about him, that I'd pretend he never existed, and yet . . .

'His name's Jack,' I say quietly. Just saying his name brings a lump to my throat. 'His name *was* Jack,' I correct myself.

Her face floods with realisation. 'What happened?' she asks.

Like watching scenes projected onto a screen, a stream of memories rushes through my mind: snippets of conversations . . . jokes . . . laughter . . . exchanged glances . . . silences . . . the first moment I saw him on the train . . . the Taj Mahal . . . glancing wordlessly across at him on the back seat of the car as we travelled across India . . . It was only a few days, but I experienced more emotions in that time than some people feel in a lifetime. Where do I even start?

'I fell in love,' I say simply.

For once my sister doesn't fire questions at me; instead she just nods.

'But now it's over,' I add. 'It was over before it ever really began,' and, pushing the feeling deep down inside me, I turn away to look out of the window.

A moment later I feel Amy reach for my hand. 'It's going to be OK,' she says quietly.

'You think so?' I search her face for reassurance.

'I know so,' she nods firmly.

I squeeze her hand gratefully. Sometimes big sisters need looking after too.

We reach the airport a few hours later. It's a new terminal, all shiny glass, huge concourses and even huger queues, but finally we make it through to departures. Our flight's already boarding. So this is it; I'm leaving India. I'm going home.

I think about everyone I've encountered and all their fascinating stories: about Rocky and his magical mystery tour, and how I never got to thank him; about the incredible journey I went on, both literally and metaphorically; and I think about Jack.

The airport is several miles outside the city, but as I walk towards the gate I catch myself glancing around, as if I might spot him amongst the crowds, see a glimpse of a battered old fedora hat, hear the strains of an American accent. But of course I'm being crazy. I'm not going to see Jack again. And I couldn't even if I wanted to. I have no address, no email, no telephone number; there's no way of getting in touch with him . . .

Handing in my boarding pass to the airport official, I follow Amy onto the plane. Besides, there's nothing left to say anyway.

Twenty minutes in to the flight they finally switch off the seatbelt signs and I get up to go to the loo. On the way back, I see Amy has already fallen asleep. That's my sister for you. She has an innate ability to sleep anywhere, at any time. Sadly I'm in the middle of the row and don't want to climb over her in case I wake her, but fortunately the two Indian women on the other side kindly get up to let me squeeze in.

'Thank you so much,' I smile, shuffling past them, 'that's very kind.'

'Oh, it's no problem,' beams the older lady, settling her large frame back down again. 'The seats are so very small, thankfully it is only a short flight to Delhi.' She pauses and looks at me with interest. 'Are you on holiday?'

'Yes . . . well, we were,' I correct myself. 'We're on our way back to London, we're getting a connecting flight after this one.'

'London?' echoes the younger girl, eagerly. 'Did you hear that, *Mummyji*?'

Of course. Now I see the resemblance between them.

'My daughter has always wanted to go to London,' explains the mother, in bemusement at her daughter's excitement.

'Well, it is a great city,' I smile.

'What do you do in London?' asks the daughter, wide-eyed.

'I write books,' I answer, somewhat reluctantly. Often, as soon as I mention what I do for a living, people insist I should write a book about their life, then proceed to tell me all about it in painstaking detail.

The daughter looks agog. 'What kind of books do you write?'

'Romances,' I reply, 'though I like to think of them more as mysteries . . .'

At the mention of romance, her face has lit up. 'Oh wow, have I got a romantic story for you!' she cries delightedly. 'You need to put this in a book!'

Oh no. I try to look enthusiastic, but I'm not really in the mood.

'Actually, it is my auntie's story,' continues the girl, excitedly, 'and it's also sort of a mystery . . .'

I nod vaguely, but I'm already glancing at the stewardesses out of the corner of my eye. How much longer before they start serving drinks? After everything's that happened, I feel like getting completely blotto.

'It is the most beautiful story, isn't it, *Mummyji*?' continues the girl, looking at her mother for confirmation.

Her mother nods. 'You will be moved to tears,' she tells me knowingly. 'It will be the most romantic story you have ever heard.'

I doubt it very much, but I nod accordingly.

'Remember what he said when we asked him why he had travelled all this way to our tiny village in India?' chatters the girl, and mother and daughter exchange looks.

'How could I forget? It always makes me cry,' nods her mother, pulling out a tissue in readiness.

There's a pause, then they both say in unison, 'I'm here to keep a promise.'

Suddenly my whole body stiffens.

'What did you say?' I stammer.

'I'm here to keep a promise,' repeats the daughter. 'That's what the American said when he gave my auntie the ring.'

I'm frozen in my seat. I can't believe what I'm hearing. It's too much of a coincidence.

'A ring?' My voice is almost a whisper.

'Yes, a beautiful ruby with little diamonds on each side,' she nods, her eyes wide with excitement. 'It was the most beautiful ring I have ever seen.'

Oh my god. *The ring.* The engagement ring.

'What else did he say?' I manage, my mind racing. Her aunt must be the girl he told me about . . . these women must be her relations. I feel as if my heart is being squeezed. *He must have proposed.*

'Well, that's the story I was going to tell you,' grins the girl, pleased to have my attention.

'Don't forget to tell her how they met,' interrupts her mother.

'*Mummyji!*' she exclaims, and rolls her eyes. 'As if I am going to forget that part. You are never trusting me to do anything right – it was like today with the suitcases—'

'The story?' I prompt urgently, seeing they are going to get into an argument. Part of me doesn't want to know anything, but the other part of me wants to know everything.

'Ah yes, I'm sorry,' she smiles apologetically, turning back to me. 'Well, it was over thirty-five years ago, my auntie was only a young girl—'

'She was twenty-one,' interrupts her mother, then adds in explanation, 'she's my sister, we are only two years apart.'

I'm suddenly thrown for a loop. 'But . . . but I don't understand . . .'

'It was back in the Seventies,' she explains.

'The Seventies?' Now I'm really confused. This isn't making any sense.

'She met a young engineer from America. He was in India working on a three-month contract, and she was a secretary in the office.' The daughter, who's obviously enjoying regaling me with this story, quickly picks it up again. 'It was love at first sight,' she declares, 'and for a few months everything was wonderful.'

'Then my father found out and he was very angry.' Her mother shakes her head. 'He told her she had to stop seeing this man—'

'But my auntie would not listen.'

'My big sister was always very headstrong,' nods the mother in agreement.

They're talking over each other, finishing one another's sentences.

'Shortly afterwards, his contract finished and he had to go back to America, but he promised he would return—' continues the daughter.

'He promised to marry her,' interrupts her mother. 'She confided in me—'

'And he said he would bring with him a ring—'

'But he never came back—'

'And she never heard from him again,' finishes the daughter.

I've been listening to the story in a sort of stunned bewilderment, trying to make sense of it all. If this happened years ago, how on earth does Jack fit into all of this?

'So, what happened?' I ask, finally.

'No one knew,' says the daughter, shaking her head.

'She wrote letters,' adds her mother. 'I remember my sister always writing letters, but he never replied. Her heart was broken. My father told her she must never mention the American's name again, that she had brought shame on the family . . .' She breaks off and sighs. 'She never married. I don't think she felt she could ever love again.'

'Gosh, that's so sad,' I say quietly, trying to imagine how she must have felt. 'She must have been heartbroken.'

'*Mummyji* said my auntie never spoke of it again,' nods the daughter. 'I only know this because I would always play at her house when I was younger, and one day I found some photographs of them together. She let me take them, she said she had no use for them anymore. Look, do you want to see?' Without waiting for my answer, she digs out her purse. 'It's one of those strips from a photo booth, they must have torn it in half . . .'

My chest tightens. It's the girl in the photograph. And Jack.

As she passes it to me, I realise it's the other half of the strip of photographs I found in the rucksack. I stare at the two faces in the pictures, smiling for the camera, so happy and in love. Only now, looking at it more closely and in the daylight, I can see the man isn't Jack at all, but someone who bears an uncanny resemblance to him.

Someone, perhaps, like his father.

'All these years, she assumed he had broken his promise, that he didn't love her, that he had gone back to America and forgotten about her—'

'But he hadn't, he had never forgotten, he told his son . . .'

I can hear my heart thudding loudly in my ears as it all starts to fall into place. This was the promise. This was why Jack was in India. *It was his father's promise, not his.*

' . . .all about how he had fallen in love with a girl in India and promised to marry her, but that when he had returned to America he discovered something that would change everything—'

'What?' I demand, almost angrily. 'What could stop him from being with the woman he loved?'

'He'd had a girlfriend in college. They broke up before he left for India, but on his return she contacted him . . .' The daughter breaks off, looking scandalised, then in a low voice adds, 'She was pregnant.'

'So he did the right thing by her and the child, and married her,' nods her mother, shooting her daughter a look. 'He felt it was his duty. Times were different then.'

As I listen, I feel an immense sense of sadness. 'And he never told your sister the real reason why he didn't come back to India?'

'No.' Her eyes meet mine and she shakes her head, sadly. 'She never heard from him again. She thought it was because he had changed his mind, because he didn't love her any more . . . yet it turns out he loved her all his life. He felt so ashamed and guilty that he ruined her life because he had promised to marry her . . . he thought it was better this way, that she would just forget him.'

I listen wordlessly, taking all this in.

'I think the saddest part is his marriage didn't work out anyway,' she continues, shaking her head. 'They were divorced some years later.'

'But why did he come back now to tell her?' I ask in confusion. 'Why now, all these years later?'

'Because it was only on his father's deathbed that his son learned of this secret.'

Of course, Jack's father died. As I remember him telling me on the rooftop in Udaipur, my heart twists inside of me.

'It was his father's dying wish that my sister would know he never abandoned her, she was always in his heart, and that he loved her until the day he died.' Her eyes welling up, the mother breaks off and begins dabbing her eyes with a tissue. 'He wanted his son to find her, to give her the engagement ring he had bought for her all those years before, but that he'd never been able to give her . . . He wanted to keep his promise . . .'

'Because a promise is a promise,' they chorus together.

Hearing the words spoken by Jack, I feel a lump in my throat. Oh, Jack. I feel a wave of regret. It all makes sense now. His reluctance to share his secret, because it wasn't his secret to share. His desire to keep a promise. *Life's complicated.* That's what he'd said to me. Yet I'd got it all wrong. I should have believed in love, like he did. I should have trusted him.

'Isn't it the most romantic story you have ever heard?' asks the daughter, eagerly, misinterpreting my glistening eyes.

Instead I ran out. I left without even saying goodbye.

'Did he leave you a number?' Snapping back, I look at them both urgently.

Mother and daughter look back at me in confusion.

'I mean, so you can get in touch with him again . . . if you need to,' I fluster hopefully.

'There was no need.' The mother shakes her head, smiling. 'He'd kept his promise, there was nothing else either one needed to say.'

I nod, feeling the tears pricking my eyelashes and, as the women turn to talk amongst themselves, I quickly brush them away.

'Madam, would you like anything?' I glance up to see the stewardess with her drinks trolley.

'No . . . no thanks,' I manage, shaking my head.

I don't want anything now, I just want Jack. But it's too late.

As the stewardess moves away, a tear rolls silently down my cheek, but this time I don't wipe it away. And turning to look out of the window, I stare at the clouds as India and Jack and everything that's happened recedes further and further into the distance.

40

Four weeks later. London.

'Incredible.'

Turning the last page, Diana reaches for a tissue and blows her nose loudly.

'So do you like it?'

I'm sitting in my literary agency in London, tucked away in Diana's corner office. She's on the other side of a huge mahogany and leather desk that takes up most of the room, the rest of which is crowded with piles of paper that tower from floor to ceiling, filling every available inch. She's just finished reading the manuscript of my latest book, which I finished late last night and emailed straight over.

'Like it? I loved it,' she sniffles, dabbing her eyes. 'But, for the record, I'm not crying,' she adds sternly. 'I never cry; it's just allergies . . . Hay fever.'

'In February?' I raise an eyebrow.

'Global warming,' she replies, shooting me a look.

I smile.

Since returning from India a month ago, I've been holed up in my flat, writing. And this time, I couldn't stop. The writer's block – or whatever it was that was preventing me from writing – just disappeared, and I was back to my old self again. People talk about coming back from holiday 'a new person', but for me, India had the opposite effect. It sounds such a cliché to say I found myself in India, but I did. Only

I found the *old* me. The me I thought I'd lost through heart-break and disappointment. The hopeless romantic and great believer I feared was gone forever. The journey to find my sister in the end became a journey to find myself.

But I'm not the only one who returned home different to when they left. Amy came back to London no longer a single unemployed graduate, but a fiancée with a fantastic new job that she loves. Even more, she loves the fact that on Shine's recent visit, he secured a job at a prestigious yoga studio in Primrose Hill. Admittedly, she was a bit nervous about intro-ducing him to Mum and Dad, but she needn't have worried. At first they were a little surprised, but when he officially asked for her hand in marriage, Mum started crying, and Dad gave him a hug and called him 'son'.

Saying that, it seems Amy isn't the only one in our family with all the surprises. When she and Shine confessed that they'd originally eloped, we all expected Mum and Dad to be angry. Or, at the least, disappointed. But instead my parents looked at each other sheepishly and made a star-tling confession: they'd eloped too. To Gretna Green, of all places! Apparently their own parents had been furious and later made them do it properly – properly being at the local register office – and those are the only wedding pictures Amy and I had ever seen.

Until now. Crowding around the kitchen table, we pored over faded photographs of the two of them in Gretna Green . . . Dad in a bell-bottom corduroy suit and Mum in a white minidress – who would have ever believed it? Seems I got it wrong. But then I was wrong about a lot of things.

Like Jack.

I only have to think his name and my heart twists. So I try hard not to. After all, what's the point? But late at night when I'm drifting off to sleep, or in the morning before I'm fully awake, my mind slips into its default setting and I dream about us together in the desert, on a rooftop in Udaipur, in a hotel room . . . And I can't stop beating myself up for not believing in him, *in us.* That I ran out on him and on love. If only I could explain . . .

But I can't. I have no idea where he is. I don't even know his full name. I did try and find him, but typing 'Jack, architect, American', into my search engine brought up over nine million results. Sometimes Google just isn't enough. And yet maybe it's the hopeless romantic in me that I couldn't keep down, or *wanted* to keep down, but there's a part of me that can't help thinking that love will find a way. Isn't that what they say? All those sayings about all you need is love, or how the course of true love never did run smooth.

But there's not running smooth and there's two people in India meeting on a road trip, not swapping numbers, and one of them – an idiot English girl – running away in the dead of night. Forget being a hopeless romantic, the only thing that's hopeless are my chances of seeing Jack again.

'And the bit at the end when he's waiting for her on her doorstep . . .'

I zone back in to see Diana dabbing her eyes.

'He's tracked her down from India to the other side of the world because he can't live without her . . . and the line where he says, "Things happen that you don't expect, like I never expected to fall in love with you".' She breaks off and starts crying again.

See. That's what I love about my job. I get to write the ending I want to have, but never will. I get to live through my characters' happy-ever-afters.

'So is Steve Archer the guy?' she sniffs. 'The one you met in India. Is it him?' She looks at me fervently.

'Let's just say I had some inspiration,' I say vaguely.

'So are you going to see him again? I gotta meet him!'

'I don't think so,' I smile sadly.

'Seriously?' Diana looks at me aghast.

I nod. 'I'm afraid I don't get to write this ending.'

Diana blows her nose violently one more time. 'Well, it's nice to have you back,' she says cheerfully, and gestures to the manuscript, 'in more ways than one.'

'Thanks,' I smile gratefully.

'I reckon it's going to be your best seller yet.'

I feel a flush of pleasure. 'You think so?'

'I know so,' she nods. 'You wrote this one from the heart.'

There's a pause and for a moment a look passes between us, before Diana suddenly notices the time.

'Shoot, I gotta go.' Jumping up, she begins randomly grabbing things from her messy desk and stuffing them into her huge handbag. 'I've arranged to meet someone for a drink—' She breaks off, as if remembering something. 'Actually, it's the same guy I asked you to meet, remember? But you said no.' She shoots me a look and I blush. 'Anyway, it's a favour for a friend of a friend; this guy's in town and doesn't know anyone, so I said I'd meet up with him.' She pauses to raise an eyebrow. 'Why don't you come along?'

'I don't think so,' I shake my head hurriedly. Before, I didn't want to meet anyone because I didn't believe in love; now it's for the very opposite reason. I do believe in love, I'm in love with Jack, and, even though it's hopeless, I don't want to meet another man.

Diana, who's busily buttoning up her duvet coat, pulls a face. 'Fair enough, I'm sure he's no Steve Archer anyway.'

I smile, despite myself, and together we take the lift downstairs.

'So what are your plans now?'

'Oh, I've got a long list of things to do,' I hear myself saying, though in actual fact my long list consists of 1) pick up dog food and 2) buy flowers for Mrs Flannegan, as it's her birthday. I've been so busy working that I haven't stopped to think about much else for weeks, but now I do, I feel at a bit of a loss.

'OK, well, bye, sweetie, I'll be in touch.' Giving me one of her rib-squeezing hugs, Diana flags down a taxi and jumps inside. 'And congratulations on the book again,' she hollers out of the window. 'Go celebrate!'

Standing on the street I wave her off, watching as the cab disappears around the corner. Diana's right, this calls for a celebration. Plus, I haven't had a chance to see anyone since I've been back. I emailed the gang when I returned from India, but I've been so busy with work, now's a good opportunity to finally catch up. I could text Rachel and see if she's free, invite Milly to a Skype drink, or even take the Eurostar to Paris for the weekend and visit Harriet . . . I pull out my phone, then pause.

And yet, to be honest, I don't feel much like celebrating. Because if the truth be told, the only person I want to celebrate with is Jack.

Slipping my phone back into my pocket, I set off walking towards the Tube, my breath making little white clouds in the evening dusk. The forecast is snow and, pulling up my collar, I wrap my scarf around me, trying to stuff the gaps to keep out the frozen air. Regent Street is bustling with traffic and people and my eyes flick over the droves of men and women in smart business suits, glossy designer stores, fashionable restaurants . . .

Plunged into the fast pace of modern London, it's hard now to imagine Rajasthan exists. The ancient land of fortresses, maharajas, sweeping deserts and holy lakes seems almost like a fairy tale. Yet it exists inside of me. People bring back souvenirs to remember their holiday, but I brought back something else – something less tangible, but something much more profound.

Before I went to India, I felt as if I was sleepwalking

through life. After Sam, it wasn't just my heart that was bruised, it was my soul that was shaken. I lost my faith in love and the joy from my life. Oh, I did all the things you're supposed to do. I drank wine, I bought a new lipstick, I partied with friends. But there was no quick fix. It wasn't like in the movies – there was no fast-forwarding to the I-will-survive moment of rebirth. Instead, I had to plod slowly through the days until, eventually, my eyes stopped welling up, I stopped hoping for some miracle that could put it all right, and I just got on with it.

Getting on with it is a way of life for so many people. People you see every day, pinning on smiles and saying they're fine, are actually really lost, deep down inside. But life moves so fast there's no time to be lost, so you've got to push it down, square your shoulders and get on with it.

So that's what I did. And I was good at it. In fact, I was so good at it I convinced myself that that's how life should be. How *I* should be. But India changed everything. It awakened my senses, lifted my soul and brought joy and beauty back into my life. It brought *me* back to life. But, most importantly of all, it opened my heart and gave me back my belief in the one thing none of us can do without.

Love.

'Hello luv, can I help you?'

I stop by a flower stall on a busy street corner, the bright blooms an explosion of colour on a dark grey wintery day.

'Yes, please,' I nod, casting my eyes across long-stemmed red roses, fluffy yellow chrysanthemums and bold bunches of purple hyacinths, and wondering what kind of flowers Mrs Flannegan would like. I go with the hyacinths: they always smell so wonderful.

'That'll be seven pounds fifty,' nods the stallholder, briskly wrapping them up in paper.

I reach into my bag for my wallet, but it's not there. It

must be in a different pocket. I start rummaging . . . Hang on, where is it? My phone begins to ring, but I ignore it. OK, I'm not going to panic, it must be here somewhere. Doubts start to mushroom. When did I last have it? Oh, I know, I used it to top up my Oyster card, then I went straight to Diana's office.

My phone's incessant burbling is stopping me thinking straight, and with my free hand I impatiently snatch it from my pocket.

It's Diana.

'I'm so sorry, I must have picked it up by mistake.'

'Excuse me?'

'Your wallet. You must have left it on my desk.'

My other hand stops rummaging. I suddenly remember the person with a bucket collecting for charity outside the office and emptying my wallet of loose change. I was still holding it in my hand when I walked into Diana's office.

'I'm such an idiot.'

I snap to. 'Don't worry about it, I'm just glad it's not been stolen!' I say with relief. Well, it wouldn't be the first time. 'Where are you? I'll come and pick it up.'

'Would you?' She sounds relieved. 'Oh sweetie, that would be so helpful. I'm in a pub in Covent Garden, the red something or other, you can't miss it – it's the big white building right across from the Tube . . .'

'OK, I'll see you soon.'

'Thing is, I've got to dash off from here in ten minutes to go to a publishers' dinner.'

Ten minutes? I do a quick calculation. If I run I think I can make it. 'Hang on. I'll be straight over.'

Apologising profusely to the vendor at the flower stall, I dash across the street and start heading towards Soho. It's rush hour and the pavements are packed with pedestrians. Dodging people and taxis I race through the back streets, my heart thumping in my chest. God, I'm really quite unfit. In my head I try to create a mental map to work out the fastest route. Now's one of those times I wish I had an iPhone.

No sooner has the thought fired across my brain than I think about Jack. My mind flashes back to the day we spent together in Pushkar looking for that silly phone charger, and for a moment I'm back there again. I drag myself reluctantly into the present moment. I have to stop this. It's hopeless.

Reaching Charing Cross Road, I slow down and hit the pedestrian crossing. Two lanes of traffic are streaming past. *Come on, come on . . .* I hop up and down impatiently. Oh, sod it. Without waiting for the green light, I start to cross, dodging between a space in the cars. A double-decker bus lurches forwards, blocking my way, and for a moment I'm stranded in the middle of the road, caught between the lanes of traffic jostling for space.

Then suddenly it moves, revealing a little white Ambassador car.

I do a double take.

It appears, as if from nowhere, and I stare at it in disbelief. That's so weird, it looks just like . . . but I don't finish the thought as I raise my eyes and I suddenly get a straight view of the driver.

It's Rocky.

Everything seems to freeze and the noise of London disappears, as if someone just hit mute. He's staring straight ahead. I can see his side profile, the familiar outline of his glasses perched on his nose, the tufts of white hair ... then almost as if he knows I'm here, he abruptly turns towards me. Our gazes meet and, dipping his head, he looks right at me above his glasses. His eyes are a piercing blue, bluer than I even remember, and taking a hand off his steering wheel he gives a small wave of hello – or is it goodbye?

Despite my thick woollen coat and scarf, I feel a shiver run down my spine. *What the ...?* But it's impossible. Rocky can't be here, in his little white car. I'm seeing things. I'm going crazy.

Suddenly I can hear him speaking. 'You must have faith, Ruby,' he's saying quietly. 'Faith, Ruby, you must have faith. You must trust in the universe ...'

Suddenly a blast of horns snaps me back. I come to, the traffic moves, there is no little white car, it's gone, vanished as quickly as it appeared. My head spinning, I quickly make it to the other side of the road, and for a moment I lean dizzily against a wall, trying to collect my thoughts.

What just happened there? I close my eyes, my mind reeling, and I'm suddenly reminded of his prediction, him reading my palm. I'd forgotten all about it, but now it comes rushing back. What was it he said? Without any prompting, I hear him as clearly as if he were standing right next to me.

'*You will meet another man, but there will be some problem, see how the line breaks here?*'

I think about Jack. Well, he was right about that.

'*A break in this line signifies a setback, a difficulty to be overcome.*'

And for a split second I'm transported back to India, back to that tiny restaurant in Agra, with its vivid blue walls and aroma of exotic spices.

'*What kind of difficulty?*'

'*You have said no to him once.*'

I wrack my brains. But that doesn't make any sense.

'*I see a lion, a big lion, but this lion is red . . .*'

Oh for god's sake, none of it makes any sense! Snapping to, I open my eyes. Grey inner-city London greets me and I quickly pull myself together. Come on, Ruby, what are you doing? This is crazy. I look back into the road, but the traffic has moved. The double-decker bus is far up the road and there's no sign of any white Ambassador car. Honestly, I'm seeing things. What next? A lion in the middle of central London? I mean, come on.

Giving myself a brisk shake, I glance at my watch. Shit, and now I'm late. Setting off quickly down a street, I soon find myself in the middle of Covent Garden. I race towards the Tube. Gosh, there are so many tourists! Weaving in and out, I finally reach the station and look across the street to the large white building on the corner. I stop dead.

'*Sometimes it is difficult to understand now, but it will all make sense one day.*'

There, ahead of me, is a painted sign outside the pub. 'THE RED LION.'

My whole body breaks out in goose bumps. It's a coincidence. A freaky coincidence. It has to be. But I don't stop to think about it, I can't, I don't have time. Pushing open the door, I hurry inside. It's one of those upmarket gastro pubs, with stripped oak floors and a recessed dining area. It's already full and I briefly scan the tables, but I can't see her. Or more to the point I can't hear her.

'Excuse me!' Spotting a waiter, I charge over. 'I'm looking for Diana Diamond?'

The waiter looks at me blankly.

'Tall, grey-haired lady, American,' I add, still catching my breath.

His face registers. 'I'm afraid she just left.'

'Left?' My voice comes out a little more high-pitched than I would like and I look at him in surprise. 'Did she leave a wallet?'

The waiter furrows his brow, doubtfully. 'A wallet? No, I don't think so . . .'

She must have had to dash off; she's probably left it behind the bar or something. Still, it's funny she didn't text to tell me that. 'Could you check?' I ask urgently.

The waiter pulls an impatient expression that makes it clear, in no uncertain terms, that he's got better things to do than look for some girl's missing wallet, but he nods dutifully and disappears.

Meanwhile I dig out my phone. Nope, no messages.

'Ruby?'

I hear a voice behind me. Low and distinctive, it makes the hairs on my neck stand up. I'd recognise that voice anywhere.

Jack?

I turn around. He's standing just a couple of feet away. What the . . .?

'I believe I just met your agent, Diana. She had to rush off to a dinner. She asked me to give you this.' He reaches into his pocket and holds out my wallet.

My heart is thudding loudly in my ears, only this time it's not from running. I can't believe it. I'm seeing things again. This can't be real.

'Cat got your tongue?' he jokes, but I can tell he's nervous. Our eyes meet. *No, this is real.*

'I'm sorry.' My words come tumbling out. 'I didn't mean to leave without saying goodbye—'

'Hey, it's fine, you don't need to explain,' he shrugs it off quickly, looking embarrassed.

'No, but I do,' I say desperately. 'You see my sister called and I was trying to find my phone and I knew you had a torch in your backpack . . .' I've rehearsed this speech a million times in my head, imagined what I would say *if* I saw him again, but now it all comes out in one breathless stream, my words tripping over themselves. 'I found the engagement ring,' I blurt.

For a moment, there's a pause, then his face floods with realisation.

'You didn't think . . .?' he begins, and I nod.

'I thought a lot of things,' I say quietly.

And then I tell him. About how I'd jumped to all the wrong conclusions, the message from my sister, catching the bus to Jodhpur, their decision to wait to get married. In the darkened corner of a pub in Covent Garden, over several glasses of white wine and as many hours, it all comes pouring out. Then I tell him about the women on the plane . . .

'You met them?' He's incredulous.

'Yes,' I nod, 'isn't that a coincidence?'

'Or serendipity,' he says quietly.

And then it's his turn. He tells me about his father and how he'd learned of his secret, about the ring and how he'd arranged to meet with a jeweller in Jaipur to get the stone re-set and cleaned, 'Because Dad wanted it to be perfect,' and why it was important to him to travel to India to keep his promise. 'He gave up everything for me,' he says, shaking his head. 'He sacrificed the woman he loved and I wanted her to know why. Not just because it was Dad's dying wish, but because I felt somehow responsible.'

'Responsible, how?' I ask.

'Because I was the reason Dad never went back to India and married the woman he loved,' Jack replies quietly. 'I was that unborn child.'

And all at once I understand what he meant by life being complicated, and yet love, real true love, is strong enough to withstand it all.

Then he talks about us. About how the morning after I'd gone, he'd driven around the city with Rocky for hours looking for me, 'Until I figured you'd run out on me because you'd changed your mind about us,' he says, his gaze meeting mine to confirm that he's wrong. 'Though Rocky said I shouldn't give up, he said I had to say hello from him when I saw you again.'

I look at him, surprised. 'He did?'

'Yeah, he seemed pretty convinced I'd see you again,' he smiles, almost shyly, then peers at me. 'What is it?'

'Oh nothing,' I shake my head. 'It's just something really weird happened on my way here.'

'Weird, *how*?'

'Well, I know this is going to sound totally nuts . . .' I pause, wondering how I can say it, then give up and just come out with it. 'I saw Rocky driving his Ambassador through the middle of London. I mean, I know it couldn't have been, but I could have sworn it was him . . .' I break off with an embarrassed laugh. 'Isn't that bizarre?'

Jack looks at me, as if deep in thought.

'Not as bizarre as the email I found this morning,' he replies after a moment. 'It was sent weeks ago but had somehow ended up in my junk folder. It was from the car rental company in India I'd booked, asking me why I'd never turned up at Delhi Railway Station to meet the driver.'

'What? But . . .' I break off in confusion. 'But then who was Rocky?'

Jack shakes his head. 'Who knows? Our fairy godmother?'

It's a joke and I laugh. But maybe he's right, I reflect, thinking back to our road trip across Rajasthan. If it hadn't been for Rocky and his little white car, none of it would ever have happened: the Taj Mahal, the desert, Udaipur . . . I recall his words when he saw us together in Udaipur. 'My job is done.' At the time I dismissed it, but now . . .

Now I can't help wondering if he appeared to us at Delhi Station for a reason; if we didn't really break down in the desert; if sitting next to the women on the plane wasn't just some bizarre coincidence; if somehow it was all part of his plan to bring me and Jack together. It sounds crazy, *more* than crazy, and maybe it's just my overactive imagination blurring the lines between reality and fantasy. I mean, it must be, *mustn't it?* That kind of stuff's impossible.

And yet, there's something about India. Something about that mystical land that makes anything and everything seem possible; a faraway place of sacred lakes and romantic legends in which you can travel back in time; of kingdoms where astrologists are able to read your fortunes in the stars, and palm readers tell you of your destiny.

'So I hear you turned me down.'

'What?' I look up to see Jack smiling at me ruefully.

'Diana wanted you to meet me for a coffee, but you said no.'

My face floods with sudden comprehension. Of course, that day Diana and I had lunch, the friend she wanted me to meet for coffee—

'That was you?' I gasp incredulously, but already I can feel the incredulity falling away. Of course. It all makes perfect sense now.

He laughs good-naturedly but, before I can explain, we're interrupted by a rowdy after-work crowd, who spill over onto our table. 'Come on, let's get out of here,' he says. Standing up, he holds out my coat so I can slip my arms inside, then walking over to the bar he pulls out his wallet. 'I just need to pay the bill.' A waiter hands him a card terminal and, as he puts in his credit card, I glance at it. *Jack Simon.*

I have a flashback to the last prediction and my breath catches inside me. 'Your last name's Simon?'

Jack turns to look at me. 'Yes, why?'

Inside I feel a little explosion of joy, but I just smile nonchalantly and shake my head. 'Oh, no reason, it was just something Rocky said.'

We walk outside into the evening darkness. For once the forecasters were right, it's started snowing, sugar-coating the pavements and whirling snowflakes around our heads.

'So why are you in London?' I ask, as we pause under a streetlight.

'I've got a connecting flight,' he replies evenly.

I feel a crush of disappointment. That wasn't the answer I was hoping for.

'What time?'

He checks his watch. 'Oh, about an hour ago.'

You see, that's the thing about love – just when you think you've got it all worked out, it has a habit of surprising you.

'So, what else did Rocky say?' As he moves towards me, I feel his warm breath on my cheek.

'That I was very lucky,' I reply, lifting my face to his.

Our eyes meet and, as he holds my gaze, he smiles. 'Well in that case . . .' Wrapping his arms around me, he pulls me against him. 'That makes two of us,' he says, kissing me.

And it's there, a million miles from India, on a snowy pavement in London, that the mystery of love finally works its magic.